EVERYMAN,
I WILL GO WITH THEE,
AND BE THY GUIDE,
IN THY MOST NEED
TO GO BY THY SIDE

JOHN BANVILLE

THE BOOK OF EVIDENCE

THE SEA

WITH AN INTRODUCTION
BY ADAM PHILLIPS

EVERYMAN'S LIBRARY
Alfred A. Knopf New York London Toronto

THIS IS A BORZOI BOOK
PUBLISHED BY ALFRED A. KNOPF

First included in Everyman's Library, 2015

Book design by Barbara de Wilde and Carol Devine Carson

Typeset in the UK by AccComputing, Wincanton, Somerset

Printed and bound in Germany by GGP Media GmbH, Pössneck

JOHN BANVILLE

INTRODUCTION

'From childhood onwards', John Banville wrote in a piece on Raymond Chandler, 'I had been keen on crime fiction: like many boys I was fascinated by puzzles, eager to find out everything I could about adult passions, and unslakeably bloodthirsty.' 'Although', he acknowledges, 'I would hardly have been able to articulate the thought at the time, what I found most attractive in Chandler's work was the sumptuousness of the prose style.' As a portrait of the artist as a young man and as an older man – it is from childhood 'onwards' that he has been fascinated by these things – it is a remarkably succinct account. Many of Banville's characters are vampyric; all of them are radically puzzled by adult passions, their own and other people's, whether they know it or not; and all his narrators are trying to work something out, fascinated by the puzzle their lives have turned into.

But it is the pathos of people trying to solve things that they know to be insoluble – who they really are, what they are doing, why they want what they want – that Banville is obsessed by in his fiction. And that *The Book of Evidence* and *The Sea* are so eloquent about. His narrators are doomed investigators of things they know to be beyond them. They crave revelations that they fear and distrust, and they mock their ambitions. The drama of these novels, then, is the drama of self-exposure, referred to in *The Book of Evidence* as 'that constant, hot, excitement, like a fever in the blood, that was half the fear of being unmasked and half the longing for it'. His protagonists – 'if that is the word', as Banville once remarked of Beckett's characters – are a strange compound of the criminal, his victim, and the detective on the case. These are the different voices we need to listen for in these two compelling artful monologues.

Both books are about men interested in paintings (Banville himself wanted to be a painter as a young man), and fascinated by women. Of antic disposition, they are men confounded by their own seriousness; or rather, men not quite sure how, if at all, to take themselves seriously. Full of a riddling self-conscious evasiveness – 'everything for me is something else,' the narrator of *The Sea* remarks, 'it is a thing I notice increasingly' – we never quite know where we are with these characters (if everything is something else, what is the thing he notices increasingly?). We never know quite how to take what they are saying. It is almost as if they want us to do something with what they are saying, other than just believing them, or disbelieving them. In the strange soliloquies that are these two novels there is an uncanny sense in which, as readers, something is being asked of us that we can't work out. They engage us by puzzling us. Banville, that is to say, is the great modern novelist of just how baffled people are about what they want from each other. And so suspicion is his theme (as if to say: one is more suspicious of oneself than of anyone else; or, seeing is never believing). Each of these novels then, in its own way, trades in mistrust, in the trickiness of character.

The Book of Evidence is in a sense a crime novel, narrated by a man, Freddie Montgomery, who is on trial for stealing a valuable painting by a Dutch master, and murdering the chambermaid who caught him. The book is, apparently, a kind of testament to a court; it is addressed, archly, to 'My Lord', but we discover that this is Freddie's 'defence' written, for the trial, from prison. He is writing when he is going to have to speak anyway. It is, therefore, redundant as yet, as evidence, but is nevertheless evidence of something, which it is for the reader to decide. With 'no explanation, and no excuse', the more he makes his case the less sure he is of what the case may be, or whether his case is worth the making. '[I am] an explorer,' Freddie writes, 'that's what I am, glimpsing a new continent from the prow of a sinking ship.'

The Sea, like *The Book of Evidence*, is written in the aftermath of a catastrophe, and in anticipation of future catastrophe. It too is a strange mixture of memoir and confession, told by (and about) Max, an academic art historian, who has recently lost his wife (both novels, that is to say, are partly organized around the death of a woman). The stolen painting is *Portrait of a Woman with Gloves*, of uncertain attribution (the narrators of both novels are exercised, as the reader is, by what they can attribute to themselves and other people by way of motive or character). 'The picture has been variously attributed to Rembrandt and Frans Hals, even to Vermeer. However, it is safest to regard it as the work of an anonymous master. None of this means anything.' Banville is fascinated by people's anonymity, by their being unnameable despite their names (the names in Banville's novels are always doing a lot of sly work). Sceptical of the faux mastery of naming, he is duly suspicious of masters: of people who can tell us what things really are. And particularly, perhaps, of that fabled master of the nineteenth-century novel, the so-called omniscient narrator (the novelist as God). Indeed, Banville's novels, whatever else they are, are parodies of omniscience. So we also need to note the deadpan theology of these books, what Max refers to in *The Sea* as 'the numerous sly references I have sprinkled through these pages', with all that 'sprinkling' might allude to.

No one, not even the experts, knows who has painted this stolen picture and it supposedly doesn't matter anyway. What does matter is that when Freddie looks at the painting his 'heart contracts. There is something in the way the woman regards me, the querulous, mute insistence of her eyes, which I can neither escape nor assuage. I squirm in the grasp of her gaze.' Looking and being looked at, even by an absent woman, by an image, undoes him. As does his relationship with his wife, but in a different way (the wives in both these novels, it should be noted, are marvellously realized by their monstrously self-absorbed husbands). It is the always enigmatic, sometimes horrifying demand in looking and being looked at that Freddie and Max, like many of Banville's characters, are gripped by. What do people want when they look at someone or something, or when they describe – i.e. look with words – which is a looking to make someone see? Being looked at, even by a woman in a painting, makes Freddie feel overexposed, ashamed of himself, or of the self he assumes she has seen. Perhaps looking, Banville intimates – and the looking that is reading and writing – is the wish to expose. And what then is the wish to expose oneself or others a wish to do? This is Banville's question in these novels. What is someone actually doing when they describe themselves? Or, as novelists do, when they describe themselves by describing others? What are they hoping for?

Max, which is not his real name but the name he gave himself – thereby cancelling his origins, and reinventing himself – is working on his 'Big Book on Bonnard', which has in fact 'got no farther than half of a putative first chapter and a notebook filled with derivative and half-baked would-be aperçus. Well, it is no matter.' His book has no real author, and it doesn't matter (there is, of course, very little matter in a book barely written). But Bonnard was an artist obsessed by painting his wife and Max is a man obsessed by, as it were, painting a picture in words of his dead wife, and indeed of a significant love from his past (Bonnard went on painting his wife after she died). Both Freddie and Max are obsessed by images of women without quite knowing what to make of these women, or of their obsession with them. Both of them seem to sense that whoever, if anyone, they happen to be is somehow bound up with these women, or at least with what they feel about these women. But for Freddie and Max the claims and the disclaimers go hand in hand. They keep telling us (and therefore themselves) what does and doesn't matter to them. But something to do with childhood (their own), women, and questions of authorship and identity preoccupies both these storytellers. They have frequent recourse to the past, but with no sense of there being a promising future.

Questions of authorship, as Banville knows, are questions of origins and of authority, of who the masters are and what they want us for. But because his fiction always makes great play with portentousness, with the comedy of grandiosity – and in this sense he follows on from Beckett – Banville is wary of the false notes prompted by the larger questions. 'I do like fiction that thinks,' he has said in an interview, 'and this is a great failing. It really is. To be infected by the bacillus of philosophizing, of thinking, is a bad thing for a novelist.'* (Banville's fiction, like Beckett's, teaches us to be wary of disclaimers and of what they claim, and, also like Beckett, to be more impressed by failure.) Banville intimates in these novels that tragedy is

---

* Quotations are from *An Interview with John Banville* by Hugh Haughton and Bryan Radley, in *Modernism/Modernity*, vol. 18, no. 4, Nov. 2011, pp. 855–69.

the way we dignify self-importance, but that it is very difficult for us to think ourselves out of our own significance. Unless, that is, we are sufficiently amused by our exorbitant self-absorption. 'I feel viscerally', Banville said in the same interview, 'that the novel is a comic form, that it's essentially a burlesque form.' We need to take in the word 'burlesque' here, if not take it too seriously. But how do we take seriously our embarrassment about being serious? It is one of the great boons of Banville's narrators, that they leave us never quite knowing what seriousness is, while knowing how much some things seem to matter to us. That we don't know where we stand, and we are utterly preoccupied. That we are prone to have our attention caught, to be struck by things. And once we notice things they have their way with us. 'It is not that I am lost for words, but the opposite,' Freddie remarks in *The Book of Evidence*. But we don't say that we are found for words, or that we are lost to words; we know what he means and we don't. We could miss this, or attend to it. The novel may be an amused and amusing form, at least in Banville's sense of it, but he wants us to have a good look at what the words are doing. And at the same time to register that there is something comic, something burlesque about all this close, attentive, suspicious reading and writing.

So Banville is a writer fascinated by fascination, by states of attention, intensely curious about people's curiosity. People looking and being looked at; people being looked at when they are looking; people distracted or immersed or absorbed; people desiring and being desired. And of course, by implication, the reader reading, lost in a book. This, for Banville the novelist, is the evidence. And there are wonderful descriptions on virtually every page of people entranced, or struck, or captivated, or intrigued, staring and glimpsing and glancing in these particularly intent ways. What it all might be evidence of, though – our capacity to be, as it were, possessed by our attention, so absorbed by our distraction – is not clear. And we are not simply and solely in the grip of these states of mind and perception, they are the stuff of art. We can describe them, and reflect on them. Art wants to hold our attention by showing us what held the artist's attention. We want to represent our preoccupations

– what occupies us before we are occupied: what is there before we are – in words and painting, and other media.

So these novels are self-consciously about artists and the writer as artist – and as criminal, thief and historian – not because Banville idealizes the peculiarly modern artist-as-hero, but because his narrators are endlessly exercised about what they might be up to in telling their stories (what he has called 'that wonderful vulgar desire to tell stories'; and again, with a similar twist, the 'low desire to write stories'). The child who wants to believe that curiosity can be satisfied – that there are detectives who can work things out, who know what the evidence is and what it points to, who know what happened – becomes the novelist, the narrator, the always failing, slightly absurd detective (and latterly, of course, Banville under a well-known pseudonym has also been writing detective stories). In Banville's fiction the unreliable narrator – a variant of the omniscient narrator, making the reader, this time, seem specially intelligent – becomes knowingly unreliable to himself. The reader can't trust him because he knows (and keeps saying) he can't trust himself. As though he needs to alert the reader. 'I cannot rid myself of the conviction', the narrator of *The Sea* writes, '. . . that I missed something, only I do not know what it might have been'; 'Why do I torment myself', he asks, 'with these insoluble equivocations?'

So if Banville's characters, in these two remarkable novels, seem to be at once in a trance and wholly engaged with the realities they encounter, lucid and utterly baffled at the same time – both Freddie and Max are entirely plausible as they keep reminding us just how implausible they are – it is because for Banville character is a kind of delirium. A delirium of words. Banville has written enthusiastically, in his introduction to Hofmannsthal's *The Lord Chandos Letter*, of Viennese intellectuals such as Karl Kraus and Fritz Mouthner, who in the early twentieth century, 'revealed a profound misconception in Western thinking. Suddenly the world-that-we-speak was no longer the world-as-it-is, and language, far from being a tool to unlock reality, was a gauze of illusion held up between us and the world of existing things.' For Banville's narrators, too, this is an essential and horrifying puzzle (though if the phrase 'a profound misconception in Western thinking' had been said by one of Banville's narrators it would have been ironized out of existence). Language is both an adaptation to circumstance and an evasion of circumstance; a tool and a refuge. 'I am just amusing myself, musing, losing myself in a welter of words,' Freddie writes in *The Book of Evidence*, 'For words in here are a form of luxury, of sensuousness, they are all we have been allowed to keep of the rich, wasteful world from which we are shut away.' Because Freddie is in prison, and in the prison that is himself, words are the last remnant from a lost world; masturbatory in their intensity and their emptiness, a substitute and a reminder. And so to read *The Book of Evidence* and *The Sea* is, in a very literal sense, to enter into the delirium of their narrators; a delirium in which words can make a world while seeming to describe the world, yet can sometimes seem to be merely words, leading to nothing but more words. A delirium is by definition coherently incoherent, riddled with blind spots. It requires a certain fluency, a logic of its own, and it needs to feel inexhaustible ('I don't work by plot, or dialogue, or character,' Banville has said, 'I work by sentence, and each sentence generates the next one.') We often wonder, as they themselves do, just how deluded Banville's narrators may be. Just how seduced they are by their own language, that is so utterly compelling, and so wholly questionable? Are they a bit mad? In Banville's fictions, at least, there is no Master available to tell us.

It is not incidental, then, that Banville's extraordinary prose style is at once startlingly evocative and wildly informative, so vivid and subtle that many of his sentences are as arresting and puzzling as aphorisms, or riddles (Chambers Dictionary has for 'sumptuous', the quality the young Banville so admired in Chandler, 'costly, magnificent, luxurious'). It is the style of a fascinated man; it has the bizarre, hallucinatory precision of dreams. His narrators can be arch and stagey – 'What an actor the world has lost in me!' Freddie declares at one point like the Cretan Liar declaring he is lying – but there is, indeed, always something fascinating about Banville's characters; though we often get the sense that rather like actors they have had to work at being fascinating; they have had to make themselves characters out of an underlying sense of invisibility (or wordlessness:

they go in fear of their anonymity). They have the vividness of people who may have once doubted that they could find a place in other people's minds. Like orphans who have had to imagine themselves into the world. Indeed many of Banville's male characters are haunted by the suspicion that there is really nothing to them. They can act, but without ever knowing what the alternative to acting is ('You know, we are all acting,' Banville has said, 'Behind that there is a shimmering creature biting its nails saying, "Oh my god, I'm going to be found out." That's what novelists do.') Both Freddie and Max are tormented and exhilarated by the sense that they are merely performing something. And both are interested, as are many of Banville's narrators, in the idea of doubles: of there being someone else who is oneself, but also not oneself (Banville, pointedly, rarely uses the word 'unconscious': his characters more often seem to be haunted by a dark, unknown twin). If you were once worried about being forgotten – or, indeed, about forgetting yourself – you may have to work at making your presence felt (or even at doubling it). And you may become fascinated by the workings of memory. A detective is someone who reconstructs a past he wasn't present at.

It can't help but occur to us that Freddie and Max are also stand-ins for the novelist who – as his reference to the novel as a burlesque form suggests – is performing something, if only the recreation of the past in words ('almost all novels are historical novels,' Banville has remarked). And each of these novels is an extraordinary meditation on memory. Banville has something of Proust's sense that the past is more vivid, more real than the present; and that the present is really only there to remind us of the past. That the present exists as a trigger for memory. Both these novels start with the past. Their very first sentences warn us that something about the past is at stake. Which is why we also need to remember, at the outset, Banville's own warning: 'Your attention can't slip when you're reading my books. That's why I work for so long on the first paragraph, because the first paragraph is saying to the reader, "This is how this must be read, and if you don't read it this way, you know, go and do something else,"' (and then, by way of qualification, 'And most people, amazingly, go and do

xiv

something else.') And yet the first paragraphs of *The Book of Evidence* and *The Sea*, like their first lines, actually offer us very few clues. As instructions go these are – perhaps appropriately, given Banville's preoccupations – notably oblique.

The first line of *The Book of Evidence* is: 'My Lord, when you ask me to tell the court in my own words, this is what I shall say.' A future request, from a kind of master, is being imagined and recruited to give an account of the past. What Freddie will say in that present moment in court he will have written in the past; as though he is writing his script, or his part in a forth-coming drama. The past is being prepared for recitation in the future. Freddie will need his script in court. It will be in his own words, but nobody's words are entirely their own words; all our own words are borrowed or stolen from other people. The book we are reading is prompted by Freddie imagining a demand a very powerful person is going to make on him, and on which his life may depend; a demand to give an account of himself. He is preparing himself, rehearsing. The past is what we use to prepare with; it is a strange kind of rehearsal, a rehearsal for an unknowable future. But at this stage we, the readers, are in the place of the judge. Somebody is on trial; judgements will unavoidably be made. How must this be read? We shall see, but we will also not see, as we read the book. *The Sea*, an odd pun suggested as is often Banville's way, is similar.

The first line of *The Sea* is: 'They departed, the gods, on the day of the strange tide.' A past, however mythical, is being referred to here, of significant consequence. Again, the authori-ties are immediately invoked, this time as gods (though 'My Lord', of course, plays on this too). As always in Banville's fiction, allusions are being made, and being alluded to, without our ever knowing quite how knowing the narrator is being (is the notorious allusiveness of Modernist literature also being burlesqued here? Is he alluding to the idea of literature as allu-sive? There is no way of knowing.) It could be the German poet Hölderlin, or Wallace Stevens or a whole host of other post-Enlightenment writers that the narrator wants us to think about (and he could also be showing off, wanting to impress us). The intellectual as entertainer and anti-entertainer is something Banville always makes much of in his novels. But suggestions are being made, hints offered, without being clarified. The departure of the gods is a common theme in Romantic and Modernist literature; if the gods have departed, though, the pagan gods may be making way for the Judeo-Christian God, the ultimate Master. Or perhaps all the gods have gone, their insignificance now requiring no capital letters, and we are fairly and squarely in the world in which god is dead, though the narrator's word is 'departed', so they could possibly return. And this departure seems to have been connected with a change in the natural world; but it was the 'day of the strange tide' so it may just have been a coincidence. But clearly we don't know what kind of future is going to come out of such an unreadably ambiguous past. As with *The Book of Evidence*, a fraught past is clearly taking its course. But nothing else is clear.

And again, as with *The Book of Evidence* the rest of the first paragraph of *The Sea* clarifies nothing of the 'insoluble equivocations' that have been broached. It is, perhaps, unsurprising that Banville's instruction to his reader is so confounding; not misleading, but somehow tantalizing. We need him to instruct us about his instruction. He hasn't told us how these openings must be read; he has just written them in his extraordinary way. But by issuing his instruction he has made us look for evidence, for clues. He wants us to concentrate, but on what exactly? It is the kind of instruction that one of his fictional narrators might have given us. There is a suspicion, everywhere in these great novels, though never said in so many words, that perhaps our masters, our 'anonymous masters', are always telling us what to attend to, what to concentrate on. That this is what our masters do: they force our attention. Banville's riveting and confounding and confiding narrators, in these brilliant fictions, keep showing us what it is like to live with and without our masters, anonymous or otherwise.

Adam Phillips

C H R O N O L O G Y

———

DATE	AUTHOR'S LIFE	LITERARY CONTEXT
1945	Birth of William John Banville (8 December) in Wexford, Ireland, youngest of the three children of Agnes (neé Doran) and Martin Banville. Educated at Christian Brothers schools and later at St Peter's College, Wexford.	Green: *Loving.* Orwell: *Animal Farm.* Waugh: *Brideshead Revisited.*
1947		Camus: *The Plague.* Compton-Burnett: *Manservant and Maidservant.* Mann: *Doctor Faustus.*
1948		Greene: *The Heart of the Matter.* Mailer: *The Naked and the Dead.* Ó'Faoláin: *The Man Who Invented Sin.* Simenon: *Dirty Snow.*
1949		Borges: *The Aleph.* Bowen: *The Heat of the Day.* Chandler: *The Little Sister.* Miller: *Death of a Salesman.* O'Casey: *Cock-a-Doodle Dandy.* Orwell: *Nineteen Eighty-Four.*
1951		Powell: *A Question of Upbringing.* Salinger: *The Catcher in the Rye.*
1952		Beckett: *Waiting for Godot.* Hemingway: *The Old Man and the Sea.* O'Connor: *The Stories of Frank O'Connor.*
1953		Bellow: *The Adventures of Augie March.* Chandler: *The Long Goodbye.*
1954		K. Amis: *Lucky Jim.* Behan: *The Quare Fellow.* Golding: *Lord of the Flies.* Thomas: *Under Milk Wood.*
1955		Highsmith: *The Talented Mr Ripley.* Nabokov: *Lolita.*

Unconditional surrender of Germany. US drops atomic bombs on Hiroshima and Nagasaki; end of World War II (Eire had remained neutral). United Nations founded. Death of Roosevelt; Truman becomes US president. Seán O'Kelly becomes Irish president (to 1959).

Marshall Plan: US aid for European postwar recovery. The Truman doctrine proclaimed, to check the worldwide spread of Communism. Beginning of Cold War.

Inter-party government formed in Ireland under John Costello as taoiseach (prime minister) following the defeat of Fianna Fáil founder Eamon De Valera. Jewish state of Israel comes into existence. Russian blockade of West Berlin. Communist coup in Czechoslovakia. Assassination of Gandhi in India. Apartheid introduced in South Africa.

Republic of Ireland Act (1948) comes into force: Eire withdraws from the Commonwealth and becomes fully independent. Britain recognizes the Republic but guarantees that the North will remain part of the UK unless its parliament decides otherwise. Federal Republic of Germany established. NATO founded (Ireland does not join). Communist Revolution in China. Soviet Union detonates its first atomic bomb.

De Valera returns as taoiseach. Irish Arts Council established. Economic depression in the Republic of Ireland throughout the 1950s; emigration increases.

Accession of Elizabeth II in UK. Eisenhower is elected US president. Britain produces its first atomic bomb.

Death of Stalin. End of Korean War (began 1950). European Court of Human Rights set up in Strasbourg. Hillary and Tenzing reach the summit of Everest.

John Costello becomes taoiseach in Ireland for the second time. Vietnam War begins (to 1975). Senator Joseph McCarthy begins his hearings on the infiltration of Communism into the American administration, the military and the entertainment industry.

Ireland joins United Nations. Warsaw Pact formed.

DATE	AUTHOR'S LIFE	LITERARY CONTEXT
1956		Beckett: *Malone Dies.*
		Osborne: *Look Back in Anger.*
1957		Beckett: *Endgame.*
		Nabokov: *Pnin.*
		Ó'Faoláin: *The Finest Stories of Séan Ó'Faoláin.*
		Pasternak: *Doctor Zhivago.*
1958		Beckett: *Krapp's Last Tape.*
		Behan: *The Hostage; Borstal Boy.*
		Lampedusa: *The Leopard.*
1959		Burroughs: *Naked Lunch.*
		Grass: *The Tin Drum.*
1960		Lee: *To Kill a Mockingbird.*
		Edna O'Brien: *The Country Girls.*
		Updike: *Rabbit, Run.*
1961		Heller: *Catch-22.*
		Murphy: *A Whistle in the Dark.*
		Flann O'Brien: *The Hard Life.*
		Spark: *The Prime of Miss Jean Brodie.*
1962	Writes his first story, 'The Party', which is published by *The Kilkenny Magazine* in 1966.	Burgess: *A Clockwork Orange.* Nabokov: *Pale Fire.* Solzhenitsyn: *One Day in the Life of Ivan Denisovich.*
1963	After school Banville decides not to go to university and instead works as a clerk for Aer Lingus, enabling him to travel widely.	Le Carré: *The Spy Who Came in from the Cold.* Frank O'Connor: *My Oedipus Complex and Other Stories.* Pynchon: *V.*
1964		Bellow: *Herzog.*
		Friel: *Philadelphia, Here I Come!*
		Larkin: *Whitsun Weddings.*
		Flann O'Brien: *The Dalkey Archive.*
1965		McGahern: *The Dark..*
		Waugh: *Sword of Honour Trilogy.*
1966		Capote: *In Cold Blood.*
		Heaney: *Death of a Naturalist.*
		Higgins: *Langrishe, Go Down.*
1967		Márquez: *One Hundred Years of Solitude.*
		Nabokov: *Speak, Memory.*
		Flann O'Brien: *The Secret Policeman.*

CHRONOLOGY

DATE	AUTHOR'S LIFE	LITERARY CONTEXT
1968	Visits California and remains in the United States until 1969.	Edna O'Brien: *The Love Object and Other Stories.* Updike: *Couples.*
1969	Becomes a sub-editor at *The Irish Press.* Marries Janet Dunham, an American textile artist, with whom he has two sons (Banville later goes on to live with Patricia Quinn, former Head of the Arts Council of Ireland, with whom he has two daughters.)	Nabokov: *Ada.* Roth: *Portnoy's Complaint.* Vonnegut: *Slaughterhouse-Five.*
1970	*Long Lankin* (short stories and a novella) published.	Farrell: *Troubles.*
1971	*Nightspawn*, first novel, published.	Powell: *Books Do Furnish a Room.* Updike: *Rabbit Redux.*
1972		Trevor: *The Ballroom of Romance and Other Stories.*
1973	*Birchwood* (novel) published. Wins the Allied Irish Banks' Prize and the Irish Arts Council Macaulay Fellowship.	Farrell: *The Siege of Krishnapur.* Greene: *The Honorary Consul.* Leonard: *Da.* Powell: *Temporary Kings.* Pynchon: *Gravity's Rainbow.*
1974		Larkin: *High Windows.* Leonard: *Summer.*
1975		Bellow: *Humboldt's Gift.* Bradbury: *The History Man.* Levi: *The Periodic Table.* Murphy: *The Sanctuary Lamp.*
1976	*Doctor Copernicus*, first part of *The Revolutions Trilogy*, published. Wins the James Tait Black Memorial Prize, the Whitbread Prize and the American Ireland Fund Literary Award.	Carver: *Will You Please Be Quiet, Please?*
1978		Greene: *The Human Factor.* Murdoch: *The Sea, The Sea.*
1979		Calvino: *If on a winter's night a traveller.* Flanagan: *The Year of the French.* Johnston: *The Old Jest.* Ó'Faoláin: *And Again?*
1980		Beckett: *Company.* Bowen: *Collected Stories.* Eco: *The Name of the Rose.*

CHRONOLOGY

Student unrest throughout Europe and the US. Soviet-led invasion of Czechoslovakia. Assassination of Martin Luther King. Nixon elected president in US.
Beginning of conflict in Northern Ireland (and occasionally the Republic) known as the Troubles; British troops made responsible for security.
US astronaut Neil Armstrong becomes first man on moon.

Chilean Salvador Allende becomes world's first democratically elected Marxist head of state.

Bloody Sunday in Northern Ireland. Direct rule imposed by Britain.
Strategic Arms Limitation Treaty (SALT I) signed by USSR and US.
Liam Cosgrove becomes taoiseach. Ireland joins the European Economic Community (EEC). Intensification of violence in Northern Ireland; IRA bombing campaign hits London. Miners' strike in UK; energy crisis prompts state of emergency.

Nixon resigns in wake of Watergate scandal; Ford becomes US president.

End of Vietnam war. USSR and Western powers sign Helsinki Agreement.

Death of Chairman Mao in China. Soweto massacre in South Africa.
Saddam Hussein becomes president of Iraq. Carter elected US president.

Camp David agreement between Carter (US), Begin (Israel) and Sadat (Egypt).
Charles Haughey becomes taoiseach in Ireland. Margaret Thatcher becomes Britain's first woman prime minister. Soviet forces invade Afghanistan.
Iran hostage crisis (to 1981). Carter and Brezhnev sign SALT II.
INLA/IRA assassinations of Airey Neave and Lord Mountbatten.
Health (Family Planning) Act: contraception made available in Ireland though only with a doctor's prescription (amended to allow sale without prescription six years later).
Lech Walesa leads strikes in Gdansk, Poland. Iran–Iraq war (to 1988).

DATE	AUTHOR'S LIFE	LITERARY CONTEXT
1981	*Kepler* (novel) published; wins the Guardian Fiction Prize.	Gordimer: *July's People.* Keane: *Good Behaviour.* McEwan: *The Comfort of Strangers.* Rushdie: *Midnight's Children.* Spark: *Loitering with Intent.*
1982	*The Newton Letter* (novel) published.	Allende: *The House of the Spirits.* Beckett: *Ill Seen Ill Said.* Binchy: *Light a Penny Candle.* Munro: *The Moons of Jupiter.*
1983		Bishop: *The Complete Poems.* Coetzee: *The Life and Times of Michael K.* Swift: *Waterland.* Trevor: *Fools of Fortune.*
1984	Film version of *The Newton Letter*, titled *Reflections*, broadcast on UK and Irish TV.	Barnes: *Flaubert's Parrot.* Beckett: *Worstward Ho.* Carter: *Nights at the Circus.* Heaney: *Station Island.* Kundera: *The Unbearable Lightness of Being.* Lodge: *Small World.*
1985		Márquez: *Love in the Time of Cholera.* Winterson: *Oranges Are Not the Only Fruit.*
1986	*Mefisto* (novel) published.	K. Amis: *The Old Devils.* Updike: *Roger's Version.*
1987		Doyle: *The Commitments.* Heaney: *The Haw Lantern.*
1988	Becomes literary editor of *The Irish Times* (to 1999).	Carey: *Oscar and Lucinda.* Eco: *Foucault's Pendulum.* Rushdie: *The Satanic Verses.*
1989	*The Book of Evidence* (novel) published; shortlisted for the Booker Prize; wins the first Guinness Peat Aviation Award.	M. Amis: *London Fields.* Barnes: *A History of the World in 10½ Chapters.* Ishiguro: *The Remains of the Day.*
1990	Begins writing for *The New York Review of Books* as a reviewer and essayist.	Byatt: *Possession.* Friel: *Dancing at Lughnasa.* McEwan: *The Innocent.* McGahern: *Amongst Women.* Updike: *Rabbit at Rest.*
1991	*The Book of Evidence* awarded the Premio Ennio Flaiano in Italy.	Carter: *Wise Children.* Heaney: *Seeing Things.* Trevor: *Two Lives.*

CHRONOLOGY

Beginning of severe economic problems in Ireland, with rising unemployment and debt. Provisional IRA hunger strike culminates in the death of Bobby Sands in Long Kesh internment prison. Reagan becomes US president. President Sadat killed by Islamic fundamentalists in Egypt.

Garret Fitzgerald becomes taoiseach in Ireland. Falklands War between Britain and Argentina.

Constitutional ban on abortion in Ireland. US troops invade Grenada.

Famine in Ethiopia. Indira Gandhi assassinated in India. Reagan re-elected as US president in landslide victory. British miners begin year-long strike.

Signing of Anglo-Irish Agreement, giving the Republic of Ireland a consultative role in Northern Ireland's government. Gorbachev becomes General Secretary in USSR; period of reform begins.

Gorbachev–Reagan summit. Nuclear explosion at Chernobyl.

Charles Haughey serves as taoiseach for the third time in Ireland. Margaret Thatcher wins her third successive general election in UK.
George Bush elected US president. Gorbachev announces Russian withdrawal from Afghanistan. Benazir Bhutto is elected prime minister of Pakistan. Terrorist bomb destroys Pan Am flight 103 over Lockerbie.
Collapse of Communist empire in Eastern Europe. Fall of the Berlin Wall. First democratic elections in USSR. Tiananmen Square massacre in China. De Klerk becomes president of South Africa. Radio Iran announces Ayatollah Khomeini's fatwa against Salman Rushdie.
Mary Robinson is elected first woman president of Ireland. Margaret Thatcher ousted; John Major becomes prime minister in UK. Iraq invades Kuwait. Nelson Mandela released from gaol after 27 years' imprisonment. Yeltsin elected first leader of Russian Federation.

Ireland signs Treaty on European Union at Maastricht. Gulf War. Bush and Gorbachev sign START arms reduction treaty. Central government in USSR suspended. War begins in former Yugoslavia. End of apartheid in South Africa.

JOHN BANVILLE

DATE	AUTHOR'S LIFE	LITERARY CONTEXT
1992		McCabe: *The Butcher Boy*.
1993	*Ghosts* (novel) published; shortlisted for the Whitbread Fiction Prize.	Doyle: *Paddy Clarke Ha Ha Ha*. Welsh: *Trainspotting*.
1994	*The Broken Jug*, adaptation of *Der zerbrochne Krug*, a comedy by Heinrich von Kleist, premières in Dublin.	Trevor: *Felicia's Journey*. Winterson: *Art and Lies*.
1995	*Athena* (novel) published. Works as sub-editor at *The Irish Times*.	M. Amis: *The Information*. Atkinson: *Behind the Scenes at the Museum*.
1996	*The Ark* (children's story) published.	Ford: *Independence Day*. Doyle: *The Woman Who Walked Into Doors*. Swift: *Last Orders*.
1997	*The Untouchable* (novel) published; shortlisted for the Whitbread Prize; receives the Lannan Literary Award.	McEwan: *Enduring Love*. Roth: *American Pastoral*.
1998		Bainbridge: *Master Georgie*. Binchy: *Tara Road*.
1999	Adapts Elizabeth Bowen's *The Last September* for the screen.	Coetzee: *Disgrace*. Doyle: *A Star Called Henty*. Tóibín: *The Blackwater Lightship*.
2000	*Eclipse* (novel) published. *Doctor Copernicus, Kepler* and *The Newton Letter* published in a single volume as *The Revolutions Trilogy*. Adaptation of Kleist's *Amphitryon* premières in Dublin.	Atwood: *The Blind Assassin*. Ní Dhuibhne: *The Pale Gold of Alaska*. Roth: *The Human Stain*. Smith: *White Teeth*.
2001	*The Book of Evidence, Ghosts* and *Athena* published in a single volume as *Frames*.	Bainbridge: *According to Queeney*. Kinsella: *Collected Poems*. McEwan: *Atonement*.
2002	*Shroud* (novel) published. *Stardust: Three Monologues of the Dead* broadcast on BBC Radio 3. *Dublin 1742* (children's play) performed in Dublin. Stage version of *The Book of Evidence* premières in Kilkenny.	Muldoon: *Moy Sand and Gravel*. Trevor: *The Story of Lucy Gault*.

CHRONOLOGY

Albert Reynolds becomes taoiseach in Ireland. Supreme Court decision in 'X Case' establishes right to abortion where the mother's life is under threat. Irish referendum approves the right to travel abroad for an abortion and the right to obtain information on abortion. Bill Clinton elected US president. Irish and British prime ministers agree the Downing Street Declaration, which offers talks on future peace in Northern Ireland if violence is renounced by all parties. Palestinian leader Arafat and Israeli prime minister Rabin sign peace agreement in the US. Discovery of a mass grave at a Dublin convent eventually leads to the Magdalene laundries scandal. Decriminalization of homosexuality in Ireland.
IRA ceasefire announced. John Bruton becomes taoiseach in Ireland. Mandela and ANC sweep to victory in South African elections. Civil war in Rwanda. Russian military action against Chechen Republic.

Rise of the 'Celtic Tiger' – beginning of rapid economic growth in Ireland, driven by foreign investment and a subsequent property bubble. Israeli prime minister Rabin assassinated.
A huge bomb blast in Canary Wharf, London, brings to an end the uneasy truce in Northern Ireland. President Clinton re-elected.

Bertie Ahern becomes taoiseach in Ireland. Divorce is made legal in Ireland under certain circumstances. Tony Blair leads first Labour government in 18 years in the UK.

Northern Ireland Referendum accepts the Good Friday Agreement; an assembly is elected. Omagh Bomb in August kills 29 people. US air strikes against Iraq. Impeachment of President Clinton begins.
Serbs attack ethnic Albanians in Kosovo; US leads NATO in bombing of Belgrade.

Milošević's regime in the former Yugoslavia collapses. George W. Bush elected US president.

Al-Qaeda terrorist attacks of 9/11. The Nice Treaty providing for an enlargement of the European Union is rejected by Irish voters.

The Punt is replaced by the Euro as the national currency in Ireland (Jan). Fianna Fail's Bertie Ahern is re-elected as Irish taoiseach (May). Second referendum in Ireland endorses Nice Treaty (Oct). US troops invade Afghanistan.

DATE	AUTHOR'S LIFE	LITERARY CONTEXT
2003	*Prague Picture: Portrait of a City* (non-fiction) published. Awarded the Premio Nonino.	
2004		Tóibín: *The Master.* Joseph O'Connor: *Star of the Sea.*
2005	*The Sea* (novel) published; wins the Booker Prize. *A World Too Wide* (radio play) broadcast by RTE. *Love in the Wars* (adaptation of Kleist's *Penthesilia*) published.	Barnes: *Arthur & George.* Barry: *A Long, Long Way.* Delaney: *Ireland, A Novel.* Ishiguro: *Never Let Me Go.* Mantel: *Beyond Black.*
2006	Awarded the Premio Grinzane-Francesco Biamonti. *The Sea* shortlisted for British Book Awards Author of the Year. *Todtnauberg* (radio play) broadcast by BBC Radio 4. *Christine Falls,* the first of his crime novels, is published, written under the pen name Benjamin Black.	Ford: *The Lay of the Land.* McCabe: *Winterwood.*
2007	*The Sea* nominated for the Man Booker International Prize. Becomes a Fellow of the Royal Society of Literature. Awarded the Madeleine Zepter Prix Littéraire Européen. *The Silver Swan* (crime novel) published.	Enright: *The Gathering.* Keegan: *Walk the Blue Fields.*
2008	*The Lemur* (crime novel) published after being serialized in *The New York Times.*	Barry: *The Secret Scripture.* Carson: *For All We Know.* Doyle: *The Dead Republic.* Mahon: *Life on Earth.* O'Neill: *Netherland.* Roth: *Indignation.*
2009	*The Infinities* (novel) published.	McCann: *Let the Great World Spin.* Mantel: *Wolf Hall.* Munro: *Too Much Happiness.* Tóibín: *Brooklyn.* Trevor: *Love and Summer.*
2010	*The Infinities* wins the Kerry Group Irish Fiction Award; *The Sea* is shortlisted for the Irish Book of the Decade. *Elegy for April* (crime novel) published.	Carey: *Parrot and Olivier in America.* Donoghue: *Room.*

CHRONOLOGY

Iraq weapons crisis. American and British troops invade Iraq. Population of Ireland reaches 4 million, driven by the return of many emigrants during the 'Celtic Tiger' years.

Terrorist bombings in Madrid. Beslan school hostage crisis. George W. Bush re-elected as US president. Indian Ocean tsunami.

Al-Qaeda terrorist bombings in London. Provisional IRA formally orders end to its armed campaign (since 1969). European Union recognizes Irish as an official working language. First parliamentary elections in Iraq since US-led invasion.

Saddam Hussein is executed in Baghdad after being convicted of crimes against humanity by an Iraqi court.

Bertie Ahern heads coalition government in his third term of office. End of direct rule of Northern Ireland by London. In the UK Blair resigns and is succeeded by Gordon Brown. Benazir Bhutto, leader of Pakistan People's Party, killed in a suicide bomb attack.

Bertie Ahern steps down as taoiseach in Ireland following a controversy over his financial affairs; he is succeeded by Brian Cowen. Largest global recession since the Great Depression begins; Ireland becomes first country in Western Europe to officially fall into recession. Barack Obama becomes the first African-American to be elected US president.

Unemployment rate in Ireland reaches 11%, highest since 1996; rally in Dublin against government handling of economic crisis. Having gained their requested concessions, Irish voters accept the EU's Lisbon Treaty (overturning referendum of 2008). Murphy Report criticizes the Irish Catholic Church hierarchy for its handling of allegations of child abuse against a sample 46 priests in the archdiocese of Dublin. Ryan Commission reports on child abuse in institutions operated by the Church and supervised by the Irish government.

Irish government agrees an 85 billion euro rescue package with the EU and the IMF; strict austerity measures to be imposed. In the UK Conservative leader David Cameron forms a coalition government with the Liberal Democrats.

DATE	AUTHOR'S LIFE	LITERARY CONTEXT
2011	*A Death in Summer* (crime novel) published. Awarded the Franz Kafka Prize. Works on the film script for *Albert Nobbs*, starring Glenn Close.	Barnes: *The Sense of an Ending.* Hollinghurst: *The Stranger's Child.* Edna O'Brien: *Saints and Sinners.* Swift: *Wish You Were Here.*
2012	*Ancient Light* (novel) and *Vengeance* (crime novel) published.	M. Amis: *Lionel Asbo: State of England.* Mantel: *Bring up the Bodies.*
2013	Receives the Irish PEN Award for Outstanding Achievement in Irish Literature and the Austrian State Prize for European Literature. *Holy Orders* (crime novel) published.	Atwood: *MaddAddam.* Doyle: *The Guts.* Larkin: *The Complete Poems.*
2014	Becomes first Irish writer to win Spain's prestigious Prince of Asturias award for literature. Created a chevalier de l'Ordre des Arts et des Lettres by the French government. *Love in the Wars* staged at the Fisher Center, Bard College in New York State.	

CHRONOLOGY

THE BOOK OF
EVIDENCE

I

MY LORD, when you ask me to tell the court in my own words, this is what I shall say. I am kept locked up here like some exotic animal, last survivor of a species they had thought extinct. They should let in people to view me, the girl-eater, svelte and dangerous, padding to and fro in my cage, my terrible green glance flickering past the bars, give them something to dream about, tucked up cosy in their beds of a night. After my capture they clawed at each other to get a look at me. They would have paid money for the privilege, I believe. They shouted abuse, and shook their fists at me, showing their teeth. It was unreal, somehow, frightening yet comic, the sight of them there, milling on the pavement like film extras, young men in cheap raincoats, and women with shopping bags, and one or two silent, grizzled characters who just stood, fixed on me hungrily, haggard with envy. Then a Guard threw a blanket over my head and bundled me into a squad car. I laughed. There was something irresistibly funny in the way reality, banal as ever, was fulfilling my worst fantasies.

By the way, that blanket. Did they bring it specially, or do they always keep one handy in the boot? Such questions trouble me now, I brood on them. What an interesting figure I must have cut, glimpsed there, sitting up in the back like a sort of mummy, as the car sped through the wet, sunlit streets, bleating importantly.

Then this place. It was the noise that impressed me first of all. A terrible racket, yells and whistles, hoots of laughter, arguments, sobs. But there are moments of stillness, too, as if a great fear, or a great sadness, has fallen suddenly, striking us all speechless. The air stands motionless in the corridors, like stagnant water. It is laced with a faint stink of carbolic, which bespeaks the charnel house. In the beginning I fancied it was me, I mean I thought this smell was mine, my contribution. Perhaps it is? The daylight too is strange, even outside, in the yard, as if something has happened to it, as if something has been done to it, before it is allowed to reach us. It has an acid, lemony cast, and comes in two intensities: either it is not enough to see by or it sears the sight. Of the various kinds of darkness I shall not speak.

My cell. My cell is. Why go on with this.

Remand prisoners are assigned the best cells. This is as it should be. After all, I might be found innocent. Oh, I mustn't laugh, it hurts too much, I get a terrible twinge, as if something were pressing on my heart – the burden of my guilt, I suppose. I have a table and what they call an easy chair. There is even a television set, though I rarely watch it, now that my case is *sub judice* and there is nothing about me on the news. The sanitation facilities leave something to be desired. Slopping out: how apt, these terms. I must see if I can get a catamite, or do I mean a neophyte? Some young fellow, nimble and willing, and not too fastidious. That shouldn't be difficult. I must see if I can get a dictionary, too.

Above all I object to the smell of semen everywhere. The place reeks of it.

I confess I had hopelessly romantic expectations of how things would be in here. Somehow I pictured myself a sort of celebrity, kept apart from the other prisoners in a special wing, where I would receive parties of grave, important people and hold forth to them about the great issues of the day, impressing the men and charming the ladies. What insight! they would cry. What breadth! We were told you were a beast, cold-blooded, cruel, but now that we have seen you, have heard you, why – ! And there am I, striking an elegant pose, my ascetic profile lifted to the light in the barred window, fingering a scented handkerchief and faintly smirking, Jean-Jacques the cultured killer.

Not like that, not like that at all. But not like other clichés either. Where are the mess-hall riots, the mass break-outs, that kind of thing, so familiar from the silver screen? What of the scene in the exercise yard in which the stoolie is done to death with a shiv while a pair of blue-jawed heavyweights stage a diversionary fight? When are the gang-bangs going to start? The fact is, in here is like out there, only more so. We are obsessed with physical comfort. The place is always overheated, we might be in an incubator, yet there are endless complaints of draughts and sudden chills and frozen feet at night. Food is important too, we pick over our plates of mush, sniffing and sighing, as if we were a convention of gourmets. After a parcel delivery word goes round like wildfire. *Psst! She's sent him a Battenberg! Homemade!* It's just like school, really, the mixture of misery and cosiness, the numbed longing, the noise, and everywhere, always, that particular smelly grey warm male fug.

It was different, I'm told, when the politicals were here. They used to goose-step up and down the corridors, barking at each other in bad Irish, causing much merriment among the ordinary criminals. But then they all went on hunger strike or something, and were moved away to a place of their own, and life returned to normal.

Why are we so compliant? Is it the stuff they are said to put in our tea to dull the libido? Or is it the drugs. Your Honour, I know that no one, not even the prosecution, likes a squealer, but I think it is my duty to apprise the court of the brisk trade in proscribed substances which is carried on in this institution. There are screws, I mean warders, involved in it, I can supply their numbers if I am guaranteed protection. Anything can be had, uppers and downers, tranqs, horse, crack, you name it – not that you, of course, your Worship, are likely to be familiar with these terms from the lower depths, I have only learned them myself since coming here. As you would imagine, it is mainly the young men who indulge. One recognises them, stumbling along the gangways like somnambulists, with that little, wistful, stunned smile of the truly zonked. There are some, however, who do not smile, who seem indeed as if they will never smile again. They are the lost ones, the goners. They stand gazing off, with a blank, preoccupied expression, the way that injured animals look away from us, mutely, as if we are mere phantoms to them, whose pain is taking place in a different world from ours.

But no, it's not just the drugs. Something essential has gone, the stuffing has been knocked out of us. We are not exactly men any more. Old lags, fellows who have committed some really impressive crimes, sashay about the place like dowagers, pale, soft, pigeon-chested, big in the beam. They squabble over library books, some of them even knit. The young too have their hobbies, they approach me in the recreation room, their calf eyes fairly brimming, and shyly display their handiwork. If I have to admire one more ship in a bottle I shall scream. Still, they are so sad, so vulnerable, these muggers, these rapists, these baby-batterers. When I think of them I always picture, I'm not sure why, that strip of stubbly grass and one tree that I can glimpse from my window if I press my cheek against the bars and peer down diagonally past the wire and the wall.

Stand up, please, place your hand here, state your name clearly. Frederick Charles St John Vanderveld Montgomery. Do you swear to tell the truth, the whole truth and nothing but the truth? Don't make me laugh. I want straight away to call my first witness. My wife. Daphne. Yes, that was, is, her name. For some reason people have always found it faintly comic. I think it matches very well her damp, dark, myopic beauty. I see her, my lady of the laurels, reclining in a sun-dazed glade, a little vexed, looking away with a small frown, while some minor god in the shape of a faun, with a reed pipe, prances and capers, vainly playing his heart out for her. It was that abstracted, mildly dissatisfied air which first drew my attention to her. She was not nice, she was not good. She suited me. Perhaps I was already thinking of a time to come when I would need to be pardoned – by someone, anyone – and who better to do that than one of my own kind.

When I say she was not good I do not mean she was wicked, or corrupt. The flaws in her were nothing compared with the jagged cracks that run athwart my soul. The most one could accuse her of was a sort of moral laziness. There were things she could not be bothered to do, no matter what imperatives pro-pelled them to her jaded attention. She neglected our son, not because she was not fond of him, in her way, but simply because his needs did not really interest her. I would catch her, sitting on a chair, looking at him with a remote expression in her eyes, as if she were trying to remember who or what precisely he was, and how he had come to be there, rolling on the floor at her feet in one of his own many messes. Daphne! I would murmur, for Christ's sake! and as often as not she would look at me then in the same way, with the same blank, curiously absent gaze.

I notice that I seem unable to stop speaking of her in the past tense. It feels right, somehow. Yet she often visits me. The first time she came she asked what it was like in here. Oh, my dear! I said, the noise! – and the people! She just nodded a little and smiled wanly, and looked about her idly at the other visitors. We understand each other, you see.

In southern climes her indolence was transformed into a kind of voluptuous languor. There is a particular room I remember, with green shutters and a narrow bed and a Van Gogh chair, and a Mediterranean noon pulsing outside in the white streets. Ibiza? Ischia? Mykonos perhaps? Always an island, please note that, clerk, it may mean something. Daphne could get out of her clothes with magical swiftness, with just a sort of shrug, as if skirt, blouse, pants, everything, were all of a piece. She is a big woman, not fat, not heavy, even, but yet weighty, and beautifully balanced: always when I saw her naked I wanted to caress her, as I would want to caress a piece of sculpture, hefting the curves in the hollow of my hand, running a thumb down the long smooth lines, feeling the coolness, the velvet texture of the stone. Clerk, strike that last sentence, it will seem to mean too much.

Those burning noons, in that room and countless others like it – my God, I tremble to think of them now. I could not resist her careless nudity, the weight and density of that glimmering flesh. She would lie beside me, an abstracted *maya*, gazing past me at the shadowy ceiling, or at that chink of hot white light between the shutters, until at last I managed, I never understood exactly how, to press a secret nerve in her, and then she would turn to me heavily, quickly, with a groan, and cling to me as if she were falling, her mouth at my throat, her blind-man's finger-tips on my back. She always kept her eyes open, their dim soft grey gaze straying helplessly, flinching under the tender damage I was inflicting on her. I cannot express how much it excited me, that pained, defenceless look, so unlike her at any other time. I used to try to have her wear her spectacles when we were in bed like this, so she would seem even more lost, more defenceless, but I never succeeded, no matter what sly means I might employ. And of course I could not ask. Afterwards it would be as though nothing at all had happened, she would get up and stroll to the bathroom, a hand in her hair, leaving me prostrate on the soaked sheet, convulsed, gasping, as if I had suffered a heart attack, which I suppose I had, in a way.

She never knew, I believe, how deeply she affected me. I was careful that she should not know it. Oh, don't mistake me, it was not that I was afraid I would give myself into her power, or anything like that. It was just that such knowledge would have been, well, inappropriate between us. There was a reticence, a tactfulness, which from the first we had silently agreed to preserve. We understood each other, yes, but that did not mean we knew each other, or wanted to. How would we have maintained that unselfconscious grace that was so important to us both, if we had not also maintained the essential secretness of our inner selves?

How good it was to get up then in the cool of afternoon and amble down to the harbour through the stark geometry of sun and shadow in the narrow streets. I liked to watch Daphne walking ahead of me, her strong shoulders and her hips moving in a muffled, complex rhythm under the light stuff of her dress. I liked to watch the island men, too, hunched over their pastis and their thimbles of turbid coffee, swivelling their lizard eyes as she went past. That's right, you bastards, yearn, yearn.

On the harbour there was always a bar, always the same one whatever the island, with a few tables and plastic chairs outside, and crooked sun-umbrellas advertising Stella or Pernod, and a swarthy, fat proprietor leaning in the doorway picking his teeth. It was always the same people, too: a few lean, tough types in bleached denim, hard-eyed women gone leathery from the sun, a fat old guy with a yachting cap and grizzled sideburns, and of course a queer or two, with bracelets and fancy sandals. They were our crowd, our set, our friends. We rarely knew their names, or they ours, we called each other pal, chum, captain, darling. We drank our brandies or our ouzos, whatever was the cheapest local poison, and talked loudly of other friends, characters every one, in other bars, on other islands, all the while eyeing each other narrowly, even as we smiled, watching for we knew not what, an opening, perhaps, a soft flank left momentarily unguarded into which we might sink our fangs. Ladies and gentlemen of the jury, you have seen us, we were part of the local colour on your package holiday, you passed us by with wistful glances, and we ignored you.

We presided among this rabble, Daphne and I, with a kind of grand detachment, like an exiled king and queen waiting daily for word of the counter-rebellion and the summons from the palace to return. People in general, I noticed it, were a little afraid of us, now and again I detected it in their eyes, a worried, placatory, doggie sort of look, or else a resentful glare, furtive and sullen. I have pondered this phenomenon, it strikes me as significant. What was it in us – or rather, what was it *about* us – that impressed them? Oh, we are large, well-made, I am handsome, Daphne is beautiful, but that cannot have been the whole of it. No, after much thought the conclusion I have come to is this, that they imagined they recognised in us a coherence and wholeness, an essential authenticity, which they lacked, and of which they felt they were not entirely worthy. We were – well, yes, we were heroes.

I thought all this ridiculous, of course. No, wait, I am under oath here, I must tell the truth. I enjoyed it. I enjoyed sitting at ease in the sun, with my resplendent, disreputable consort at my side, quietly receiving the tribute of our motley court. There was a special, faint little smile I had, calm, tolerant, with just the tiniest touch of contempt, I bestowed it in particular on the sillier ones, the poor fools who prattled, cavorting before us in cap and bells, doing their pathetic tricks and madly laughing. I looked in their eyes and saw myself ennobled there, and so could forget for a moment what I was, a paltry, shivering thing, just like them, full of longing and loathing, solitary, afraid, racked by doubts, and dying.

That was how I got into the hands of crooks: I allowed myself to be lulled into believing I was inviolable. I do not seek, my Lord, to excuse my actions, only to explain them. That life, drifting from island to island, encouraged illusions. The sun, the salt air, leached the significance out of things, so that they lost their true weight. My instincts, the instincts of our tribe, those coiled springs tempered in the dark forests of the north, went slack down there, your Honour, really, they did. How could anything be dangerous, be wicked, in such tender, blue, watercolour weather? And then, bad things are always things that take place elsewhere, and bad people are never the people that one knows. The American, for instance, seemed no worse than any of the others among that year's crowd. In fact, he seemed to me no worse than I was myself – I mean, than I imagined myself to be, for this, of course, was before I discovered what things I was capable of.

I refer to him as the American because I did not know, or cannot remember, his name, but I am not sure that he was American at all. He spoke with a twang that might have been learned from the pictures, and he had a way of looking about him with narrowed eyes while he talked which reminded me of some film star or other. I could not take him seriously. I did a splendid impression of him – I have always been a good mimic – which made people laugh out loud in surprise and recognition. At first I thought he was quite a young man, but Daphne smiled and asked had I looked at his hands. (She noticed such things.) He was lean and muscular, with a hatchet face and boyish, close-cropped hair. He went in for tight jeans and high-heeled boots and leather belts with huge buckles. There was a definite touch of the cowpoke about him. I shall call him, let me see, I shall call him – Randolph. It was Daphne he was after. I watched him sidle up, hands stuck in his tight pockets, and start to sniff around her, at once cocksure and edgy, like so many others before him, his longing, like theirs, evident in a certain strained whiteness between the eyes. Me he treated with watchful affability, addressing me as friend, and even – do I imagine it? – as *pardner*. I remember the first time he sat himself down at our table, twining his spidery legs around the chair and leaning forward on an elbow. I expected him to fetch out a tobacco pouch and roll himself a smoke with one hand. The waiter, Paco, or Pablo, a young man with hot eyes and aristocratic pretensions, made a mistake and brought us the wrong drinks, and Randolph seized the opportunity to savage him. The poor boy stood there, his shoulders bowed under the lashes of invective, and was what he had always been, a peasant's son. When he had stumbled away, Randolph looked at Daphne and grinned, showing a side row of long, fulvous teeth, and I thought of a hound sitting back proud as Punch after delivering a dead rat at its mistress's feet. Goddamned spics, he said carelessly, and made a spitting noise out of the side of his mouth. I jumped up and seized the edge of the table and overturned it, pitching the drinks into his lap, and shouted at him to get up and reach for it, you sonofabitch! No, no, of course I didn't. Much as I might have liked to dump a table full of broken glass into his ludicrously overstuffed crotch, that was not the way I did things, not in those days. Besides, I had enjoyed as much as anyone seeing Pablo or Paco get his comeuppance, the twerp, with his soulful glances and his delicate hands and that horrible, pubic moustache.

Randolph liked to give the impression that he was a very dangerous character. He spoke of dark deeds perpetrated in a far-off country which he called Stateside. I encouraged these tales of derring-do, secretly delighting in the aw-shucks, 'tweren't-nuthin' way he told them. There was something wonderfully ridiculous about it all, the braggart's sly glance and slyly modest inflexion, his air of euphoric self-regard, the way he opened like a flower under the warmth of my silently nodding, awed response. I have always derived satisfaction from the little wickednesses of human beings. To treat a fool and a liar as if I esteemed him the soul of probity, to string him along in his poses and his fibs, that is a peculiar pleasure. He claimed he was a painter, until I put a few innocent questions to him on the subject, then he suddenly became a writer instead. In fact, as he confided to me one night in his cups, he made his money by dealing in dope among the island's transient rich. I was shocked, of course, but I recognised a valuable piece of information, and later, when –

But I am tired of this, let me get it out of the way. I asked him to lend me some money. He refused. I reminded him of that drunken night, and said I was sure the *Guardia* would be interested to hear what he had told me. He was shocked. He thought about it. He didn't have the kind of dough I was asking for, he said, he would have to get it for me somewhere, maybe from some people that he knew. And he chewed his lip. I said that would be all right, I didn't mind where it came from. I was amused, and rather pleased with myself, playing at being a blackmailer. I had not really expected him to take me seriously, but it seemed I had underestimated his cravenness. He produced the cash, and for a few weeks Daphne and I had a high old time, and everything was grand except for Randolph dogging my steps wherever I went. He was distressingly literal-minded in his interpretation of words such as *lend* and *repay*. Hadn't I kept his grubby little secret, I said, was that not a fair return? These people, he said, with an awful, twitching attempt at a grin, these people didn't fool around. I said I was glad to hear it, one wouldn't want to think one had been dealing, even at second-hand, with the merely frivolous. Then he threatened to give them my name. I laughed in his face and walked away. I still could not take any of it seriously. A few days later a small package wrapped in brown paper arrived, addressed to me in a semi-literate hand. Daphne

made the mistake of opening it. Inside was a tobacco tin – Balkan
Sobranie, lending an oddly cosmopolitan touch – lined with
cotton wool, in which nestled a curiously whorled, pale, gristly
piece of meat crusted with dried blood. It took me a moment to
identify it as a human ear. Whoever had cut it off had done a
messy job, with something like a breadknife, to judge by the
ragged serration. Painful. I suppose that was the intention.
I remember thinking: How appropriate, an ear, in this land of
the toreador! Quite droll, really.

I went in search of Randolph. He wore a large lint pad pressed
to the left side of his head, held in place by a rakishly angled and
none-too-clean bandage. He no longer made me think of the
Wild West. Now, as if fate had decided to support his claim of
being an artist, he bore a striking resemblance to poor, mad
Vincent in that self-portrait made after he had disfigured himself
for love. When he saw me I thought he was going to weep, he
looked so sorry for himself, and so indignant. You deal with them
yourself now, he said, you owe them, not me, I've paid, and he
touched a hand grimly to his bandaged head. Then he called me
a vile name and skulked off down an alleyway. Despite the noon-
day sun a shiver passed across my back, like a grey wind swarming
over water. I tarried there for a moment, on that white corner,
musing. An old man on a burro saluted me. Nearby a tinny
churchbell was clanging rapidly. Why, I asked myself, why am
I living like this?

That is a question which no doubt the court also would like
answered. With my background, my education, my – yes – my
culture, how could I live such a life, associate with such people,
get myself into such scrapes? The answer is – I don't know the
answer. Or I do, and it is too large, too tangled, for me to attempt
here. I used to believe, like everyone else, that I was determining
the course of my own life, according to my own decisions, but
gradually, as I accumulated more and more past to look back on,
I realised that I had done the things I did because I could do no
other. Please, do not imagine, my Lord, I hasten to say it, do not
imagine that you detect here the insinuation of an apologia, or
even of a defence. I wish to claim full responsibility for my
actions – after all, they are the only things I can call my own –
and I declare in advance that I shall accept without demur the

verdict of the court. I am merely asking, with all respect, whether it is feasible to hold on to the principle of moral culpability once the notion of free will has been abandoned. It is, I grant you, a tricky one, the sort of thing we love to discuss in here of an evening, over our cocoa and our fags, when time hangs heavy.

As I've said, I did not always think of my life as a prison in which all actions are determined according to a random pattern thrown down by an unknown and insensate authority. Indeed, when I was young I saw myself as a master builder who would one day assemble a marvellous edifice around myself, a kind of grand pavilion, airy and light, which would contain me utterly and yet wherein I would be free. Look, they would say, distinguishing this eminence from afar, look how sound it is, how solid: it's him all right, yes, no doubt about it, the man himself. Meantime, however, unhoused, I felt at once exposed and invisible. How shall I describe it, this sense of myself as something without weight, without moorings, a floating phantom? Other people seemed to have a density, a thereness, which I lacked. Among them, these big, carefree creatures, I was like a child among adults. I watched them, wide-eyed, wondering at their calm assurance in the face of a baffling and preposterous world. Don't mistake me, I was no wilting lily, I laughed and whooped and boasted with the best of them – only inside, in that grim, shadowed gallery I call my heart, I stood uneasily, with a hand to my mouth, silent, envious, uncertain. They understood matters, or accepted them, at least. They knew what they thought about things, they had opinions. They took the broad view, as if they did not realise that everything is infinitely divisible. They talked of cause and effect, as if they believed it possible to isolate an event and hold it up to scrutiny in a pure, timeless space, outside the mad swirl of things. They would speak of whole peoples as if they were speaking of a single individual, while to speak even of an individual with any show of certainty seemed to me foolhardy. Oh, they knew no bounds.

And as if people in the outside world were not enough, I had inside me too an exemplar of my own, a kind of invigilator, from whom I must hide my lack of conviction. For instance, if I was reading something, an argument in some book or other, and agreeing with it enthusiastically, and then I discovered at the end that I had misunderstood entirely what the writer was saying, had in fact got the whole thing arse-ways, I would be compelled at once to execute a somersault, quick as a flash, and tell myself, I mean my other self, that stern interior sergeant, that what was being said was true, that I had never really thought otherwise, and, even if I had, that it showed an open mind that I should be able to switch back and forth between opinions without even noticing it. Then I would mop my brow, clear my throat, straighten my shoulders and pass on delicately, in stifled dismay. But why the past tense? Has anything changed? Only that the watcher from inside has stepped forth and taken over, while the puzzled outsider cowers within.

Does the court realise, I wonder, what this confession is costing me?

I took up the study of science in order to find certainty. No, that's not it. Better say, I took up science in order to make the lack of certainty more manageable. Here was a way, I thought, of erecting a solid structure on the very sands that were everywhere, always, shifting under me. And I was good at it, I had a flair. It helped, to be without convictions as to the nature of reality, truth, ethics, all those big things – indeed, I discovered in science a vision of an unpredictable, seething world that was eerily familiar to me, to whom matter had always seemed a swirl of chance collisions. Statistics, probability theory, that was my field. Esoteric stuff, I won't go into it here. I had a certain cold gift that was not negligible, even by the awesome standards of the discipline. My student papers were models of clarity and conciseness. My professors loved me, dowdy old boys reeking of cigarette smoke and bad teeth, who recognised in me that rare, merciless streak the lack of which had condemned them to a life of drudgery at the lectern. And then the Americans spotted me.

How I loved America, the life there on that pastel, sun-drenched western coast, it spoiled me forever. I see it still in dreams, all there, inviolate, the ochre hills, the bay, the great delicate red bridge wreathed in fog. I felt as if I had ascended to some high, fabled plateau, a kind of Arcady. Such wealth, such ease, such innocence. From all the memories I have of the place I select one at random. A spring day, the university cafeteria. It is lunchtime. Outside, on the plaza, by the fountain, the marvellous girls disport themselves in the sun. We have listened that morning to a lecture by a visiting wizard, one of the grandmasters of the arcanum, who sits with us now at our table, drinking coffee from a paper cup and cracking pistachio nuts between his teeth. He is a lean, gangling person with a wild mop of frizzed hair going grey. His glance is humorous, with a spark of malice, it darts restlessly here and there as if searching for something that will make him laugh. The fact is, friends, he is saying, the whole damn thing is chance, pure chance. And he flashes suddenly a shark's grin, and winks at me, a fellow outsider. The faculty staff sitting around the table nod and say nothing, big, tanned, serious men in short-sleeved shirts and shoes with broad-rimmed soles. One scratches his jaw, another consults idly a chunky wristwatch. A boy wearing shorts and no shirt passes by outside, playing a flute. The girls rise slowly, two by two, and slowly walk away, over the grass, arms folded, their books pressed to their chests like breastplates. My God, can I have been there, really? It seems to me now, in this place, more dream than memory, the music, the mild maenads, and us at our table, faint, still figures, the wise ones, presiding behind leaf-reflecting glass.

They were captivated by me over there, my accent, my bow-ties, my slightly sinister, old-world charm. I was twenty-four, among them I felt middle-aged. They threw themselves at me with solemn fervour, as if engaging in a form of self-improvement. One of their little foreign wars was in full swing just then, everyone was a protester, it seemed, except me – I would have no truck with their marches, their sit-downs, the ear-splitting echolalia that passed with them for argument – but even my politics, or lack of them, were no deterrent, and flower children of all shapes and colours fell into my bed, their petals trembling. I remember few of them with any precision, and when I think of them I see a sort of hybrid, with this one's hands and that one's eyes and yet another's sobs. From those days, those nights, only a faint, bittersweet savour remains, and a trace, the barest afterglow, of that state of floating ease, of, how shall I say, of balanic, ataraxic bliss – yes, yes, I have got hold of a dictionary – in which they left me, my muscles aching from their strenuous ministrations, my flesh bathed in the balm of their sweat.

It was in America that I met Daphne. At a party in some professor's house one afternoon I was standing on the porch with a treble gin in my hand when I heard below me on the lawn the voice of home: soft yet clear, like the sound of water falling on glass, and with that touch of lethargy which is the unmistakable note of our set. I looked, and there she was, in a flowered dress and unfashionable shoes, her hair done up in the golliwog style of the day, frowning past the shoulder of a man in a loud jacket who was replying with airy gestures to something she had asked, while she nodded seriously, not listening to a word he said. I had just that glimpse of her and then I turned away, I don't quite know why. I was in one of my bad moods, and halfway drunk. I see that moment as an emblem of our life together. I would spend the next fifteen years turning away from her, in one way or another, until that morning when I stood at the rail of the island steamer, snuffling the slimed air of the harbour and waving half-heartedly to her and the child, the two of them tiny below me on the dockside. That day it was she who turned away from me, with what seems to me now a slow and infinitely sad finality.

I felt as much foolishness as fear. I felt ridiculous. It was unreal, the fix I had got myself into: one of those mad dreams that some ineffectual fat little man might turn into a third-rate film. I would dismiss it for long periods, as one dismisses a dream, no matter how awful, but presently it would come slithering back, the hideous, tentacled thing, and there would well up in me a hot flush of terror and shame – shame, that is, for my own stupidity, my wanton lack of prescience, that had landed me in such a deal of soup.

Since I had seemed, with Randolph, to have stumbled into a supporting feature, I had expected it would be played by a comic cast of ruffians, scarified fellows with low foreheads and little thin moustaches who would stand about me in a circle with their hands in their pockets, smiling horribly and chewing toothpicks. Instead I was summoned to an audience with a silver-haired hidalgo in a white suit, who greeted me with a firm, lingering handshake and told me his name was Aguirre. His manner was courteous and faintly sad. He fitted ill with his surroundings. I had climbed a narrow stairs to a dirty, low room above a bar. There was a table covered with oilcloth, and a couple of cane chairs. On the floor under the table a filthy infant was sitting, sucking on a wooden spoon. An outsize television set squatted in a corner, on the blank, baleful screen of which I saw myself reflected, immensely tall and thin, and curved like a bow. There was a smell of fried food. Señor Aguirre, with a little moue of distaste, examined the seat of one of the chairs and sat down. He poured out wine for us, and tipped his glass in a friendly toast. He was a businessman, he said, a simple businessman, not a great professor – and smiled at me and gently bowed – but all the same he knew there were certain rules, certain moral imperatives. One of these in particular he was thinking of: perhaps I could guess which one? Mutely I shook my head. I felt like a mouse being toyed with by a sleek, bored old cat. His sadness deepened. Loans, he said softly, loans must be repaid. That was the law on which commerce was founded. He hoped I would understand his position. There was a silence. A kind of horrified amazement had taken hold of me: this was the real world, the world of fear and pain and retribution, a serious place, not that sunny playground in which I had frittered away fistfuls of someone else's money. I would have to go home, I said at last, in a voice that did not seem to be mine, there were people who would help me, friends, family, I could borrow from them. He considered. Would I go alone? he wondered. For a second I did not see what he was getting at. Then I looked away from him and said slowly yes, yes, my wife and son would probably stay here. And as I said it I seemed to hear a horrible cackling, a jungle hoot of derision, just behind my shoulder. He smiled, and poured out carefully another inch of wine. The infant, which had been playing with my shoelaces, began to howl. I was agitated, I had not meant to kick the creature. Señor Aguirre frowned, and shouted something over his shoulder. A door behind him opened and an enormously fat, angry-looking young woman put in her head and grunted at him. She wore a black, sleeveless dress with a crooked hem, and a glossy black wig as high as a beehive, with false eyelashes to match. She waddled forward, and with an effort bent and picked up the infant and smacked it hard across the face. It started in surprise, and, swallowing a mighty sob, fixed its round eyes solemnly on me. The woman glared at me too, and took the wooden spoon and threw it on the table in front of me with a clatter. Then, planting the child firmly on one tremendous hip, she stumped out of the room and slammed the door behind her. Señor Aguirre gave a slight, apologetic shrug. He smiled again, twinkling. What was my opinion of the island women? I hesitated. Come come, he said gaily, surely I had an opinion on such an important matter. I said they were lovely, quite lovely, quite the loveliest of their species I had ever encountered. He nodded happily, it was what he had expected me to say. No, he said, no, too dark, too dark all over, even in those places never exposed to the sun. And he leaned forward with his crinkled, silvery smile and tapped a finger lightly on my wrist. Northern women, now, ah, those pale northern women. Such white skin! So delicate! So fragile! Your wife, for instance, he said. There was another, breathless silence. I could hear faintly the brazen strains of music from a radio in the bar downstairs. Bullfight music. My chair made a crackling noise under me, like a muttered warning. Señor Aguirre joined his El Greco hands and looked at me over the spire of his fingertips. Your whife, he said, breathing on the word, your beautiful whife, you will come back quickly to her? It was not really a question. What could I say to him, what could I do? These are not really questions either.

I told Daphne as little as possible. She seemed to understand. She made no difficulties. That has always been the great thing about Daphne: she makes no difficulties.

It was a long trip home. The steamer landed in Valencia harbour at dusk. I hate Spain, a brutish, boring country. The city smelled of sex and chlorine. I took the night train, jammed in a third-class compartment with half a dozen reeking peasants in cheap suits. I could not sleep. I was hot, my head ached. I could feel the engine labouring up the long slope to the plateau, the wheels drumming their one phrase over and over. A washed-blue dawn was breaking in Madrid. I stopped outside the station and watched a flock of birds wheeling and tumbling at an immense height, and, the strangest thing, a gust of euphoria, or something like euphoria, swept through me, making me tremble, and bringing tears to my eyes. It was from lack of sleep, I suppose, and the effect of the high, thin air. Why, I wonder, do I remember so clearly standing there, the colour of the sky, those birds, that shiver of fevered optimism? I was at a turning point, you will tell me, just there the future forked for me, and I took the wrong path without noticing – that's what you'll tell me, isn't it, you, who must have meaning in everything, who lust after meaning, your palms sticky and your faces on fire! But calm, Frederick, calm. Forgive me this outburst, your Honour. It is just that I do not believe such moments mean anything – or any other moments, for that matter. They have significance, apparently. They may even have value of some sort. But they do not mean anything.

There now, I have declared my faith.

Where was I? In Madrid. On my way out of Madrid. I took another train, travelling north. We stopped at every station on the way, I thought I would never get out of that terrible country. Once we halted for an hour in the middle of nowhere. I sat in the ticking silence and stared dully through the window. Beyond the littered tracks of the up-line there was an enormous, high, yellow field, and in the distance a range of blue mountains that at first I took for clouds. The sun shone. A tired crow flapped past. Someone coughed. I thought how odd it was to be there, I mean just there and not somewhere else. Not that being somewhere else would have seemed any less odd. I mean – oh, I don't know what I mean. The air in the compartment was thick. The seats gave off their dusty, sat-upon smell. A small, swarthy, low-browed man opposite me caught my eye and did not look away. At that instant it came to me that I was on my way to do something very bad, something really appalling, something for which there would be no forgiveness. It was not a premonition, that is too tentative a word. I knew. I cannot explain how, but I knew. I was shocked at myself, my breathing quickened, my face pounded as if from embarrassment, but as well as shock there was a sort of antic glee, it surged in my throat and made me choke. That *campesino* was still watching me. He sat canted forward a little, hands resting calmly on his knees, his brow lowered, at once intent and remote. They stare like that, these people, they have so little sense of themselves they seem to imagine their actions will not register on others. They might be looking in from a different world.

I knew very well, of course, that I was running away.

I HAD expected to arrive in rain, and at Holyhead, indeed, a fine, warm drizzle was falling, but when we got out on the channel the sun broke through again. It was evening. The sea was calm, an oiled, taut meniscus, mauve-tinted and curiously high and curved. From the forward lounge where I sat the prow seemed to rise and rise, as if the whole ship were straining to take to the air. The sky before us was a smear of crimson on the palest of pale blue and silvery green. I held my face up to the calm sea-light, entranced, expectant, grinning like a loon. I confess I was not entirely sober, I had already broken into my allowance of duty-free booze, and the skin at my temples and around my eyes was tightening alarmingly. It was not just the drink, though, that was making me happy, but the tenderness of things, the simple goodness of the world. This sunset, for instance, how lavishly it was laid on, the clouds, the light on the sea, that heartbreaking, blue-green distance, laid on, all of it, as if to console some lost, suffering wayfarer. I have never really got used to being on this earth. Sometimes I think our presence here is due to a cosmic blunder, that we were meant for another planet altogether, with other arrangements, and other laws, and other, grimmer skies. I try to imagine it, our true place, off on the far side of the galaxy, whirling and whirling. And the ones who were meant for here, are they out there, baffled and homesick, like us? No, they would have become extinct long ago. How could they survive, these gentle earthlings, in a world that was made to contain *us*?

The voices, that was what startled me first of all. I thought they must be putting on this accent, it sounded so like a caricature. Two raw-faced dockers with fags in their mouths, a customs man in a cap: my fellow countrymen. I walked through a vast, corrugated-iron shed and out into the tired gold of the summer evening. A bus went past, and a workman on a bike. The clock-tower, its addled clock still showing the wrong time. It was all so affecting, I was surprised. I liked it here when I was a child, the pier, the promenade, that green bandstand. There was always a sweet sense of melancholy, of mild regret, as if some quaint, gay music, the last of the season, had just faded on the air. My father never referred to the place as anything but Kingstown: he had no time for the native jabber. He used to bring me here on Sunday afternoons, sometimes on weekdays too in the school holidays. It was a long drive from Coolgrange. He would park on the road above the pier and give me a shilling and slope off, leaving me to what he called my own devices. I see myself, the frog prince, enthroned on the high back seat of the Morris Oxford, consuming a cornet of ice cream, licking the diminishing knob of goo round and round with scientific application, and staring back at the passing promenaders, who blanched at the sight of my baleful eye and flickering, creamy tongue. The breeze from the sea was a soft, salt wall of air in the open window of the car, with a hint of smoke in it from the mailboat berthed below me. The flags on the roof of the yacht club shuddered and snapped, and a thicket of masts in the harbour swayed and tinkled like an oriental orchestra.

My mother never accompanied us on these jaunts. They were, I know now, just an excuse for my father to visit a poppet he kept there. I do not recall him behaving furtively, or not any more so than usual. He was a slight, neatly-made man, with pale eyebrows and pale eyes, and a small, fair moustache that was faintly indecent, like a bit of body fur, soft and downy, that had found its way inadvertently on to his face from some other, secret part of his person. It made his mouth startlingly vivid, a hungry, violent, red-coloured thing, grinding and snarling. He was always more or less angry, seething with resentment and indignation. Behind the bluster, though, he was a coward, I think. He felt sorry for himself. He was convinced the world had used him badly. In recompense he pampered himself, gave himself treats. He wore expensive shoes and Charvet ties, drank good claret, smoked cigarettes specially imported in airtight tins from a shop in the Burlington Arcade. I still have, or had, his malacca walking-cane. He was enormously proud of it. He liked to demonstrate to me how it was made, from four or was it eight pieces of rattan prepared and fitted together by a master craftsman. I could hardly keep a straight face, he was so laughably earnest. He made the mistake of imagining that his possessions were a measure of his own worth, and strutted and crowed, parading his things like a schoolboy with a champion catapult. Indeed, there was something of the eternal boy about him, something tentative and pubertal. When I think of us together I see him as impossibly young and me already grown-up, weary, embittered. I suspect he was a little afraid of me. By the age of twelve or thirteen I was as big as he, or as heavy, anyway, for although I have his fawn colouring, in shape I took after my mother, and already at that age was inclined towards flab. (Yes, m'lud, you see before you a middling man inside whom there is a fattie trying not to come out. For he was let slip once, was Bunter, just once, and look what happened.)

I hope I do not give the impression that I disliked my father. We did not converse much, but we were perfectly companionable, in the way of fathers and sons. If he did fear me a little, I too was wise enough to be wary of *him*, a relation easily mistaken, even by us at times, for mutual esteem. We had a great distaste for the world generally, there was that much in common between us. I notice I have inherited his laugh, that soft, nasal snicker which was his only comment on the large events of his time. Schisms, wars, catastrophes, what did he care for such matters? – the world, the only worthwhile world, had ended with the last viceroy's departure from these shores, after that it was all just a wrangle among peasants. He really did try to believe in this fantasy of a great good place that had been taken away from us and our kind – our kind being Castle Catholics, as he liked to say, yes, sir, Castle Catholics, and proud of it! But I think there was less pride than chagrin. I think he was secretly ashamed not to be a Protestant: he would have had so much less explaining, so much less justifying, to do. He portrayed himself as a tragic figure, a gentleman of the old school displaced in time. I picture him on those Sunday afternoons with his mistress, an ample young lady, I surmise, with hair unwisely curled and a generous décolletage, before whom he kneels, poised trembling on one knee, gazing rapt into her face, his moustache twitching, his moist red mouth open in supplication. Oh but I must not mock him like this. Really, really, I did not think unkindly of him – apart, that is, from wanting deep down to kill him, so that I might marry my mother, a novel and compelling notion which my counsel urges on me frequently, with a meaning look in his eye.

But I digress.

The charm I had felt in Kingstown, I mean Dun Laoghaire, did not endure into the city. My seat at the front on the top deck of the bus – my old seat, my favourite! – showed me scenes I hardly recognised. In the ten years since I had last been here something had happened, something had befallen the place. Whole streets were gone, the houses torn out and replaced by frightening blocks of steel and black glass. An old square where Daphne and I lived for a while had been razed and made into a vast, cindered car park. I saw a church for sale – a church, for sale! Oh, something dreadful had happened. The very air itself seemed damaged. Despite the late hour a faint glow of daylight lingered, dense, dust-laden, like the haze after an explosion, or a great conflagration. People in the streets had the shocked look of survivors, they seemed not to walk but reel. I got down from the bus and picked my way among them with lowered gaze, afraid I might see horrors. Barefoot urchins ran along beside me, whining for pennies. There were drunks everywhere, staggering and swearing, lost in joyless befuddlement. An amazing couple reared up out of a pulsating cellar, a minatory, pockmarked young man with a crest of orange hair, and a stark-faced girl in gladiator boots and ragged, soot-black clothes. They were draped about with ropes and chains and what looked like cartridge belts, and sported gold studs in their nostrils. I had never seen such creatures, I thought they must be members of some fantastic sect. I fled before them, and dived into Wally's pub. Dived is the word.

I had expected it to be changed, like everything else. I was fond of Wally's. I used to drink there when I was a student, and later on, too, when I worked for the government. There was a touch of sleaze to the place which I found congenial. I know much has been made of the fact that it was frequented by homosexuals, but I trust the court will dismiss the implications which have been tacitly drawn from this, especially in the gutter press. I am not queer. I have nothing against those who are, except that I despise them, of course, and find disgusting the thought of the things they get up to, whatever those things may be. But their presence lent a blowsy gaiety to the atmosphere in Wally's and a slight edge of threat. I liked that shiver of embarrassment and gleeful dread that ran like a bead of mercury up my spine when a bevy of them suddenly exploded in parrot shrieks of laughter, or when they got drunk and started howling abuse and breaking things. Tonight, when I hurried in to shelter from the stricken city, the first thing I saw was a half dozen of them at a table by the door with their heads together, whispering and giggling and pawing each other happily. Wally himself was behind the bar. He had grown fatter, which I would not have thought possible, but apart from that he had not changed in ten years. I greeted him warmly. I suspect he remembered me, though of course he would not acknowledge it: Wally prided himself on the sourness of his manner. I ordered a large, a gargantuan, gin and tonic, and he sighed grudgingly and heaved himself off the high stool on which he had been propped. He moved very slowly, as if through water, billowing in his fat, like a jellyfish. I was feeling better already. I told him about the church I had seen for sale. He shrugged, he was not surprised, such things were commonplace nowadays. As he was setting my drink before me the huddled circle of queers by the door flew apart suddenly in a loud splash of laughter, and he frowned at them, pursing his little mouth so that it almost disappeared in the folds of his fat chin. He affected contempt for his clientele, though it was said he kept a bevy of boys himself, over whom he ruled with great severity, jealous and terrible as a Beardsleyan queen.

I drank my drink. There is something about gin, the tang in it of the deep wildwood, perhaps, that always makes me think of twilight and mists and dead maidens. Tonight it tinkled in my mouth like secret laughter. I looked about me. No, Wally's was not changed, not changed at all. This was my place: the murmurous gloom, the mirrors, the bottles ranged behind the bar, each one with its bead of ruby light. Yes, yes, the witch's kitchen, with a horrid fat queen, and a tittering band of fairy-folk. Why, there was even an ogre – Gilles the Terrible, *c'est moi*. I was happy. I enjoy the inappropriate, the disreputable, I admit it. In low dives such as this the burden of birth and education falls from me and I feel, I feel – I don't know what I feel. I don't know. The tense is wrong anyway. I turned to Wally and held out my glass, and watched in a kind of numbed euphoria as he measured out another philtre for me in a little silver chalice. That flash of blue when he added the ice, what am I thinking of? Blue eyes. Yes, of course.

I did say dead maidens, didn't I. Dear me.

So I sat in Wally's pub and drank, and talked to Wally of this and that – his side of the conversation confined to shrugs and dull grunts and the odd malevolent snigger – and gradually the buzz that travel always sets going in my head was stilled. I felt as if, instead of journeying by ship and rail, I had been dropped somehow through the air to land up in this spot at last, feeling groggy and happy, and pleasantly, almost voluptuously, vulnerable. Those ten years I had passed in restless wandering were as nothing, a dream voyage, insubstantial. How distant all that seemed, those islands in a blue sea, those burning noons, and Randolph and Señor Aguirre, even my wife and child, how distant. Thus it was that when Charlie French came in I greeted him as if I had seen him only yesterday.

I know Charlie insists that he did not meet me in Wally's pub, that he never went near the place, but all I am prepared to admit is the possibility that it was not on that particular night that I saw him there. I remember the moment with perfect clarity, the queers whispering, and Wally polishing a glass with a practised and inimitably contemptuous wrist-action, and I sitting at the bar with a bumper of gin in my fist and my old pigskin suitcase at my feet, and Charlie pausing there in his chalkstripes and his scuffed shoes, a forgetful Eumaeus, smiling uneasily and eyeing me with vague surmise. All the same, it is possible that my memory has conflated two separate occasions. It is possible. What more can I say? I hope, Charles, this concession will soothe, even if only a little, your sense of injury.

People think me heartless, but I am not. I have much sympathy for Charlie French. I caused him great distress, no doubt of that. I humiliated him before the world. What pain that must have been, for a man such as Charlie. He behaved very well about it. He behaved beautifully, in fact. On that last, appalling, and appallingly comic occasion, when I was being led out in handcuffs, he looked at me not accusingly, but with a sort of sadness. He almost smiled. And I was grateful. He is a source of guilt and annoyance to me now, but he was my friend, and –

He was my friend. Such a simple phrase, and yet how affecting. I don't think I have ever used it before. When I wrote it down I had to pause, startled. Something welled up in my throat, as if I might be about to, yes, to weep. What is happening to me?

Is this what they mean by rehabilitation? Perhaps I shall leave here a reformed character, after all.

Poor Charlie did not recognise me at first, and was distinctly uneasy, I could see, at being addressed in this place, in this familiar fashion, by a person who seemed to him a stranger. I was enjoying myself, it was like being in disguise. I offered to buy him a drink, but he declined, with elaborate politeness. He had aged. He was in his early sixties, but he looked older. He was stooped, and had a little egg-shaped paunch, and his ashen cheeks were inlaid with a filigree of broken veins. Yet he gave an impression of, what shall I call it, of equilibrium, which seemed new to him. It was as if he were at last filling out exactly his allotted space. When I knew him he had been a small-time dealer in pictures and antiques. Now he had presence, it was almost an air of imperium, all the more marked amid the gaudy trappings of Wally's bar. It's true, there was still that familiar expression in his eye, at once mischievous and sheepish, but I had to look hard to find it. He began to edge away from me, still smiling uneasily, but then he in turn must have caught something familiar in my eye, and he knew me at last. Relieved, he gave a breathy laugh and glanced around the bar. That I did remember, that glance, as if he had just discovered his flies were open and was looking to see if anyone had noticed. Freddie! he said. Well well! He lit a cigarette with a not altogether steady hand, and released a great whoosh of smoke towards the ceiling. I was trying to recall when it was I had first met him. He used to come down to Coolgrange when my father was alive and hang about the house looking furtive and apologetic. They had been young together, he and my parents, in their cups they would reminisce about hunt balls before the war, and dashing up to Dublin for the Show, and all the rest of it. I listened to this stuff with boundless contempt, curling an adolescent's villous lip. They sounded like actors flogging away at some tired old drawing room comedy, projecting wildly, my mother especially, with her scarlet fingernails and metallic perm and that cracked, gin-and-smoke voice of hers. But to be fair to Charles, I do not think he really subscribed to this fantasy of the dear dead days. He could not ignore the tiny trill of hysteria that made my mother's goitrous throat vibrate, nor the way my father looked at her sometimes, poised on the edge of his chair, tense as a whippet, pop-eyed and pale, with an expression of incredulous loathing. When they got going like this, the two of them, they forgot everything else, their son, their friend, everything, locked together in a kind of macabre trance. This meant that Charlie and I were often thrown into each other's company. He treated me tentatively, as if I were something that might blow up in his face at any moment. I was very fierce in those days, brimming with impatience and scorn. We must have been a peculiar pair, yet we got on, at some deep level. Perhaps I seemed to him the son he would never have, perhaps he seemed to me the father I had never had. (This is another idea put forward by my counsel. I don't know how you think of them, Maolseachlainn.) What was I saying? Charlie. He took me to the races one day, when I was a boy. He was all kitted out for the occasion, in tweeds and brown brogues and a little trilby hat tipped at a raffish angle over one eye. He even had a pair of binoculars, though he did not seem to be able to get them properly in focus. He looked the part, except for a certain stifled something in his manner that made it seem all the time as if he were about to break down in helpless giggles at himself and his pretensions. I was fifteen or sixteen. In the drinks marquee he turned to me blandly and asked what I would have, Irish or Scotch – and brought me home in the evening loudly and truculently drunk. My father was furious, my mother laughed. Charlie maintained an unruffled silence, pretending nothing was amiss, and slipped me a fiver as I was stumbling off to bed.

Ah Charles, I am sorry, truly I am.

Now, as if he too were remembering that other time, he insisted on buying a drink, and pursed his lips disapprovingly when I asked for gin. He was a whiskey man, himself. It was part of his disguise, like the striped suit and the worn-down, hand-made shoes, and that wonderful, winged helmet of hair, now silvered all over, which, so my mother liked to say, had destined him for greatness. He had always managed to avoid his destiny, however. I asked him what he was doing these days. Oh, he said, I'm running a gallery. And he glanced about him with an abstracted, wondering smile, as if he were himself surprised at such a notion. I nodded. So that was what had bucked him up, what had given him that self-sufficient air. I saw him in some dusty room, a forgotten backwater, with a few murky pictures on the wall, and a frosty spinster for a secretary who bickered with him over tea money and gave him a tie wrapped in tissue paper every Christmas. Poor Charlie, forced to take himself seriously at last, with a business to take care of, and painters after him for their money. Here, I said, let me, and peeled a note from my rapidly dwindling wad and slapped it on the bar.

To be candid, however, I was thinking of asking him for a loan. What prevented me was – well, there will be laughter in court, I know, but the fact is I felt it would be in bad taste. It is not that I am squeamish about these matters, in my time I have touched sadder cases than Charlie for a float, but there was something in the present circumstances that held me back. We might indeed have been a father and son – not *my* father, of course, and certainly not *this* son – meeting by chance in a brothel. Constrained, sad, obscurely ashamed, we blustered and bluffed, knocking our glasses together and toasting the good old days. But it was no use, in a little while we faltered, and fell gloomily silent. Then suddenly Charlie looked at me, with what was almost a flash of pain, and in a low, impassioned voice said, Freddie, what have you done to yourself? At once abashed, he leaned away from me in a panic, desperately grinning, and puffed a covering cloud of smoke. First I was furious, and then depressed. Really, I was not in the mood for this kind of thing. I glanced at the clock behind the bar and, purposely misunderstanding him, said yes, it was true, it had been a long day, I was overdoing it, and I finished my drink and shook his hand and took up my bag and left.

There it was again, in another form, the same question: why, Freddie, why are you living like this? I brooded on it next morning on the way to Coolgrange. The day looked as I felt, grey and flat and heavy. The bus plunged laboriously down the narrow country roads, pitching and wallowing, with a dull zip and roar that seemed the sound of my own blood beating in my brain. The myriad possibilities of the past lay behind me, a strew of wreckage. Was there, in all that, one particular shard – a decision reached, a road taken, a signpost followed – that would show me just how I had come to my present state? No, of course not. My journey, like everyone else's, even yours, your Honour, had not been a thing of signposts and decisive marching, but drift only, a kind of slow subsidence, my shoulders bowing down under the gradual accumulation of all the things I had not done.

Yet I can see that to someone like Charlie, watching from the ground, I must have seemed a creature of fable scaling the far peaks, rising higher and ever higher, leaping at last from the pinnacle into marvellous, fiery flight, my head wreathed in flames. But I am not Euphorion. I am not even his father.

The question is wrong, that's the trouble. It assumes that actions are determined by volition, deliberate thought, a careful weighing-up of facts, all that puppet-show twitching which passes for consciousness. I was living like that because I was living like that, there is no other answer. When I look back, no matter how hard I try I can see no clear break between one phase and another. It is a seamless flow – although flow is too strong a word. More a sort of busy stasis, a sort of running on the spot. Even that was too fast for me, however, I was always a little way behind, trotting in the rear of my own life. In Dublin I was still the boy growing up at Coolgrange, in America I was the callow young man of Dublin days, on the islands I became a kind of American. And nothing was enough. Everything was coming, was on the way, was about to be. Stuck in the past, I was always peering beyond the present towards a limitless future. Now, I suppose, the future may be said to have arrived.

None of this means anything. Anything of significance, that is. I am just amusing myself, musing, losing myself in a welter of words. For words in here are a form of luxury, of sensuousness, they are all we have been allowed to keep of the rich, wasteful world from which we are shut away.

O God, O Christ, release me from this place.

O Someone.

I must stop, I am getting one of my headaches. They come with increasing frequency. Don't worry, your Lordship, no need to summon the tipstaff or the sergeant-at-arms or whatever he's called – they are just headaches. I shall not suddenly go berserk, clutching my temples and bawling for my – but speak of the devil, here she is, Ma Jarrett herself. Come, step into the witness box, mother.

IT WAS early afternoon when I reached Coolgrange. I got down at the cross and watched the bus lumber away, its fat back-end looking somehow derisive. The noise of the engine faded, and the throbbing silence of summer settled again on the fields. The sky was still overcast, but the sun was asserting itself somewhere, and the light that had been dull and flat was now a tender, pearl-grey glow. I stood and looked about me. What a surprise the familiar always is. It was all there, the broken gate, the drive, the long meadow, the oak wood – home! – all perfectly in place, waiting for me, a little smaller than I remembered, like a scale-model of itself. I laughed. It was not really a laugh, more an exclamation of startlement and recognition. Before such scenes as this – trees, the shimmering fields, that mild soft light – I always feel like a traveller on the point of departure. Even arriving I seemed to be turning away, with a lingering glance at the lost land. I set off up the drive with my raincoat over my shoulder and my battered bag in my hand, a walking cliché, though it's true I was a bit long in the tooth, and a bit on the beefy side, for the part of the prodigal son. A dog slid out of the hedge at me with a guttural snarl, teeth bared to the gums. I halted. I do not like dogs. This was a black-and-white thing with shifty eyes, it moved back and forth in a half-circle in front of me, still growling, keeping its belly close to the ground. I held the suitcase against my knees for a shield, and spoke sharply, as to an unruly child, but my voice came out a broken falsetto, and for a moment there was a sense of general merriment, as if there were faces hidden among the leaves, laughing. Then a whistle sounded, and the brute whined and turned guiltily towards the house. My mother was standing on the front steps. She laughed. Suddenly the sun came out, with a kind of soundless report. Good God, she said, it is you, I thought I was seeing things.

*   *   *

I hesitate. It is not that I am lost for words, but the opposite. There is so much to be said I do not know where to begin. I feel myself staggering backwards slowly, clutching in my outstretched arms a huge, unwieldy and yet weightless burden. She is so much, and, at the same time, nothing. I must go carefully, this is perilous ground. Of course, I know that whatever I say will be smirked at knowingly by the amateur psychologists packing the court. When it comes to the subject of mothers, simplicity is not permitted. All the same, I shall try to be honest and clear. Her name is Dorothy, though everyone has always called her Dolly, I do not know why, for there is nothing doll-like about her. She is a large, vigorous woman with the broad face and heavy hair of a tinker's wife. In describing her thus I do not mean to be disrespectful. She is impressive, in her way, at once majestic and slovenly. I recall her from my childhood as a constant but remote presence, statuesque, blank-eyed, impossibly handsome in an Ancient Roman sort of way, like a marble figure at the far side of a lawn. Later on, though, she grew to be top-heavy, with a big backside and slim legs, a contrast which, when I was an adolescent and morbidly interested in such things, led me to speculate on the complicated architecture that must be necessary to bridge the gap under her skirt between those shapely knees and that thick waist. Hello, mother, I said, and looked away from her, casting about me crossly for something neutral on which to concentrate. I was annoyed already. She has that effect on me, I have only to stand before her and instantly the irritation and resentment begin to seethe in my breast. I was surprised. I had thought that after ten years there would be at least a moment of grace between our meeting and the first attack of filial heartburn, but not a bit of it, here I was, jaw clenched, glaring venomously at a tuft of weed sprouting from a crack in the stone steps where she stood. She was not much changed. Her bosom, which cries out to be called ample, had descended to just above her midriff. Also she had grown a little moustache. She wore baggy corduroy trousers and a cardigan with sagging pockets. She came down the steps to me and laughed again. You have put on weight, Freddie, she said, you've got fat. Then she reached out and – this is true, I swear it – and took hold of a piece of my stomach and rolled it playfully between a finger and thumb. This woman, this woman – what can I say? I was thirty-eight, a man of parts, with a wife and a son and an impressive Mediterranean tan, I carried myself with gravitas and a certain faint air of menace, and she, what did she do? – she pinched my belly and laughed her phlegmy laugh. Is it any wonder I have ended up in jail? Is it? The dog, seeing that I was to be accepted, sidled up to me and tried to lick my hand, which gave me an opportunity to deliver it a good hard kick in the ribs. That made me feel better, but not much, and not for long.

Is there anything as powerfully, as piercingly evocative, as the smell of the house in which one's childhood was spent? I try to avoid generalisations, as no doubt the court has noticed, but surely this is a universal, this involuntary spasm of recognition which comes with the first whiff of that humble, drab, brownish smell, which is hardly a smell at all, more an emanation, a sort of sigh exhaled by the thousands of known but unacknowledged tiny things that collectively constitute what is called home. I stepped into the hall and for an instant it was as if I had stepped soundlessly through the membrane of time itself. I faltered, tottering inwardly. Hatstand with broken umbrella, that floor tile, still loose. Get out, Patch, damn you! my mother said behind me, and the dog yelped. The taste of apples unaccountably flooded my mouth. I felt vaguely as if something momentous had happened, as if in the blink of an eye everything around me had been whipped away and replaced instantly with an exact replica, perfect in every detail, down to the last dust mote. I walked on, into this substitute world, tactfully keeping a blank expression, and seemed to hear a disembodied held breath being let go in relief that the difficult trick had worked yet again.

We went into the kitchen. It looked like the lair of some large, scavenging creature. Lord, mother, I said, are you *living* in here? Items of clothing, an old woman's nameless rags, were stuffed between the dishes on the dresser. The toes of three or four pairs of shoes peeped out from under a cupboard, an unnerving sight, as if the wearers might be huddled together in there, stubby arms clasped around each other's hunched shoulders, listening. Pieces of furniture had migrated here from all over the house, the narrow little bureau from my father's study, the walnut cocktail cabinet from the drawing room, the velvet-covered recliner with balding armrests in which my Great-Aunt Alice, a tiny, terrible woman, had died without a murmur one Sunday afternoon in summer. The huge old wireless that used to lord it over the

lounge stood now at a drunken tilt on the draining board, crooning softly to itself, its single green eye pulsing. The place was far
from clean. A ledger was open on the table, and bills and things
were strewn amid the smeared plates and the unwashed teacups.
She had been doing the accounts. Briefly I considered bringing
up the main matter straight away – money, that is – but thought
better of it. As if she had an inkling of what was in my mind she
glanced from me to the papers and back again with amusement.
I turned away from her, to the window. Out on the lawn a stocky
girl in jodhpurs was leading a string of Connemara ponies in a
circle. I recalled dimly my mother telling me, in one of her infrequent and barely literate letters, about some harebrained
venture involving these animals. She came and stood beside me.
We watched in silence the ponies plodding round and round.
Ugly brutes, aren't they, she said cheerfully. The simmering
annoyance I had felt since arriving was added to now by a sense
of general futility. I have always been prone to accidie. It is a state,
or, I might even say, a force, the significance of which in human
affairs historians and suchlike seem not to appreciate. I think
I would do anything to avoid it – anything. My mother was talking about her customers, mostly Japs and Germans, it seemed –
They're taking over the bloody country, Freddie, I'm telling you.
They bought the ponies as pets for their spoilt offspring, at what
she happily admitted were outrageous prices. Cracked, the lot of
them, she said. We laughed, and then fell vacantly silent again.
The sun was on the lawn, and a vast white cloud was slowly
unfurling above the sweltering beeches. I was thinking how
strange it was to stand here glooming out at the day like this,
bored and irritable, my hands in my pockets, while all the time,
deep inside me somewhere, hardly acknowledged, grief dripped
and dripped, a kind of silvery ichor, pure, and strangely precious.
Home, yes, home is always a surprise.

She insisted that I come and look the place over, as she put it.
After all, my boy, she said, someday all this will be yours. And
she did her throaty cackle. I did not remember her being so easily
amused in the past. There was something almost unruly in her
laughter, a sort of abandon. I was a little put out by it, I thought
it was not seemly. She lit up a cigarette and set off around the
house, with the cigarette box and matches clutched in her left
claw, and me trailing grimly in her smoking wake. The house

was rotting, in places so badly, and so rapidly, that even she was startled. She talked and talked. I nodded dully, gazing at damp walls and sagging floors and mouldering window-frames. In my old room the bed was broken, and there was something growing in the middle of the mattress. The view from the window – trees, a bit of sloping field, the red roof of a barn – was exact and famil-iar as an hallucination. Here was the cupboard I had built, and at once I had a vision of myself, a small boy with a fierce frown, blunt saw in hand, hacking at a sheet of plywood, and my griev-ing heart wobbled, as if it were not myself I was remembering, but something like a son, dear and vulnerable, lost to me forever in the depths of my own past. When I turned round my mother was not there. I found her on the stairs, looking a little odd around the eyes. She set off again. I must see the grounds, she cried, the stables, the oak wood. She was determined I would see everything, everything.

Out of doors my spirits rose somewhat. How soft the air of summer here. I had been too long under harsh southern skies. And the trees, the great trees! those patient, quietly suffering crea-tures, standing stock-still as if in embarrassment, their tragic gazes somehow turned away from us. Patch the dog – I can see I am going to be stuck with this brute – Patch the dog appeared, rolling its mad eyes and squirming. It followed silently behind us across the lawn. The stable-girl, watching sidelong as we approached, seemed on the point of taking to her heels in fright. Her name was Joan, or Jean, something like that. Big bum, big chest – obviously mother had felt an affinity. When I spoke to her the poor girl turned crimson, and wincingly extended a callused little paw as if she were afraid I might be going to keep it. I gave her one of my special, slow smiles, and saw myself through her eyes, a tall, tanned hunk in a linen suit, leaning over her on a summer lawn and murmuring dark words. Tinker! she yelped, get off! The lead pony, a stunted beast with a truculent eye, was edging sideways in that dully determined way that they have, nudging heavily against me. I put my hand on its flank to push it away, and was startled by the solidity, the actuality of the animal, the coarse dry coat, the dense unyielding flesh beneath, the blood warmth. Shocked, I took my hand away quickly and stepped back. Suddenly I had a vivid, queasy sense of myself, not the tanned pin-up now, but something else, something pallid and slack and soft. I was aware of my toenails, my anus, my damp, constricted crotch. And I was ashamed. I can't explain it. That is, I could, but won't. Then the dog began to bark, rushing at the pony's hoofs, and the pony snorted, peeling back its muzzle and snapping its alarming teeth. My mother kicked the dog, and the girl hauled the pony's head sideways. The dog howled, the line of ponies plunged and whinnied. What a racket! Everything, always, turns to farce. I remembered my hangover. I needed a drink.

Gin first, then some sort of awful sherry, then successive jorums of my late father's fine Bordeaux, the last, alas, of the bin. I was already half-soused when I went down to the cellar to fetch more claret. I sat on a crate amid the must and gloom, breathing gin fumes out of flared nostrils. A streaming lance of sunlight, seething with dust, pierced the low, cobwebbed window above my head. Things thronged around me in the shadows – a battered rocking horse, an old high bicycle, a bundle of antique tennis racquets – their outlines blurred, greyish, fading, as if this place were a way-station where the past paused on its way down into oblivion. I laughed. Old bastard, I said aloud, and the silence rang like a rapped glass. He was always down here in those last months before he died. He had become a potterer, he who all his life had been driven by fierce, obsessive energies. My mother would send me down to look for him, in case something might have happened to him, as she delicately put it. I would find him poking about in corners, fiddling with things, or just standing, canted at an odd angle, staring at nothing. When I spoke he would give a great start and turn on me angrily, huffing, as if he had been caught at something shameful. But these spurts of animation did not last long, and after a moment he would drift off again into vagueness. It was as if he were not dying of an illness, but of a sort of general distraction: as if one day in the midst of his vehement doings something had caught his attention, had beckoned to him out of the darkness, and, struck, he had turned aside and walked towards it, with a sleepwalker's pained, puzzled concentration. I was, what, twenty-two, twenty-three. The long process of his dying wearied and exasperated me in equal measure. Of course I pitied him, too, but I think pity is always, for me, only the permissible version of an urge to give weak things a good hard shake. He began to shrink. Suddenly his shirt collars were too big for that wobbly tortoise-neck with its two slack harp-strings. Everything was too big for him, his clothes had more substance than he did, he seemed to rattle about inside them. His eyes were huge and haunted, already clouding. It was summer then, too. Light was not his medium any more, he preferred it down here, in the mossy half-dark, among the deepening shades.

I hauled myself to my feet and gathered an armful of dusty bottles and staggered with them up the damp stone steps.

Yet he died upstairs, in the big front bedroom, the airiest room in the house. It was so hot all that week. They opened wide the window, and he made them move his bed forward until the foot of it was right out on the balcony. He lay with the covers thrown back, his meagre chest bared, giving himself up to the sun, the vast sky, dying into the blue and gold glare of summer. His hands. The rapid beat of his breathing. His –

Enough. I was speaking of my mother.

I had set the bottles on the table, and was clawing the dust and cobwebs off them, when she informed me that she did not drink now. This was a surprise – in the old days she could knock it back with the best of them. I stared at her, and she shrugged and looked away. Doctor's orders, she said. I examined her with renewed attention. There was something wrong with her left eye, and her mouth drooped a little on that side. I recalled the odd way she had clutched the cigarette box and matches in her left hand when she was conducting me around the house. She shrugged again. A slight stroke, she said, last year. I thought what an odd term that is: a slight stroke. As if a benevolent but clumsy power had dealt her a fond, playful blow and accidentally damaged her. She glanced at me sidelong now with a tentative, almost girlish, melancholy little smile. She might have been confessing to something, some peccadillo, trivial but embarrassing. Sorry to hear it, old thing, I said, and urged her to go on, take a drop of wine, the doctors be damned. She seemed not to hear me. And then a really surprising thing happened. The girl, Joan or Jean – I'll compromise, and call her Jane – got up suddenly from her place, with a gulp of distress, and put her arm awkwardly around my mother's head, clutching her in a sort of wrestling hold, and laying a hand along her brow. I expected my mother to give her a good push and tell her to get off, but no, she sat there, suffering calmly the girl's embrace and looking at me still with that small smile. I stared back at her in startlement, holding the wine bottle suspended above my glass. It was the strangest thing. The girl's great hip was beside my mother's shoulder, and I thought irresistibly of the pony pressing against me on the lawn with that stubborn, brute weight. There was a silence. Then the girl, I mean Jane, caught my eye, and blenched, and withdrew her arm and sat down again hurriedly. Here is a question: if man is a sick animal, an insane animal, as I have reason to believe, then how account for these small, unbidden gestures of kindness and of care? Does it occur to you, my Lord, that people of our kind – if I may be permitted to scramble up and join you on the bench for a moment – that we have missed out on something, I mean something in general, a universal principle, which is so simple, so obvious, that no one has ever thought to tell us about it? They all know what it is, my learned friend, this knowledge is the badge of their fellowship. And they are everywhere, the vast, sad, initiated crowd. They look up at us from the well of the court and say nothing, only smile a little, with that mixture of compassion and sympathetic irony, as my mother was smiling at me now. She reached across and patted the girl's hand and told her not to mind me. I stared. What had I done? The child sat with eyes fixed on her plate, groping blindly for her knife and fork. Her cheeks were aflame, I could almost hear them hum. Had a look from me done all that? I sighed, poor ogre, and ate a potato. It was raw and waxen at the heart. More drink.

You're not getting into one of your moods, are you, Freddie? my mother said.

Have I mentioned my bad moods, I wonder. Very black, very black. As if the world had grown suddenly dim, as if something had dirtied the air. Even when I was a child my depressions frightened people. In them again, is he? they would say, and they would chuckle, but uneasily, and edge away from me. In school I was a terror – but no, no, I'll spare you the schooldays. I noticed my mother was no longer much impressed by my gloom. Her smile, with that slight droop at the side, was turning positively sardonic. I said I had seen Charlie French in town. Oh, Charlie, she said, and shook her head and laughed. I nodded. Poor Charlie, he is the kind of person about whom people say, Oh, like that, and laugh. Another, listless silence. Why on earth had

I come back here. I picked up the bottle, and was surprised to find it empty. I opened another, clamping it between my knees and swaying and grunting as I yanked at the cork. Ah! and out it came with a jolly pop. Outside on the lawn the last of the day's sunlight thickened briefly, then faded. My mother was asking after Daphne and the child. At the thought of them something like a great sob, lugubrious, faintly comical, ballooned under my breastbone. Jane – no, I can't call her that, it doesn't fit – Joan cleared the table, and my mother produced, of all things, a decanter of port and pushed it across the table to me. You won't want us to withdraw, will you? she said, with that grin – you can think of me as a man, anyway, I'm ancient enough. I began earn- estly to tell her about my financial troubles, but got into a muddle and had to stop. Besides, I suspected she was not really listening. She sat with her face half-turned to the nickel light of evening from the window, rheum-eyed and old, showing the broad brow and high cheekbones of her Dutch forebears, King Billy's henchmen. You should have a ruff, ma, I said, and a lace cap. I laughed loudly, then frowned. My face was going numb. Jean carefully offered me a cup of coffee. No, thank you, my dear, I said gravely, in my grandee's voice, indicating my port glass, which, I noticed, was unaccountably empty. I refilled it, admir- ing the steadiness of the hand that held the decanter. Time passed. Birds were calling through the blue-grey dusk. I sat bemused, bolt-upright, in happy misery, listening to them. Then with a snort and a heave I roused myself and looked about me, smacking my lips and blinking. My mother and the girl were gone.

He died at evening. The room was still heavy with the long day's heat. I sat on a chair beside his bed in the open window and held his hand. His hand. The waxen feel of. How bright the air above the trees, bright and blue, like the limitless skies of child- hood. I put my arm around him, laid a hand on his forehead. He said to me: don't mind her. He said to me –

Stop this, stop it. I was not there. I have not been present at anyone's death. He died alone, slipped away while no one was looking, leaving us to our own devices. By the time I arrived from the city they had trussed him up, ready for the coffin. He lay on the bed with his hands folded on his breast and his eyes shut tight, like a child being good. His hair was brushed in a neat lick across his forehead. His ears, I remember, were very white.

Extraordinary: all that anger and resentment, that furious, un-focused energy: gone.

I took what remained of the port and staggered away upstairs. My knees quaked, I felt as if I were lugging a body on my back. The light-switches seemed to have been moved, in the half-darkness I kept banging into things, swearing and laughing. Then I found my way by mistake into Joanne's room. (Joanne: that's it!) She must have been awake, listening to me barging about, I hardly got the door open before she switched on her lamp. I stood teetering on the threshold, goggling at her. She lay in a vast, sagg-ing bed with the sheet pulled to her chin, and for some reason I was convinced that she was still wearing her jodhpurs and her baggy pullover, and even her riding boots. She said nothing, only smiled at me in fright, and for a wild moment I considered climb-ing in beside her, shoes and all, so that now she might cradle *my* poor whirling head in her plump young accommodating arm. I had not really noticed before her extraordinary flame-red hair, the sight of it spread out on the pillow in the lamplight almost made me cry. Then the moment was gone, and with a grave nod I withdrew silently, like an old sad grey fading ghost, and marched at a careful, dignified pace across the landing to the room where a bed had been made up for me. There I discovered that somewhere along the way I had mislaid the port.

I sat on the side of the bed, arms dangling between my knees, and was suddenly exhausted. My head fizzed, my eyes burned, but yet I could not make myself lie down to sleep. I might have been a child come home after a day of wild excursions. I had travelled far. Slowly, with underwater movements, I untied my shoelaces. One shoe dropped, and then –

I WOKE with a dreadful start, my ears ringing, as if there had been an explosion in my head. A dream: something about meat. It was light, but whether it was dawn or still dusk I was not sure. Grey. Nor did I know where I was. Even when I realised it was Coolgrange I did not recognise the room at first. Very high and long, with lofty windows that came down to the floor. Shabby, too, in a peculiar, offended way, as if it were conscious of once having been an important place. I got up carefully from the bed and went and looked down at the lawn. The grass was pale, and there were pigeon-coloured shadows under the trees. My brain thudded. It must be dawn: in the oak wood, under an iron sky, a solitary bird was testing out the lightening air with a single repeated flute-note. I pressed my forehead against the window-pane, and shivered at the clammy, cold touch of the glass. I had been travelling for the best part of a week, with scant food and too much alcohol, and now it was all catching up with me. I felt sick, sodden, reamed. My eyelids were scalding, my spit tasted of ash. It seemed to me the garden was watching me, in its stealthy, tight-lipped way, or that it was at least somehow aware of me, framed here in the window, wringing my hands, a stricken starer-out – how many other such there must have been, down the years! – with the room's weightless dark pressing at my back. I had slept in my clothes.

The dream. (The court will need to hear about my dreams.) It came back to me suddenly. Nothing very much happened in it. My dreams are not the riotous tumble of events that others claim to enjoy, but states of feeling, rather, moods, particular humours, gusts of emotion, accompanied often by extreme physical effects: I weep, or thrash my limbs, grind my teeth, laugh, cry out. On this occasion it had been a dry retching, the ache in my throat when I woke was what brought it back to me. I had dreamed I was gnawing the ripped-out sternum of some creature, possibly human. It seemed to have been boiled, for the meat on it was soft and white. Barely warm now, it crumbled in my mouth like suet, making me gag. Believe me, your Lordship, I do not enjoy relating these things any more than the court enjoys hearing them. And there is worse to come, as you know. Anyway, there I was, mumbling these frightful gobs of flesh, my stomach heaving even as I slept. That is all there was, really, except for an underlying sensation of enforced yet horribly pleasurable transgression. Wait a moment. I want to get this right, it is important, I'm not sure why. Some nameless authority was making me do this terrible thing, was standing over me implacably with folded arms as I sucked and slobbered, yet despite this – or perhaps, even, because of it – despite the horror, too, and the nausea – deep inside me something exulted.

By the way, leafing through my dictionary I am struck by the poverty of the language when it comes to naming or describing badness. Evil, wickedness, mischief, these words imply an agency, the conscious or at least active doing of wrong. They do not signify the bad in its inert, neutral, self-sustaining state. Then there are the adjectives: dreadful, heinous, execrable, vile, and so on. They are not so much descriptive as judgmental. They carry a weight of censure mingled with fear. Is this not a queer state of affairs? It makes me wonder. I ask myself if perhaps the thing itself – *badness* – does not exist at all, if these strangely vague and imprecise words are only a kind of ruse, a kind of elaborate cover for the fact that nothing is there. Or perhaps the words are an attempt to make it be there? Or, again, perhaps there *is* something, but the words invented it. Such considerations make me feel dizzy, as if a hole had opened briefly in the world. What was I talking about? My dreams, yes. There was the recurring one, the one in which – but no, no, leave that to another time.

I am standing by the window, in my parents' bedroom. Yes, I had realised that it was, used to be, theirs. The grey of dawn was giving way to a pale wash of sunlight. My lips were tacky from last night's port. The room, the house, the garden and the fields, all was strange to me, I did not recognise it today – strange, and yet known, too, like a place in – yes – in a dream. I stood there in my wrinkled suit, with my aching head and soiled mouth, wide-eyed but not quite awake, staring fixedly into that patch of sunlit garden with an amnesiac's numbed amazement. But then, am I not always like that, more or less? When I think about it, I seem to have lived most of my life that way, stalled between sleep and waking, unable to distinguish between dream and the daylight world. In my mind there are places, moments, events, which are so still, so isolated, that I am not sure they can be real, but which if I had recalled them that morning would have struck me with more vividness and force than the real things surrounding me. For instance, there is the hallway of a farmhouse where I went once as a child to buy apples. I see the polished stone floor, cardinal red. I can smell the polish. There is a gnarled geranium in a pot, and a big pendulum clock with the minute-hand missing. I can hear the farmer's wife speaking in the dim depths of the house, asking something of someone. I can sense the fields all around, the light above the fields, the vast, slow, late-summer day. I am there. In such remembered moments I am there as I never was at Coolgrange, as I seem never to have been, or to be, anywhere, at any time, as I, or some essential part of me, was not there even on that day I am remembering, the day I went to buy apples from the farmer's wife, at that farm in the midst of the fields. Never wholly anywhere, never with anyone, either, that was me, always. Even as a child I seemed to myself a traveller who had been delayed in the middle of an urgent journey. Life was an unconscionable wait, walking up and down the platform, watching for the train. People got in the way and blocked my view, I had to crane to see past them. Yes, that was me, all right.

I picked my way down through the silent house to the kitchen. In the morning light the room had a scrubbed, eager aspect. I moved about warily, unwilling to disturb the atmosphere of hushed expectancy, feeling like an uninitiate at some grand, rapt ceremony of light and weather. The dog lay on a dirty old rug beside the stove, its muzzle between its paws, watching me, a crescent of white showing in each eye. I made a pot of tea, and was sitting at the table, waiting for it to draw, when Joanne came in. She was wearing a mouse-grey dressing-gown belted tightly about her midriff. Her hair was tied up at the back in a thick, appropriately equine plume. It really was remarkable in colour, a vernal russet blaze. Immediately, and not for the first time, I found myself picturing how she must be flossed elsewhere, and then was ashamed, as if I had misused the poor child. Seeing me, she halted, of course, ready to bolt. I lifted the teapot in a friendly gesture, and invited her to join me. She shut the door and edged around me with a panic-stricken smile, keeping the table between us, and took down a cup and saucer from the dresser. She had red heels and very white, thick calves. I thought she must be about seventeen. Through the fog of my hangover it occurred to me that she would be bound to know something about the state of my mother's finances – whether, for instance, those ponies were making money. I gave her what was intended to be a boyish, encouraging smile, though I suspect it came out a broken leer, and told her to sit down, that we must have a chat. The tea, however, was not for her, but for my mother – for Dolly, she said. Well! I thought, Dolly, no less! She made off at once, with the saucer grasped in both hands and her agitated smile fixed on the trembling liquid in the cup.

When she was gone I poked about morosely for a while, looking for the papers that had been on the table yesterday, the bills and ledgers and chequebook stubs, but found nothing. A drawer of the little bureau from my father's study was locked. I considered forcing it open, but restrained myself: in my hungover mood I might have smashed the whole thing to bits.

I wandered off through the house, carrying my teacup with me. In the drawing room the carpet had been taken up, and a pane of glass in one of the windows was broken, and there was glass on the floor. I noticed I had no shoes on. I opened the garden door and stepped outside in my socks. There was a smell of sun-warmed grass and a faint tang of dung in the rinsed, silky air. The black shadow of the house lay across the lawn like a fallen stage-flat. I ventured a step or two on the yielding turf, the dew seeping up between my toes. I felt like an old man, going along shakily with my cup and saucer rattling and my trouser-cuffs wet and crumpled around my ankles. The rosebeds under the window had not been tended for years, and a tangle of briars rioted at the sills. The faded roses hung in clusters, heavy as cloth. Their particular wan shade of pink, and the chiaroscuro of the scene in general, put me in mind of something. I halted, frowning. The pictures – of course. I went back into the drawing room. Yes, the walls were empty, with here and there a square patch where the wallpaper was not as faded as elsewhere. Surely she hadn't –? I put my cup down carefully on the mantelpiece, taking slow, deep breaths. The bitch! I said aloud, I bet she has! My feet had left wet, webbed prints behind me on the floorboards.

I went through room after room, scanning the walls. Then I tackled the upstairs. But I knew there would be nothing. I stood on the first-floor landing, cursing under my breath. There were voices nearby. I flung open a bedroom door. My mother and Joanne were sitting up side by side in the girl's big bed. They looked at me in mild astonishment, and for a moment I faltered as something brushed past my consciousness, a wingbeat of incredulous speculation. My mother wore a knitted yellow bed-jacket with bobbles and tiny satin bows, which made her look like a monstrously overgrown Easter chick. Where, I said, with a calm that surprised me, where are the pictures, pray? There followed a bit of comic patter, with my mother saying *What? What?* and I shouting *The pictures! The pictures, damn it!* In the end we both had to shut up. The girl had been watching us, turning her eyes slowly from one to the other of us, like a spectator at a tennis match. Now she put a hand over her mouth and laughed. I stared at her, and she blushed. There was a brief silence. I will see you downstairs, mother, I said, in a voice so stiff with ice it fairly creaked.

As I was going away from the door I thought I heard them both sniggering.

My mother arrived in the kitchen barefoot. The sight of her bunions and her big yellow toenails annoyed me. She had wrapped herself in an impossible, shot-silk tea-gown. She had the florid look of one of Lautrec's ruined doxies. I tried not to show too much of the disgust I felt. She pottered about with a show of unconcern, ignoring me. Well? I said, but she only raised her eyebrows blandly and said, Well what? She was almost smirking. That did it. I shouted, I waved my fists, I stamped about stiff-legged, beside myself. Where were they, the pictures, I cried, what had she done with them? I *demanded* to know. They were mine, my inheritance, my future and my son's future. And so on. My anger, my sense of outrage, impressed me. I was moved. I might almost have shed tears, I felt so sorry for myself. She let me go on like this for a while, standing with a hand on her hip and her head thrown back, contemplating me with sardonic calm. Then, when I paused to take a breath, she started. Demand, did I? – I, who had gone off and abandoned my widowed mother, who had skipped off to America and married without even informing her, who had never once brought my child, her grandson, to see her – I, who for ten years had stravaged the world like a tinker, never doing a hand's turn of work, living off my dead father's few pounds and bleeding the estate dry – what right, she shrilled, what right had I to demand anything here? She stopped, and waited, as if really expecting an answer. I fell back a pace. I had forgotten what she is like when she gets going. Then I gathered myself and launched at her again. She rose magnificently to meet me. It was just like the old days. Hammer and tongs, oh, hammer and tongs! So stirring was it that even the dog joined in, barking and whining and dancing up and down on its front paws, until my mother gave it a clout and roared at it to lie down. I called her a bitch and she called me a bastard. I said if I was a bastard what did that make her, and quick as a flash she said, If I'm a bitch what does that make *you*, you cur! Oh, it was grand, a grand match. We were like furious children – no, not children, but big, maddened, primitive creatures – mastodons, something like that – tearing and thrashing in a jungle clearing amidst a storm of whipping lianas and uprooted vegetation. The air throbbed between us, blood-dimmed and thick. There was a sense of things ranged around us, small creatures cowering in the undergrowth, watching us in a trance of terror and awe. At last, sated, we disengaged tusks and turned aside. I nursed my pounding head in my hands. She stood at the sink, holding on to one of the taps and looking out of the window at the garden, her chest heaving. We could hear ourselves breathe. The upstairs lavatory flushed, a muted, tentative noise, as if the girl were tactfully reminding us of her presence in the house. My mother sighed. She had sold the pictures to Binkie Behrens. I nodded to myself. Behrens: of course. All of them? I said. She did not answer. Time passed. She sighed again. You got the money, she said, what there was of it – he left me only debts. Suddenly she laughed. I should have known better, she said, than to marry a mick. She looked at me over her shoulder and shrugged. Now it was my turn to sigh. Dear me, I said. Oh, dear me.

Coincidences come out strangely flattened in court testimony – I'm sure you have noticed this, your Honour, over the years – rather like jokes that should be really funny but fail to raise a single laugh. Accounts of the most bizarre doings of the accused are listened to with perfect equanimity, yet the moment some trivial simultaneity of events is mentioned feet begin to shuffle in the gallery, and counsel clear their throats, and reporters take to gazing dreamily at the mouldings on the ceiling. These are not so much signs of incredulity, I think, as of embarrassment. It is as if someone, the hidden arranger of all this intricate, amazing affair, who up to now never put a foot wrong, has suddenly gone that bit too far, has tried to be just a little too clever, and we are all disappointed, and somewhat sad.

I am struck, for instance, by the frequent appearance which paintings make in this case. It was through art that my parents knew Helmut Behrens – well, not art, exactly, but the collecting of it. My father fancied himself a collector, did I mention that? Of course, he cared nothing for the works themselves, only for their cash value. He used his reputation as a horseman and erstwhile gay blade to insinuate himself into the houses of doddering acquaintances, on whose walls thirty or forty years before he had spotted a landscape, or a still life, or a kippered portrait of a cross-eyed ancestor, which by now might be worth a bob or two. He had an uncanny sense of timing, often getting in only a step ahead of the heirs. I imagine him, at the side of a four-poster, in candlelight, still breathless from the stairs, leaning down and pressing a fiver urgently into a palsied, papery hand. He accumulated a lot of trash, but there were a few pieces which I thought were not altogether bad, and probably worth something. Most of these he had wheedled out of a distraite old lady whom his own father had courted briefly when she was a girl. He was hugely proud of this piece of chicanery, imagining, I suppose, that it put him on a par with the great robber barons of the past whom he so much admired, the Guggenheims and Pierpont Morgans and, indeed, the Behrenses. Perhaps these were the very pictures that led to his meeting Helmut Behrens. Perhaps they tussled for them over the old lady's deathbed, narrowing their eyes at each other, mouths pursed in furious determination.

It was through painting also that I met Anna Behrens – or met her again, I should say. We knew each other a little when we were young. I seem to remember once at Whitewater being sent outside to play with her in the grounds. Play! That's a good one. Even in those days she had that air of detachment, of faint, remote amusement, which I have always found unnerving. Later on, in Dublin, she would appear now and then, and glide through our student roisterings, poised, silent, palely handsome. She was nicknamed the Ice Queen, of course. I lost sight of her, forgot about her, until one day in Berkeley – this is where the coincidences begin – I spotted her in a gallery on Shattuck Avenue. I had not known she was in America, yet there was no sense of surprise. This is one of the things about Anna, she belongs exactly wherever she happens to be. I stood in the street for a moment watching her – admiring her, I suppose. The gallery was a large high white room with a glass front. She was leaning against a desk with a sheaf of papers in her hand, reading. She wore a white dress. Her hair, bleached silver by the sun, was done in a complicated fashion, with a single heavy braid hanging down at her shoulder. She might have been a piece on show, standing there so still in that tall, shadowless light behind sun-reflecting glass. I went in and spoke to her, admiring again that long, slightly off-centre, melancholy face with its close-set grey eyes and florentine mouth. I remembered the two tiny white spots on the bridge of her nose where the skin was stretched tight over the bone. She was friendly, in her distant way. She watched my lips as I talked. On the walls there were two or three vast canvases, done in the joky, minimalist style of the time, hardly distinguishable in their pastel bareness from the blank spaces surrounding them. I asked her if she was thinking of buying something. This amused her. I work here, she said, pushing back the blonde braid from her shoulder. I invited her to lunch, but she shook her head. She gave me her telephone number. When I stepped out into the sunlit street a jet plane was passing low overhead, its engines making the air rattle, and there was a smell of cypresses and car exhaust, and a faint whiff of tear gas from the direction of the campus. All this was fifteen years ago. I crumpled the file card on which she had written her phone number, and started to throw it away. But I kept it.

She lived in the hills, in a mock-Tyrolean, shingled wooden house which she rented from a mad widow. More than once on the way there I stood up to get off the bus and go home, bored and half-annoyed already at the thought of Anna's amused, appraising glance, that impenetrable smile. When I called her she had spoken hardly a dozen words, and twice she put a hand over the phone and talked to someone with her in the room. Yet that morning I had shaved with particular care, and put on a new shirt, and selected an impressive volume on mathematical theory to carry with me. Now, as the bus threaded its way up these narrow roads, I was assailed by a sense of revulsion, I seemed to myself an obscurely shameful, lewd object, exposed and cringing, with my palped and powdered flesh, my baby-blue shirt, the floppy book clutched in my hand like a parcel of meat. The day was overcast, and there was mist in the pines. I climbed a zigzag of damp steps to the door, looking about me with an expression of bland interest, trying to appear blameless, as I always seem to do when I am on unfamiliar territory. Anna wore shorts, and her hair was loose. The sight of her there suddenly in the doorway, ash-blonde, at ease, her long legs bare, caused an ache at the root of my tongue. The house was dim inside. A few books, prints on the wall, a straw hat on a hook. The widow's cats had left a trace of themselves on the carpets and the chairs, a sharp, citrus stink, not wholly unpleasant.

Daphne was sitting cross-legged in a canvas chair, shelling peas into a nickel bowl. She wore a bathrobe, and her hair was wrapped in a towel. Another coincidence, you see.

What did we talk about that day, the three of us? What did I do? Sat down, I suppose, drank a beer, stretched out my legs and leaned back, playing at being relaxed. I cannot see myself. I am a sort of floating eye, watching, noting, scheming. Anna came and went between the living room and the kitchen, bringing cheese and oranges and sliced avocados. It was Sunday. The place was quiet. I watched through the window the mist moving among the trees. The telephone rang and Anna answered it, turning away and murmuring into the receiver. Daphne smiled at me. Her glance was unfocused, a kind of soft groping among the objects around her. She rose and handed me the bowl and the remaining unshelled peas, and went away upstairs. When she came back in a while she was dressed, her hair was dried and she was wearing her spectacles, and at first I did not recognise her, and thought she was yet another tenant of the house. It was only then that I realised it was she I had seen on the lawn that day at Professor Something's party. I started to tell her about it, about having seen her, but I changed my mind, for the same, unknown reason that I had turned away that first time without speaking to her. She took the bowl of peas from me and sat down again. Anna answered another phonecall, murmuring, quietly laughing. It occurred to me that my presence was hardly impinging on their day, that they would have done just these same things if I were not there. It was a soothing thought. I had not been invited to dinner, but it seemed accepted that I would stay. After we had eaten we sat on at the table for a long time. The fog thickened, pressing against the windows. I see the two of them opposite me there in that milky twilight, the dark one and the fair: they have an air of complicity, of secret amusement, as if they are sharing a mild, not very unkind joke at my expense. How distant it all seems, an age away, when we were still innocent, if that is the word, which I doubt.

I was, I confess it, captivated by them, their looks, their composure, their casual selfishness. They embodied an ideal that I had not known I harboured until now. I was still working at my science in those days, I was going to be one of those great, cold technicians, the secret masters of the world. Now suddenly another future had opened up, as if these two had caused a whole rockface before me to fall away and reveal beyond the swirling dust a vast, radiant distance. They were splendid, at once languorous and dashing. They reminded me of a pair of adventuresses out of the last century. They had arrived in New York the previous winter, and drifted by stages across the country to this tawny, sunlit shore, where they were poised now, as if on tiptoe, hands joined and arms extended, with the Pacific all before them. Though they had been in this house nearly half a year their impress was so light, so fleeting, that the rooms had barely registered their presence. They seemed to have no belongings – even the straw hat hanging on the door had been left behind by a previous tenant. There must have been friends, or acquaintances at least – I'm thinking of those phonecalls – but I never met them. Once in a while their landlady would descend on them, a darkly dramatic person with soulful eyes and very black hair twisted tight into a bun and skewered with a carved wooden pin. She dressed like an Indian squaw, festooning herself with beads and brightly coloured scarves. She would surge about the house distractedly, talking over her shoulder and trailing a dense, musky perfume, then fling herself with a balletic leap on to the couch in the living room and sit for an hour telling of her woes – the result mostly of what with a throb in her voice she referred to as *man trouble* – meanwhile getting steadily, tearfully

drunk on Calvados, a supply of which she kept in a locked cupboard in the kitchen. A ghastly woman, I could not abide her,
that leathery skin and daubed mouth, all that hysteria, that messy
loneliness. The girls, however, found her greatly entertaining.
They liked to do imitations of her, and made catchphrases of
things she said. Sometimes, listening to them mimicking her,
I wondered if perhaps, when I was not there, they treated *me* like
this, lobbing remarks at each other in a comically solemn version
of my voice and laughing softly, in that jaded way they had, as if
the joke were not really funny, just ridiculous.

They thought the country, too, was a scream, especially California. We had a lot of fun together laughing at the Americans,
who just then were entering that stage of doomed hedonistic
gaiety through which we, the gilded children of poor old raddled
Europe, had already passed, or so we believed. How innocent
they seemed to us, with their flowers and their joss sticks and
their muddled religiosity. Of course, I felt a secret twinge of guilt,
sneering at them like this. I had been captivated by the country
when I first came there, now it was as if I had joined in mocking
some happy, good-hearted creature, the fat girl at the party
against whom only a moment ago I had been pressing myself,
under cover of the general romp, in wordless, swollen ecstasy.

Perhaps contempt was for us a form of nostalgia, of home-
sickness, even? Living there, amid those gentle, paintbox colours,
under that dome of flawless blue, was like living in another
world, a place out of a storybook. (I used to dream of rain – real,
daylong, Irish rain – as if it were something I had been told about
but had never seen.) Or perhaps laughing at America was a means
of defence? It's true, at times it crossed our minds, or it crossed
my mind, at least, that we might be just the teeniest bit laughable
ourselves. Was there not a touch of the preposterous about us,
with our tweeds and our sensible shoes, our extravagant accents,
our insolently polite manners? More than once I thought I
detected a suppressed smile twitching the lips of some person
who was supposed to be the unknowing butt of our ridicule.
Even among ourselves there were moments of silence, of awkwardness, when a half-formed admission hovered between us,
like a bad, embarrassing smell. A trio of expatriates meeting in
this mellow playground – what could be more novelettish? We
were a triangle, for God's sake!

We were a triangle. It happened, the inevitable, one afternoon a month or so after we met. We had been sitting on the porch at the back of the house drinking gin and smoking something with a horrid taste and the oddest effects. The day was hot and hazy. Above us a coin-coloured sun was stuck in the middle of a white sky. I was watching a cloud of hummingbirds sipping at a honeysuckle bush beside the porch steps. Daphne, in shorts and halter and high-heeled sandals, stood up, a little unsteadily, blinking, and wandered into the house. I followed her. I was not thinking of anything – I was fetching more ice, something like that. After the glare outside I could hardly see indoors, everywhere I turned the air had a huge dark hole in it. Idly I looked about for Daphne, following the sound of the ice tinkling in her glass, from the kitchen through the living room to the bedroom. The blind was drawn. She was sitting on the side of the bed, gazing before her in the amber half-light. My head suddenly began to ache. She drained her drink in one long gulp, and was still holding the glass when we lay down together, and a bead of ice slid out of it and dropped into the hollow of my shoulder. Her lips were chill and wet. She began to say something, and laughed softly into my mouth. Our clothes seemed tight as bandages, I clawed at them, snorting. Then abruptly we were naked. There was a startled pause. Somewhere nearby children were playing. Daphne laid her hand on my hip. Her eyes were closed, and she was smiling with her eyebrows raised, as if she were listening to a distant, dreamy, and slightly funny melody. I heard a sound, and looked over my shoulder. Anna was standing in the doorway. I had a glimpse of myself as she would see me, my glimmering flanks and pale backside, my fish-mouth agape. She hesitated a moment, and then walked to the bed with her eyes on the ground, as if deep in thought, and sat down beside us and began to undress. Daphne and I lay quietly in each other's arms and watched her. She pulled her blouse over her head, and surfaced like a swimmer, tossing her hair. A metal clasp left its mauve imprint in the centre of her back. Why did she seem to me so much older now than us, world-weary, a little used, an adult joining tolerantly in a children's not quite permissible game? Daphne hardly breathed, her fingers steadily tightening on my hip. Her lips were parted, and she frowned a little, gazing at Anna's bared flesh, lost in a sort of vague amazement. I could

feel her heartbeat, and my own. We might have been attending
a ritual disrobing.

A ritual, yes, that's how it was. We strove together slowly on
the bed, the three of us, as if engaged in an archaic ceremonial of
toil and worship, miming the fashioning and raising of something, a shrine, say, or a domed temple. How grave we were, how
pensive, with what attentiveness we handled each other's flesh.
No one spoke a word. The women had begun by exchanging a
chaste kiss. They smiled, a little bashfully. My hands were trembling. I had felt this choking sense of transgression once before,
long ago, when as a child I tussled with two girl cousins in the
dark on the stairs one winter evening at Coolgrange – the same
dread and incredulity, the same voluptuous, aching, infantile
glee. Dreamily we delved and nuzzled, shivering, sighing. Now
and then one of us would clutch at the other two with a child's
impatient, greedy fervour and cry out softly, tinily, as if in pain
or helpless sorrow. It seemed to me at times that there were not
two women but one, a strange, remote creature, many-armed,
absorbed behind an enamelled mask in something I could not
begin to know. At the end, the final spasm gathering itself inside
me, I raised myself up on trembling arms, with Daphne's heels
pressed in the small of my back, and looked down at the two of
them gnawing at each other with tender avidity, mouth on open
mouth, and for a second, as the blood welled up in my eyes, I saw
their heads merge, the fair one and the dark, the tawny and the
panther-sleek. At once the shudder started in my groin, and I fell
upon them, exultant and afraid.

But afterwards it was Daphne alone who lay in my arms, still
holding me inside her, while Anna got up and walked to the window, and lifted the canvas blind at the side with one finger and
stood gazing out into the hazy glare of afternoon. The children
were still at play. There's a school, Anna murmured, up the hill.
She laughed quietly and said, *But what do I know, I ask you?* It was
one of the mad widow's catchphrases. Suddenly everything
was sad and grey and waste. Daphne put her face against my
shoulder and began to weep silently. I will always remember
those children's voices.

It was a strange encounter, never to be repeated. I brood on it
now, not for the obvious reasons, but because it puzzles me. The

act itself, the troilism, was not so remarkable: in those days everyone was doing that sort of thing. No, what struck me then, and
strikes me still, is the curious passiveness of my role in that afternoon's doings. I was the man among the three of us, yet I felt that
it was I who was being softly, irresistibly penetrated. The wise
will say that I was only the link along which the two of them
had negotiated their way, hand over hand, into each other's arms.
It may be true, but it is not of much significance, and certainly
not the central thing. I could not rid myself of the feeling that
a rite was being performed, in which Anna Behrens was the
priestess and Daphne the sacrificial offering, while I was a mere
prop. They wielded me like a stone phallus, bowing and writhing
about me, with incantatory sighs. They were –

They were saying goodbye. Of course. It's just occurred to me.
They were not finding each other, but parting. Hence the sadness
and the sense of waste, hence Daphne's bitter tears. It was nothing to do with me, at all.

Well well. That's the advantage of jail, one has the time and
leisure really to get to the heart of things.

The illusion of their melting into each other which I had
experienced at the end of our bout on the bed that day was to last
for a long time. Even yet when I think of them together it is a kind
of double-headed coin that I see, on which are stamped their twin
profiles, serene, emblematic, looking away, a stylised representa-
tion of paired virtues – Calm and Fortitude, let's say, or, better
still, Silence and Sacrifice. I am remembering a certain moment,
when Anna lifted her bruised, glistening mouth from between
Daphne's legs and, glancing back at me with a complicitous, wry
little smile, leaned aside so that I might see the sprawled girl's lap
lying open there, intricate and innocent as a halved fruit. Everything was present, I see now, in that brief passage of renunciation
and discovery. A whole future began just there.

I do not recall proposing to Daphne. Her hand, so to speak,
had already been granted me. We were married one misty, hot
afternoon in August. The ceremony was quick and squalid. I had
a headache all through it. Anna and a colleague of mine from the
university acted as witnesses. Afterwards the four of us went back
to the house in the hills and drank cheap champagne. The occasion was not a success. My colleague made a limp excuse and
departed after half an hour, leaving the three of us together in a

restless, swirling silence. All sorts of unspoken things swam in the air between us like slithery, dangerous fish. Then Anna, with that smile, said she supposed we young things would want to be alone, and left. Suddenly I was prey to an absurd embarrassment. I jumped up and began collecting the empty bottles and the glasses, avoiding Daphne's eye. There was sun and mist in the kitchen window. I stood at the sink looking out at the blue-black ghosts of trees on the hillside, and two great, fat, inexplicable tears gathered on the rims of my eyelids, but would not fall.

I do not know that I loved Daphne in the manner that the world understands by that word, but I do know that I loved her ways. Will it seem strange, cold, perhaps even inhuman, if I say that I was only interested really in what she was on the surface? Pah, what do I care how it seems. This is the only way another creature can be known: on the surface, that's where there is depth. Daphne walking through a room searching for her spectacles, touching things gently, quickly, reading things with her fingertips. The way she had of turning aside and peering into her purse, frowning, lips compressed, like a maiden aunt fetching up a shilling for sweets. Her stinginess, her sudden rushes of greed, childish and endearing. That time, years ago, I can't remember where, when I came upon her at the end of a party, standing by a window in a blue dress in the half-light of an April dawn, lost in a dream – a dream from which I, tipsy and in a temper, unceremoniously woke her, when I could – dear Christ! when I could have hung back in the shadows and painted her, down to the tiniest, tenderest detail, on the blank inner wall of my heart, where she would be still, vivid as in that dawn, my dark, mysterious darling.

We quickly agreed – tacitly, as always – to leave America. I gave up my studies, the university, my academic career, everything, with hardly a second thought, and before the year was out we had sailed for Europe.

MAOLSEACHLAINN MAC Giolla Gunna, my counsel and, he insists, my friend, has a trick of seizing on the apparently trivial in the elaboration of his cases. Anecdotes of his methods circulate in the corridors of chancery, and around the catwalks in here. Details, details are his obsession. He is a large, lumbering, unhandy man – yards, literally yards of pinstripe – with a big square head and raggedy hair and tiny, haunted eyes. I think a life spent poking in the crevices of other people's nasty little tragedies has damaged something in him. He exudes an air of injured longing. They say he is a terror in court, but when he sits at the scarred table in the counsel room here, with his half-glasses hooked on that big head, crouched over his papers and writing out notes in a laborious, minute hand, panting a little and muttering to himself, I am reminded irresistibly of a certain fat boy from my schooldays, who was disconsolately in love with me, and whom I used to get to do my homework for me.

At present Maolseachlainn is deeply interested in why I went to Whitewater in the first place. But why should I not have gone there? I knew the Behrenses – or God knows I knew Anna, anyway. I had been away for ten years, I was paying a social call, as a friend of the family. This, however, is not good enough, it seems. Maolseachlainn frowns, slowly shaking his great head, and without realising it goes into his court routine. Is it not true that I left my mother's house in anger only a day after my arrival there? Is it not the case that I was in a state of high indignation because I had heard my father's collection of pictures had been sold to Helmut Behrens for what I considered a paltry sum? And is it not further the case that I had reason already to feel resentment against the man Behrens, who had attempted to cuckold my father in – But hold on there, old man, I said: that last bit only came to light later on. He always looks so crestfallen when I stop him in his tracks like this. All the same, facts are facts.

It is true, I did fight with my mother again, I did storm out of the house (with the dog after me, of course, trying to bite my heels). However, Binkie Behrens was not the cause of the row, or not directly, anyway. As far as I remember it was the same old squabble: money, betrayal, my going to the States, my leaving the States, my marriage, my abandoned career, all that, the usual – and, yes, the fact that she had flogged my birthright for the price of a string of plug-ugly ponies out of which she had imagined she would make a fortune to provide for herself in the decrepitude of her old age, the deluded bloody bitch. There was as well the business of the girl Joanne. As I was leaving I paused and said, measuring my words, that I thought it hardly appropriate for a woman of my mother's position in society – her position! – in society! – to be so chummy with a stable-girl. I confess I had intended to cause outrage, but I am afraid I was the one who ended up goggle-eyed. My mother, after a moment's silence, stared me straight in the face, with brazen insouciance, and said that Joanne was not a child, that she was in fact twenty-seven years of age. She is – with a pause here for effect – she is like a son to me, the son I never had. Well, I said, swallowing hard, I'm happy for you both, I'm sure! and flounced out of the house. On the drive, though, I had to stop and wait for my indignation and resentment to subside a little before I could get my breath back. Sometimes I think I am an utter sentimentalist.

I got to Whitewater that evening. The last leg of the journey I made by taxi from the village. The driver was an immensely tall, emaciated man in a flat cap and an antique, blue-flannel suit. He studied me with interest in the driving-mirror, hardly bothering to watch the road ahead of us. I tried staring back at him balefully, but he was unabashed, and only grinned a little on one side of his thin face with a peculiarly friendly air of knowing. Why do I remember people like this so vividly? They clutter my mind, when I look up from the page they are thronged around me in the shadows, silent, mildly curious – even, it might be, solicitous. They are witnesses, I suppose, the innocent bystanders who have come, without malice, to testify against me.

I can never approach Whitewater without a small, involuntary gasp of admiration. The drive leads up from the road in a long, deep, treeless curve, so that the house seems to turn, slowly, dreamily, opening wide its Palladian colonnades. The taxi drew to a stop on the gravel below the great front steps, and with the sudden silence came the realisation – yes, Maolseachlainn, I admit it – that I had no reasonable cause to be there. I sat for a moment looking about me in groggy consternation, like a wakened sleepwalker, but the driver was watching me in the mirror now with rapt expectancy, and I had to pretend to know what I was about. I got out of the car and stood patting my pockets and frowning, but I could not fool him, his lopsided grin grew slyer still, for a second I thought he was going to wink at me. I told him brusquely to wait, and mounted the steps pursued by an unshakeable sensation of general mockery.

After a long time the door was opened by a wizened little angry man in what appeared at first to be a bus conductor's uniform. A few long strands of very black hair were plastered across his skull like streaks of boot polish. He looked at me with deep disgust. Not open today, he said, and was starting to shut the door in my face when I stepped smartly past him into the hall. I gazed about me, rubbing my hands slowly and smiling, playing the returned expatriate. Ah, I said, the old place! The great Tintoretto on the stairs, swarming with angels and mad-eyed martyrs, blared at me its vast chromatic chord. The door-man or whatever he was danced about anxiously behind me. I turned and loomed at him, still grinning, and said no, I wasn't a tripper, but a friend of the family – was Miss Behrens at home, by any chance? He dithered, distrustful still, then told me to wait, and scuttled off down the hall, splaying one flat foot as he went and carefully smoothing the oiled hairs on his pate.

I waited. All was silent save for the ticking of a tall, seventeenth-century German clock. On the wall beside me there was a set of six exquisite little Bonington watercolours, I could have put a couple of them under my arm there and then and walked out. The clock took a laboured breath and pinged the half-hour, and then, all about me, in farther and farther rooms, other clocks too let fall their single, silvery chimes, and it was as if a tiny tremor had passed through the house. I looked again at the Tintoretto. There was a Fragonard, too, and a Watteau. And this was only the hallway. What was going on, what had happened, that it was all left unattended like this? I heard the taximan outside sounding his horn, a tentative, apologetic little toot. He must have thought I had forgotten about him. (I had.) Somewhere at the back of the house a door banged shut, and a second later a breath of cool air brushed past my face. I advanced creakingly along the hall, a hot, almost sensuous thrill of apprehensiveness pulsing behind my breastbone. I am at heart a timid man, and large deserted places make me nervous. One of the figures in the Fragonard, a silken lady with blue eyes and a plump lower lip, was watching me sidelong with what seemed an expression of appalled but lively speculation. Cautiously I opened a door. The fat knob turned under my hand with a wonderful, confiding smoothness. I entered a long, high, narrow, many-windowed room. The wallpaper was the colour of tarnished gold. The air was golden too, suffused with the heavy soft light of evening. I felt as if I had stepped straight into the eighteenth century. The furnishings were sparse, there were no more than five or six pieces – some delicate, lyre-backed chairs, an ornate sideboard, a small ormolu table – placed just so, in such a way that not the things but the space around them, the light itself, seemed arranged. I stood quite still, listening, I did not know for what. On the low table there was a large and complicated jigsaw puzzle, half-assembled. Some of the pieces had fallen to the floor. I gazed at them, sprinkled on the parquet like puddles of something that had spilled, and once again a faint shiver seemed to pass through the house. At the far end of the room a french window stood wide-open, and a gauze curtain billowed in the breeze. Outside there was a long slope of lawn, whereon, in the middle distance, a lone, heraldic horse was prancing. Farther off was the river bend, the water whitening in the shallows, and beyond that there were trees, and then vague mountains, and then the limitless, gilded blue of summer. It struck me that the perspective of this scene was wrong somehow. Things seemed not to recede as they should, but to be arrayed before me – the furniture, the open window, the lawn and river and far-off mountains – as if they were not being looked at but were themselves looking, intent upon a vanishing point here, inside the room. I turned then, and saw myself turning as I turned, as I seem to myself to be turning still, as I sometimes imagine I shall be turning always, as if this might be my punishment, my damnation, just this breathless, blurred, eternal turning towards her.

You have seen the picture in the papers, you know what she looks like. A youngish woman in a black dress with a broad white collar, standing with her hands folded in front of her, one gloved, the other hidden except for the fingers, which are flexed, ringless. She is wearing something on her head, a cap or clasp of some sort, which holds her hair drawn tightly back from her brow. Her prominent black eyes have a faintly oriental slant. The nose is large, the lips full. She is not beautiful. In her right hand she holds a folded fan, or it might be a book. She is standing in what I take to be the lighted doorway of a room. Part of a couch can be seen, or maybe a bed, with a brocade cover. The darkness behind her is dense and yet mysteriously weightless. Her gaze is calm, inexpectant, though there is a trace of challenge, of hostility, even, in the set of her mouth. She does not want to be here, and yet cannot be elsewhere. The gold brooch that secures the wings of her wide collar is expensive and ugly. All this you have seen, all this you know. Yet I put it to you, gentle connoisseurs of the jury, that even knowing all this you still know nothing, next to nothing. You do not know the fortitude and pathos of her presence. You have not come upon her suddenly in a golden room on a summer eve, as I have. You have not held her in your arms, you have not seen her asprawl in a ditch. You have not – ah no! – you have not killed for her.

I stood there, staring, for what seemed a long time, and gradually a kind of embarrassment took hold of me, a hot, shamefaced awareness of myself, as if somehow I, this soiled sack of flesh, were the one who was being scrutinised, with careful, cold attention. It was not just the woman's painted stare that watched me. Everything in the picture, that brooch, those gloves, the flocculent darkness at her back, every spot on the canvas was an eye fixed on me unblinkingly. I retreated a pace, faintly aghast. The silence was fraying at the edges. I heard cows lowing, a car starting up. I remembered the taxi, and turned to go. A maid was standing in the open french window. She must have come in just then and seen me there and started back in alarm. Her eyes were wide, and one knee was flexed and one hand lifted, as if to ward off a blow. For a moment neither of us stirred. Behind her a sudden breeze burnished the grassy slope. We did not speak. Then slowly, with her hand still raised, she stepped backwards carefully through the window, teetering a little as her heels blindly sought the level of the paved pathway outside. I felt an inexplicable, brief rush of annoyance – a presentiment, perhaps, a stray zephyr sent ahead

of the storm that was to come. A telephone was ringing somewhere. I turned quickly and left the room.

There was no one in the hall. The telephone rang and rang,
with peevish insistence. I could still hear it going as I descended
the front steps. The taxi had left, of course. I swore, and set off
down the drive, hobbling over the stony ground in my thin-soled
Spanish shoes. The low sun glared in my face. When I looked
back at the house the windows were ablaze, and seemed to be
laughing fatly in derision. I began to perspire, and that brought
on the midges. I asked myself again what had possessed me to
come to Whitewater. I knew the answer, of course. It was the
smell of money that had attracted me, as the smell of sweat was
attracting these damned flies. I saw myself, as if from one of those
sunstruck windows, skulking along here in the dust, hot, disgruntled, overweight, head bowed and fat back bent, my white
suit rucked at the armpits and sagging in the arse, a figure of fun,
the punchline of a bad joke, and at once I was awash with self-
pity. Christ! was there no one who would help me? I halted, and
cast a troubled glance around me, as if there might be a benefactor
lurking among the trees. The silence had a sense of muffled gloating. I plunged on again, and heard the sound of engines, and
presently an enormous black limousine came around the bend,
followed by a sleek red sportscar. They were going at a stately
pace, the limousine bouncing gently on its springs, and for a
second I thought it was a funeral. I stepped on to the grass verge
but kept on walking. The driver of the limousine, a large, crop-
headed man, sat erect and vigilant, his hands lightly cupped on
the rim of the steering wheel, as if it were a projectile he might
pluck from its moorings and throw with deadly aim. Beside him
there was a stooped, shrunken figure, as the car swished past
I glimpsed a dark eye and a liver-spotted skull, and huge hands
resting one upon the other on the crook of a stick. A blonde
woman wearing dark glasses was driving the sportscar. We gazed
at each other with blank interest, like strangers, as she went by.
I recognised her, of course.

Ten minutes later I was trudging along the road with my
thumb stuck out when I heard her pull up behind me. I knew it
would be she. I stopped, turned. She remained in the car, her
wrists folded before her on the steering wheel. There was a
brief, wordless tussle to see which one of us would make the first

move. We compromised. I walked back to the car and she got out to meet me. I *thought* it was you, she said. We smiled, and were silent. She wore a cream suit and a white blouse. There was blood on her shoes. Her hair was yellower than I remembered, I wondered if she was dyeing it now. I told her she looked marvellous. I meant it, but the words sounded hollow, and I blushed. Anna, I said. I remembered, with a soft shock, how one day long ago I stole the envelope of one of her letters to Daphne, and took it into the lavatory and prised open the flap, my heart pounding, so that I might lick the gum where she had licked. The thought came to me: I loved her! and I gave a sort of wild, astonished laugh. She took off her sunglasses and looked at me quizzically. My hands were trembling. Come and see father, she said, he needs cheering up.

She drove very fast, working the controls probingly, as if she were trying to locate a pattern, a secret formula, hidden in this mesh of small, deft actions. I was impressed, even a little cowed. She was full of the impatient assurance of the rich. We did not speak. In a moment we were at the house, and pulled up in a spray of gravel. She opened her door, then paused and looked at me for a moment in silence and shook her head. Freddie Montgomery, she said. Well!

As we went up the steps to the front door she linked her arm lightly in mine. I was surprised. When I knew her, all those years ago, she was not one for easy intimacies – intimacies, yes, but not easy ones. She laughed and said, God, I'm a little drunk, I think. She had been to the hospital in the city – Behrens had suffered some sort of mild attack. The hospital was in an uproar. A bomb had gone off in a car in a crowded shopping street, quite a small device, apparently, but remarkably effective. She had wandered unchallenged into the casualty ward. There were bodies lying everywhere. She walked among the dead and dying, feeling like a survivor herself. Good God, Anna, I said. She gave a tense little laugh. What an experience, she said – luckily Flynn keeps a flask of something in the glove compartment. She had taken a few good swigs, and was beginning to regret it now.

We went into the house. The uniformed doorman was nowhere to be seen. I told Anna how he had gone off and left me to wander at will about the place. She shrugged. She supposed everyone had been downstairs watching the news of the bombing on television. All the same, I said, anyone could have got in. Why, she asked, do you think someone might come and plant a bomb here? And she looked at me with a peculiar, bitter smile.

She led the way into the gold salon. The french window was still open. There was no sign of the maid. A sort of shyness made me keep my eyes averted from the other end of the room, where the picture leaned out a little from the wall, as if listening intently. I sat down gingerly on one of the Louis Quinze chairs while Anna opened the carved and curlicued sideboard and poured out two whopping measures of gin. There was no ice, and the tonic was flat, but I didn't care, I needed a drink. I was still breathless with the notion of having been in love with her. I felt excited and bemused, and ridiculously pleased, like a child who has been given something precious to play with. I said it to myself again – *I loved her!* – trying it out for the sound of it. The thought, lofty, grand, and slightly mad, fitted well with the surroundings. She was pacing between me and the window, clutching her glass tightly in both hands. The gauze curtain bellied lazily at the edge of my vision. Something in the air itself seemed to be shaking. Suddenly the telephone on the low table beside me sprang to life with a crashing noise. Anna snatched it up and cried yes, yes, what? She laughed. It's some taximan, she said to me, looking for his fare. I took the phone and spoke harshly to the fellow. She watched me intently, with a kind of avid amusement. When I put down the receiver she said gaily, Oh, Freddie, you've got so pompous! I frowned. I was not sure how to respond. Her laughter, her glazed stare, were tinged with hysteria. But then, I too was less than calm. Look at that, she said. She was peering in annoyance at her bloodstained shoes. She clicked her tongue, and putting down her glass she quickly left the room. I waited. All this had happened before. I went and stood in the open window, a hand in my pocket, swigging my gin. Pompous, indeed – what did she mean? The sun was almost down, the light was gathering in bundles above the river. I stepped out on to the terrace. A balm of soft air breathed on my face. I thought how strange it was to be here like this, glass in hand, in the silence and calm of a summer evening, while there was so much darkness in my heart. I turned and looked up at the house. It seemed to be flying swiftly against the sky. I wanted my share of this richness, this gilded ease. From the depths of the room a pair of eyes looked out, dark, calm, unseeing.

Flynn, the crop-headed chauffeur, approached me from the side of the house with an air of tight-lipped politeness which was somehow menacing, rolling on the balls of his disproportionately dainty feet. He sported a bandit's drooping blue-black moustache, trimmed close and squared off at the ends, so that it looked as if it had been painted on to his large, pasty face. I do not like moustaches, have I mentioned that? There is something lewd about them which repels me. I have no doubt the prison shrink could explain what such an aversion signifies – and I've no doubt, too, that in my case he would be wrong. Flynn's was a particularly offensive specimen. The sight of it gave me heart suddenly, cheered me up, I don't know why. I followed him eagerly into the house. The dining room was a great dim cavern full of the glint and gleam of precious things. Behrens came in leaning on Anna's arm, a tall, delicate figure in rich tweeds and a bow-tie. He moved slowly, measuring his steps. His head, trembling a little, was smooth and steeply domed, like a marvellous, desiccated egg. It must have been twenty years since I had seen him last. I confess I was greatly taken with him now. He had the fine high patina of something lovingly crafted, like one of those exquisite and temptingly pocket-sized jade figurines which I had been eyeing only a moment ago on the mantelpiece. He took my hand and squeezed it slowly in his strangler's grip, looking deep into my eyes as if he were trying to catch a glimpse of someone else in there. Frederick, he said, in his breathy voice. So like your mother.

We dined at a rickety table in the bay of a tall window overlooking the garden. The cutlery was cheap, the plates mismatched. It was something I remembered about Whitewater, the makeshift way that life was lived in odd corners, at the edge of things. The house was not meant for people, all that magnificence would not tolerate their shoddy doings in its midst. I watched Behrens cutting up a piece of bleeding meat. Those enormous hands fascinated me. I was always convinced that at some time in the past he had killed someone. I tried to imagine him young, in flannels and a blazer, carrying a tennis racquet – *Oh look, here's Binkie!* – but it was impossible. He talked about the bombing. Five dead – or was it six by now? – from a mere two pounds of explosive! He sighed and shook his head. He seemed more impressed than shocked. Anna hardly spoke. She was pale, and looked tired and distracted. I noticed for the first time how she had aged. The woman I knew fifteen years ago was still there, but fixed inside a coarser outline, like one of Klimt's gem-encrusted lovers. I looked out into the luminous grey twilight, aghast and in an obscure way proud at the thought of what I had lost, of what might have been. Piled clouds, a last, bright strip of sky. A blackbird whistled suddenly. Someday I would lose all this too, I would die, and it would all be gone, this moment at this window, in summer, on the tender brink of night. It was amazing, and yet it was true, it would happen. Anna struck a match and lighted a candle on the table between us, and for a moment there was a sense of hovering, of swaying, in the soft, dark air.

My mother, I said to Behrens, and had to stop and clear my throat – my mother gave you some pictures, I believe. He turned his raptor's gaze on me. *Sold*, he said, and it was almost a whisper, sold, not gave. He smiled. There was a brief silence. He was quite at ease. He was sorry, he said, if I had come in the hope of seeing the pictures again. He could understand that I might be attached to them. But he had got rid of them almost at once. He smiled again, gently. There were one or two quite nice things, he said, but they would not have been comfortable, here, at Whitewater.

There you are, father, I thought, so much for your connoisseur's eye.

I wanted to do something for your mother, you see, Behrens was saying. She had been ill, you know. I gave her much more than the market value – you mustn't tell her that, of course. She wanted to set up in business of some kind, I think. He laughed. Such a spirited woman! he said. There was another silence. He fiddled with his knife, amused, waiting. I realised, with some astonishment, that he must have thought I had come to demand the return of the collection. Then, of course, I began to wonder if despite his protestations he had cheated on the price. The notion bucked me up immensely. Why, you old scoundrel, I thought, laughing to myself, you're just like all the rest of us. I looked at Anna's profile faintly reflected in the window before me. What was she, too, but an ageing spinster, with her wrinkles and her dyed hair – probably Flynn serviced her once a month or so, between hosing down the car and taking his moustache to the barber's for a trim. Damn you all! I poured myself a brimming glass of wine, and spilled some on the tablecloth, and was glad. Oh dark, dark.

I expected to be asked to stay the night, but when we had drunk our coffee Anna excused herself, and came back in a minute and said she had phoned for a taxi. I was offended. I had come all this way to see them and they would not even offer me a bed. An ugly silence fell. Behrens at my prompting had been talking about Dutch painters. Did I imagine it, or did he glance at me with a sly smile when he asked if I had been into the garden room? Before I realised it was the gilded salon that he meant he had passed on. Now he sat, head trembling, his mouth open a little, staring dully at the candle-flame. He lifted a hand, as if he were about to speak again, but let it fall slowly. The lights of a car swept the window and a horn tooted. Behrens did not get up. So good to see you, he murmured, giving me his left hand. So good.

Anna walked with me to the front door. I felt I had somehow made a fool of myself, but could not think how, exactly. In the hall our footsteps sounded very loud, a confused and faintly absurd racket. It's Flynn's night off, Anna said, or I would have had him drive you. I said stiffly that was quite all right. I was asking myself if we could be the same two people who had rolled with Daphne naked on a bed one hot Sunday afternoon on the other side of the world, on the other side of time. How could I have imagined I had ever loved her. Your father seems well, I said. She shrugged. Oh, she said, he's dying. At the door, I don't know what I was thinking of, but I fumbled for her hand and tried to kiss her. She stepped back quickly, and I almost fell over. The taxi tooted again. Anna! I said, and then could think of nothing to add. She laughed bleakly. Go home, Freddie, she said, with a wan smile, and shut the door slowly in my face.

I knew who would be driving the taxi, of course. Don't say anything, I said to him sternly, not a word! He looked at me in the mirror with a mournful, accusing eye, and we lumbered off down the drive. I realised I had nowhere to go.

IT IS SEPTEMBER. I have been here now for two months. It seems longer than that. The tree that I can glimpse from the window of my cell has a drab, dusty look, it will soon begin to turn. It trembles, as if in anticipation, at night I fancy I can hear it, rustling excitedly out there in the dark. The skies in the morning are splendid, immensely high and clear. I like to watch the clouds building and dispersing. Such huge, delicate labour. Today there was a rainbow, when I saw it I laughed out loud, as at a wonderful, absurd joke. Now and then people pass by, under the tree. It must be a shortcut, that way. At nine come the office girls with cigarettes and fancy hairdos, and, a little later, dreamy housewives lugging shopping bags and babies. At four every afternoon a schoolboy straggles by, bearing an enormous satchel on his back like a hump. Dogs come too, trotting very fast with an air of determination, stop, give the tree a quick squirt, pass on. Other lives, other lives. Lately, since the season began to change, they all seem to move, even the boy, with a lighter tread, borne up, as if they are flying, somehow, through the glassy blue autumnal air.

At this time of year I often dream about my father. It is always the same dream, though the circumstances vary. The person in it is indeed my father, but not as I ever knew him. He is younger, sturdier, he is cheerful, he has a droll sense of humour. I arrive at a hospital, or some such large institution, and, after much searching and confusion, find him sitting up in bed with a steaming mug of tea in his hand. His hair is boyishly rumpled, he is wearing someone else's pyjamas. He greets me with a sheepish smile. On impulse, because I am flustered and have been so worried, I embrace him fervently. He suffers this unaccustomed display of emotion with equanimity, patting my shoulder and laughing a little. Then I sit down on a chair beside the bed and we are silent for a moment, not quite knowing what to do, or where to look. I understand that he has survived something, an accident, or a shipwreck, or a hectic illness. Somehow it is his own foolhardiness, his recklessness (my father, reckless!), that has got him into danger, and now he is feeling silly, and comically ashamed of himself. In the dream it is always I who have been responsible for his lucky escape, by raising the alarm, calling for an ambulance, getting the lifeboat out, something like that. My deed sits between us, enormous, unmanageable, like love itself, proof at last of a son's true regard. I wake up smiling, my heart swollen with tenderness. I used to believe that in the dream it was death I was rescuing him from, but lately I have begun to think that it is, instead, the long calamity of his life I am undoing at a stroke. Now perhaps I'll have another, similar task to perform. For they told me today my mother has died.

By the time the taxi got me to the village the last bus to the city had left, as my driver, with melancholy enjoyment, had assured me would be the case. We sat in the darkened main street, beside a hardware shop, the engine purring. The driver turned around in his seat, lifting his cap for a rapid, one-finger scratch, and settled down to see what I would do next. Once again I was struck by the way these people stare, the dull, brute candour of their interest. I had better give him a name – it is Reck, I'm afraid – for I shall be stuck with him for a while yet. He would be happy, he said, to drive me into the city himself. I shook my head: it was a good thirty miles, and I already owed him money. Otherwise, he said, with an awful, ingratiating smile, his mother might put me up – Mrs Reck, it seemed, ran a public house with a room upstairs. The idea did not appeal to me, but the street was dark and grimly silent, and there was something very depressing about those tools in that shop window, and yes, I said faintly, with a hand to my forehead, yes, take me to your mother.

But she was not there, or asleep or something, and he led me up the back stairs himself, going on tiptoe like a large, shaky spider. The room had a little low window, one chair, and a bed with a hollow in the middle, as if a cadaver had lately been removed from it. There was a smell of piss and porter. Reck stood smiling at me shyly, kneading his cap in his hands. I bade him a firm goodnight, and he withdrew, lingeringly. The last I saw of him was a bony hand slowly pulling the door closed behind him. I walked back and forth once or twice gingerly, the floorboards creaking. Did I wring my hands, I wonder? The low window and the sagging bed gave me a vertiginous sense of disproportion, I seemed too tall, my feet too big. I sat on the side of the bed. A faint radiance lingered in the window. If I leaned down sideways I could see a crooked chimney pot and a silhouette of trees. I felt like the gloomy hero in a Russian novel, brooding in my bolthole above the dramshop in the village of Dash, in the year Dot, with my story all before me, waiting to be told.

I did not sleep. The sheets were clammy and somehow slippery, and I was convinced I was not the first to have tossed and turned between them since their last laundering. I tried to lie, tensed like a spring, in such a way that as little of me as possible came in contact with them. The hours were marked by a distant churchbell with a peculiarly dull note. There was the usual barking of dogs and bellowing of cattle. The sound of my own fretful sighs infuriated me. Now and then a car or a lorry passed by, and a box of lighted geometry slid rapidly over the ceiling and down the walls and poured away into a corner. I had a raging thirst. Waking dreams assailed me with grotesque and bawdy visions. Once, on the point of sleep, I had a sudden, dreadful sense of falling, and I sprang awake with a jerk. Though I tried to put her out of my mind I kept returning to the thought of Anna Behrens. What had happened to her, that she should lock herself away in that drear museum, with only a dying old man for company? But perhaps nothing had happened, perhaps that was it. Perhaps the days just went by, one by one, without a sound, until at last it was too late, and she woke up one morning and found herself stuck fast in the middle of her life. I imagined her there, sad and solitary, bewitched in her magic castle, year after year, and – oh, all sorts of mad notions came into my head, I am too embarrassed to speak of them. And as I was thinking these things, another thought, on another, murkier level, was winding and winding its dark skein. So it was out of a muddled conflation of ideas of knight errantry and rescue and reward that my plan originated. I assure you, your Honour, this is no sly attempt at exoneration: I only wish to explain my motives, I mean the deepest ones, if such a thing is possible. As the hours went on, and stars flared in the little window and then slowly faded again, Anna Behrens merged in my mind with the other women who were in some way in my care – Daphne, of course, and even my mother, even the stable-girl, too – but in the end, when the dawn came, it was that Dutch figure in the picture in the garden room who hovered over the bed and gazed at me, sceptical, inquisitive and calm. I got up and dressed, and sat on the chair by the window and watched the ashen light of day descend upon the rooftops and seep into the trees. My mind was racing, my blood fizzled in my veins. I knew now what I would do. I was excited, and at the same time I had a deep sense of dread. There were stirrings downstairs. I wanted to be out, out, being and doing. I started to leave the room, but paused and lay on the bed for a moment to calm myself, and fell at once into a profound and terrible sleep. It was as if I had been struck down. I cannot describe it. It lasted no more than a minute or two. I woke up shaking. It was as if the very heart of things had skipped a beat. So it was that the day began, as it would continue, in the horrors.

Mrs Reck was tall and thin. No, she was short and fat. I do not remember her clearly. I do not wish to remember her clearly. For God's sake, how many of these grotesques am I expected to invent? I'll call her for a witness, and you can do the job yourselves. At first I thought she was in pain, but it was only a terrible, tongue-tied shyness that was making her duck and flinch. She fed me sausages and rashers and black pudding in the parlour behind the bar (it was the executioner who ate a hearty breakfast). An intricate silence filled the room, I could hear myself swallow. Shadows hung down the walls like fronds of cobweb. There was a picture of Jesus with his dripping heart on show, done in thick shades of crimson and cream, and a photograph of some pope or other blessing the multitudes from a Vatican balcony. A feeling of gloom settled like heartburn in my breast. Reck appeared, in his braces and shirtsleeves, and asked coyly if everything was all right. Grand, I said stoutly, grand! He stood and gazed at me, smiling tenderly, with a sort of happy pride. I might have been something he had left to propagate overnight. Ah, these poor, simple lives, so many, across which I have dragged my trail of slime. He had not once mentioned the monies I owed him – even on the phone he had apologised for not waiting for me. I rose and edged past him in the doorway. Just popping out for a moment, I said, get a breath of air. I could feel my horrible smile, like something sticky that had spread over my face. He nodded, and a little flicker of sadness passed across his brow and down his sheep's muzzle. You knew I was going to

do a flit, didn't you? Why did you not stop me? I don't understand these people. I have said it before. I don't understand them.

The sun was shining through a thinning haze. It was still
impossibly early. I walked down one side of the main street and
up the other, twitching with impatience. Few people were
about. Where did the notion come from that country folk are
early risers? A van passed by, towing a trailer with a pig in it. At
the end of the street there was a bridge over a shallow brown
stream. I sat on the parapet and watched the water for a while.
I needed a shave. I thought of going back to Reck's and borrow-
ing a razor from him, but even I was not ruffian enough for such
effrontery. The day was growing hot already. I began to feel light-
headed there in the sun, watching the water squiggle and gulp
below me. Presently a large, ancient man came along and began
to address me earnestly. He wore sandals, and a torn mackintosh
slung like a kern's tartan over one shoulder, and carried a thick
ash stave. His hair was long, his beard matted. For some reason
I found myself picturing his head borne aloft on a platter. He
spoke calmly, in a loud, strong voice. I could not understand a
word he said – he seemed to have lost the power of articulation –
yet I found something oddly affecting in the way he stood there,
leaning on his ashplant, with one knee flexed, his eyes fixed on
me, speaking out his testament. I watched his mouth working in
the thicket of his beard, and nodded my head slowly, seriously.
Madmen do not frighten me, or even make me uneasy. Indeed,
I find that their ravings soothe me. I think it is because everything, from the explosion of a nova to the fall of dust in a deserted
room, is to them of vast and equal significance, and therefore
meaningless. He finished, and continued regarding me in silence
for a moment. Then he nodded gravely, and, with a last, mean-
ingful stare, turned and strode away, over the bridge.

Your Honour, I know I have spoken of having a plan, but it
was a plan only in the broadest sense. I have never been much
good at details. In the night, when the egg hatched and the thing
first flexed its sticky, brittle wings, I had told myself that when
morning came and real life started up again I would laugh at such
a preposterous notion. And I did laugh, even if it was in a
thoughtful sort of way, and I believe, I really do, that if I had not
been stranded in that hole, with nothing to pass the time except
my own dark thoughts, none of this would have happened.

I would have gone to Charlie French and borrowed some money from him, and returned to the island and paid my debt to Señor Aguirre, and then I would have taken my wife and child and come home, to Coolgrange, to make my peace with my mother, and settle down, and become a squireen like my father, and live, and be happy. Ah –

What was I saying? My plan, yes. Your Lordship, I am no mastermind. The newspapers, which from the start have been quite beside themselves – it was the silly season, after all, and I gave them a glorious, running story – have portrayed me both as a reckless thug and a meticulous, ice-cool, iron-willed blond beast. But I swear, it was all just drift, like everything else. I suppose at first I played with the idea, telling it to myself as a sort of story, as I lay there, the sleepless prince, in Mother Reck's gingerbread house, while the innocent stars crowded silently in the window. In the morning I rose and held it up to the light, and already it had begun to harden, to set. Strangely, it was like the work of someone else, which had been given to me to measure and to test. This process of distancing seems to have been an essential preliminary to action. Perhaps this accounts for the peculiar sensation which came over me there on the bridge above that gurgling river. It's hard to describe. I felt that I was utterly unlike myself. That is to say, I was perfectly familiar with this large, somewhat overweight, fair-haired man in a wrinkled suit sitting here fretfully twiddling his thumbs, yet at the same time it was as if I – the real, thinking, sentient I – had somehow got myself trapped inside a body not my own. But no, that's not it, exactly. For the person that was inside was also strange to me, stranger by far, indeed, than the familiar, physical creature. This is not clear, I know. I say the one within was strange to *me*, but which version of *me* do I mean? No, not clear at all. But it was not a new sensation. I have always felt – what is the word? – bifurcate, that's it. Today, however, this feeling was stronger, more pronounced than usual. Bunter was restive, aching to get out. He had been shut up for so long, burbling and grumbling and taunting in there, and I knew that when he burst out at last he would talk and talk and talk. I felt dizzy. Grey nausea made my insides cringe. I wonder if the court appreciates what a state my nerves were in, not just that day, but throughout that period? My wife and child were being held hostage by wicked people,

I was practically broke, my quarterly allowance from the pittance left me by my father was not due for another two months, and here I was, after a ghastly night, red-eyed, unshaven, stranded in the middle of nowhere and contemplating desperate actions. How would I not have been dizzy, how would I not have felt sick to my guts?

Eventually I sensed the village behind me coming sluggishly to life, and I walked back along the main street, keeping an eye out in case I should encounter an importunate Reck or, worse, Reck's mother. The morning was sunny and still, dew-laden, and a little dazed, as if drunk on its own newness. There were patches of damp on the pavements. It would be a glorious day. Oh yes, glorious.

I did not know until I found it that I was looking for the hardware shop where Reck had stopped the taxi the night before. My arm reached out and pushed open the door, a bell pinged, my legs walked me inside.

Gloom, a smell of paraffin and linseed oil, and clusters of things pendent overhead. A short, stout, elderly, balding man was sweeping the floor. He wore carpet slippers, and a cinnamon-coloured shopcoat such as I had not seen since I was a child. He smiled and nodded at me, and put aside his brush. He would not speak, however – professional etiquette, no doubt – until he had taken up position behind the counter, leaning forward on his arms with his head cocked to one side. Wire-rimmed glasses, I thought, would have completed the effect. I liked him straight away. Good day to you, sir, he said, in a cheery, hand-rubbing sort of voice. I felt better already. He was polite to just the correct degree, without undue subservience, or any hint of nosiness. I bought a ball of twine and a roll of brown wrapping paper. Also a hank of rope – coiled, I recall, in a tight cylinder, very like a hangman's knot – good hard smooth hemp, not that modern plastic stuff. I had little notion of what I intended to do with these things. The rope, for instance, was pure indulgence. I didn't care. It was years – decades! – since I had experienced such simple, greedy pleasure. The shopman placed my purchases lovingly before me on the counter, crooning a little under his breath, smiling, pursing his lips approvingly. It was playtime. In this pretend-world I could have anything I wanted. A tenon saw, for instance, with rosewood stock. A set of brass fire irons, their handles made in the shape of crouching monkeys. That white enamelled bucket, with a delicate, flesh-blue shadow down one side. Oh, anything! Then I spotted the hammer. One moulded, polished piece of stainless steel, like a bone from the thigh of some swift animal, with a velvety, black rubber grip and a blued head and claw. I am utterly unhandy, I do not think I could drive a nail straight, but I confess I had always harboured a secret desire to have a hammer like that. More laughter in court, of course, more ribald guffaws from the wiseacres in the gallery. But I insist, your Honour, gentle handymen of the jury, I insist it was an innocent desire, a wish, an ache, on the part of the deprived child inside me – not Bunter, not him, but the true, lost ghost of my boyhood – to possess this marvellous toy. For the first time my fairy-godfather hesitated. There are other models, he ventured, less – a hurried, breathy whisper – less expensive, sir. But no, no, I could not resist it. I must have it. That one. Yes, that one, there, with the tag on it. Exhibit A, in other words.

I stumbled out of the shop with my parcel under my arm, bleared and grinning, happy as a drunken schoolboy. The shopkeeper came to the door to watch me go. He had shaken hands with me in an odd, cryptic manner. Perhaps he was a mason, and was testing to see if I too might be a member of the brotherhood? – but no, I prefer to think he was merely a decent, kindly, well-meaning man. There are not many such, in this testimony.

I felt by now that I knew the village. I felt in fact that I had been here before, and even that I had done all these things before, walked about aimlessly in the early morning, and sat on the bridge, and gone into a shop and purchased things. I have no explanation: I only felt it. It was as if I had dreamed a prophetic dream and then forgotten it, and this was the prophecy coming true. But then, something of that sense of inevitability infected everything I did that day – inevitable, mind you, does not mean excusable, in my vocabulary. No indeed, a strong mixture of Catholic and Calvinist blood courses in my veins.

It came to me suddenly, with happy inconsequentiality, that it was midsummer day.

This is a wonderful country, a man with a decent accent can do almost anything. I thought I was heading for the bus stop, to see if there was a bus to the city, but instead – more inevitability – I found myself outside a tumbledown garage in the village square. A boy in filthy overalls a number of sizes too small for him was heaving tyres and whistling tunelessly out of the side of his face. A rusty tin sign nailed to the wall above his head proclaimed: *Melmoth's ar Hire*. The boy paused and looked at me blankly. He had stopped whistling, but kept his lips puckered. Car? I said, pointing to the sign, for hire, yes? I jiggled an invisible steering wheel. He said nothing, only frowned in deep puzzlement, as if I had asked for something utterly outlandish. Then a stout, big-bosomed woman came out of the cash office and spoke to him sharply. She wore a crimson blouse and tight black trousers and high-heeled, toeless sandals. Her hair, black as a crow's wing, was piled up in a brioche shape, with ringlets trailing down at the sides. She reminded me of someone, I could not think who. She led me into the office, where with a lurch I spied, among a cluster of gaudy postcards tacked to the wall behind her desk, a view of the island, and the harbour, and the very bar where I had first encountered Randolph the American. It was unnerving, an omen, even a warning, perhaps. The woman was studying me up and down with a sort of smouldering surmise. With another shock I realised who it was she reminded me of: the mother of the squalling baby in Señor Aguirre's apartment.

The car was a Humber, a great, heavy, high model, not old enough to be what they call vintage, just hopelessly out of fashion. It seemed to have been built for a simpler, more innocent age than this, one peopled by a species of big children. The upholstery had a vaguely fecal smell. I drove sedately through the village in third gear, perched high above the road as if I were being borne along on a palanquin. The engine made a noise like muffled cheering. I had paid a deposit of five pounds, and signed a document in the name of Smyth (I thought the y a fiendishly clever touch). The woman had not even asked to see a driving licence. As I say, this is a wonderful country. I felt extraordinarily light-hearted.

Speaking of jaunts: I went to my mother's funeral today. Three plain-clothes men took me in a closed car, I was very impressed. We sped through the city with the siren hee-hawing, it was like my arrest all over again, but in reverse. A lovely, sunny, crisp morning, pale smoke in the air, a few leaves down already on the pavements. I felt such a strange mingling of emotions – a certain rawness, of course, a certain pain, but elation, too, and something like grief that yet was not without sweetness. I was grieving not for my mother only, perhaps not for her at all, but for things in general. Maybe it was just the usual September melancholy, made unfamiliar by the circumstances. We drove by the river under a sky piled high with bundles of luminous Dutch clouds, then south through leafy suburbs. The sea surprised me, as it always does, a bowl of blue, moving metal, light rising in flakes off the surface. All three detectives were chain-smokers, they worked at it grimly, as if it were a part of their duties. One of them offered me a cigarette. Not one of my vices, I said, and they laughed politely. They seemed embarrassed, and kept glancing warily out of the windows, as if they had been forced to come on an outing with a famous and disreputable relative and were afraid of being spotted by someone they knew. Now we were in the country, and there was mist on the fields still, and the hedges were drenched. She was buried in the family plot in the old cemetery at Coolgrange. I was not allowed to leave the car, or even to open a window. I was secretly glad, for somehow I could conceive of myself stepping out suddenly, just like that, into the world. The driver parked as near as possible to the graveside, and I sat in a fug of cigarette smoke and watched the brief, hackneyed little drama unfold beyond the fogged glass, among the leaning headstones. There were few mourners: an aunt or two, and an old man who had worked years ago for my father in the stables. The girl Joanne was there, of course, red-eyed, her poor face blotched and swollen, dressed in a lumpy pullover and a crooked skirt. Charlie French stood a little apart from the rest, with his hands awkwardly clasped. I was surprised to see him. Decent of him to come, courageous, too. Neither he nor the girl looked in my direction, though they must have felt the pressure of my humid gaze. The coffin seemed to me surprisingly small, they got it down into the hole with room to spare. Poor Ma. I can't believe that she's gone, I mean the fact of it has not sunk in yet. It is somehow as if she had been bundled away to make room for something more important. Of course, the irony of the situation does not escape me: if I had only waited a few months there would have been no need to – but no, enough of that. They'll read the will without me, which is only right. The last time I saw her I fought with her. That was the day I left for Whitewater.

She did not visit me in jail. I don't blame her. I never brought the child for her to see, not once. She was not as tough as I imagined. Did I destroy her life, too? All these dead women.

When the ceremony was over Charlie walked past the car with his head down. He seemed to hesitate, but changed his mind and went on. I think he would have spoken to me, had it not been for the presence of the detectives, and my aunts agog behind him, and, oh, just the general awfulness of everything.

SO I AM driving away from the village, in the Humber Hawk, with a foolish grin on my face. I felt, for no good reason, that I was escaping all my problems, I pictured them dwindling in space and time like the village itself, a quaint jumble of things getting steadily smaller and smaller. If I had stopped for a moment to think, of course, I would have realised that what I was leaving behind me was not my tangled troubles, as I fondly imagined, but, on the contrary, a mass of evidence, obvious and unmistakable as a swatch of matted hair and blood. I had skipped Ma Reck's without paying for my lodgings, I had bought a burglar's kit in the village shop, and now I had as good as stolen a car – and all this not five miles from what would soon come to be known as the scene of the crime. The court will agree, these are hardly the marks of careful premeditation. (Why is it that every other thing I say sounds like the sly preamble to a plea of mitigation?) The fact is, I was not thinking at all, not what could really be called thinking. I was content to sail through sun and shade along these dappled back roads, one hand on the wheel and an elbow out of the window, with the scents of the countryside in my nostrils and the breeze whipping my hair. Everything would be well, everything would work itself out. I do not know why I felt so elated, perhaps it was a form of delirium. Anyway, I told myself, it was only a madcap game I was playing, I could call it off whenever I wished.

Meanwhile here was Whitewater, rising above the trees.

An empty tour bus was parked at the gate. The driver's door was open, and the driver was lounging in the stepwell, sunning himself. He watched me as I swung past him into the drive. I waved to him. He wore tinted glasses. He did not smile. He would remember me.

Afterwards the police could not understand why I showed so little circumspection, driving up brazenly like that, in broad daylight, in that unmistakable motor car. But I believed, you see,

that the matter would be entirely between Behrens and me, with
Anna perhaps as go-between. I never imagined there would be
anything so vulgar as a police investigation, and headlines in
the papers, and all the rest of it. A simple business transaction
between civilised people, that's what I intended. I would be
polite but firm, no more than that. I was not thinking in terms
of threats and ransom demands, certainly not. When later I read
what those reporters wrote – the Midsummer Manhunt, they
called it – I could not recognise myself in their depiction of me
as a steely, ruthless character. Ruthless – me! No, as I drove up
to Whitewater it was not police I was thinking of, but only the
chauffeur Flynn, with his little pig eyes and his boxer's meaty
paws. Yes, Flynn was a man to avoid.

Halfway up the drive there was

God, these tedious details.

Halfway up there was a fork in the drive. A wooden arrow
with HOUSE written on it in white paint pointed to the right,
while to the left a sign said STRICTLY PRIVATE. I stopped
the car. See me there, a big blurred face behind the windscreen
peering first this way, then that. It is like an illustration from a
cautionary tract: the sinner hesitates at the parting of the ways.
I drove off to the left, and my heart gave an apprehensive wallop.
Behold, the wretch forsakes the path of righteousness.

I rounded the south wing of the house, and parked on the
grass and walked across the lawn to the garden room. The french
window was open. Deep breath. It was not yet noon. Far off in
the fields somewhere a tractor was working, it made a drowsy,
buzzing sound that seemed the very voice of summer, I hear it
still, that tiny, distant, prelapsarian song. I had left the rope and
the hammer in the car, and brought with me the twine and
the roll of wrapping paper. It struck me suddenly how absurd the
whole thing was. I began to laugh, and laughing stepped into
the room.

The painting is called, as everyone must know by now, *Portrait
of a Woman with Gloves*. It measures eighty-two centimetres by
sixty-five. From internal evidence – in particular the woman's
attire – it has been dated between 1655 and 1660. The black dress
and broad white collar and cuffs of the woman are lightened only
by a brooch and gold ornamentation on the gloves. The face has
a slightly Eastern cast. (I am quoting from the guidebook to

Whitewater House.) The picture has been variously attributed to Rembrandt and Frans Hals, even to Vermeer. However, it is safest to regard it as the work of an anonymous master.

None of this means anything.

I have stood in front of other, perhaps greater paintings, and not been moved as I am moved by this one. I have a reproduction of it on the wall above my table here – sent to me by, of all people, Anna Behrens – when I look at it my heart contracts. There is something in the way the woman regards me, the querulous, mute insistence of her eyes, which I can neither escape nor assuage. I squirm in the grasp of her gaze. She requires of me some great effort, some tremendous feat of scrutiny and attention, of which I do not think I am capable. It is as if she were asking me to let her live.

She. There is no she, of course. There is only an organisation of shapes and colours. Yet I try to make up a life for her. She is, I will say, thirty-five, thirty-six, though people without thinking still speak of her as a girl. She lives with her father, the merchant (tobacco, spices, and, in secret, slaves). She keeps house for him since her mother's death. She did not like her mother. Her father dotes on her, his only child. She is, he proclaims, his treasure. She devises menus – father has a delicate stomach – inspects the kitchen, she even supervises his wine cellar. She keeps an inventory of the household linen in a little notebook attached to her belt by a fine gold chain, using a code of her own devising, for she has never learned to read or write. She is strict with the servants, and will permit no familiarities. Their dislike she takes for respect. The house is not enough to absorb her energies, she does good works besides: she visits the sick, and is on the board of visitors of the town's almshouse. She is brisk, sometimes impatient, and there are mutterings against her among the alms-folk, especially the old women. At times, usually in spring and at the beginning of winter, everything becomes too much for her. Notice the clammy pallor of her skin: she is prey to obscure ailments. She takes to her bed and lies for days without speaking, hardly breathing, while outside in the silvery northern light the world goes about its busy way. She tries to pray, but God is distant. Her father comes to visit her at evening, walking on tiptoe. These periods of prostration frighten him, he remembers his wife dying, her terrible silence in the last weeks. If he were to lose his daughter too – But she gets up, wills herself to it, and very soon the servants are feeling the edge of her tongue again, and he cannot contain his relief, it comes out in little laughs, roguish endearments, a kind of clumsy skittishness. She considers him wryly, then turns back to her tasks. She cannot understand this notion he has got into his head: he wants to have her portrait painted. I'm old, is all he will say to her, I am an old man, look at me! And he laughs, awkwardly, and avoids her eye. My portrait? she says, mine? – I am no fit subject for a painter. He shrugs, at which she is first startled, then grimly amused: he might at least have attempted to contradict her. He seems to realise what is going through her mind, and tries to mend matters, but he becomes flustered, and, watching him fuss and fret and pluck at his cuffs, she realises with a pang that it's true, he has aged. Her father, an old man. The thought has a touch of bleak comedy, which she cannot account for. You have fine hands, he says, growing testy, annoyed both at himself and her, your mother's hands – we'll tell him to make the hands prominent. And so, to humour him, but also because she is secretly curious, she goes along one morning to the studio. The squalor is what strikes her first of all. Dirt and daubs of paint everywhere, gnawed chicken bones on a smeared plate, a chamber pot on the floor in the corner. The painter matches the place, with that filthy smock, and those fingernails. He has a drinker's squashed and pitted nose. She thinks the general smell is bad until she catches a whiff of his breath. She discovers that she is relieved: she had expected someone young, dissolute, threatening, not this pot-bellied old soak. But then he fixes his little wet eyes on her, briefly, with a kind of impersonal intensity, and she flinches, as if caught in a burst of strong light. No one has ever looked at her like this before. So this is what it is to be known! It is almost indecent. First he puts her standing by the window, but it does not suit, the light is wrong, he says. He shifts her about, grasping her by the upper arms and walking her backwards from one place to another. She feels she should be indignant, but the usual responses do not seem to function here. He is shorter than her by a head. He makes some sketches, scribbles a colour note or two, then tells her to come tomorrow at the same time. And wear a darker dress, he says. Well! She is about to give him a piece of her mind, but already he has turned aside to another task. Her

maid, sitting by the door, is biting her lips and smirking. She lets
the next day pass, and the next, just to show him. When she does
return he says nothing about the broken appointment, only looks
at her black dress – pure silk, with a broad collar of Spanish lace
– and nods carelessly, and she is so vexed at him it surprises her,
and she is shocked at herself. He has her stand before the couch.
Remove your gloves, he says, I am to emphasise the hands. She
hears the note of amused disdain in his voice. She refuses. (*Her*
hands, indeed!) He insists. They engage in a brief, stiff little
squabble, batting icy politenesses back and forth between them.
In the end she consents to remove one glove, then promptly tries
to hide the hand she has bared. He sighs, shrugs, but has to suppress a grin, as she notices. Rain streams down the windows,
shreds of smoke fly over the rooftops. The sky has a huge silver
hole in it. At first she is restless, standing there, then she seems to
pass silently through some barrier, and a dreamy calm comes over
her. It is the same, day after day, first there is agitation, then the
breakthrough, then silence and a kind of softness, as if she were
floating away, away, out of herself. He mutters under his breath
as he works. He is choleric, he swears, and clicks his tongue,
sending up sighs and groans. There are long, fevered passages
when he works close up against the canvas, and she can only see
his stumpy legs and his old, misshapen boots. Even his feet seem
busy. She wants to laugh when he pops his head out at the side
of the easel and peers at her sharply, his potato nose twitching.
He will not let her see what he is doing, she is not allowed even
a peek. Then one day she senses a kind of soundless, settling crash
at his end of the room, and he steps back with an expression of
weary disgust and waves a hand dismissively at the canvas, and
turns aside to clean his brush. She comes forward and looks. For
a second she sees nothing, so taken is she by the mere sensation
of stopping like this and turning: it is as if – as if somehow she
had walked out of herself. A long moment passes. The brooch,
she says, is wonderfully done. The sound of her own voice
startles her, it is a stranger speaking, and she is cowed. He laughs,
not bitterly, but with real amusement and, so she feels, a curious
sort of sympathy. It is an acknowledgement, of – she does not
know what. She looks and looks. She had expected it would be
like looking in a mirror, but this is someone she does not recognise, and yet knows. The words come unbidden into her head:

Now I know how to die. She puts on her glove, and signals to her maid. The painter is speaking behind her, something about her father, and money, of course, but she is not listening. She is calm. She is happy. She feels numbed, hollowed, a walking shell. She goes down the stairs, along the dingy hall, and steps out into a commonplace world.

Do not be fooled: none of this means anything either.

I had placed the string and the wrapping paper carefully on the floor, and now stepped forward with my arms outstretched. The door behind me opened and a large woman in a tweed skirt and a cardigan came into the room. She halted when she saw me there, with my arms flung wide before the picture and peering wildly at her over my shoulder, while I tried with one foot to conceal the paper and the ball of twine on the floor. She had blue-grey hair, and her spectacles were attached to a cord around her neck. She frowned. You must stay with the party, she said loudly, in a cross voice – really, I don't know how many times I have to say it. I stepped back. A dozen gaudily dressed people were crowding in the doorway behind her, craning to get a look at me. Sorry, I heard myself say meekly, I got lost. She gave an impatient toss of the head and strode to the middle of the room and began at once to speak in a shouted singsong about Carlin tables and Berthoud clocks, and weeks later, questioned by the police and shown my photograph, she would deny ever having seen me before in her life. Her charges shuffled in, jostling surreptitiously in an effort to stay out of her line of sight. They took up position, standing with their hands clasped before them, as if they were in church, and looked about them with expressions of respectful vacancy. One grizzled old party in a Hawaiian shirt grinned at me and winked. I confess I was rattled. There was a knot in the pit of my stomach and my palms were damp. All the elation I had felt on the way here had evaporated, leaving behind it a stark sense of foreboding. I was struck, for the first time, really, by the enormity of what I was embarked on. I felt like a child whose game has led him far into the forest, and now it is nightfall, and there are shadowy figures among the trees. The guide had finished her account of the treasures in the room – the picture, *my* picture, was given two sentences, and a misattribution – and walked out now with one arm raised stiffly above her head, still talking, shepherding the party behind her. When they had gone

I waited, staring fixedly at the doorknob, expecting her to come back and haul me out briskly by the scruff of the neck. Somewhere inside me a voice was moaning softly in panic and fright. This is something that does not seem to be appreciated – I have remarked on it before – I mean how timorous I am, how easily daunted. But she did not return, and I heard them tramping away up the stairs. I set to work again feverishly. I see myself, like the villain in an old three-reeler, all twitches and scowls and wriggling eyebrows. I got the picture off the wall, not without difficulty, and laid it flat on the floor – shying away from that black stare – and began to tear off lengths of wrapping paper. I would not have thought that paper would make so much noise, such scuffling and rattling and ripping, it must have sounded as if some large animal were being flayed in here. And it was no good, my hands shook, I was all thumbs, and the sheets of paper kept rolling back on themselves, and I had nothing to cut the twine with, and anyway the picture, with its thick, heavy frame, was much too big to be wrapped. I scampered about on my knees, talking to myself and uttering little squeaks of distress. Everything was going wrong. Give it up, I told myself, oh please, please, give it up now, while there's still time! but another part of me gritted its teeth and said, no you don't, you coward, get up, get on your feet, do it! So I struggled up, moaning and snivelling, and grasped the picture in my arms and staggered with it blindly, nose to nose, in the direction of the french window. Those eyes were staring into mine, I almost blushed. And then – how shall I express it – then somehow I sensed, behind that stare, another presence, watching me. I stopped, and lowered the picture, and there she was, standing in the open window, just as she had stood the day before, wide-eyed, with one hand raised. This, I remember thinking bitterly, this is the last straw. I was outraged. How dare the world strew these obstacles in my path. It was not fair, it was just not fair! Right, I said to her, here, take this, and I thrust the painting into her arms and turned her about and marched her ahead of me across the lawn. She said nothing, or if she did I was not listening. She found it hard going on the grass, the picture was too heavy for her, and she could hardly see around it. When she faltered I prodded her between the shoulder blades. I really was very cross. We reached the car. The cavernous boot smelled strongly of fish. There was the usual

jumble of mysterious implements, a jack, and spanners and things
– I am not mechanically minded, or handed, have I mentioned
that? – and a filthy old pullover, which I hardly noticed at the
time, thrown in a corner with deceptive casualness by the hidden
arranger of all these things. I took out the tools and threw them
behind me on to the grass, then lifted the painting from the
maid's arms and placed it face-down on the worn felt matting.
This was the first time I had seen the back of the canvas, and
suddenly I was struck by the antiquity of the thing. Three hundred years ago it had been stretched and sized and left against a
lime-washed wall to dry. I closed my eyes for a second, and at
once I saw a workshop in a narrow street in Amsterdam or
Antwerp, smoky sunlight in the window, and hawkers going by
outside, and the bells of the cathedral ringing. The maid was
watching me. She had the most extraordinary pale, violet eyes,
they seemed transparent, when I looked into them I felt I was
seeing clear through her head. Why did she not run away?
Behind her, in one of the great upstairs windows, a dozen heads
were crowded, goggling at us. I could make out the guide-
woman's glasses and the American's appalling shirt. I think I must
have cried aloud in rage, an old lion roaring at the whip and chair,
for the maid flinched and stepped back a pace. I caught her wrist
in an iron claw and, wrenching open the car door, fairly flung
her into the back seat. Oh, why did she not run away! When
I got behind the wheel, fumbling and snarling, I caught a whiff
of something, a faint, sharp, metallic smell, like the smell of worn
pennies. I could see her in the mirror, crouched behind me as in
a deep glass box, braced between the door and the back of
the seat, with her elbows stuck out and fingers splayed and her
face thrust forward, like the cornered heroine in a melodrama.
A fierce, choking gust of impatience surged up inside me.
Impatience, yes, that was what I felt most strongly – that, and a
grievous sense of embarrassment. I was mortified. I had never
been so exposed in all my life. People were looking at me – she
in the back seat, and the tourists up there jostling at the window,
but also, it seemed, a host of others, of phantom spectators, who
must have been, I suppose, an intimation of all that horde
who would soon be crowding around me in fascination and
horror. I started the engine. The gears shrieked. In my agitation
I kept getting ahead of myself and having to go back and repeat

the simplest actions. When I had got the car off the grass and on to the drive I let the clutch out too quickly, and the machine sprang forward in a series of bone-shaking lurches, the bonnet going up and down like the prow of a boat caught in a wash and the shock absorbers grunting. The watchers at the window must have been in fits by now. A bead of sweat ran down my cheek. The sun had made the steering wheel almost too hot to hold, and there was a blinding glare on the windscreen. The maid was scrabbling at the door handle, I roared at her and she stopped at once, and looked at me wide-eyed, like a rebuked child. Outside the gate the bus driver was still sitting in the sun. When she saw him she tried to get the window open, but in vain, the mechanism must have been broken. She pounded on the glass with her fists. I spun the wheel and the car lumbered out into the road, the tyres squealing. We were shouting at each other now, like a married couple having a fight. She pummelled me on the shoulder, got a hand around in front of my face and tried to claw my eyes. Her thumb went up my nose, I thought she would tear off the nostril. The car was going all over the road. I trod with both feet on the brake pedal, and we sailed in a slow, dragging curve into the hedge. She fell back. I turned to her. I had the hammer in my hand. I looked at it, startled. The silence rose around us like water. Don't, she said. She was crouched as before, with her arms bent and her back pressed into the corner. I could not speak, I was filled with a kind of wonder. I had never felt another's presence so immediately and with such raw force. I saw her now, really saw her, for the first time, her mousy hair and bad skin, that bruised look around her eyes. She was quite ordinary, and yet, somehow, I don't know – somehow radiant. She cleared her throat and sat up, and detached a strand of hair that had caught at the corner of her mouth.

You must let me go, she said, or you will be in trouble.

It's not easy to wield a hammer in a motor car. When I struck her the first time I expected to feel the sharp, clean smack of steel on bone, but it was more like hitting clay, or hard putty. The word *fontanel* sprang into my mind. I thought one good bash would do it, but, as the autopsy would show, she had a remarkably strong skull – even in that, you see, she was unlucky. The first blow fell just at the hairline, above her left eye. There was not much blood, only a dark-red glistening dent with hair matted in it. She shuddered, but remained sitting upright, swaying a little, looking at me with eyes that would not focus properly. Perhaps I would have stopped then, if she had not suddenly launched herself at me across the back of the seat, flailing and screaming. I was dismayed. How could this be happening to me – it was all so *unfair*. Bitter tears of self-pity squeezed into my eyes. I pushed her away from me and swung the hammer in a wide, backhand curve. The force of the blow flung her against the door, and her head struck the window, and a fine thread of blood ran out of her nostril and across her cheek. There was blood on the window, too, a fan-shaped spray of tiny drops. She closed her eyes and turned her face away from me, making a low, guttural noise at the back of her throat. She put a hand up to her head just as I was swinging at her again, and when the blow landed on her temple her fingers were in the way, and I heard one of them crack, and I winced, and almost apologised. Oh! she said, and suddenly, as if everything inside her had collapsed, she slithered down the seat on to the floor.

There was silence again, clear and startling. I got out of the car and stood a moment, breathing. I was dizzy. Something seemed to have happened to the sunlight, everywhere I looked there was an underwater gloom. I thought I had driven only a little way, and expected to see the gates of Whitewater, and the tour bus, and the driver running towards me, but to my astonishment the road in both directions was empty, and I had no idea where I was. On one side a hill rose steeply, and on the other I could see over the tops of pine trees to far-off, rolling downs. It all looked distinctly improbable. It was like a hastily painted backdrop, especially that smudged, shimmering distance, and the road winding innocently away. I found I was still clutching the hammer. With a grand sweep of my arm I flung it from me, and watched it as it flew, tumbling slowly end over end, in a long, thrilling arc, far, far out over the blue pine-tops. Then abruptly I bent forward and vomited up the glutinous remains of the breakfast I had consumed an age ago, in another life.

I crawled back into the car, keeping my eyes averted from that crumpled thing wedged behind the front seat. The light in the windscreen was a splintered glare, I thought for a second the glass was smashed, until I put a hand to my face and discovered I was crying. This I found encouraging. My tears seemed not just a foretoken of remorse, but the sign of some more common, simpler urge, an affect for which there was no name, but which might be my last link, the only one that would hold, with the world of ordinary things. For everything was changed, where I was now I had not been before. I trembled, and all around me trembled, and there was a sluggish, sticky feel to things, as if I and all of this – car, road, trees, those distant meadows – as if we had all a moment ago struggled mute and amazed out of a birthhole in the air. I turned the key in the ignition, bracing myself, convinced that instead of the engine starting something else would happen, that there would be a terrible, rending noise, or a flash of light, or that slime would gush out over my legs from under the dashboard. I drove in second gear along the middle of the road. Smells, smells. Blood has a hot, thick smell. I wanted to open the windows, but did not dare, I was afraid of what might come in – the light outside seemed moist and dense as glair, I imagined it in my mouth, my nostrils.

I drove and drove. Whitewater is only thirty miles or so from the city, but it seemed hours before I found myself in the suburbs. Of the journey I remember little. That is to say, I do not remember changing gears, accelerating and slowing down, working the pedals, all that. I see myself moving, all right, as if in a crystal bubble, flying soundlessly through a strange, sunlit, glittering landscape. I think I went very fast, for I recall a sensation of pressure in my ears, a dull, rushing blare. So I must have driven in circles, round and round those narrow country roads. Then there were houses, and housing estates, and straggling factories, and supermarkets big as aircraft hangars. I stared through the windscreen in dreamy amazement. I might have been a visitor from another part of the world altogether, hardly able to believe how much like home everything looked and yet how different it was. I did not know where I was going, I mean I was not going anywhere, just driving. It was almost restful, sailing along like that, turning the wheel with one finger, shut off from everything. It was as if all my life I had been clambering up a steep and difficult slope, and now had reached the peak and leaped out blithely into the blue. I felt so free. At the first red traffic light the car drifted gently to a stop as if it were subsiding into air. I was at the junction of two suburban roads. On the left there was a little green rise with a chestnut tree and a neat row of new houses. Children

were playing on the grassy bank. Dogs gambolled. The sun
shone. I have always harboured a secret fondness for quiet places
such as this, unremarked yet cherished domains of building and
doing and tending. I leaned my head back on the seat and smiled,
watching the youngsters at play. The lights changed to green, but
I did not stir. I was not really there, but lost somewhere, in some
sunlit corner of my past. There was a sudden rapping on the
window beside my ear. I jumped. A woman with a large, broad,
horsy face – she reminded me, dear God, of my mother! – was
peering in at me and saying something. I rolled down the window. She had a loud voice, it sounded very loud to me, at any
rate. I could not understand her, she was talking about an
accident, and asking me if I was all right. Then she pressed her
face forward and squinnied over my shoulder, and opened her
mouth and groaned. Oh, she said, the poor child! I turned my
head. There was blood all over the back seat now, far too much,
surely, for just one person to have shed. For a mad instant, in
which a crafty spark of hope flared and died, I wondered if there
had been a crash, which somehow I had not noticed, or had
forgotten, if some overloaded vehicle had ploughed into the back
of us, flinging bodies and all this blood in through the rear window. I could not speak. I had thought she was dead, but there she
was, kneeling between the seats and groping at the window
beside her, I could hear her fingers squeaking on the glass. Her
hair hung down in bloodied ropes, her face was a clay mask
streaked with copper and crimson. The woman outside was
gabbling into my ear about telephones and ambulances and the
police – the police! I turned to her with a terrible glare. Madam!
I said sternly (she would later describe my voice as *cultured* and
authoritative), will you please get on about your business! She
stepped back, staring in shock. I confess I was myself impressed,
I would not have thought I could muster such a commanding
tone. I rolled up the window and jammed the car into gear and
shot away, noticing, too late, that the lights had turned to red.
A tradesman's van coming from the left braked sharply and let
out an indignant squawk. I drove on. However, I had not gone
more than a street or two when suddenly an ambulance reared
up in my wake, its siren yowling and blue light flashing. I was
astonished. How could it have arrived so promptly? In fact, this
was another of those appalling coincidences in which this case

abounds. The ambulance, as I would later learn, was not looking for me, but was returning from – yes – from the scene of a car crash, with – I'm sorry, but, yes – with a dying woman in the back. I kept going, haring along with my head down, my nose almost touching the rim of the wheel. I do not think I could have stopped, locked in fright as I was. The ambulance drew alongside, swaying dangerously and trumpeting like a frenzied big beast. The attendant in the passenger seat, a burly young fellow in shirtsleeves, with a red face and narrow sideburns, looked at the blood-streaked window behind me with mild, professional interest. He conferred briefly with the driver, then signalled to me, with complicated gestures, nodding and mouthing, to follow them. They thought I was coming from the same crash, ferrying another victim to hospital. They surged ahead. I followed in their wake, befuddled with alarm and bafflement. I could see nothing but this big square clumsy thing scudding along, whooshing up dust and wallowing fatly on its springs. Then abruptly it braked and swung into a wide gateway, and an arm appeared out of the side window and beckoned me to follow. It was the sight of that thick arm that broke the spell. With a gulp of demented laughter I drove on, past the hospital gate, plunging the pedal to the floor, and the noise of the siren dwindled behind me, a startled plaint, and I was free.

I peered into the mirror. She was sitting slumped on the seat with her head hanging and her hands resting palm upwards on her thighs.

Suddenly the sea was on my left, far below, blue, unmoving. I drove down a steep hill, then along a straight cement road beside a railway track. A pink and white hotel, castellated, with pennants flying, rose up on my right, enormous and empty. The road straggled to an end in a marshy patch of scrub and thistles, and there I stopped, in the midst of a vast and final silence. I could hear her behind me, breathing. When I turned she lifted her sibyl's fearsome head and looked at me. *Help me*, she whispered. *Help me*. A bubble of blood came out of her mouth and burst. *Tommy!* she said, or a word like that, and then: *Love*. What did I feel? Remorse, grief, a terrible – no no no, I won't lie. I can't remember feeling anything, except that sense of strangeness, of being in a place I knew but did not recognise. When I got out of the car I was giddy, and had to lean on the door for a moment with my eyes shut tight. My jacket was bloodstained, I wriggled out of it and flung it into the stunted bushes – they never found it, I can't think why. I remembered the pullover in the boot, and put it on. It smelled of fish and sweat and axle-grease. I picked up the hangman's hank of rope and threw that away too. Then I lifted out the picture and walked with it to where there was a sagging barbed-wire fence and a ditch with a trickle of water at the bottom, and there I dumped it. What was I thinking of, I don't know. Perhaps it was a gesture of renunciation or something. Renunciation! How do I dare use such words. The woman with the gloves gave me a last, dismissive stare. She had expected no better of me. I went back to the car, trying not to look at it, the smeared windows. Something was falling on me: a delicate, silent fall of rain. I peered upwards in the glistening sunlight and saw a cloud directly overhead, the merest smudge of grey against the summer blue. I thought: I am not human. Then I turned and walked away.

II

ALL MY adult life I have had a recurring dream (yes, yes, dreams again!), it comes once or twice a year and leaves me feeling disturbed for days afterwards. As usual it is not a dream in the ordinary sense, for not much happens in it, really, and nothing is explicit. There is mainly an undefined but profound and mounting sensation of unease, which rises at the end to full-fledged panic. A long time ago, it seems, I have committed a crime. No, that is too strong. I have done something, it is never clear what, precisely. Perhaps I stumbled upon something, it may even have been a corpse, and covered it up, and almost forgot about it. Now, years later, the evidence has been found, and they have come to question me. As yet there is nothing to suggest that I was directly involved, not a hint of suspicion attaches to me. I am merely another name on a list. They are mild, soft-spoken, stolidly deferential, a little bored. The young one fidgets. I respond to their questions politely, with a certain irony, smiling, lifting an eyebrow. It is, I tell myself smugly, the performance of my life, a masterpiece of dissembling. Yet the older one, I notice, is regarding me with deepening interest, his shrewd eyes narrowing. I must have said something. What have I said? I begin to blush, I cannot help it. A horrible constriction takes hold of me. I babble, what is intended as a relaxed little laugh turns into a strangled gasp. At length I run down, like a clockwork toy, and sit and gape at them helplessly, panting. Even the younger one, the Sergeant, is interested now. An appalling silence descends, it stretches on and on, until at last my sleeping self makes a bolt for it and I start awake, aghast and sweating. What is peculiarly awful in all this is not the prospect of being dragged before the courts and put in jail for a crime I am not even sure I have committed, but the simple, terrible fact of having been found out. This is what makes me sweat, what fills my mouth with ashes and my heart with shame.

And now, as I hurried along the cement road, with the railway track beside me and the sea beyond, I had that same feeling of ignominy. What a fool I had been. What trouble there would be in the days, the weeks, the years ahead. Yet also there was a sensation of lightness, of buoyancy, as if I had thrown off an awkward burden. Ever since I had reached what they call the use of reason I had been doing one thing and thinking another, because the weight of things seemed so much greater than that of thoughts. What I said was never exactly what I felt, what I felt was never what it seemed I should feel, though the feelings were what felt genuine, and right, and inescapable. Now I had struck a blow for the inner man, that guffawing, fat foulmouth who had been telling me all along I was living a lie. And he had burst out at last, it was he, the ogre, who was pounding along in this lemon-coloured light, with blood on his pelt, and me slung helpless over his back. Everything was gone, the past, Coolgrange, Daphne, all my previous life, gone, abandoned, drained of its essence, its significance. To do the worst thing, the very worst thing, that's the way to be free. I would never again need to pretend to myself to be what I was not. The thought made my head spin and my empty stomach heave.

I was prey to a host of niggling worries. This pullover was smelly, and too tight for me. The knee of my left trouser-leg had a small rip in it. People would notice that I had not shaved today. And I needed, I positively longed, to wash my hands, to plunge up to the elbows in scalding suds, to sluice myself, to drench, rinse, scour – to be clean. Opposite the deserted hotel there was a jumble of grey buildings that had once been a railway station. Weeds were growing on the platform, and all the windows in the signal box were smashed. A pockmarked enamel sign with a lovingly painted pointing hand indicated a cement blockhouse set at a discreet distance down the platform. A clump of purple buddleia was flourishing by the doorway of the gents. I went into the ladies – there were no more rules, after all. The air here was chill and dank. There was a quicklime smell, and something green and glistening was growing up the walls. The fittings had been ripped out long ago, even the stall doors were gone. It was apparent from the state of the floor, however, that the place was still in frequent use. In a corner there was a little heap of stuff – used condoms, I think, and discoloured wads of cotton, even bits of clothing – from which I quickly averted my eyes. A single tap on a green copper pipe stuck out of the wall where the handbasins had been. When I turned the spigot there was a distant groaning and clanking, and presently a rusty dribble came out. I washed my hands as best I could and dried them on the tail of my shirt. Yet when I had finished, and was about to leave, I discovered a drop of blood between my fingers. I don't know where it came from. It may have been on the pullover, or even in my hair. The blood was thick by now, dark, and sticky. Nothing, not the stains in the car, the smears on the windows, not her cries, not even the smells of her dying, none of it affected me as did this drop of brownish gum. I plunged my fists under the tap again, whining in dismay, and scrubbed and scrubbed, but I could not get rid of it. The blood went, but something remained, all that long day I could feel it there, clinging in the fork of tender flesh between my fingers, a moist, warm, secret stain.

I am afraid to think what I have done.

For a while I sat on a broken bench on the platform in the sun. How blue the sea was, how gay the little flags fluttering and snapping on the hotel battlements. All was quiet, save for the sea-breeze crooning in the telegraph wires, and something some-where that creaked and knocked, creaked and knocked. I smiled. I might have been a child again, daydreaming here, in these toy surroundings. I could smell the sea, and the sea-wrack on the beach, and the cat-smell of the sand. A train was on the way, yes, a puff-puff, the rails were humming and shivering in anticipa-tion. Not a soul to be seen, not a grown-up anywhere, except, away down the beach, a few felled sunbathers on their towels. I wonder why the place was so deserted? Perhaps it wasn't, per-haps there were seaside crowds all about, and I didn't notice, with my inveterate yearning towards backgrounds. I closed my eyes, and something swam up dreamily, a memory, an image, and sank again without breaking the surface. I tried to catch it before it was gone, but there was only that one glimpse: a doorway, I think, opening on to a darkened room, and a mysterious sense of expectancy, of something or someone about to appear. Then the train came through, a slow, rolling thunder that made my diaphragm shake. The passengers were propped up in the wide windows like manikins, they gazed at me blankly as they were borne slowly past. It occurred to me I should have turned my face away: everyone was a potential witness now. But I thought it did not matter. I thought I would be in jail within hours. I looked about me, taking great breaths, drinking my fill of the world that I would soon be losing. A gang of boys, three or four, had appeared in the grounds of the hotel. They straggled across the unkempt lawns, and stopped to throw stones at a 'For Sale' sign. I rose, with a leaden sigh, and left the station and set off along the road again.

I took a bus into the city. It was a single-decker, on an infrequent route, coming from far out. The people on it all seemed to know each other. At each stop when someone got on there was much banter and friendly raillery. An old chap with a cap and a crutch was the self-appointed host of this little travelling club. He sat near the front, behind the driver, his stiff left leg stuck out into the aisle, and greeted each newcomer with a start of feigned surprise and a rattle of his crutch. Oh! watch out! here he comes! he would say, mugging at the rest of us over his shoulder, as if to alert us to the arrival of some terrible character, when what had appeared up the step was a ferret-faced young man with a greasy season-ticket protruding from his fist like a discoloured tongue. Girls provoked gallantries, which made them smirk, while for the housewives off to town to do their shopping there were winks and playful references to that stiff limb of his. Now and again he would let a glance slide over me, quick, tentative, uneasy, like that of an old trouper spotting a creditor in the front row. It struck me, indeed, that there was something faintly theatrical about the whole thing. The rest of the passengers had the self-conscious nonchalance of a first-night audience. They too had a part of sorts to play. Behind the chatter and the jokes and the easy familiarity they seemed worried, their eyes were full of uncertainty and tiredness, as if they had got the text by heart but still were not sure of their cues. I studied them with deep interest. I felt I had discovered something significant, though what it was, or what it signified, I was not sure. And I, what was I among them? A stage-hand, perhaps, standing in the wings envying the players.

When we reached town I could not decide where to get off, one place seemed as good as another. I must say something about the practicalities of my situation. I should have been shaking in fear. I had a five-pound note and some coins – mostly foreign – in my pocket, I looked, and smelled, like a tramp, and I had nowhere to go. I did not even have a credit card with which to bluff my way into a hotel. Yet I could not worry, could not make myself be concerned. I seemed to float, bemused, in dreamy detachment, as if I had been given a great dose of local anaesthetic. Perhaps this is what it means to be in shock? No: I think it was just the certainty that at any moment a hand would grasp me by the shoulder while a terrible voice boomed out an official caution. By now they would have my name, a description would be in circulation, hard-eyed men in bulging jackets would be cruising the streets on the look-out for me. That none of this was so is still a puzzle to me. The Behrenses must have known at once who it was that had that particular picture, yet they said nothing. And what about the trail of evidence I left behind me? What about the people who saw me, the Recks, the señorita at the garage, the man in the hardware shop, that woman who looked like my mother who came upon me sitting like a waxwork model of myself at the traffic lights? Your Lordship, I would not wish to encourage potential wrongdoers, but I must say, it is easier to get away with wrongdoing, for a time at least, than is generally acknowledged. Vital days – how easily one slips into the lingo! – *vital days* were to pass before they even began to know who it was they were after. If I had not continued to be as rash as I was at the start, if I had stopped and taken stock, and considered carefully, I believe I might not be here now, but in some sunnier clime, tending my guilt under an open sky. But I did not stop, did not consider. I got off the bus and set off at once in the direction in which I happened to be facing, since my fate, I was convinced, awaited me all around, in the open arms of the law. Capture! I nursed the word in my heart. It comforted me. It was the promise of rest. I dodged along through the crowds like a drunk, surprised that they did not part before me in horror. All round me was an inferno of haste and noise. A gang of men stripped to the waist was gouging a hole in the road with pneumatic drills. The traffic snarled and bellowed, sunlight flashing like knives off the windshields and the throbbing roofs of cars. The air was a poisonous hot blue haze. I had become unused to cities. Yet I was aware that even as I struggled here I was simultaneously travelling smoothly forward in time, it seemed a kind of swimming without effort. Time, I thought grimly, time will save me. Here is Trinity, the Bank. Fox's, where my father used to

come on an annual pilgrimage, with great ceremony, to buy his
Christmas cigars. My world, and I an outcast in it. I felt a deep,
dispassionate pity for myself, as for some poor lost wandering
creature. The sun shone mercilessly, a fat eye stuck in the haze
above the streets. I bought a bar of chocolate and devoured it,
walking along. I bought an early edition of an evening paper,
too, but there was nothing in it. I dropped it on the ground and
shambled on. An urchin picked it up – Eh, mister! – and ran after
me with it. I thanked him, and he grinned, and I almost burst
into tears. I stood there, stalled, and looked about me blearily, a
baffled hulk. People crowded past me, all faces and elbows. That
was my lowest point, I think, that moment of helplessness and
dull panic. I decided to give myself up. Why had I not thought
of it before? The prospect was wonderfully seductive. I imagined
myself being lifted tenderly and carried through a succession of
cool white rooms to a place of calm and silence, of luxurious
surrender.

In the end, instead, I went to Wally's pub.

It was shut. I did not understand. At first I thought wildly that it
must be something to do with me, that they had found out I had
been there and had closed it down. I pushed and pushed at the
door, and tried to see through the bottle-glass of the windows,
but all was dark inside. I stepped back. Next door there was a
tiny fashion boutique where a pair of pale girls, frail and blank
as flowers, stood motionless, staring at nothing, as if they were
themselves a part of the display. When I spoke they turned their
soot-rimmed eyes on me without interest. Holy hour, one said,
and the other giggled wanly. I retreated, simpering, and went
back to the pub and pounded on the door with renewed force.
After some time there were dragging footsteps inside and the
sound of locks being undone. What do you want, Wally said
crossly, blinking in the harsh sunlight slanting down from the
street. He was wearing a purple silk dressing-gown and shapeless
slippers. He looked me up and down with distaste, noting the
stubble and the filthy pullover. I told him my car had broken
down, and that I needed to make a phonecall. He gave a sardonic
snort and said, A phonecall! as if it were the richest thing he had
heard in ages. He shrugged. It was nearly opening time anyway.
I followed him inside. His calves were plump and white and

hairless, I wondered where I had seen others like them recently. He switched on a pink-shaded lamp behind the bar. There's the phone, he said with a wave, pursing his lips derisively. I asked if I could have a gin first. He sniffed, his sceptic's heart gratified, and permitted himself a thin little smile. Have a smash-up, did you? he said. For a second I did not know what he was talking about. Oh, the car, I said, no, no it just – stopped. And I thought, with bleak amusement: There's the first question answered and I haven't lied. He turned away to make my drink, priest-like in his purple robe, then set it before me and propped himself on the edge of his stool with his fat arms folded. He knew I had been up to something, I could see it from the look in his eye, at once eager and disdainful, but he could not bring himself to ask. I grinned at him and drank my drink, and gleaned a grain of enjoyment from his dilemma. I said it was a good idea, wasn't it, the siesta. He raised an eyebrow. I pointed a finger at his dressing-gown. A nap, I said, in the middle of the day: good idea. He did not think that was funny. From somewhere in the shadowy reaches behind me a tousle-haired young man appeared, clad only in a drooping pair of underpants. He gave me a bored glance and asked Wally if the paper was in yet. Here, I said, take mine, go ahead. I must have been twisting it in my hands, it was rolled into a tight baton. He prised it open and read the headlines, his lips moving. Fucking bombers, he said, fucking lunatics. Wally had fixed him with a terrible glare. He threw the paper aside and wandered off, scratching his rump. I held out my glass for a refill. We still charge for drinks, you know, Wally said. We'll accept money. I gave him my last fiver. A thin blade of light had got in through a chink in a shutter somewhere and stood at a slant beside me, embedded in the floor. I watched Wally's plump back as he refilled my glass. I wondered if I might tell him what I had done. It seemed perfectly possible. Nothing, I told myself, nothing shocks Wally, after all. I could almost believe it. I imagined him looking at me with a twist of the mouth and one eyebrow arched, trying not to laugh as I recounted my horrid tale. The thought of confessing gave me a little lift, it was so splendidly irresponsible. It made the whole thing seem no more than a spot of high jinks, a jape that had gone wrong. I chuckled mournfully into my glass. You look like shit, Wally said complacently. I asked for another gin, a double this time.

Distinctly in my head her voice again said: Don't.

The boy with the curls came back, now wearing tight jeans and a shiny tight green shirt. He was called Sonny. Wally left him in charge of the bar and waddled off to his quarters, his dressing-gown billowing behind him. Sonny poured a generous measure of crème de menthe into a tumbler and filled it up with ice cubes, then perched himself on the stool, squirming his narrow little nates, and examined me without much enthusiasm. You're new, he said, making it sound like an accusation. No I'm not, I said, you are, and I smirked, pleased with myself. He made a wide-eyed face. Well excuse me, he said, I'm sure. Wally came back, dressed and coiffed and reeking of pomade. I had another double. My face was growing taut, it felt like a mud mask. I had reached that stage of inebriation where everything was settling into another version of reality. It seemed not drunkenness, but a form of enlightenment, almost a sobering-up. A crowd of theatre people came in, prancing and squawking. They looked at my appearance and then at each other, brimming with merriment. Talk about rough trade, one said, and Sonny tittered. And I thought, that's what I'll do, I'll get one of them to take me home and hide me, Lady Macbeth there with the mascara and the blood-red nails, or that laughing fellow in the harlequin shirt – why not? Yes, that's what I should do, I should live henceforth among actors, practise among them, study their craft, the grand gesture and the fine nuance. Perhaps in time I would learn to play my part sufficiently well, with enough conviction, to take my place among the others, the naturals, those people on the bus, and all the rest of them.

It was only when Charlie French came in that I realised it was for him I had been waiting. Good old Charlie. My heart flooded with fondness, I felt like embracing him. He was in his chalkstripes, carrying a battered, important-looking briefcase. Although he had seen me three days ago he tried at first not to know me. Or perhaps he really didn't recognise me, in my dishevelled, wild-eyed state. He said he had thought I was going down to Coolgrange. I said I had been there, and he asked after my mother. I told him about her stroke. I laid it on a bit, I think – I may even have shed a tear. He nodded, looking past my left ear and jingling the coins in his trousers pocket. There was a pause, during which I snuffled and sighed. So, he said brightly, you're off on your travels again, are you? I shrugged. His car's broke down, isn't it, Wally said, and expelled an unpleasant little chuckle. Charlie assumed a sympathetic frown. Is that right? he said slowly, with a dreamy lack of emphasis. The crowd of actors behind us suddenly shrieked, so piercingly that glasses chimed, but he might not have heard them, he did not even blink. He had perfected a pose for places and occasions such as this, by which he managed to be at once here and not here. He stood very straight, his black brogues planted firmly together and his briefcase leaning against his leg, with one fist on the bar – oh, I can see him! – and the other hand holding his whiskey glass suspended halfway to his lips, just as if he had stumbled in here by mistake and was too much the gentleman to cut and run before partaking of a snifter and exchanging a few civilities with the frantic denizens of the place. He could maintain this air of being just about to leave throughout a whole night's drinking. Oh yes, Charlie could act them all into a cocked hat.

The more I drank the fonder I became of him, especially as he kept paying for gins as fast as I could drink them. But it was not just that. I was – I am – genuinely fond of him, I think I have said so already. Did I mention that he got me my job at the Institute? We had kept in touch during my years in college – or at least *he* had kept in touch with *me*. He liked to think of himself as the wise old family friend watching over with an avuncular eye the brilliant only son of the house. He took me out for treats. There were teas at the Hibernian, the odd jaunt to the Curragh, the dinner at Jammet's every year on my birthday. They never quite worked, these occasions, they smacked too much of contrivance. I was always afraid that someone would see me with him, and while I squirmed and scowled he would sink into a state of restless melancholy. When we were ready to part there would be a sudden burst of hearty chatter which was nothing but relief badly disguised, then we would each turn and slink away guiltily. Yet he was not deterred, and the day after my return with Daphne from America he took me for a drink in the Shelbourne and suggested that, as he put it, I might like to give the chaps at the Institute a hand. I was still feeling groggy – we had made a hideous winter crossing, on what was hardly more than a tramp steamer – and he was so diffident, and employed such elaborate depreciations, that it was a while before I realised he was offering me a job. The work, he assured me hurriedly, would be right up my street – hardly work at all, and to such as I, he fancied, more a form of play – the money was decent, the prospects were limitless. I knew at once, of course, from his suppliant, doggy manner, that all this was at my mother's prompting. Well, he said, showing his big yellow teeth in a strained smile, what do you think? First I was annoyed, then amused. I thought: why not?

If the court pleases, I shall skim lightly over this period of my life. It is a time that is still a source of vague unease in my mind, I cannot say why, exactly. I have the feeling of having done something ridiculous by taking that job. It was unworthy of me, of course, of my talent, but that is not the whole source of my sense of humiliation. Perhaps that was the moment in my life at which – but what am I saying, there are no moments, I've said that already. There is just the ceaseless, slow, demented drift of things. If I had any lingering doubts of that the Institute extinguished them finally. It was housed in a great grey stone building from the last century which always reminded me, with its sheer flanks, its buttresses and curlicues and blackened smokestacks, of a grand, antiquated ocean liner. No one knew what exactly it was we were expected to achieve. We did statistical surveys, and produced thick reports bristling with graphs and flow-charts and complex appendices, which the government received with grave words of praise and then promptly forgot about. The director was a large, frantic man who sucked fiercely on an enormous black pipe and had a tic in one eye and tufts of hair sprouting from his ears. He plunged about the place, always on his way elsewhere. All queries and requests he greeted with a harsh, doomed laugh. Try that on the Minister! he would cry over his shoulder as he strode off, emitting thick gusts of smoke and sparks in his wake. Inevitably there was a high incidence of looniness among the staff. Finding themselves with no fixed duties, people embarked furtively on projects of their own. There was an economist, a tall, emaciated person with a greenish face and unruly hair, who was devising a foolproof system for betting on the horses. He offered one day to let me in on it, clutching my wrist in a trembling claw and hissing urgently into my ear, but then something happened, I don't know what, he grew suspicious, and in the end would not speak to me, and avoided me in the corridors. This was awkward, for he was one of a select band of savants with whom

I had to treat in order to gain access to the computer. This machine was at the centre of all our activities. Time on it was strictly rationed, and to get an uninterrupted hour at it was a rare privilege. It ran all day and through the night, whirring and crunching in its vast white room in the basement. At night it was tended by a mysterious and sinister trio, a war criminal, I think, and two strange boys, one with a damaged face. Three years I spent there. I was not violently unhappy. I just felt, and feel, as I say, a little ridiculous, a little embarrassed. And I never quite forgave Charlie French.

It was late when we left the pub. The night was made of glass. I was very drunk. Charlie helped me along. He was worrying about his briefcase, and clutched it tightly under his arm. Every few yards I had to stop and tell him how good he was. No, I said, holding up a hand commandingly, no, I want to say it, you're a good man, Charles, a good man. I wept copiously, of course, and retched drily a few times. It was all a sort of glorious, grief-stricken, staggering rapture. I remembered that Charlie lived with his mother, and wept for that, too. But how is she, I shouted sorrowfully, tell me, Charlie, how is she, that sainted woman? He would not answer, pretended not to hear, but I kept at it and at last he shook his head irritably and said, She's dead! I tried to embrace him, but he walked away from me. We came upon a hole in the street with a cordon of red and white plastic ribbon around it. The ribbon shivered and clicked in the breeze. It's where the bomb in the car went off yesterday, Charlie said. Yesterday! I laughed and laughed, and knelt on the road at the edge of the hole, laughing, with my face in my hands. Yesterday, the last day of the old world. Wait, Charlie said, I'll get a taxi. He went off, and I knelt there, rocking back and forth and crooning softly, as if I were a child I was holding in my arms. I was tired. It had been a long day. I had come far.

I WOKE in splintered sunlight with a shriek fading in my ears. Big sagging bed, brown walls, a smell of damp. I thought I must be at Coolgrange, in my parents' room. For a moment I lay without moving, staring at sliding waterlights on the ceiling. Then I remembered, and shut my eyes tight and hid my head in my arms. The darkness drummed. I got up and dragged myself to the window, and stood amazed at the blue innocence of sea and sky. Far out in the bay white sailboats were tacking into the wind. Below the window was a little stone harbour, and beyond that the curve of the coast road. An enormous seagull appeared and flung itself on flailing pinions at the glass, shrieking. They must think you are Mammy, Charlie said behind me. He was standing in the doorway. He wore a soiled apron, and held a frying pan in his hand. The gulls, he said, she used to feed them. At his back a white, impenetrable glare. This was the world I must live in from now on, in this searing, inescapable light. I looked at myself and found I was naked.

I sat in the vast kitchen, under a vast, grimy window, and watched Charlie making breakfast in a cloud of fat-smoke. He did not look too good in daylight, he was hollow and grey, with flakes of dried shaving soap on his jaw and bruised bags under his phlegm-coloured eyes. Besides the apron he wore a woollen cardigan over a soiled string vest, and sagging flannel trousers. Used to wait till I was gone, he said, then throw the food out of the window. He shook his head and laughed. A terrible woman, he said, terrible. He brought a plate of rashers and fried bread and a swimming egg and set it down in front of me. There, he said, only thing for a sore head. I looked up at him quickly. *A sore head?* Had I blurted something out to him last night, some drunken confession? But no, Charlie would not make that kind of joke. He went back to the stove and lit a cigarette, fumbling with the matches.

Look, Charlie, I said, I may as well tell you, I've got into a bit of a scrape.

I thought at first he had not heard me. He went slack, and a dreamy vacancy came over him, his mouth open and drooping a little on one side and his eyebrows mildly lifted. Then I realised that he was being tactful. Well, if he didn't want to know, that was all right. But I wish to have it in the record, m'lud, that I would have told him, if he had been prepared to listen. As it was I merely let a silence pass, and then asked if I might borrow a razor, and perhaps a shirt and tie. Of course, he said, of course, but he would not look me in the eye. In fact, he had not looked at me at all since I had got up, but edged around me with averted gaze, busying himself with the teapot and the pan, as if afraid that if he paused some awful awkward thing would arise which he would not know how to deal with. He suspected something, I suppose. He was no fool. (Or not a great fool, anyway.) But I think too it was simply that he did not quite know how to accommodate my presence. He fidgeted, moving things about, putting things away in drawers and cupboards and then taking them out again, murmuring to himself distractedly. People did not come often to this house. Some of the weepy regard I had felt for him last night returned. He seemed almost maternal, in his apron and his old felt slippers. He would take care of me. I gulped my tea and gloomed at my untouched fry congealing on its plate. A car horn tooted outside, and Charlie with an exclamation whipped off his apron and hurried out of the kitchen. I listened to him blundering about the house. In a surprisingly short time he appeared again, in his suit, with his briefcase under his arm, and sporting a raffish little hat that made him look like a harassed bookie. Where are you based, he said, frowning at a spot beside my left shoulder, Coolgrange, or –? I said nothing, only looked at him appealingly, and he said, Ah, and nodded slowly, and slowly withdrew. Suddenly, though, I did not want him to go – alone, I would be alone! – and I rushed after him and made him come back and tell me how the stove worked, and where to find a key, and what to say if the milkman called. He was puzzled by my vehemence, I could see, and faintly alarmed. I followed him into the hall, and was still talking to him as he backed out through the front door, nodding at me warily, with a fixed smile, as if I were – ha! I was going to say, a dangerous criminal. I scampered up the stairs to the bedroom, and watched as he came out on the footpath below, a clownishly foreshortened figure in his hat and his baggy suit. A large black car was waiting at the kerb, its twin exhaust pipes discreetly puffing a pale-blue mist. The driver, a burly, dark-suited fellow with no neck, hopped out smartly and held open the rear door. Charlie looked up at the window where I stood, and the driver followed his glance. I saw myself as they would see me, a blurred face floating behind the glass, blear-eyed, unshaven, the very picture of a fugitive. The car slid away smoothly and passed along the harbour road and turned a corner and was gone. I did not stir. I wanted to stay like this, with my forehead against the glass and the summer day out there before me. How quaint it all seemed, the white-tipped sea, and the white and pink houses, and the blurred headland in the distance, quaint and happy, like a little toy world laid out in a shop window. I closed my eyes, and again that fragment of memory swam up out of the depths – the doorway, and the darkened room, and the sense of something imminent – but this time it seemed to be not my own past I was remembering.

The silence was swelling like a tumour at my back.

Hurriedly I fetched my plate with the fried egg and greying rashers from the kitchen, taking the stairs three at a time, and came back and opened the window and clambered on to the narrow, wrought-iron balcony outside. A strong, warm wind was blowing, it startled me, and left me breathless for a moment. I picked up the pieces of food and flung them into the air, and watched the gulls swooping after the rich tidbits, crying harshly in surprise and greed. From behind the headland a white ship glided soundlessly into view, shimmering in the haze. When the food was gone I threw the plate away too, I don't know why, skimmed it like a discus out over the road and the harbour wall. It slid into the water with hardly a splash. There were strings of lukewarm fat between my fingers and egg-yolk under my nails. I climbed back into the room and wiped my hands on the bedclothes, my heart pounding in excitement and disgust. I did not know what I was doing, or what I would do next. I did not know myself. I had become a stranger, unpredictable and untrustworthy.

I explored the house. I had never been here before. It was a great gaunt shadowy place with dark drapes and big brown furniture and bald spots in the carpets. It was not exactly dirty, but there was a sense of staleness, of things left standing for too long in the same spot, and the air had a grey, dull feel to it, as if a vital essence in it had been used up long ago. There was a smell of must and stewed tea and old newspapers, and, everywhere, a flattish, faintly sweet something which I took to be the afterglow of Mammy French. I suppose there will be guffaws if I say I am a fastidious man, but it's true. I was already in some distress before I started poking among Charlie's things, and I feared what I might find. His sad little secrets were no nastier than mine, or anyone else's, yet when here and there I turned over a stone and they came scuttling out, I shivered, and was ashamed for him and for myself. I steeled myself, though, and persevered, and was rewarded in the end. There was a rolltop desk in his bedroom, which took me ten minutes of hard work with a kitchen knife to break into, squatting on my heels and sweating beads of pure alcohol. Inside I found some banknotes and a plastic wallet of credit cards. There were letters, too – from my mother, of all people, written thirty, forty years before. I did not read them, I don't know why, but put them back carefully, along with the credit cards, and even the cash, and locked the desk again. As I was going out I exchanged a shamefaced little grin with my reflection in the wardrobe mirror. That German, what's his name, was right: money is abstract happiness.

The bathroom was on the first-floor return, a sort of wooden lean-to with a gas geyser and a gigantic, claw-footed bath. I crouched over the handbasin and scraped off two days' growth of stubble with Charlie's soap-encrusted razor. I had thought of growing a beard, for disguise, but I had lost enough of myself already, I did not want half of my face to disappear as well. The shaving-glass had a concave, silvery surface in which my magnified features – a broad, pitted jaw, one black nose-hole with hairs, a single, rolling eyeball – bobbed and swayed alarmingly, like things looming in the window of a bathysphere. When I had finished I got into the tub and lay with my eyes shut while the water cascaded down on me from the geyser. It was good, at once a solace and a scalding chastisement, and if the gas had not eventually gone out I might have stayed there all day, lost to myself and everything else in that roaring, steamy darkness. When I opened my eyes tiny stars were whizzing and popping in front of me. I padded, dripping, into Charlie's room, and spent a long time deciding what to wear. In the end I chose a dark-blue silk shirt and a somewhat louche, flowered bow-tie to go with it. Black socks, of course – silk again: Charlie is not one to stint himself – and a pair of dark trousers, baggy but well cut, of a style which was antique enough to have come back into fashion. For the present I would do without underwear: even a killer on the run has his principles, and mine precluded getting into another man's drawers. My own clothes – how odd they looked, thrown on the bedroom floor, as if waiting to be outlined in chalk – I gathered in a bundle, and with my face averted carried them to the kitchen and stuffed them into a plastic rubbish bag. Then I washed and dried the breakfast things, and was standing in the middle of the floor with a soiled tea-towel in my hand when the image of her bloodied face shot up in front of me like something in a fairground stall, and I had to sit down, winded and shaking. For I kept forgetting, you see, forgetting all about it, for quite long periods. I suppose my mind needed respite, in order to cope. Wearily I looked about the big dank kitchen. I wondered if Charlie would notice there was a plate missing. Why did I throw it into the sea, why did I do that? It was not yet noon. Time opened its black maw in my face. I went into one of the front rooms – net curtains, vast dining table, a stuffed owl under glass – and stood at the window looking out at the sea. All that blue out there was daunting. I paced the floor, stopped, stood listening, my heart in my mouth. What did I expect to hear? There was nothing, only the distant noise of other lives, a tiny ticking and plinking, like the noise of an engine cooling down. I remembered days like this in my childhood, strange, empty days when I would wander softly about the silent house and seem to myself a kind of ghost, hardly there at all, a memory, a shadow of some more solid version of myself living, oh, living marvellously, elsewhere.

I must stop. I'm sick of myself, all this.

Time. The days.

Go on, go on.

Disgust, now, that is something I know about. Let me say a word or two about disgust. Here I sit, naked under my prison garb, wads of pallid flesh trussed and bagged like badly packaged meat. I get up and walk around on my hind legs, a belted animal, shedding an invisible snow of scurf everywhere I move. Mites live on me, they lap my sweat, stick their snouts into my pores and gobble up the glop they find there. Then the split skin, the cracks, the crevices. Hair: just think of hair. And this is only the surface. Imagine what is going on inside, the purple pump shuddering and squelching, lungs fluttering, and, down in the dark, the glue factory at its ceaseless work. Animate carrion, slick with gleet, not ripe enough yet for the worms. Ach, I should –

Calm, Frederick. Calm.

My wife came to see me today. This is not unusual, she comes every week. As a remand prisoner I have the right to unrestricted visiting, but I have not told her this, and if she knows it she has said nothing. We prefer it this way. Even at its most uneventful the Thursday visiting hour is a bizarre, not to say uncanny ritual. It is conducted in a large square lofty room with small windows set high up under the ceiling. A partition of plywood and glass, an ugly contraption, separates us from our loved ones, with whom we converse as best we can by way of a disinfected plastic grille. This state of virtual quarantine is a recent imposition. It is meant to keep out drugs, we're told, but I think it is really a way of keeping *in* those interesting viruses which lately we have begun to incubate in here. The room has a touch of the aquarium about it, with that wall of greenish glass, and the tall light drifting down from above, and the voices that come to us out of the plastic lattices as if bubbled through water. We inmates sit with shoulders hunched, leaning grimly on folded arms, wan, bloated, vague-eyed, like unhoused crustaceans crouching at the bottom of a tank. Our visitors exist in a different element from ours, they seem more sharply defined than we, more intensely present in their world. Sometimes we catch a look in their eyes, a mixture of curiosity and compassion, and faint repugnance, too, which strikes us to the heart. They must feel the force of our longing, must hear it, almost, the mermen's song, a high needle-note of pure woe buzzing in the glass that separates us from them. Their concern for our plight is not a comfort, but distresses us, rather. This is the tenderest time of our week, we desire tranquillity, decorum, muted voices. We are constantly on edge, worried that someone's wife or girlfriend out there will make a scene, jump up and shout, pound her fists on the partition, weep. When such a thing does happen it is awful, just awful, and afterwards the one that it happened to is an object of sympathy and awe amongst us, as if he had suffered a bereavement.

No fear of Daphne making a scene. She maintains an admirable poise at all times. Today, for instance, when she told me about the child, she spoke quietly, looking away from me with her usual air of faint abstraction. I confess I was annoyed at her, I couldn't hide it. She should have told me she was having him tested, instead of just presenting me with the diagnosis out of the blue like this. She gave me a quizzical look, tilting her head to one side and almost smiling. Are you surprised? she said. I turned my face away crossly and did not answer. Of course I was not surprised. I knew there was something wrong with him, I always knew − I told her so, long before she was ready to admit it. From the start there was the way he moved, warily, quaking, on his scrawny little legs, as if trying not to drop some large, unmanageable thing that had been dumped into his arms, looking up at us in bewilderment and supplication, like a creature looking up out of a hole in the ground. Where did you take him, I said, what hospital, and what did they say exactly? She shrugged. They were very nice, she said, very sympathetic. The doctor had talked to her for a long time. It is a very rare condition, somebody's syndrome, I have forgotten the name already, some damn Swiss or Swede − what does it matter. He will never speak properly. He'll never do anything properly, it seems. There is something wrong with his brain, something is missing, some vital bit. She explained it all to me, repeating what the doctor told her, but I was only half-listening. A sort of weariness had come over me, a sort of lethargy. Van is his name, have I mentioned that? Van. He's seven. When I get out he will probably be, what, thirty-something? Jesus, almost as old as I am now. A big child, that's what the country people will call him, not without fondness, at Coolgrange. A big child.

I will not, I will not weep. If I start now I'll never stop.

In the afternoon I broke into Charlie's desk again, and took some cash and ventured out to the newsagent's on the harbour. What a strange, hot thrill of excitement I felt, stepping into the shop. My stomach wobbled, and I seemed to be treading slowly through some thick, resistant medium. I think a part of me hoped − no, expected − that somehow I would be saved, that as in a fairy-tale everything would be magically reversed, that the wicked witch would disappear, that the spell would be lifted, that the maid would wake from her enchanted sleep. And when I picked up the papers it seemed for a moment as if some magic had indeed been worked, for at first I could see nothing in them except more stuff about the bombing and its aftermath. I bought three mornings, and an early-evening edition, noting (is this only hindsight?) the hard look that the pimpled girl behind the counter gave me. Then I hurried back to the house, my heart going at a gallop, as if it were some choice erotica I was clutching under my arm. Indoors again, I left the papers on the kitchen table and ran to the bathroom, where in my agitation I managed to pee on my foot. After a lengthy, feverish search I found a quarter-full bottle of gin and took a good slug from the neck. I tried to find something else to do, but it was no good, and with leaden steps I returned to the kitchen and sat down slowly at the table and spread out the papers in front of me. There it was, a few paragraphs in one of the mornings, squeezed under a photograph of a bandaged survivor of the bombing sitting up in a hospital bed. In the evening edition there was a bigger story, with a photograph of the boys I had seen playing in the hotel grounds. It was they who had found her. There was a photograph of her, too, gazing out solemn-eyed from a blurred background, it must have been lifted from a group shot of a wedding, or a dance, for she was wearing a long, ugly dress with an elaborate collar, and was clutching something, flowers, perhaps, in her hands. Her name was Josephine Bell. There was more inside, a file picture of Behrens and a view of Whitewater House, and an article on the Behrens collection, littered with misspellings and garbled dates. A reporter had been sent down the country to talk to Mrs Brigid Bell, the mother. She was a widow. There was a photograph of her standing awkwardly in front of her cottage, a big, raw-faced woman in an apron and an old cardigan, peering at the camera in a kind of stolid dismay. Her Josie, she said, was a good girl, a decent girl, why would anyone want to kill her. And suddenly I was back there, I saw her sitting in the mess of her own blood, looking at me, a bleb of pink spittle bursting on her lips. *Mammy* was what she said, that was the word, not Tommy, I've just this moment realised it. *Mammy*, and then: *Love*.

I THINK the time I spent in Charlie French's house was the strangest period of my life, stranger even and more disorienting than my first days here. I felt, in the brownish gloom of those rooms, with all that glistening marine light outside, as if I were suspended somehow in mid-air, in a sealed flask, cut off from everything. Time was split in two: there was clock time, which moved with giant slowness, and then there was that fevered rush inside my head, as if the mainspring had broken and all the works were spinning madly out of control. I did sentry-go up and down the kitchen for what seemed hours on end, shoulders hunched and hands stuck in my pockets, furiously plotting, unaware how the distance between turns was steadily decreasing, until in the end I would find myself at a shuddering stop, glaring about me in bafflement, like an animal that had blundered into a net. I would stand in the big bedroom upstairs, beside the window, with my back pressed to the wall, watching the road, for so long that sometimes I forgot what it was I was supposed to be watching for. There was little traffic in this backwater, and I soon got to recognise the regular passers-by, the girl with the orange hair from the flat in the house next door, the smooth, shady-looking fellow with the salesman's sample-case, the few old bodies who walked their pugs or shuffled to the shops at the same hour every day. Anyway, there would be no mistaking the others, the grim ones, when they came for me. Probably I would not even see them coming. They would surround the house, and kick in the door, and that would be the first I would know of it. But still I stood there, watching and watching, more like a pining lover than a man on the run.

Everything was changed, everything. I was estranged from myself and all that I had once supposed I was. My life up to now had only the weightless density of a dream. When I thought about my past it was like thinking of what someone else had been, some-one I had never met but whose history I knew by heart. It all seemed no more than a vivid fiction. Nor was the present any more solid. I felt light-headed, volatile, poised at an angle to everything. The ground under me was stretched tight as a trampoline, I must keep still for fear of unexpected surges, dangerous leaps and bounces. And all around me was this blue and empty air.

I could not think directly about what I had done. It would have been like trying to stare steadily into a blinding light. It was too big, too bright, to contemplate. It was incomprehensible. Even still, when I say *I did it*, I am not sure I know what I mean. Oh, do not mistake me. I have no wish to vacillate, to hum and haw and kick dead leaves over the evidence. I killed her, I admit it freely. And I know that if I were back there today I would do it again, not because I would want to, but because I would have no choice. It would be just as it was then, this spider, and this moonlight between the trees, and all, all the rest of it. Nor can I say I did not mean to kill her – only, I am not clear as to when I began to mean it. I was flustered, impatient, angry, she attacked me, I swiped at her, the swipe became a blow, which became the prelude to a second blow – its apogee, so to speak, or perhaps I mean perigee – and so on. There is no moment in this process of which I can confidently say, there, that is when I decided she should die. Decided? – I do not think it was a matter of deciding. I do not think it was a matter of thinking, even. That fat monster inside me just saw his chance and leaped out, frothing and flailing. He had scores to settle with the world, and Josie Bell, at that moment, was world enough for him. I could not stop him. Or could I? He is me, after all, and I am he. But no, things were too far gone for stopping. Perhaps that is the essence of my crime, of my culpability, that I let things get to that stage, that I had not been vigilant enough, had not been enough of a dissembler, that I left Bunter to his own devices, and thus allowed him, fatally, to understand that he was free, that the cage door was open, that nothing was forbidden, that everything was possible.

After my first appearance in court the newspapers said I showed no sign of remorse when the charges were read out. (What did they expect, that I would weep, rend my garments?) They were on to something, in their dim-witted way. Remorse implies the expectation of forgiveness, and I knew that what I had done was unforgivable. I could have feigned regret and sorrow, guilt, all that, but to what end? Even if I had felt such things, truly, in the deepest depths of my heart, would it have altered anything? The deed was done, and would not be cancelled by cries of anguish and repentance. Done, yes, finished, as nothing ever before in my life had been finished and done – and yet there would be no end to it, I saw that straight away. I was, I told myself, responsible, with all the weight that word implied. In killing Josie Bell I had destroyed a part of the world. Those hammer-blows had shattered a complex of memories and sensations and possibilities – a life, in short – which was irreplaceable, but which, somehow, must be replaced. For the crime of murder I would be caught and put away, I knew this with the calmness and certainty which only an irrelevance could inspire, and then they would say I had paid my debt, in the belief that by walling me up alive they had struck a sort of balance. They would be right, according to the laws of retribution and revenge: such balance, however, would be at best a negative thing. No, no. What was required was not my symbolic death – I recognised this, though I did not understand what it meant – but for her to be brought back to life. That, and nothing less.

That evening when Charlie returned he put his head cautiously around the door as if he feared there might be a bucket of water balanced on it. I leered at him, swaying. I had finished the gin, and moved on, reluctantly, to whiskey. I was not drunk, exactly, but in a kind of numbed euphoria, as if I had just come back from a lengthy and exquisitely agonising visit to the dentist. Under the new buzz the old hangover lurked, biding its time. My skin was hot and dry all over, and my eyes felt scorched. Cheers! I cried, with a fatuous laugh, and the ice cubes chuckled in my glass. Charlie was darting sidelong looks at my outfit. Hope you don't mind, I said. Didn't think we'd be the same size. Ah, he said, yes, well, I've shrunk in my old age, you see. And he gave a graveyard laugh. I could see he had been hoping I would be gone when he came home. I followed him out to the hall, where he took off his bookie's titfer and put it with his briefcase on the bog-oak hallstand. He went into the dining room and poured himself a modest whiskey, adding a go of flattish soda from a screw-top bottle. He took a sip, and stood for a little while as if stalled, with a hand in his pocket, frowning at his feet. My presence was interfering with his evening rituals. He put away the whiskey bottle without offering me a refill. We traipsed back to the kitchen, where Charles donned his apron and rooted about in cupboards and on murky shelves for the makings of a stew. While he worked he talked distractedly over his shoulder, with a cigarette hanging from a corner of his lopsided mouth and one eye screwed shut against the smoke. He was telling me about a sale he had made, or a picture he had bought, or something like that. I think he only spoke for fear of the prospect of silence. Anyway I was not really listening. I watched him glugging the better half of a fifty-pound bottle of Pomerol into the stew. An inch of cigarette ash went into the pot as well, he tried vainly to fish it out with a spoon, clucking in annoyance. You can imagine what it's like for me, he said, actually parting with pictures! I nodded solemnly. In fact, what I was imagining was Charlie in his poky gallery, bowing and scraping and wringing his hands in front of some fur-coated bitch reeking of face-powder and perspiration, whose hubby had given her the money to bag a bauble for her birthday. I was depressed suddenly, and suddenly tired.

He served up the stew, spilling some on the floor. He was not good with implements, they tended to turn treacherous in his hands, to wobble and veer and let things slither off. We carried our plates into the dining room and sat down at the table under the stuffed owl's virulent, glassy stare. We drank the rest of the Pomerol, and Charles fetched another bottle. He continued to make an elaborate business of avoiding my eye, smiling about him at the floor, the furniture, the fire irons in the grate, as if the commonplace had suddenly presented itself to his attention with a new and unexpected charm. The lowering sun was shining full upon me through the tall window at my back. The stew tasted of burnt fur. I pushed my plate aside and turned and looked out at the harbour. There was a shimmering flaw in the windowpane. Something made me think of California, something about the light, the little yachts, the gilded evening sea. I was so tired, so tired, I could have given up then and there, could have drifted out into that summer dusk as easily as a breeze, unknown, planless, free. Charlie squashed out a sodden fag-end on the rim of his plate. Did you see that thing about Binkie Behrens in the paper? he said. I poured myself another fill of wine. No, I said, what was that, Charles?

By the by, what would I have done in all this affair without the solace of drink and its deadening effect? I seem to have got over those days in a series of quaking lunges from one brief state of drunken equilibrium to another, like a fugitive fleeing across a zigzag of slimed stepping-stones. Even the colours, gin-blue and claret-red, are they not the very emblems of my case, the court-colours of my testimony? Now that I have sobered up forever I look back not only on that time but on all my life as a sort of tipsy but not particularly happy spree, from which I knew I would have to emerge sooner or later, with a bad headache. This, ah yes, this is hangover time with a vengeance.

The rest of that evening, as I recall it, was a succession of distinct, muffled shocks, like falling downstairs slowly in a dream. That was when I learned that my father had kept a mistress. I was first astonished, then indignant. I had been his alibi, his camouflage! While I sat for hours in the back of the car above the yacht club in Dun Laoghaire on Sunday afternoons, he was off fucking his fancy-woman. Penelope was her name – Penelope, for God's sake! Where did they meet, I wanted to know, was there a secret love nest where he kept her, a bijou little hideaway with roses round the door and a mirror on the bedroom ceiling? Charlie shrugged. Oh, he said, they used to come here. At first I could not take it in. Here? I cried. Here? But what about –? He shrugged again, and gave a sort of grin. Mammy French, it seems, did not mind. On occasion she even had the lovers join her for tea. She and Penelope exchanged knitting patterns. You see, she knew – Charlie said, but stopped, and a spot of colour appeared in the cracked skin over each cheekbone, and he ran a finger quickly around the inside of his shirt collar. I waited. She knew I was fond of your – of Dolly, he said at last. By now I was fairly reeling. Before I could speak he went on to tell me how Binkie Behrens too had been after my mother, how he would invite her and my father to Whitewater and ply my father with drink so he would not notice Binkie's gamy eye and wandering hands. And then my mother would come and tell Charlie all about it, and they would laugh together. Now he shook his head and sighed. Poor Binkie, he said. I sat aghast, lost in wonderment and trying to hold my wine glass straight. I felt like a child hearing for the first time of the doings of the gods: they crowded in my buzzing head, these tremendous, archaic, flawed figures with their plots and rivalries and impossible loves. Charlie was so matter-of-fact about it all, half wistful and half amused. He spoke mostly as if I were not there, looking up now and then in mild surprise at my squeaks and snorts of astonishment. And you, I said, what about you and my —? I could not put it into words. He gave me a look at once arch and sly.

Here, he said, finish the bottle.

I think he told me something more about my mother, but I don't remember what it was. I do remember phoning her later that night, sitting cross-legged in the dark on the floor in the hall, with tears in my eyes and the telephone squatting in my lap like a frog. She seemed immensely far away, a miniature voice booming at me tinily out of a thrumming void. Freddie, she said, you're drunk. She asked why had I not come back, to collect my bag if for nothing else. I wanted to say to her, Mother, how could I go home, now? We were silent for a moment, then she said Daphne had called her, wondering where I was, what I was doing. Daphne! I had not thought of her for days. Through the doorway at the end of the hall I watched Charlie pottering about in the kitchen, rattling the pots and pans and pretending he was not trying to hear what I was saying. I sighed, and the sigh turned into a thin little moan. Ma, I said, I've got myself into such trouble. There was a noise on the line, or maybe it was in my head, like a great rushing of many wings. What? she said, I can't hear you – what? I laughed, and two big tears ran down the sides of my nose. Nothing, I shouted, nothing, forget it! Then I said, Listen, do you know who Penelope is – was – do you know about her? I was shocked at myself. Why did I say such a thing, why did I want to wound her? She was silent for a moment, and then she laughed. That bitch? she said, of course I knew about her. Charlie had come to the doorway, and stood, with a rag in one hand and a plate in the other, watching me. The light was behind him, I could not see his face. There was another pause. You're too hard on yourself, Freddie, my mother said at last, in that reverberant, faraway voice, you make things too hard on yourself. I did not know what she meant. I still don't. I waited a moment, but she said nothing more, and I could not speak. Those were the last words we would ever exchange. I put down the receiver gently, and got to my feet, not without difficulty. One of my knees was asleep. I limped into the kitchen. Charlie was bent over the sink doing the washing-up, with yet another cigarette dangling from his lip, sleeves rolled, his waistcoat unbuckled at the back. The sky in the window in front of him was a pale shade of indigo, I thought I had never seen anything so lovely in my life.

Charlie, I said, swaying, I need a loan.

I had always been a weeper, but now any hint of kindness could make me blub like a babe. When there and then he sat down at the kitchen table and wrote out a cheque – I have it still: spidery black scrawl, an illegible signature, a stewy thumb-print in one corner – I tried to seize his liver-spotted hand, I think I meant to kiss it. He made a little speech, I don't remember it well. My mother figured in it, Daphne too. I think even Penelope's name was mentioned. I wonder if he was drunk? He kept looming into focus and fading out again, yet I felt this was less an effect of my blurred vision than of a sort of tentativeness on his part. Oh, Charlie, you should have heeded that niggle of suspicion, you should have thrown me out that night, fuddled and defenceless though I was.

The next thing I recall is being on my knees in the lavatory, puking up a ferruginous torrent of wine mixed with fibrous strands of meat and bits of carrot. The look of this stuff gushing out filled me with wonder, as if it were not vomit, but something rich and strange, a dark stream of ore from the deep mine of my innards. Then there is an impression of everything swaying, of glistening darkness and things in it spinning past me, as though I were being whirled round and round slowly on a wobbly carousel made of glass. Next I was lying on my back on the big, disordered bed upstairs, shivering and sweating. There was a light on, and the window was a box of deep, gleaming darkness. I fell asleep, and after what seemed a moment woke again with the sun shining in my face. The house was silent around me, but there was a thin, continuous ringing which I seemed to feel rather than hear. The sheets were a sodden tangle. I did not want to move, I felt as fragile as crystal. Even my hair felt breakable, a shock of erect, minute filaments bristling with static. I could feel the blood rushing along my veins, quick and heavy as mercury. My face was swollen and hot, and strangely smooth to the touch: a doll's face. When I closed my eyes a crimson shape pulsed and faded and pulsed again on the inside of my lids, like the repeated afterimage of a shell bursting in blackness. When I swallowed, the ringing in my ears changed pitch. I dozed, and dreamed I was adrift in a hot lake. When I woke it was afternoon. The light in the window, dense, calm, unshadowed, was a light shining straight out of the past. My mouth was dry and swollen, my head seemed packed with air. Not since childhood had I known this particular state of voluptuous distress. It was not really illness, more a kind of respite. I lay for a long time, hardly stirring, watching the day change, listening to the little noises of the world. The brazen sunlight slowly faded, and the sky turned from lilac to mauve, and a single star appeared. Then suddenly it was late, and I lay in a sleepy daze in the soft summer darkness and would not have been surprised if my mother had appeared, young and smiling, in a rustle of silk, with a finger to her lips, to say goodnight to me on her way out for the evening. It was not Maman who came, however, but only Charlie, he opened the door cautiously on its wheezy hinges and peered in at me, craning his tortoise-neck, and I shut my eyes and he withdrew softly and creaked away down the stairs. And I saw in my mind another doorway, and another darkness – that fragment of memory, not mine, yet again – and waited, hardly breathing, for something or someone to appear. But there was nothing.

I think of that brief bout of ague as marking the end of an initial, distinct phase of my life as a murderer. By the morning of the second day the fever had abated. I lay in a clammy tangle of sheets with my arms flung wide, just breathing. I felt as if I had been wading frantically through waist-high water, and now at last I had gained the beach, exhausted, trembling in every limb, and yet almost at peace. I had survived. I had come back to myself. Outside the window the seagulls were crying, looking for Mammy French, they rose and fell with stiff wings spread wide, as if suspended on elastic cords. I rose shakily and crossed the room. There was wind and sun, and the sea glared, a rich, hazardous blue. Below in the little stone harbour the yachts bobbed and slewed, yanking at their mooring-ropes. I turned away. There was something in the gay, bright scene that seemed to rebuke me. I put on Charlie's dressing-gown and went down to the kitchen. Silence everywhere. In the calm matutinal light everything stood motionless as if under a spell. I could not bear the thought of food. I found an open bottle of Apollinaris in the refrigerator and drank it off. It was flat, and tasted faintly of metal. I sat down at the table and rested my forehead in my hands. My skin felt grainy, as if the surface layer had crumpled to a sort of clinging dust. Charlie's breakfast things were still on the table, and there was spilled cigarette ash and a saucer of crushed butts. The newspapers I had bought on Thursday were stuffed in the rubbish bin. This was Saturday. I had missed, what, nearly two days, two days of accumulating evidence. I looked for the plastic bag in which I had put my clothes, but it was gone. Charlie must have put it out for the binmen, it would be on some dump by now. Perhaps at this very moment a rag-picker was rummaging in it. A spasm of horror swarmed over me. I jumped up and paced the floor, my hands clasped together to keep them from shaking. I must do something, anything. I ran upstairs and swept from room to room like a mad king, the tail of the dressing-gown flying out behind me. I shaved, glaring at myself in the fish-eye mirror, then I put on Charlie's clothes again, and broke into his desk and took his cash and his wallet of credit cards, and went down the stairs three at a time and stormed out into the world.

And paused. Everything was in its place, the boats in the harbour, the road, the white houses along the coast, the far headland, those little clouds on the horizon, and yet – and yet it was all different somehow from what I had expected, from what something inside me had expected, some nice sense of how things should be ordered. Then I realised it was I, of course, who was out of place.

I went into the newsagent's, with the same cramp of fear and excitement in my breast as I had felt the first time. When I picked up the papers the ink came off on my hands, and the coins slipped in my sweaty fingers. The girl with the pimples gave me another look. She had a curious, smeared sort of gaze, it seemed to pass me by and take me in at the same time. Pre-menstrual, I could tell by her manner, that tensed, excitable air. I turned my back on her and scanned the papers. By now the story had seeped up from the bottom of the front pages like a stain, while reports on the bombing dwindled, the injured having stopped dying off. There was a photograph of the car, looking like a wounded hippo, with a stolid Guard standing beside it and a detective in Wellington boots pointing at something. The boys who had found it had been interviewed. Did they remember me, that pallid stranger dreaming on the bench in the deserted station?

They did, they gave a description of me: an elderly man with black hair and a bushy beard. The woman at the traffic lights was sure I was in my early twenties, well-dressed, with a moustache and piercing eyes. Then there were the tourists at Whitewater who saw me make off with the painting, and Reck and his ma, of course, and the idiot boy and the woman at the garage where I hired the car: from each of their accounts another and more fantastic version of me emerged, until I became multiplied into a band of mustachioed cutthroats, rushing about glaring and making threatening noises, like a chorus of brigands in an Italian opera. I nearly laughed. And yet I was disappointed. Yes, it's true, I was disappointed. Did I want to be found out, did I hope to see my name splashed in monster type across every front page? I think I did. I think I longed deep down to be made to stand in front of a jury and reveal all my squalid little secrets. Yes, to be found out, to be suddenly pounced upon, beaten, stripped, and set before the howling multitude, that was my deepest, most ardent desire. I hear the court catching its breath in surprise and disbelief. But ah, do you not also long for this, in your hearts, gentlepersons of the jury? To be rumbled. To feel that heavy hand fall upon your shoulder, and hear the booming voice of authority telling you the game is up at last. In short, to be unmasked. Ask yourselves. I confess (I confess!), those days that passed while I waited for them to find me were the most exciting I have ever known, or ever hope to know. Terrible, yes, but exciting too. Never had the world appeared so unstable, or my place in it so thrillingly precarious. I had a raw, lascivious awareness of myself, a big warm damp thing parcelled up in someone else's clothes. At any moment they might catch me, they might be watching me even now, murmuring into their handsets and signalling to the marksmen on the roof. First there would be panic, then pain. And when everything was gone, every shred of dignity and pretence, what freedom there would be, what lightness! No, what am I saying, not lightness, but its opposite: weight, gravity, the sense at last of being firmly grounded. Then finally I would be me, no longer that poor impersonation of myself I had been doing all my life. I would be real. I would be, of all things, human.

I took the bus to town, and got off at a street where I used to live years ago, when I was a student, and walked along by the railings of the park in the warm wind under the seething trees, my heart filled with nostalgia. A man in a cap, with terrible, soiled eyes, stood on the pavement shaking a fist in the air and roaring obscene abuse at the cars passing by. I envied him. I would have liked to stand and shout like that, to pour out all that rage and pain and indignation. I walked on. A trio of light-clad girls came tripping out of a bookshop, laughing, and for a second I was caught up in their midst, my side-teeth bared in a frightful grin, a beast among the graces. In a bright new shop I bought a jacket and trousers, two shirts, some ties, underwear, and, in a flourish of defiance, a handsome but not altogether unostentatious hat. I thought I detected a slight stiffening of attention when I produced Charlie's credit cards – my God, did they know him, did he shop here? – but I turned up my accent to full force and dashed off his signature with aplomb, and everyone relaxed. I was not really worried. In fact, I felt ridiculously excited and happy, like a boy on a birthday spree. (What is it about the mere act of buying things, that it can afford me so much simple pleasure?) I seemed to swim along the street, upright as a seahorse, breasting the air. I think I must have been feverish still. The people among whom I moved were strange to me, stranger than usual, I mean. I felt I was no longer of their species, that something had happened since I had last encountered a crowd of them together, that an adjustment had occurred in me, a tiny, amazingly swift and momentous evolutionary event. I passed through their midst like a changeling, a sport of nature. They were beyond me, they could not touch me – could they see me, even, or was I now outside the spectrum of their vision? And yet how avidly I observed them, in hunger and wonderment. They surged around me at a sort of stumble, dull-eyed and confused, like refugees. I saw myself, bobbing head and shoulders above them, disguised, solitary, nursing my huge secret. I was their un-recognised and their unacknowledged dream – I was their Moos-brugger. I came to the river, and dawdled on the bridge, among the beggars and the fruit-sellers and the hawkers of cheap jewel-lery, admiring the wind-blurred light above the water and tasting the salt air on my lips. The sea! To be away, out there, out over countless fathoms, lost in all that blue!

I went – everything was so simple – I went into a bar and bought a drink. Each sip was like a sliver of precious metal, chill

and smooth. It was a cavernous place, very dark. The light from
the street glared whitely in the open doorway. I might have been
somewhere in the south, in one of those dank, tired ports I used
to know so well. At the back, in a lighted place like a stage, some
youths with shaven heads and outsize lace-up boots were playing
a game of billiards. The balls whirred and clacked, the young
men softly swore. It was like something out of Hogarth, a group
of wigless surgeons, say, intent over the dissecting table. The
barman, arms folded and mouth open, was watching a horse race
on the television set perched high up on a shelf in a corner above
him. A tubercular young man in a black shortie overcoat came
in and stood beside me, breathing and fidgeting. I could tell from
the tension coming off him that he was working himself up to
something, and for a moment I was pleasurably alarmed. He
might do anything, anything. But he only spoke. *I've lived here
thirty-three years*, he said, in a tone of bitter indignation, *and everyone is afraid*. The barman glanced at him with weary contempt
and turned back to the television. Blue horses galloped in silence
over bright-green turf. *I* am afraid, the young man said, resentful
now. He gave a tremendous twitch, hunching his shoulders and
ducking his head and throwing up one arm, as if something had
bitten him on the neck. Then he turned and went out hurriedly,
clutching his coat about him. I followed, leaving my drink half-
finished. It was blindingly bright outside. I spotted him, a good
way off already, dodging along through the crowds with his
elbows pressed to his sides, taking tight, swift little steps, nimble
as a dancer. Nothing could stop him. In the thickest surge of
bodies he would find a chink at once, and swivel deftly from the
waist up and dive through without altering his pace. What a pair
we would have made, if anyone had thought to link us, he in his
tight shabby coat and I with my fancy hat and expensive clutch
of carrier bags. I could hardly keep up with him, and after a
minute or two I was puffing and in a sweat. I had an unaccountable sense of elation. Once he paused, and stood glaring into the
window of a chemist's shop. I waited, loitering at a bus stop,
keeping him in the corner of my eye. He was so intent, and
seemed to quiver so, that I thought he was going to do something
violent, turn and attack someone, maybe, or kick in the window
and stamp about among the cameras and the cosmetic displays.
But he was only waiting for another shudder to pass through him.

This time when he flung up his arm his leg shot up as well, as if elbow and knee were connected by an invisible string, and a second later his heel came down on the pavement with a ringing crack. He cast a quick look up and down the street, to see if anyone had noticed, and gave himself a casual little shake, as if by that he would make the previous spasm appear to have been intentional too, and then he was off again like a whippet. I wanted to catch up with him, I wanted to speak to him. I did not know what I would say. I would not offer him sympathy, certainly not. I did not pity him, I saw nothing in him to merit my pity. No, that's not true, for he was pathetic, a maimed and mad poor creature. Yet I was not sorry for him, my heart did not go out to him in that way. What I felt was, how shall I say, a kind of brotherly regard, a strong, sustaining, almost cheerful sense of oneness with him. It seemed the simplest thing in the world for me to walk up now and put my hand on that thin shoulder and say: *my fellow sufferer, dear friend, compagnon de misères!* And so it was with deep disappointment and chagrin that at the next corner I stopped and looked about me in the jostling crowd and realised that I had lost him. Almost at once, however, I found a substitute, a tall fat girl with big shoulders and a big behind, and big, tubular legs ending in a pair of tiny feet, like a pig's front trotters, wedged into high-heeled white shoes. She had been to the hairdresser's, her hair was cropped in a fashionable, boyish style that was, on her, grotesque. The stubbled back of her neck, with its fold of fat, was still an angry shade of red from the dryer, it seemed to be blushing for her. She was so brave and sad, clumping along in her ugly shoes, and I would have followed her all day, I think, but after a while I lost her, too. Next I took up with a man with a huge strawberry mark on his face, then a tiny woman wheeling a tiny dog in a doll's pram, then a young fellow who marched resolutely along, as if he could see no one, with a visionary's fixed glare, swinging his arms and growling to himself. In a busy pedestrian thoroughfare I was surrounded suddenly by a gang of tinker girls, what my mother would have called *big rawsies*, with red hair and freckles and extraordinary, glass-green eyes, who pushed against me in truculent supplication, plucking at my sleeve and whining. It was like being set upon by a flock of importunate large wild birds. When I tried to shoo them away one of them knocked my hat off, while another deftly snatched out of my hand the carrier bag containing my new jacket. They fled, shoving each other and laughing shrilly, their raw, red heels flying. I laughed too, and picked up my hat from the pavement, ignoring the looks of the passers-by, who appeared to find my merriment unseemly. I did not care about the jacket – in fact, the loss of it chimed in a mysteriously apt way with that of its discarded predecessor – but I would have liked to see where those girls would go. I imagined a lean-to made of rags and bits of galvanised iron on a dusty patch of waste ground, with a starving dog and snot-nosed infants, and a drunken hag crouched over a steaming pot. Or perhaps there was a Fagin somewhere waiting for them, skulking in the shadows in some derelict tenement, where the light of summer fingered the shutters, and dust motes drifted under lofty ceilings, and the rat's claw in the wainscoting scratched at the silence, scratched, stopped, and scratched again. So I went along happily for a little while, dreaming up other lives, until I spotted a whey-faced giant with rubber legs clomping ahead of me on two sticks, and I set off after him in eager pursuit.

What was I doing, why was I following these people – what enlightenment was I looking for? I did not know, nor care. I was puzzled and happy, like a child who has been allowed to join in an adults' game. I kept at it for hours, criss-crossing the streets and the squares with a drunkard's dazed single-mindedness, as if I were tracing out a huge, intricate sign on the face of the city for someone in the sky to read. I found myself in places I had not known were there, crooked alleyways and sudden, broad, deserted spaces, and dead-end streets under railway bridges where parked cars basked fatly in the evening sun, their toy-coloured roofs agleam. I ate a hamburger in a glass-walled café with moulded plastic chairs and tinfoil ashtrays, where people sat alone and gnawed at their food like frightened children abandoned by their parents. The daylight died slowly, leaving a barred, red and gold sunset trembling in the sky, and as I walked along it was like walking under the surface of a broad, burning river. The evening crowds were out, girls in tight trousers and high heels, and brawny young men with menacing haircuts. In the hot, hazy dusk the streets seemed wider, flattened, somehow, and the cars scudded along, sleek as seals in the sodium glare. I got back late to Charlie's house, footsore, hot and dishevelled, my hat awry, but filled with a mysterious sense of achievement. And that night I dreamed about my father. He was a miniature version of himself, a wizened child with a moustache, dressed in a sailor suit, his pinched little face scrubbed and his hair neatly parted, leading by the hand a great, tall, dark-eyed matron wearing Greek robes and a crown of myrtle, who fixed me with a lewd, forgiving smile.

I HAVE HAD a shock. My counsel has been to see me today, bringing an extraordinary piece of news. Usually I enjoy our little conferences, in a lugubrious sort of way. We sit at a square table in a small airless room with no windows. The walls are painted filing-cabinet grey. Light from a strip of neon tubing above our heads sifts down upon us like a fine-grained mist. The bulb makes a tiny, continuous buzzing. Maolseachlainn at first is full of energy, rooting in his bag, shuffling his papers, muttering. He is like a big, worried bear. He works at finding things to talk to me about, new aspects of the case, obscure points of law he might bring up, the chances of our getting a sympathetic judge, that sort of thing. He speaks too fast, stumbling over his words as if they were so many stones. Gradually the atmosphere of the place gets in at him, like damp, and he falls silent. He takes off his specs and sits and blinks at me. He has a way of squeezing the bridge of his nose between two fingers and a thumb which is peculiarly endearing. I feel sorry for him. I think he truly does like me. This puzzles him, and, I suspect, disturbs him too. He believes he is letting me down when he runs out of steam like this, but really, there is nothing left to say. We both know I will get life. He cannot understand my equanimity in the face of my fate. I tell him I have taken up Buddhism. He smiles carefully, unsure that it is a joke. I divert him with tales of prison life, fleshing them out with impersonations – I do our governor here very convincingly. When Maolseachlainn laughs there is no sound, only a slow heaving of the shoulders and a stretched, shiny grin.

By the way, what an odd formulation that is: to get life. Words so rarely mean what they mean.

Today I saw straight away he was in a state about something. He kept clawing at the collar of his shirt and clearing his throat, and taking off his half-glasses and putting them back on again. Also there was a smeary look in his eye. He hummed and hawed, and mumbled about the concept of justice, and the discretion of the courts, and other such folderol, I hardly listened to him. He was so mournful and ill at ease, shifting his big backside on the prison chair and looking everywhere except at me, that I could hardly keep from laughing. I pricked up my ears, though, when he started to mutter something about the possibility of my making a guilty plea – and this after all the time and effort he expended at the beginning in convincing me I should plead not guilty. Now when I caught him up on it, rather sharply, I confess, he veered off at once, with an alarmed look. I wonder what he's up to? I should have kept at it, and got it out of him. As a diversionary measure he dived into his briefcase and brought out a copy of my mother's will. I had not yet heard the contents, and was, I need hardly say, keenly interested. Maolseachlainn, I noticed, found this subject not much easier than the previous one. He coughed a lot, and frowned, and read out stuff about gifts and covenants and minor bequests, and was a long time getting to the point. I still cannot credit it. The old bitch has left Coolgrange to that stable-girl, what's-her-name, Joanne. There is some money for Daphne, and for Van's schooling, but for me, nothing. I suppose I should not be surprised, but I am. I was not a good son, but I was the only one she had. Maolseachlainn was watching me with compassion. I'm sorry, he said. I smiled and shrugged, though it was not easy. I wished he would go away now. Oh, I said, it's understandable, after all, that she would make a new will. He said nothing. There was a peculiar silence. Then, almost tenderly, he handed me the document, and I looked at the date. The thing was seven, nearly eight years old. She had cut me out long ago, before ever I came back to disgrace her and the family name. I recalled, with shocking clarity, the way she looked at me that day in the kitchen at Coolgrange, and heard again that cackle of raucous laughter. Well, I'm glad she enjoyed her joke. It's a good one. I find a surprising lack of bitterness in my heart. I am smiling, though probably it seems more as if I am wincing. This is her contribution to the long course of lessons I must learn.

Maolseachlainn stood up, assuming his heartiest manner, as always, in an attempt to disguise his relief at the prospect of getting away. I watched him struggle into his navy-blue overcoat and knot his red woollen muffler around his neck. Sometimes, when he first arrives, his clothes give off little wafts and slivers of the air of outdoors, I snuff them up with surreptitious pleasure, as if they were the most precious of perfumes. What's it like, out-side? I said now. He paused, and blinked at me in some alarm. I think he thought I was asking him for an overall picture, as if I might have forgotten what the world looked like. The day, I said, the weather. His brow cleared. He shrugged. Oh, he said, grey, just grey, you know. And I saw it at once, with a pang, the late November afternoon, the dull shine on the wet roads, and the children straggling home from school, and rooks tossing and wheeling high up against ragged clouds, and the tarnished glow in the sky off behind bare, blackened branches. These were the times I used to love, the weather's unconsidered moments, when the vast business of the world just goes on quietly by itself, as if there were no one to notice, or care. I see myself as a boy out there, dawdling along that wet road, kicking a stone ahead of me and dreaming the enormous dream of the future. There was a path, I remember, that cut off through an oak wood a mile or so from home, which I knew must lead to Coolgrange eventually. How green the shadows, and deep the track, how restless the silence seemed, that way. Every time I passed by there, coming up from the cross, I said to myself, Next time, next time. But always when the next time came I was in a rush, or the light was fading, or I was just not in the mood to break new ground, and so I kept to the ordinary route, along the road. In the end I never took that secret path, and now, of course, it is too late.

I have been doing calculations in my head – it keeps my mind off other things – and I find to my surprise that I spent no more than ten days in all at Charlie's house, from midsummer day, or night, rather, until the last, momentous day of June. That *is* ten, isn't it? Thirty days hath September, April, June – yes, ten. Or is it nine. It's nine nights, certainly. But where does the day end and the night start, and vice versa? And why do I find the night a more easily quantifiable entity than day? I have never been any good at this kind of thing. The simpler the figures the more they fox me. Anyway. Ten days, thereabouts, more or less, is the length of my stay with Charlie French, whose hospitality and kindness I did not mean to betray. It seemed a longer time than that. It seemed weeks and weeks. I was not unhappy there. That's to say, I was no more unhappy there than I would have been somewhere else. Unhappy! What a word! As the days went on

I grew increasingly restless. My nerves seethed, and there was a permanent knot of pain in my guts. I suffered sudden, furious attacks of impatience. Why didn't they come for me, what were they doing? In particular I resented the Behrenses' silence, I was convinced they were playing a cruel game with me. But all the time, behind all these agitations, there was that abiding, dull, flat sensation. I felt disappointed. I felt let down. The least I had expected from the enormities of which I was guilty was that they would change my life, that they would make things happen, however awful, that there would be a constant succession of heart-stopping events, of alarms and sudden frights and hair-breadth escapes. I do not know how I got through the days. I awoke each morning with an anguished start, as if a pure, dis-tilled drop of pain had plopped on to my forehead. That big old house with its smells and cobwebs was oppressive. I drank a lot, of course, but not enough to make myself insensible. I tried to achieve oblivion, God knows, I poured in the booze until my lips went numb and my knees would hardly bend, but it was no good, I could not escape myself. I waited with a lover's rapt expectancy for the evenings, when I would put on my hat and my new clothes – my new mask! – and step forth gingerly, a quavering Dr Jekyll, inside whom that other, terrible creature chafed and struggled, lusting for experience. I felt I had never until now looked at the ordinary world around me, the people, places, things. How innocent it all seemed, innocent, and doomed. How can I express the tangle of emotions that thrashed inside me as I prowled the city streets, letting my monstrous heart feed its fill on the sights and sounds of the commonplace? The feeling of power, for instance, how can I communicate that? It sprang not from what I had done, but from the fact that I had done it and *no one knew.* It was the secret, the secret itself, *that* was what set me above the dull-eyed ones among whom I moved as the long day died, and the streetlights came on, and the traffic slid away homeward, leaving a blue haze hanging like the smoke of gunfire in the darkening air. And then there was that constant, hot excitement, like a fever in the blood, that was half the fear of being unmasked and half the longing for it. Somewhere, I knew, in dayrooms and in smoke-filled, shabby offices, faceless men were even now painstakingly assembling the evidence against me. I thought about them at night, as I lay in Charlie's mother's big lumpy bed. It was strange to be the object of so much meticulous attention, strange, and not entirely unpleasant. Does that seem perverse? But I was in another country now, where the old rules did not apply.

It was hard to sleep, of course. I suppose I did not want to sleep, afraid of what I would encounter in my dreams. At best I would manage a fitful hour or two in the darkness before dawn, and wake up exhausted, with an ache in my chest and my eyes scalding. Charlie too was sleepless, I would hear at all hours his creaking step on the stair, the rattle of the teapot in the kitchen, the laborious, spasmodic tinkle as he emptied his old man's bladder in the bathroom. We saw little of each other. The house was big enough for us both to be in it at the same time and yet feel we were alone. Since that first, drunken night he had been avoiding me. He seemed to have no friends. The phone never rang, no one came to the house. I was surprised, then, and horribly alarmed, to return early one evening from my rambles in town and find three big black cars parked on the road, and a uniformed Guard loitering in the company of two watchful men in anoraks at the harbour wall. I made myself walk past slowly, an honest citizen out for a stroll at end of day, though my heart was hammering and my palms were damp, and then skipped around the back way and got in through the mews. Halfway up the jungly garden I tripped and fell, and tore my left hand on a rose bush that had run wild. I crouched in the long grass, listening. Smell of loam, smell of leaves, the thick feel of blood on my wounded hand. The yellow light in the kitchen window turned the dusk around me to tenderest blue. There was a strange woman inside, in a white apron, working at the stove. When I opened the back door she turned quickly and gave a little shriek. Holy God, she said, who are you? She was an elderly person with a henna wig and ill-fitting dentures and a scattered air. Her name, as we shall discover presently, was Madge. They're all upstairs, she said, dismissing me, and turned back to her steaming saucepans.

There were five of them, or six, counting Charlie, though at first it seemed to me there must be twice that number. They were in the big gaunt drawing room on the first floor, standing under the windows with drinks in their hands, ducking and bobbing at each other like nervous storks and chattering as if their lives depended on it. Behind them the lights of the harbour glimmered, and in the far sky a huge bank of slate-blue cloud was shutting down like a lid on the last, smouldering streak of sunset fire. At my entrance the chattering stopped. Only one of them was a woman, tall, thin, with foxy red hair and an extraordinary stark white face. Charlie, who was standing with his back to me, saw me first reflected in their swivelling glances. He turned with a pained smile. Ah, he said, there you are. His winged hair gleamed like a polished helm. He was wearing a bow-tie. Well, I heard myself saying to him, in a tone of cheery truculence, well, you might have told me! My hands were trembling. There was a moment of uncertain silence, then the talk abruptly started up again. The woman went on watching me. Her pale colouring and vivid hair and long, slender neck gave her a permanently startled look, as if at some time in the past she had been told a shocking secret and had never quite absorbed it. Charlie, mumbling apologetically, had put a shaky old hand under my elbow and was gently but firmly steering me backwards out of the room. The fear I had felt earlier had turned into annoyance. I felt like giving him a clout, and putting a dent in that ridiculous praetorian helmet of hair. Tell Madge, he was saying, tell Madge to give you something to eat, and I'll be down presently. He was so worried I thought he was going to weep. He stood on the top step and watched me make my way downstairs, as if he were afraid I would come scampering back up again if he took his eye off me, and only when I had safely reached the bottom and was heading for the kitchen did he turn back to the drawing room and his guests.

The kitchen was filled with steam, and Madge, her wig awry, looked even hotter and more harassed than before. This place, she said bitterly, honest to God! She was, as she picturesquely put it, Mr French's occasional woman, and came in when there were dinner parties, and that. This was interesting. Dinner parties, indeed! I helped her by opening the wine, and sat down at the table with a bottle for myself. I had drunk half of it when there was a loud knock at the front door that set my heart thumping again. I went into the hall, but Charlie was already rattling hurriedly down the stairs. When he opened the door I could see the two anoraks outside, guarding the way for a burly man and a tall, sleek woman, as they advanced at a regal pace into the hall. Ah,

Max, Charlie said, and stepped forward with clumsy eagerness. The woman he ignored. Max shook hands with him briefly, and then took back his hand and ran it upwards quickly over his low, truculent brow. Christ, he said, you're far enough out, I thought we were never going to get here. They moved towards the stairs, Charlie and Max in front and the woman behind them. She wore an ugly blue gown and a triple rope of pearls. She glanced along the hall and caught my eye, and held it until I looked away. Madge had come out of the kitchen, and hovered at my shoulder. There's his nibs, she whispered, and the missus too.

I waited a while after they had gone up, and when Madge returned to her cooking I followed them, and slipped into the drawing room again. Charlie and Max and Mrs Max were standing at one of the windows admiring the view, while the others bobbed and clucked and tried not to stare too openly in their direction. I seized an armful of bottles from the mantelpiece and passed among them, topping up their glasses. The men had an eager, slightly anxious air, like that of big, blue-suited schoolboys on their first adult outing, except for one old chap with a nose like a blood-orange and stains down the front of his waistcoat, who stood to one side all on his own, glazed and dejected. The others carefully looked through me, but he brightened up at once, and was ready for a chat. What do you think, anyway, he said loudly, will we win, will we? I understood it to be a rhetorical question. We will, I said stoutly, and gave him a broad wink. He raised his eyebrows and stepped back a pace, however, peering at me doubtfully. By God, he said, I don't know, now. I shrugged, and passed on blandly. Charlie had caught sight of me, and was smiling fixedly in alarm. Mine was a vodka, Mrs Max said coldly when I offered her gin. My attention was on her husband. He had a raw, scrubbed look to him, as if he had been exposed for a long time to some far rougher form of light and weather than the others in the room had ever known. His movements, too, the way he held himself, the slow, deliberate way he turned his glance or lifted his hand to his brow, all these bore a unique stamp, and were weighted with a kind of theatrical awareness. His voice was slow and guttural, and he had a violent manner of speaking that was impressive, and even, in an odd way, seductive. It was the voice of a man moving inexorably forward through a forest of small obstacles. I imagined him carelessly crunching things underfoot, flowers, or snails, or the insteps of his enemies. Well, Charlie, he was saying, still buying cheap and selling dear? Charlie blushed, and glanced at me. That's right, Mrs Max said, embarrass everyone. She spoke loudly, with a dull emphasis, and did not look at him. It was as if she were lobbing remarks past his shoulder at a sardonic ally listening there. Nor did he look at her, it might have been a disembodied voice that had spoken. He laughed harshly. Have you acquired that Dutch job for me yet? he said. Charlie, grinning in anguish, shook his head, speechless. His left eyelid began to flutter, as if a moth had suddenly come to life under it. I proffered the whiskey bottle but he put a hand quickly over his glass. Max also waved me away. The woman with the foxy hair had come up behind me. Your hand, she said, you've cut it. For a moment we all stood in silence, Max and his missus, and Charlie and Foxy and me, contemplating the beaded scratch across my knuckles. Yes, I said, I fell over a rose bush. I laughed. That half-bottle of wine had gone straight to my head. Charlie was shifting stealthily from foot to foot, afraid, I suppose, that I was about to do something outrageous. It struck me for the first time how frightened of me he was. Poor Charlie. A lighted yacht was gliding silently across the inky harbour. Lovely view, Max said grimly.

In the dining room the stuffed owl looked out of its bell-jar at the company with an expression of surprise and some dismay. By now Patch, I mean Madge, was in a state of panic. I carried plates for her, and serving dishes, and plonked them down on the table with extravagant, waiterly flourishes. I confess, I was enjoying myself. I was light-headed, brimming with manic glee, like a child in a dressing-up game. I seemed to move as if under a magic spell, I do not know how it worked, but for a while, for an hour or two, posing as Charlie's factotum, I was released from myself and the terrors that had been pursuing me relentlessly for days. I even invented a history for myself as I went along, I mean I – how shall I express it – I fell into a certain manner that was not my own and that yet seemed, even to me, no less authentic, or plausible, at least, than my real self. (My real self!) I became Frederick the Indispensable, Mr French's famous man, without whom that crusty, moneyed old bachelor would not be able to survive. He had rescued me from uncongenial circumstances when I was a young man – tending the bar, say, in some sleazy downtown pub – and now I was devoted to him, and loyal to the point of ferocity. I bullied him too, of course, and could be a terror when he had people in. (Jealousy? Acquaintances did sometimes speculate among themselves, but no, they decided, Charlie was not that way inclined: remember that horsy woman down the country, the lost love of his life?) Really, we were like father and son, except that no son would be so steadfast, and no father so forgiving of my little ways. At times it was hard to tell which was master and which the man. Tonight, for instance, when the main course was finished, I sat myself down among the guests and poured a glass of wine as if it were the most natural thing in the world. A silence fell, and Charlie frowned, and rolled a breadcrumb about on the tablecloth, pretending he was thinking about something else, and Max stared balefully out of the window at the harbour lights while his henchmen around him fidgeted and glanced at each other nervously, and at last I took up my glass, and rose and said, Well! I suppose us ladies better withdraw, and fairly flounced out of the room. In the hall, of course, I leaned against the wall and laughed. All the same, my hands were shaking. Stage fright, I suppose. What an actor the world has lost in me!

Now what shall I do?

I went upstairs to the drawing room. No, I went into the kitchen. Madge: wig, false teeth, white apron, I have done all that. Out again. In the hall I found Foxy. She had wandered out of the dining room. Under the stairs was a dark place, there we met. I could see her face in the gloom, her eyes watching me, so solemn and fearful. Why are you sad? I said, and for a moment she did not know what to do with her hands, then she put them behind her back, and flexed one knee and briefly swayed her shoulders and her hips, like a schoolgirl playing the coquette. Who says I'm sad? she said. I'm not sad. And I thought she was going to cry. Did she see it in me, the terror and the shame, had she seen it from the first? For she had sought me out, I knew that. I reached behind her and opened a door, and we stepped suddenly on to bare floorboards in an empty room. There was a smell, dry and oniony, that was the smell of a certain attic room at Coolgrange. A parallelogram of moonlight was propped against one wall like a broken mirror. I am still holding these damned plates. I put them on the floor at our feet, and while I was still bending she touched my shoulder and said something which I did not catch. She laughed softly, in surprise, it seemed, as if the sound of her own voice were unexpected. Nothing, she said, nothing. She shook in my arms. She was all teeth, breath, clutching fingers. She held my head between her hands as if she would crush it. She had kicked off her shoes, they clattered where they fell. She raised one foot behind her and pressed it against the door, pressed, and pressed. Her thighs were cold. She wept, her tears fell on my hands. I bit her throat. We were like – I don't know. We were like two messengers, meeting in the dark to exchange our terrible news. O God, she said, O God. She put her forehead against my shoulder. Our hands were smeared with each other. The room came back, the moonlight, the oniony smell. No thought, except: her white face, her hair. Forgive me, I said. I don't know why I laughed. Anyway, it wasn't really a laugh.

How peaceful the days are now, here at the dead end of the year. Sitting in the fastness of this grey room I sometimes imagine I am utterly alone, that there is no one around me for miles and miles. It is like being in the deep hold of a great grey ship. The air is heavy and still, it presses in my ears, on my eyes, on the base of my skull. A trial date has been fixed at last. I know this should concentrate my mind, give me a purpose and so on, make me excited, or afraid, but it does not. Something has happened to my sense of time, I think in aeons now. The days, the weeks of this banal little courtroom drama will register as no more than a pinprick. I have become a lifer.

Again today Maolseachlainn brought up the topic of how I should plead. I let him maunder on for a while, then I got fed up and told him I would dispense with his services if he did not come straight out and say whatever it was he had on his mind. This was disingenuous of me, for I had realised, of course, since his last visit, that he was hinting at the possibility of an arrangement – I understand, from the conversations I have had in here, that there is hardly a sentence handed down that has not been prearranged among counsel. I was curious to know what the court could want from me. Now, as I watched poor old Mac squirm and sweat, I thought I had it: Charlie, of course – they were trying to salvage something of Charlie's reputation. (How could I have imagined they would care a fig for Charlie, or his

reputation?) I would do all I could for him, that went without
saying, though it seemed to me a bit late now. All right, Mac,
I said, holding up a hand, I'll plead guilty – and what then? He
gave me one of his over-the-spectacles looks. Then it'll be an
open-and-shut case, won't it? he said. This, I realised after a
moment, was intended as a witticism. He grinned dolefully.
What he meant was that the trial would open, I would deny the
charges as stated, plead guilty to manslaughter or something, the
judge would pass sentence, with a bit lopped off in return for my
co-operation, and then, presto, it would all be over, the hearing
would end, the case would be closed. He could guarantee nothing, he said, but he had a duty to his client to try to secure the
best judgment that was possible within the law. He is very charming when he waxes pompous like this. What's the point, I said,
what's the trick? He shrugged. The trick is that no evidence will
be heard. Simple as that. For a moment we were silent. And will
that work, I said, will that save him? He frowned in puzzlement,
and at once I saw I had been wrong, that Charlie and his embarrassment were not the subject here. I laughed. I've said it before,
sometimes I think I am hopelessly innocent. Maolseachlainn
glanced over his shoulder – he did, he really did – and leaned
across the table conspiratorially. No one is worrying about
Charlie French, he said, no one is worrying about *him*.

Your honour, I do not like this, I do not like this at all. I'll
plead guilty, of course – haven't I done so all along? – but I do
not like it that I may not give evidence, no, that I don't like. It's
not fair. Even a dog such as I must have his day. I have always
seen myself in the witness box, gazing straight ahead, quite calm,
and wearing casual clothes, as the newspapers will have it. And
then that authoritative voice, telling my side of things, in my own
words. Now I am to be denied my moment in the spotlight, the
last such, surely, that I'll know in this life. No, it's not right.

Look, the fact is I hardly remember that evening at Charlie
French's. I mean, I remember the evening, but not the people,
not with any clarity. I see far more vividly the lights on the water
outside, and the last streak of sunset and the dark bank of cloud,
than I do the faces of those hearty boy-men. Even Max Molyneaux is not much more, in my recollection, than an expensive
suit and a certain sleek brutishness. What do I care for him and his
ilk, for God's sake? Let them keep their reputations, it's nothing

to me, one way or the other, I have no interest in stirring up
scandal. The occasion passed before me in a glassy blur, like so
much else over those ten days. Why, even poor Foxy was hardly
more substantial to me in my frantic condition than a prop in a
wet dream. No, wait, I take that back. However much they may
hoot in ribald laughter, I must declare that I remember her
clearly, with tenderness and compassion. She is, and will most
likely remain, the last woman I made love to. Love? Can I call it
that? What else can I call it. She trusted me. She smelled the
blood and the horror and did not recoil, but opened herself like
a flower and let me rest in her for a moment, my heart shaking,
as we exchanged our wordless secret. Yes, I remember her. I was
falling, and she caught me, my Gretchen.

In fact, her name was Marian. Not that it matters.

They stayed very late, all except Mrs Max, who left directly
dinner was over. I watched as she was driven away, sitting up very
straight in the back of one of the black limousines, a ravaged
Nefertiti. Max and his pals went upstairs again, and caroused
until the dawn was breaking. I spent the night in the kitchen
playing cards with Madge. Where was Marian? I don't know –
I got blotto, as usual. Anyway, our moment was over, if we were
to encounter each other now we would only be embarrassed. Yet
I think I must have gone to look for her, for I recall blundering
about upstairs, in the bedrooms, and falling over repeatedly in
the dark. I remember, too, standing at a wide-open window, very
high up, listening to the strains of music outside on the air, a mysterious belling and blaring, that seemed to move, to fade, as if a
clamorous cavalcade were departing into the night. I suppose it
came from some dancehall, or some nightclub on the harbour.
I think of it, however, as the noise of the god and his retinue,
abandoning me.

NEXT DAY the weather broke. At mid-morning, when my hang-over and I got up, the sun was shining as gaily and as heartlessly as it had all week, and the houses along the coast shimmered in a pale-blue haze, as if the sky had crumbled into airy geometry there. I stood at the window in my drawers, scratching and yawn-ing. It struck me that I had become almost accustomed to this strange way of life. It was as if I were adapting to an illness, after the initial phase of frights and fevers. A churchbell was ringing. Sunday. The strollers were out already, with their dogs and children. Across the road, at the harbour wall, a man in a raincoat stood with his hands clasped behind his back, gazing out to sea. I could hear voices downstairs. Madge was in the kitchen doing last night's washing-up. She gave me a peculiar glance. I was wearing Charlie's dressing-gown. How is it, I wonder, that I did not catch it then, that new, speculative note in Madge's voice, which should have alerted me? She had a helper with her this morning, her niece, a dim-looking child of twelve or so with – with what, what does it matter what she had, what she was like. All these minor witnesses, none of whom will ever be called now. I sat at the table drinking tea and watched them as they worked. The child I could see was frightened of me. Fe fi fo fum. He's gone out, you know, Madge said, her arms plunged in suds, Mr French, he went out as I was coming in. Her tone was un-accountably accusing, as if Charlie had fled the house because of me. But then, he had.

In the afternoon a huge cloud grew up on the horizon, grey and grainy, like a deposit of silt, and the sea swarmed, a blackish blue flecked with white. I watched an undulant curtain of rain sweep in slowly from the east. The man at the harbour wall buttoned his raincoat. The Sunday morning crowd was long gone, but he, *he* was still there.

*   *   *

Strange how it felt, now that it was here at last. I had expected
terror, panic, cold sweat, the shakes, but there was none of that.
Instead, a kind of wild-eyed euphoria took hold of me. I strode
about the house like the drunken captain of a storm-tossed ship.
All sorts of mad ideas came into my head. I would barricade the
doors and windows. I would take Madge and her niece hostage,
and barter them for a helicopter to freedom. I would wait until
Charlie came back, and use him as a human shield, marching him
out ahead of me with a knife at his throat – I even went down to
the kitchen to find a blade for the purpose. Madge had finished
the washing-up, and was sitting at the table with a pot of tea and
a Sunday tabloid. She watched me apprehensively as I rummaged
in the cutlery drawer. She asked if I would be wanting my lunch,
or would I wait for Mr French. I laughed wildly. Lunch! The
niece laughed too, a little parrot squawk, her top lip curling up
to reveal a half-inch of whitish, glistening gum. When I looked
at her she shut her mouth abruptly, it was like a blind coming
down. Jacintha, Madge said to her sharply, you go home. Stay
where you are! I cried. They both flinched, and Jacintha's chin
trembled and her eyes filled up with tears. I abandoned the search
for a knife, and plunged off upstairs again. The man in the mackintosh was gone. I gave a great gasp of relief, as if I had been
holding my breath all this time, and slumped against the window-
frame. The rain teemed, big drops dancing on the road and
making the surface of the water in the harbour seethe. I heard the
front door open and bang shut, and Madge and the girl appeared
below me and scampered away up the street with their coats over
their heads. I laughed to see them go, the child leaping the
puddles and Madge wallowing in her wake. Then I spotted the
car, parked a little way up the road, on the other side, with two
dim, large, motionless figures seated in the front, their faces
blurred behind the streaming windscreen.

I sat in a chair in the drawing room, gazing before me, my
hands gripping the armrests and my feet placed squarely side by
side on the floor. I do not know how long I stayed like that, in
that glimmering, grey space. I have an impression of hours passing, but surely that cannot be. There was a smell of cigarettes and
stale drink left over from last night. The rain made a soothing
noise. I sank into a kind of trance, a waking sleep. I saw myself,
as a boy, walking across a wooded hill near Coolgrange. It was in

March, I think, one of those blustery, Dutch days with china-blue sky and tumbling, cindery clouds. The trees above me swayed and groaned in the wind. Suddenly there was a great quick rushing noise, and the air darkened, and something like a bird's vast wing crashed down around me, thrashing and whipping. It was a branch that had fallen. I was not hurt, yet I could not move, and stood as if stunned, aghast and shaking. The force and swiftness of the thing had appalled me. It was not fright I felt, but a profound sense of shock at how little my presence had mattered. I might have been no more than a flaw in the air. Ground, branch, wind, sky, world, all these were the precise and necessary co-ordinates of the event. Only I was misplaced, only I had no part to play. And nothing cared. If I had been killed I would have fallen there, face down in the dead leaves, and the day would have gone on as before, as if nothing had happened. For what would have happened would have been nothing, or nothing extraordinary, anyway. Adjustments would have been made. Things would have had to squirm out from under me. A stray ant, perhaps, would explore the bloody chamber of my ear. But the light would have been the same, and the wind would have blown as it had blown, and time's arrow would not have faltered for an instant in its flight. I was amazed. I never forgot that moment. And now another branch was about to fall, I could hear that same rushing noise above me, and feel that same dark wing descending.

The telephone rang, with a sound like glass breaking. There was a hubbub of static on the line. Someone seemed to be asking for Charlie. No, I shouted, no, he's not here! and threw down the receiver. Almost at once the thing began to shrill again. Wait, wait, don't hang up, the voice said, this *is* Charlie. I laughed, of course. I'm down the road, he said, just down the road. I was still laughing. Then there was a silence. The Guards are here, Freddie, he said, they want to speak to you, there's been some sort of mis-understanding. I closed my eyes. Part of me, I realised, had been hoping against hope, unable quite to believe that the game was up. The hum in the wires seemed the very sound of Charlie's anxiety and embarrassment. Charlie, I said, Charlie, Charlie, why are you hiding in a phone box, what did you think I would do to you? I hung up before he could answer.

I was hungry. I went down to the kitchen and made an enor-mous omelette, and devoured half a loaf of bread and drank a

pint of milk. I sat hunched over the table with my elbows planted
on either side of the plate and my head hanging, stuffing the food
into myself with animal indifference. The rain-light made a kind
of dusk in the room. I heard Charlie as soon as he entered the
house – he never was very good at negotiating his way around
the furniture of life. He put his head in at the kitchen door and
essayed a smile, without much success. I motioned to the chair
opposite me and he sat down gingerly. I had started on the cold
remains of last night's boiled potatoes. I was ravenous, I could
not get enough to eat. Charles, I said, you look terrible. He did.
He was grey and shrunken, with livid hollows under his eyes.
The collar of his shirt was buttoned though he wore no tie. He
ran a hand over his jaw and I heard the bristles scrape. He had
been up early, he said, they had got him up and asked him to go
to the station. For a second I did not understand, I thought he
meant the train station. He kept his eyes on my plate, the mess
of spuds there. Something had happened to the silence around
us. I realised that the rain had stopped. God almighty, Freddie,
he said softly, what have you done? He seemed more bemused
than shocked. I fetched another, half-full bottle of milk from the
back of the fridge. Remember, Charlie, I said, those treats you
used to stand me in Jammet's and the Paradiso? He shrugged.
It was not clear if he was listening. The milk had turned. I drank
it anyway. I enjoyed them, you know, those occasions, I said,
even if I didn't always show it. I frowned. Something wrong
there, something off, like the milk. Mendacity always makes my
voice sound curiously dull, a flat blaring at the back of the throat.
And why resurrect now an ancient, unimportant lie? Was I just
keeping my hand in, getting a bit of practice for the big tourney
that lay ahead? No, that's too hard. I was trying to apologise,
I mean in general, and how was I supposed to do that without
lying? He looked so old, sitting slumped there with his head
drooping on its stringy neck and his mouth all down at one
side and his bleared eyes fixed vaguely before him. Oh, fuck it,
Charlie, I said, I'm sorry.

Was it coincidence, I wonder, that the policeman made his
move just at that moment, or had he been listening outside the
door? In films, I have noticed, the chap with the gun always waits
in the corridor, back pressed to the wall, the whites of his eyes
gleaming, until the people inside have had their say. And this one

was, I suspect, a keen student of the cinema. He had a hatchet face and lank black hair and wore a sort of padded military jacket. The sub-machine gun he was holding, a blunt squarish model with only about an inch of barrel, looked remarkably like a toy. Of the three of us he seemed the most surprised. I could not help admiring the deft way he had kicked in the back door. It hung quivering on its hinges, the broken latch lolling like a hound's tongue. Charlie stood up. It's all right, officer, he said. The policeman advanced into the doorway. He was glaring at me. You're fucking under arrest, you are, he said. Behind him, in the yard, the sun came out suddenly, and everything shone and glittered wetly.

More policemen came in then by the front way, there seemed to be a large crowd of them, though they were in fact only four. One of them was the fellow I had seen standing at the harbour wall that morning, I recognised the raincoat. All were carrying guns, of assorted shapes and sizes. I was impressed. They ranged themselves around the walls, looking at me with a kind of bridling curiosity. The door to the hall stood open. Charlie made a move in that direction and one of the policemen in a flat voice said: Hang on. There was silence except for the faint, metallic nattering of police radios outside. We might have been awaiting the entrance of a sovereign. The person who came in at last was a surprise. He was a slight, boyish man of thirty or so, with sandy hair and transparent blue eyes. I noticed at once his hands and feet, which were small, almost dainty. He approached me at an angle somehow, looking at the floor with a peculiar little smile. His name, he said, was Haslet, Detective Inspector Haslet. (Hello, Gerry, hope you don't mind my mentioning your dainty hands – it's true, you know, they are.) The oddness of his manner – that smile, the oblique glance – was due, I realised, to shyness. A shy policeman! It was not what I had expected. He looked about him. There was a moment of awkwardness. No one seemed to know quite what to do next. He turned his downcast eyes in my direction again. Well, he said to no one in particular, are we right? Then all was briskness suddenly. The one with the machine gun – Sergeant Hogg, let's call him – stepped forward and, laying his weapon down on the table, deftly clapped a pair of handcuffs on my wrists. (By the way, they are not as uncomfortable as they might seem – in fact, there was something about being manacled that I found almost soothing, as if it were a more natural state than that of untrammelled freedom.) Charlie frowned. Is that necessary, Inspector? he said. It was such a grand old line, and so splendidly delivered, with just the right degree of solemn hauteur, that for a second I thought it might elicit a small round of applause. I looked at him with renewed admiration. He had thrown off that infirm air of a minute or two ago, and looked, really, quite impressive there in his dark suit and silver wings of hair. Even his unshaven cheeks and tieless collar only served to give him the appearance of a statesman roused from his bed to deal with some grave crisis in the affairs of the nation. Believe me, I am sincere when I say I admire his expertise as a quick-change artist. To place all faith in the mask, that seems to me now the true stamp of refined humanity. Did I say that, or someone else? No matter. I caught his eye, to show him my appreciation, and to ask him – oh, to ask some sort of pardon, I suppose. Afterwards I worried that my glance might have seemed to him more derisive than apologetic, for I think I must have worn a smirk throughout that grotesque kitchen comedy. His mouth was set grimly, and a nerve was twitching in his jaw – he had every right to be furious – but in his eyes all I could see was a sort of dreamy sadness. Then Hogg prodded me in the back, and I was marched quickly down the hall and out into the dazzling light of afternoon.

There was a moment of confusion as the policemen milled on the pavement, craning their stumpy necks and peering sharply this way and that about the harbour. What did they expect, a rescue party? I noticed that they all wore running shoes, except Haslet, the good country boy, in his stout brown brogues. One of his men bumped into him. Too many cops spoil the capture, I said brightly. No one laughed, and Haslet pretended he had not heard. I thought it was awfully witty, of course. I was still in that mood of mad elation, I cannot explain it. I seemed not to walk but bound along, brimful of tigerish energy. Everything sparkled in the rinsed sea-air. The sunlight had a flickering, hallucinatory quality, and I felt I was seeing somehow into the very process of it, catching the photons themselves in flight. We crossed the road. The car I had seen from the upstairs window was still there, the windscreen stippled with raindrops. The two figures sitting in the front watched us with cautious curiosity as we went past.

I laughed – they were not police, but a large man and his large missus, out for a Sunday spin. The woman, chewing slowly on a sweet, goggled at the handcuffs, and I raised my wrists to her in a friendly salute. Hogg poked me again between the shoulder blades and I almost stumbled. I could see I was going to have trouble with him.

There were two cars, unmarked and nondescript, a blue one and a black. The comedy of car doors opening, like beetles' wings. I was put into the back seat with Sergeant Hogg on one side of me and a big, baby-faced bruiser with red hair on the other. Haslet leaned on the door. Did you caution him? he enquired mildly. There was silence. The two detectives in the front seat went very still, as if afraid to stir for fear of laughing. Hogg stared grimly before him, his mouth set in a thin line. Haslet sighed and walked away. The driver carefully started up the engine. You have the right to remain silent blah blah blah, Hogg said venomously, without looking at me. Thank you, Sergeant, I said. I thought this another splendid bit of repartee. We took off from the kerb with a squeal, leaving a puff of tyre-smoke behind us on the air. I wondered if Charlie was watching from the window. I did not look back.

I pause to record that Helmut Behrens has died. Heart. Dear me, this is turning into the Book of the Dead.

How well I remember that journey. I had never travelled so fast in a car. We fairly flew along, weaving through the sluggish Sunday traffic, roaring down the inside lanes, taking corners on two wheels. It was very hot, with all the windows shut, and there was a musky, animal stink. The atmosphere bristled. I was entranced, filled with terror and a kind of glee, hurtling along like this, packed in with these big, sweating, silent men, who sat staring at the road ahead with their arms tightly folded, clasping to them their excitement and their pent-up rage. I could feel them breathing. Speed soothed them: speed was violence. The sun shone in our eyes, a great, dense glare. I knew that at the slightest provocation they would set on me and beat me half to death, they were just waiting for the chance. Even this knowledge, though, was bracing. I had never in my life been so entirely the centre of attention. From now on I would be watched over, I would be tended and fed and listened to, like a big, dangerous baby. No more running, no more hiding and waiting, no more decisions. I snuggled down between my captors, enjoying the hot chafe of metal on my wrists. Yet all the while another part of my mind was registering another version of things – was thinking, for instance, of all that I was losing. I looked at the streets, the buildings, the people, as if for the last time. I, who am a countryman at heart – yes, yes, it's true – and never really knew or cared for the city, even when I lived here, had come to love it now. Love? That is not a word I use very often. Perhaps I mean something else. It was the loss, yes, the imminent loss of – of what, I don't know. I was going to say, *of the community of men*, something solemn and grand like that, but when was I ever a part of *that* gathering? All the same, as we travelled along, some deep cavern of my heart was filling up with the grief of renunciation and departure. I recall especially a spot, near the river, where we were held up for a minute by a faulty traffic light. It was a street of little houses wedged between grey, featureless buildings, warehouses and the like. An old man sat on a window-sill, an infant played in the gutter with a grimy pup. Lines of brilliant washing were strung like bunting across an alleyway. All was still. The light stayed red. And then, as if a secret lever somewhere had been pressed, the whole rackety little scene came slowly, shyly to life. First a green train passed over a red metal bridge. Then two doors in two houses opened at once, and two girls in their Sunday best stepped out into the sunlight. The infant crowed, the pup yapped. A plane flew overhead, and an instant later its shadow skimmed the street. The old man hopped off the window-sill with surprising sprightliness. There was a pause, as if for effect, and then, with a thrilling foghorn blast, there glided into view above the rooftops the white bridge and black smokestack of an enormous, stately ship. It was all so quaint, so innocent and eager, like an illustration from the cover of a child's geography book, that I wanted to laugh out loud, though if I had, I think what would have come out would have sounded more like a sob. The driver swore then, and drove on through the red light, and I turned my head quickly and saw the whole thing swirling away, bright girls and ship, child and dog, old man, that red bridge, swirling away, into the past.

The police station was a kind of mock-Renaissance palace

with a high, grey, many-windowed stone front and an archway leading into a grim little yard where surely once there had been a gibbet. I was hauled brusquely out of the car and led through low doorways and along dim corridors. There was a Sunday-afternoon air of lethargy about the place, and a boarding-school smell. I confess I had expected that the building would be agog at my arrival, that there would be clerks and secretaries and policemen in their braces crowding the hallways to get a look at me, but hardly a soul was about, and the few who passed me by hardly looked at me, and I could not help feeling a little offended. We stopped in a gaunt, unpleasant room, and had to wait some minutes for Inspector Haslet to arrive. Two tall windows, extremely grimy, their lower panes reinforced with wire mesh, gave on to the yard. There was a scarred desk, and a number of wooden chairs. No one sat. We shuffled our feet and looked at the ceiling. Someone cleared his throat. An elderly Guard in shirtsleeves came in. He was bald, and had a sweet, almost child-like smile. I noticed he was wearing a pair of thick black boots, tightly laced and buffed to a high shine. They were a comforting sight, those boots. In the coming days I was to measure my captors by their footwear. Brogues and boots I felt I could trust, running shoes were sinister. Inspector Haslet's car arrived in the yard. Once again we stood about awaiting his entrance. He came in as before, with the same diffident half-smile. I stood in front of the desk while he read out the charges. It was an oddly formal little ceremony. I was reminded of my wedding day, and had to suppress a grin. The bald old Guard typed out the charge sheet on an ancient upright black machine, as if he were laboriously picking out a tune on a piano, the tip of his tongue wedged into a corner of his mouth. When Inspector Haslet asked if I had any-thing to say I shook my head. I would not have known where to begin. Then the ritual was over. There was a kind of general relaxing, and the other detectives, except Hogg, shuffled out. It was like the end of Mass. Hogg produced cigarettes, and offered the grinning packet to Haslet and the Guard at the type-writer, and even, after a brief hesitation, to me. I felt I could not refuse. I tried not to cough. Tell me, I said to Haslet, how did you find me? He shrugged. He had the air of a schoolboy who has scored an embarrassingly high mark in his exams. The girl in the paper shop, he said. You never read only the one story, every day. Ah, I said, yes, of course. It struck me, however, as not at all convincing. Was he covering up for Binkie Behrens, for Anna, even? (He wasn't. They kept silent, to the end.) We smoked for a while, companionably. Twin shafts of sunlight leaned in the windows. A radio was squawking somewhere. I was suddenly, profoundly bored.

Listen, Hogg said, tell us, why did you do it?

I stared at him, startled, and at a loss. It was the one thing I had never asked myself, not with such simple, unavoidable force. Do you know, Sergeant, I said, that's a very good question. His expression did not change, indeed he seemed not to move at all, except that his lank forelock lifted and fell, and for an instant I thought I had suffered a seizure, that something inside me, my liver, or a kidney, had burst of its own accord. More than anything else I felt amazement – that, and a curious, perverse satisfaction. I sank to my knees in a hot mist. I could not breathe. The elderly Guard came from behind the desk and hauled me to my feet – did he say Oops-a-daisy, surely I imagine it? – and led me, stumbling, through a door and down a corridor and shoved me into a noisome, cramped lavatory. I knelt over the bowl and puked up lumps of egg and greasy spuds and a string of curdled milk. The ache in my innards was extraordinary, I could not believe it, I, who should have known all about such things. When there was nothing left to vomit I lay down with my arms clasped around my knees. Ah yes, I thought, this is more like it, this is more what I expected, writhing on the floor in a filthy jakes with my guts on fire. The Guard knocked on the door and wanted to know was I done. He helped me to my feet again and walked me slowly back along the corridor. Always the same, he said, in a chatty tone, stuff comes up you think you never ate.

Hogg was standing at the window with his hands in his pockets, looking out at the yard. He glanced at me over his shoulder. Better now? he said. Inspector Haslet sat in front of the desk, wearing a faraway frown and drumming his fingers on a jumble of papers. He indicated the chair beside him. I sat down gingerly. When he turned sideways to face me our knees were almost touching. He studied a far corner of the ceiling. Well, he said, do you want to talk to me? Oh, I did, I did, I wanted to talk and talk, to confide in him, to pour out all my poor secrets. But what could I say? What secrets? The bald Guard was at his typewriter again, blunt fingers poised over the keys, his eyes fixed on my lips in lively expectation. Hogg too was waiting, standing by the window and jingling the coins in his trousers pocket. I would not have cared what I said to them, they meant nothing to me. The Inspector was a different matter. He kept reminding me of someone I might have known at school, one of those modest, inarticulate heroes who were not only good at sport but at maths as well, yet who shrugged off praise, made shy by their own success and popularity. I had not the heart to confess to him that there was nothing to confess, that there had been no plan worthy of the name, that I had acted almost without thinking from the start. So I made up a rigmarole about having intended to make the robbery seem the work of terrorists, and a lot of other stuff that I am ashamed to repeat here. And then the girl, I said, the woman – for a second I could not think of her name! – and then *Josie*, I said, had ruined everything by trying to stop me taking the picture, by attacking me, by threatening to to to – I ran out of words, and sat and peered at him helplessly, wringing my hands. I so much wanted him to believe me. At that moment his credence seemed to me almost as desirable as forgiveness. There was a silence. He was still considering the corner of the ceiling. He might not have been listening to me at all. Jesus, Hogg said quietly, with no particular emphasis, and the Guard behind the desk cleared his throat. Then Haslet stood up, wincing a little and flexing one knee, and ambled out of the room, and shut the door softly behind him. I could hear him walk away along the corridor at the same leisurely pace. There were voices faintly, his and others. Hogg was looking at me over his shoulder in disgust. You're a right joker, aren't you, he said. I thought of answering him, but decided on prudence instead. Time passed. Someone laughed in a nearby room. A motorcycle started up in the yard. I studied a yellowed notice on the wall dealing with the threat of rabies. I smiled, Mad-dog Montgomery, captured at last.

Inspector Haslet came back then, and held open the door and ushered in a large, red-faced, sweating man in a striped shirt, and another, younger, dangerous-looking fellow, one of Hogg's breed. They gathered round and looked at me, leaning forward intently, breathing, their hands flat on the desk. I told my story again, trying to remember the details so as not to contradict myself. It sounded even more improbable this time.

When I finished there was another silence. I was becoming
accustomed already to these interrogative and, as it seemed to
me, deeply sceptical pauses. The red-faced man, a person of large
authority, I surmised, appeared to be in a rage which he was
controlling only with great difficulty. His name will be – Barker.
He looked at me hard for a long moment. Come on, Freddie, he
said, why did you kill her? I stared back at him. I did not like his
contemptuously familiar tone – *Freddie*, indeed! – but decided to
let it go. I recognised in him one of my own kind, the big, short-
tempered, heavy-breathing people of this world. And anyway,
I was getting tired of all this. I killed her because I could, I said,
what more can I say? We were all startled by that, I as much
as they. The younger one, Hickey – no, Kickham, gave a sort
of laugh. He had a thin, piping, almost musical voice that was
peculiarly at odds with his menacing look and manner. What's-
his-name, he said, he's a queer, is he? I looked at him helplessly.
I did not know what he was talking about. Pardon? I said. French,
he said impatiently, is he a fairy? I laughed, I could not help it.
I did not know whether it was more comic or preposterous, the
idea of Charlie prancing into Wally's and pinching the bottoms
of his boys. (It appears that Wally's creature, Sonny of the emer-
ald hues, had been telling scurrilous lies about poor Charlie's
predilections. Truly, what a wicked world this is.) Oh no, I said,
no – he has an occasional woman. It was just nervousness and
surprise that made me say it, I had not meant to attempt a joke.
No one laughed. They all just went on looking at me, while the
silence tightened and tightened like something being screwed
shut, and then, as if at a signal, they turned on their heels and
trooped out and the door slammed behind them, and I was left
alone with the elderly Guard, who smiled his sweet smile at me
and shrugged. I told him I was feeling nauseous again, and he
went off and fetched me a mug of sticky-sweet tea and a lump of
bread. Why is it that tea, just the look of it, always makes me
feel miserable, like an abandoned waif? And how lost and lonely
everything seemed, this stale room, and the vague noises of
people elsewhere going about their lives, and the sunlight in the
yard, that same thick steady light that shines across the years out
of farthest childhood. All the euphoria I had felt earlier was
gone now.

Haslet returned, alone this time, and sat down beside me at the

desk as before. He had removed his jacket and tie and rolled up
his sleeves. His hair was tousled. He looked more boyish than
ever. He too had a mug of tea, the mug looking enormous in that
small, white hand. I had an image of him as a child, out on some
bog in the wastes of the midlands, stacking turf with his da: quake
of water in the cuttings, smell of smoke and roasting spuds, and
the flat distances the colour of a hare's pelt, and then the enormous, vertical sky stacked with luminous bundles of cloud.

Now, he said, let's start again.

We went on for hours. I was almost happy, sitting there with
him, pouring out my life story, as the shafts of sunlight in the
windows lengthened and the day waned. He was infinitely
patient. There seemed to be nothing, no detail, however minute
or enigmatic, that did not interest him. No, that's not quite it.
It was as if he were not really interested at all. He greeted everything, every strand and knot of my story, with the same passive
air of toleration and that same faint bemused little smile. I told
him about knowing Anna Behrens, and about her father, about
his diamond mines and his companies and his priceless art collection. I watched him carefully, trying to judge how much of this
was new to him, but it was no good, he gave nothing away. Yet
he must have spoken to them, must have taken statements and all
the rest of it. Surely they would have told him about me, surely
they were not protecting me still. He rubbed his cheek, and
gazed again into the corner of the ceiling. Self-made man, is he,
he said, this Behrens? Oh Inspector, I said, aren't we all? At that
he gave me a peculiar look, and stood up. I noticed again that
brief grimace of pain. Bad knee. Footballer. Sunday afternoons,
the shouts muffled in grey air, the flat thud of leather on leather.
Now what, I said, what happens now? I did not want him to
leave me yet. What would I do when the darkness came? He said
I should give the Guard my solicitor's name, so he could be
told I was here. I nodded. I had no solicitor, of course, but I felt
I could not say so – everything was so relaxed and chummy,
and I did not want to create any awkwardnesses. Anyway, I was
fully intending to conduct my own defence, and already saw
myself making brilliant and impassioned speeches from the dock.
Is there anything else I should do, I said, frowning up at him
seriously, is there anyone else I should tell? (Oh, I was so good,
so compliant, what a warm thrill of agreeableness I felt, deferring

like this to this good chap!) He gave me that peculiar look again, there was irritation and impatience in it, but a certain ironic amusement too, and even a hint of complicity. What you can do, he said, is get your story straight, without the frills and fancy bits. What do you mean, I said, what do you mean? I was dismayed. Bob Cherry had suddenly turned harsh, had almost for a moment become Mr Quelch. You know very well what I mean, he said. Then he went off, and Hogg came back, and he and the elderly Guard — oh, call him something, for God's sake — he and Cunningham, old Cunningham the desk sergeant, took me down to the cells.

Am I still handcuffed?

I do not know why I say they took me *down* (well, I do, of course) for we simply walked a little way along a corridor, past the lavatory, and through a steel gate. I confess I felt a stab of fear, but that was quickly replaced by surprise: it was all just as I expected! There really are bars, there really is a bucket, and a pallet with a striped, bare mattress, and graffiti on the scarred walls. There was even a stubbled old-timer, standing white-knuckled at the door of his cell, who peered out at me in word-less, angry derision. I was given a piece of soap and a tiny towel and three pieces of shiny toilet paper. In return I surrendered my belt and shoelaces. I saw at once the importance of this ritual. Cowering there, with the tongues of my shoes hanging out, clutching in one hand the waistband of my trousers and holding in the other, for all to see, the fundamental aids to my most private functions, I was no longer wholly human. I hasten to say this seemed to me quite proper, to be, indeed, a kind of setting to rights, an official and outward definition of what had been the case, in my case, all along. I had achieved my apotheosis. Even old Cunningham, even Sergeant Hogg, seemed to recognise it, for they treated me now, brusquely, with a sort of truculent, abstracted regard, as if they were not my jailers but my keepers, rather. I might have been a sick old toothless lion. Hogg put his hands in his pockets and went off whistling. I sat down on the side of the cot. Time passed. It was very quiet. The old boy in the other cell asked me my name. I did not answer him. Well fuck you, then, he said. Dusk came on. I have always loved that hour of the day, when that soft, muslin light seeps upward, as if out of the earth itself, and everything seems to grow thoughtful and turn away. It was almost dark when Sergeant Hogg came back, and handed me a grubby sheet of foolscap. He had been eating chips, I could smell them on his breath. I peered in bafflement at the ill-typed page. That's your confession, Hogg said. Feel like signing it? The lag next door cackled grimly. What are you talking about? I said. These are not my words. He shrugged, and belched into his fist. Suit yourself, he said, you'll be going down for life anyway. Then he went off again. I sat down and examined this strange document. Oh, well-named Cunningham! Behind the mask of the bald old codger a fiendish artist had been at work, the kind of artist I could never be, direct yet subtle, a master of the spare style, of the art that conceals art. I marvelled at how he had turned everything to his purpose, misspellings, clumsy syntax, even the atrocious typing. Such humility, such deference, such ruthless suppression of the ego for the sake of the text. He had taken my story, with all its – what was it Haslet said? – with all its frills and fancy bits, and pared it down to stark essentials. It was an account of my crime I hardly recognised, and yet I believed it. He had made a mur-derer of me. I would have signed it there and then, but I had nothing to write with. I even searched my clothing for some-thing sharp, a pin or something, with which to stick myself, and scrawl my signature in blood. But what matter, it did not require my endorsement. Reverently I folded the page in four and placed it under the mattress at the end where my head would be. Then I undressed and lay down naked in the shadows and folded my hands on my breast, like a marble knight on a tomb, and closed my eyes. I was no longer myself. I can't explain it, but it's true. I was no longer myself.

That first night in captivity was turbulent. I slept fitfully, it was not really sleep, but a helpless tossing and sliding on the surface of a dark sea. I could sense the deeps beneath me, the black, boundless deeps. The hour before dawn was, as always, the worst. I masturbated repeatedly – forgive these squalid details – not for pleasure, really, but to exhaust myself. What a motley little band of manikins I conjured up to join me in these melancholy frot-tings. Daphne was there, of course, and Anna Behrens, amused and faintly shocked at the things I was making her do, and poor Foxy as well, who wept again in my arms, as I, silent and stealthy about my felon's work, pressed her and pressed her against that door in the empty, moonlit room of my imagination. But there were others, too, whom I would not have expected: Madge's niece, for instance – remember Madge's niece? – and the big girl with the red neck I had followed through the city streets – remember *her*? – and even, God forgive me, my mother and the stable-girl. And in the end, when they all had come and gone, and I lay empty on my prison bed, there rose up out of me again, like the spectre of an onerous and ineluctable task, the picture of that mysterious, dark doorway, and the invisible presence in it, yearning to appear, to be there. To live.

MONDAY MORNING. Ah, Monday morning. The ashen light, the noise, the sense of pointless but compulsory haste. I think it will be Monday morning when I am received in Hell. I was wakened early by a policeman bearing another mug of tea and lump of bread. I had been dozing, it was like being held fast in the embrace of a large, hot, rank-smelling animal. I knew at once exactly where I was, there was no mistaking the place. The policeman was young, an enormous boy with a tiny head, when I opened my eyes first and looked up at him he seemed to tower above me almost to the ceiling. He said something incomprehensible and went away. I sat on the edge of the cot and held my head in my hands. My mouth was foul, and there was an ache behind my eyes and a wobbly sensation in the region of my diaphragm. I wondered if this nausea would be with me for the rest of my life. Wan sunlight fell at a slant through the bars of my cage. I was cold. I draped a blanket around my shoulders and squatted over the bucket, my knees trembling. I would not have been surprised if a crowd had gathered in the corridor to laugh at me. I kept thinking, yes, this is it, this is how it will be from now on. It was almost gratifying, in a horrible sort of way.

Sergeant Cunningham came to fetch me for the first of that day's inquisitions. I had washed as best I could at the filthy sink in the corner. I asked him if I might borrow a razor. He laughed, shaking his head at the idea, the richness of it. He thought I really was a card. I admired his good humour: he had been here all night, his shift was only ending now. I shuffled after him along the corridor, clutching my trousers to keep them from falling down. The dayroom was filled with a kind of surly pandemonium. Typewriters clacked, and short-wave radios snivelled in adenoidal bursts, and people strode in and out of doorways, talking over their shoulders, or crouched at desks and shouted into telephones. A hush fell when I came through – no, not a hush, exactly, but a downward modulation in the noise. Word, obviously, had spread. They did not stare at me, I suppose that would have been unprofessional, but they took me in, all the same. I saw myself in their eyes, a big, confused creature, like a dancing bear, shambling along at the steel-tipped heels of Cunningham's friendly boots. He opened a door and motioned me into a square, grey room. There was a plastic-topped table and two chairs. Well, he said, I'll be seeing you, and he winked and withdrew his head and shut the door. I sat down carefully, placing my hands flat before me on the table. Time passed. I was surprised how calmly I could sit, just waiting. It was as if I were not fully there, as if I had become detached somehow from my physical self. The room was like the inside of a skull. The hubbub in the dayroom might have been coming to me from another planet.

Barker and Kickham were the first to arrive. Barker today wore a blue suit which had been cut in great broad swathes, as if it were intended not for wearing but to house a collection of things, boxes, perhaps. He was red-faced and in a sweat already. Kickham had on the same leather jacket and dark shirt that he had worn yesterday – he did not strike me as a man much given to changing his clothes. They wanted to know why I had not signed the confession. I had forgotten about it, had left it under the mattress, but I told them, I don't know why, that I had torn it up. There was another of those brief, stentorian silences, while they stood over me, clenching their fists and breathing heavily down their nostrils. The air rippled with suppressed violence. Then they trooped out and I was left alone again. Next to appear was an elderly chap in cavalry twill and a natty little hat, and a narrow-eyed, brawny young man who looked like the older one's disgruntled son. They stood just inside the door and studied me carefully for a long moment, as if measuring me for something. Then Detective Twill advanced and sat down opposite me, and crossed his legs, and took off his hat, revealing a flattish bald head, waxen and peculiarly pitted, like that of an ailing baby. He produced a pipe and lighted it with grave deliberation, then recrossed his legs and settled himself more comfortably, and began to ask me a series of cryptic questions, which after some time I realised were aimed at discovering what I might know about Charlie French and his acquaintances. I answered as circumspectly as I could, not knowing what it was they wanted to know – I suspect they didn't, either. I kept smiling at them both, to show how willing I was, how compliant. The younger one, still standing by the door, took notes. Or at least he went through the motions of writing in a notebook, for I had an odd feeling that the whole thing was a sham, intended to distract or intimidate me. All that happened, however, was that I grew bored – I could not take them seriously – and got muddled, and began to contradict myself. After a while they too seemed to grow discouraged, and eventually left. Then my chum Inspector Haslet came sidling in with his shy smile and averted glance. My God, I said, who were they? Branch, he said. He sat down, looked at the floor, drummed his fingers on the table. Listen, I said, I'm worried, my wife, I – He wasn't listening, wasn't interested. He brought up the matter of my confession. Why hadn't I signed it? He spoke quietly, he might have been talking about the weather. Save a lot of trouble, you know, he said. Suddenly I flew into a rage, I don't know what came over me, I banged my fist on the table and jumped up and shouted at him that I would do nothing, sign nothing, until I got some answers. I really did say that: *until I get some answers!* At once, of course, the anger evaporated and I sat down again sheepishly, biting on a knuckle. The ruffled air subsided. Your wife, Haslet said mildly, is getting on a plane – he consulted his watch – just about now. I stared at him. Oh, I said. I was relieved, of course, but not really surprised. I knew all along Señor what's-his-name would be too much of a gentleman not to let her go.

It was noon when Maolseachlainn arrived, though he had the rumpled air of having just got out of bed. He always looks like that, it is another of his endearing characteristics. The first thing that struck me was how alike we were in build, two big soft broad heavy men. The table groaned between us when we leaned forward over it, the chairs gave out little squeaks of alarm under our ponderous behinds. I liked him at once. He said I must be wondering who had engaged him on my behalf. I nodded vigorously, though in truth no such thought had entered my head. He grew shifty then, and mumbled something about my mother, and some work he claimed to have done for her in some unspecified period of the past. It was to be a long time before I would discover, to my surprise and no little dismay, that in fact it was Charlie French who arranged it all, who called my mother that

Sunday evening and broke the news to her of my arrest, and told her to contact straight away his good friend Maolseachlainn Mac Giolla Gunna, the famous counsel. It was Charles too who paid, and is paying still, Mac's not inconsiderable fees. He puts the money through the bank, and my mother, or it must be that stable-girl, now, I suppose, sends it on as if it were coming from Coolgrange. (Sorry to have kept this bit from you, Mac, but it's what Charlie wanted.) You made some sort of confession, Maolseachlainn was saying, is that right? I told him about Cunningham's marvellous document. I must have grown excited in the telling, for his brow darkened, and he closed his eyes behind his half-glasses as if in pain and held up a hand to silence me. You'll sign nothing, he said, nothing – are you mad? I hung my head. But I'm guilty, I said quietly, I *am* guilty. This he pretended not to hear. Listen to me, he said, listen. You will sign nothing, say nothing, do nothing. You will enter a plea of not guilty. I opened my mouth to protest, but he was not to be interrupted. You will plead not guilty, he said, and when I judge the moment opportune you will change your submission, and plead guilty to manslaughter. Do you understand? He was looking at me coldly over his glasses. (This was early days, before he had become my friend.) I shook my head. It doesn't seem right, I said. He gave a sort of laugh. Right! he said, and did not add: that's rich, coming from you. We were silent for a moment. My stomach made a pinging sound. I felt sick and hungry at the same time. By the way, I said, have you spoken to my mother, is she coming to see me? This also he pretended not to hear. He put away his papers, and took off his glasses and squeezed the bridge of his nose. Was there anything I wanted? Now it was my turn to snicker. I mean is there anything I can have them get for you, he said, in a primly disapproving tone. A razor, I said, and they could give me back my belt, I'm not going to hang myself. He stood up to leave. Suddenly I wanted to detain him. Thank you, I said, so fervently that he paused and stared at me owlishly. I meant to kill her, you know, I said, I have no explanation, and no excuse. He just sighed.

I was brought to court in the afternoon. Inspector Haslet and two uniformed Guards accompanied me. My hand where I had caught it on the rose bush had become infected. O Frederick, thou art sick. I have a strangely hazy recollection of that first appearance. I had expected the courtroom to be rather grand, something like a small church, with oaken pews and a carved ceiling and an air of pomp and seriousness, and I was disappointed when it turned out to be little more than a shabby office, the kind of place where obscure permits are issued by incompetent clerks. When I was led in, there was a sort of irritable flurry of activity which I took to be a general making-ready, but which was, as I discovered to my surprise, the hearing itself. It cannot have lasted more than a minute or two. The judge, who wore an ordinary business suit, was a jolly old boy with whiskers and a red nose. He must have had a reputation as a wit, for when he fixed me with a merry eye and said, Ah, Mr Montgomery, the whole place fairly rocked with amusement. I smiled politely, to show him I could take a joke, even if I did not get it. A Guard prodded me in the back, I stood up, sat down, stood up again, then it was over. I looked about me in surprise. I felt I must have missed something. Maolseachlainn was asking for bail. Judge Fielding gently shook his head, as if he were reproving a forward child. Ah no, he said, I think not, sir. That provoked another tremor of merriment in the court. Well, I was glad they were all having such a good time. The Guard behind me was saying something, but I could not concentrate, for there was a horrible, hollow sensation in my chest, and I realised that I was about to weep. I felt like a child, or a very old man. Maolseachlainn touched my arm. I turned away helplessly. Come on now, the Guard said, not unkindly, and I blundered after him. Everything swam. Haslet was behind me, I knew his step by now. In the street a little crowd had gathered. How did they know who I was, which court I would be in, the time at which I would appear? When they caught sight of me they gave a cry, a sort of ululant wail of awe and execration that made my skin prickle. I was so confused and frightened I forgot myself and waved – I waved to them! God knows what I thought I was doing. I suppose it was meant as a placatory gesture, an animal sign of submission and retreat. It only made them more furious, of course. They shook their fists, they howled. One or two of them seemed about to break from the rest and fly at me. A woman spat, and called me a dirty bastard. I just stood there, nodding and waving like a clockwork man, with a terrified grin fixed on my face. That was when I realised, for the first time, it was *one of theirs* I had killed.

It had rained while I was inside, and now the sun was shining again. I remember the glare of the wet road, and a cloud stealthily disappearing over the rooftops, and a dog skirting the angry crowd with a worried look in its eye. Always the incidental things, you see, the little things. Then the blanket was thrown over me and I was pushed head-first into the police car and we sped away, the tyres hissing. Hee-haw, hee-haw. In the hot, woolly darkness I wept my fill.

Prison. This place. I have described it already.

My first visitor was a surprise. When they told me it was a woman I expected Daphne, straight from the airport, or else my mother, and at first when I came into the visiting room I did not recognise her. She seemed younger than ever, in her shapeless pullover and plaid skirt and sensible shoes. She had the unformed, palely freckled look of a schoolgirl, the dullard of the class, who cries in the dorm at night and is mad on ponies. Only her marvellous, flame-coloured hair proclaimed her a woman. Jenny! I said, and she blushed. I took her hands in mine. I was absurdly pleased to see her. I did not know then that she would soon prove my usurper. Joanne, actually, she mumbled, and bit her lip. I laughed in embarrassment. Joanne, I said, of course, forgive me, I'm so confused just now. We sat down. I beamed and beamed. I felt light-hearted, almost skittish. I might have been the visitor, an old bachelor friend of the family, come to see the poor duckling on the school open day. She had brought my bag from Cool-grange. It looked strange to me, familiar and yet alien, as if it had been on an immense, transfiguring voyage, to another planet, another galaxy, since I had seen it last. I enquired after my mother. I was tactful enough not to ask why she had not come. Tell her I'm sorry, I said. It sounded ridiculous, as if I were apologising for a broken appointment, and we looked away from each other furtively and were silent for a long, awkward moment. I have a nickname in here already, I said, they call me Monty, of course. She smiled, and I was pleased. When she smiles, biting her lip like that, she is more than ever like a child. I cannot believe she is a schemer. I suspect she was as surprised as I when the will was read. I find it hard to see her as the mistress of Coolgrange. Perhaps that is what my mother intended – after *her*, the drip. Ah, that is unworthy of me, my new seriousness. I do not hate her for disinheriting me. I think that in her way she was trying to teach me something, to make me look more closely at things, perhaps, to pay more attention to people, such as this poor clumsy girl, with her freckles and her timid smile and her almost invisible eyebrows. I am remembering what Daphne said to me only yesterday, through her tears, it has lodged in my mind like a thorn: *You knew nothing about us, nothing!* She's right, of course. She was talking about America, about her and Anna Behrens and all that, but it's true in general – I know nothing. Yet I am trying. I watch, and listen, and brood. Now and then I am afforded a glimpse into what seems a new world, but which I realise has been there all along, without my noticing. In these explorations my friend Eddie is a valuable guide. I have not mentioned Eddie before, have I? He attached himself to me early on, I think he is a little in love with me. He's nineteen – muscles, oiled black hair, a killer's shapely hands, like mine. Our trials are due to open on the same day, he takes this as a lucky omen. He is charged with murder and multiple rape. He insists on his innocence, but cannot suppress a guilty little smile. I believe he is secretly proud of his crimes. Yet a kind of innocence shines out of him, as if there is something inside, some tiny, precious part, that nothing can besmirch. When I consider Eddie I can almost believe in the existence of the soul. He has been in and out of custody since he was a child, and is a repository of prison lore. He tells me of the various ingenious methods of smuggling in dope. For instance, before the glass screens were put up, wives and girlfriends used to hide in their mouths little plastic bags of heroin, which were passed across during lingering kisses, swallowed, and sicked-up later, in the latrines. I was greatly taken with the idea, it affected me deeply. Such need, such passion, such charity and daring – when have I ever known the like?

What was I saying. I am becoming so vague. It happens to all of us in here. It is a kind of defence, this creeping absent-mindedness, this torpor, which allows us to drop off instantly, anywhere, at any time, into brief, numb stretches of sleep.

Joanne. She came to see me, brought me my bag. I was glad to have it. They had confiscated most of what was in it, the prison authorities, but there were some shirts, a bar of soap – the scented smell of it struck me like a blow – a pair of shoes, my books. I clutched these things, these icons, to my heart, and grieved for the dead past.

But grief, that kind of grief is the great danger, in here. It saps the will. Those who give way to it grow helpless, a wasting lethargy comes over them. They are like mourners for whom the period of mourning will not end. I saw this danger, and determined to avoid it. I would work, I would study. The theme was there, ready-made. I had Daphne bring me big thick books on Dutch painting, not only the history but the techniques, the secrets of the masters. I studied accounts of the methods of grinding colours, of the trade in oils and dyes, of the flax industry in Flanders. I read the lives of the painters and their patrons. I became a minor expert on the Dutch republic in the seventeenth century. But in the end it was no good: all this learning, this information, merely built up and petrified, like coral encrusting a sunken wreck. How could mere facts compare with the amazing knowledge that had flared out at me as I stood and stared at the painting lying on its edge in the ditch where I dropped it that last time? That knowledge, that knowingness, I could not have lived with. I look at the reproduction, pinned to the wall above me here, but something is dead in it. Something is dead.

It was in the same spirit of busy exploration that I pored for long hours over the newspaper files in the prison library. I read every word devoted to my case, read and reread them, chewed them over until they turned to flavourless mush in my mind. I learned of Josie Bell's childhood, of her schooldays – pitifully brief – of her family and friends. Neighbours spoke well of her. She was a quiet girl. She had almost married once, but something had gone wrong, her fiancé went to England and did not return. First she worked in her own village, as a shopgirl. Then, before going to Whitewater, she was in Dublin for a while, where she was a chambermaid in the Southern Star Hotel. The Southern Star! – my God, I could have gone there when I was at Charlie's, could have taken a room, could have slept in a bed that she had once made! I laughed at myself. What would I have learned? There would have been no more of her there, for me, than there was in the newspaper stories, than there had been that day when I turned and saw her for the first time, standing in the open french window with the blue and gold of summer at her back, than there was when she crouched in the car and I hit her again and again and her blood spattered the window. This is the worst, the essential sin, I think, the one for which there will be no forgiveness: that I never imagined her vividly enough, that I never made her be there sufficiently, that I did not make her live. Yes, that failure of imagination is my real crime, the one that made the others possible. What I told that policeman is true – I killed her because I could kill her, and I could kill her because for me she was not alive. And so my task now is to bring her back to life. I am not sure what that means, but it strikes me with the force of an unavoidable imperative. How am I to make it come about, this act of parturition? Must I imagine her from the start, from infancy? I am puzzled, and not a little fearful, and yet there is something stirring in me, and I am strangely excited. I seem to have taken on a new weight and density. I feel gay and at the same time wonderfully serious. I am big with possibilities. I am living for two.

I have decided: I will not be swayed: I will plead guilty to murder in the first degree. I think it is the right thing to do. Daphne, when I told her, burst into tears at once. I was astonished, astonished and appalled. What about *me*, she cried, what about the child? I said, as mildly as I could, that I thought I had already destroyed their lives, and that the best thing I could do was to stay away from the two of them for as long as possible – forever, even – so that she might have the chance to start afresh. This, it seems, was not tactful. She just cried and cried, sitting there beyond the glass, clutching a sodden tissue in her fist, her shoulders shaking. Then it all came out, the rage and the shame, I could not make out the half of it through her sobs. She went back over the years. What I had done, and not done. How little I knew, how little I understood. I sat and gazed at her, aghast, my mouth open. I could not speak. How was it possible, that I could have been so wrong about her, all this time? How could I not have seen that behind her reticence there was all this passion, this pain? I was thinking about a pub I had passed by late on one of my night rambles through the city in that week before I was captured. It was in, I don't know, Stoneybatter, somewhere like that, a working-class pub with protective steel mesh covering the windows and old vomit-stains around the doorway. As I went past, a drunk

stumbled out, and for a second, before the door swung shut
again, I had a glimpse inside. I walked on without pausing, carrying the scene in my head. It was like something by Jan Steen:
the smoky light, the crush of red-faced drinkers, the old boys
propping up the bar, the fat woman singing, displaying a mouth-
ful of broken teeth. A kind of slow amazement came over me, a
kind of bafflement and grief, at how firmly I felt myself excluded
from that simple, ugly, roistering world. That is how I seem to
have spent my life, walking by open, noisy doorways, and passing
on, into the darkness. – And yet there are moments too that allow
me to think I am not wholly lost. The other day, for instance, on
the way to yet one more remand hearing, I shared the police van
with an ancient wino who had been arrested the night before,
so he told me, for killing his friend. I could not imagine him
having a friend, much less killing one. He talked to me at length
as we bowled along, though most of what he said was gibberish.
He had a bloodied eye, and an enormous, weeping sore on his
mouth. I looked out through the barred window at the city
streets going past, doing my best to ignore him. Then, when we
were rounding a sharp bend, he fell off his seat on top of me, and
I found myself holding the old brute in my arms. The smell was
appalling, of course, and the rags he wore had a slippery feel to
them that made me clench my teeth, but still I held him, and
would not let him fall to the floor, and I even – surely I am
embroidering – I think I may even have clasped him to me for a
moment, in a gesture of, I don't know, of sympathy, of comrade-
ship, of solidarity, something like that. Yes, an explorer, that's
what I am, glimpsing a new continent from the prow of a sinking ship. And don't mistake me, I don't imagine for a second
that such incidents as this, such forays into the new world, will
abate my guilt one whit. But maybe they signify something for
the future.

Should I destroy that last paragraph? No, what does it matter,
let it stand.

Daphne brought me one of Van's drawings. I have pinned it
up on the wall here. It is a portrait of me, she says. One huge,
club foot, sausage fingers, a strangely calm, cyclopean eye. Quite
a good likeness, really, when I think about it. She also brought
me a startling piece of news. Joanne has invited her and the child
to come and live at Coolgrange. They are going to set up house

together, my wife and the stable-girl. (How quaintly things contrive to make what seems an ending!) I am not displeased, which surprises me. Apparently I am to live there also, when I get out. Oh, I can just see myself, in Wellingtons and a hat, mucking out the stables. But I said nothing. Poor Daphne, if only – ah yes, if only.

Maolseachlainn too was horrified when I told him of my decision. Don't worry, I said, I'll plead guilty, but I don't want any concessions. He could not understand it, and I had not the energy to explain. It's what I want, that's all. It's what I must do. Apollo's ship has sailed for Delos, the stern crowned with laurel, and I must serve my term. By the way, Mac, I said, I owe a plate to Charlie French. He did not get the joke, but he smiled anyway. She wasn't dead, you know, when I left her, I said. I wasn't man enough to finish her off. I'd have done as much for a dog. (It's true – is there no end to the things I must confess?) He nodded, trying not to show his disgust, or perhaps it was just shock he was hiding. Hardy people, he said, they don't die easily. Then he gathered up his papers and turned to go. We shook hands. The occasion seemed to require that small formality.

Oh, by the way, the plot: it almost slipped my mind. Charlie French bought my mother's pictures cheap and sold them dear to Binkie Behrens, then bought them cheap from Binkie and sold them on to Max Molyneaux. Something like that. Does it matter? Dark deeds, dark deeds. Enough.

Time passes. I eat time. I imagine myself a kind of grub, calmly and methodically consuming the future, what the world outside calls the future. I must be careful not to give in to despair, to that aboulia which has been a threat always to everything I tried to do. I have looked for so long into the abyss, I feel sometimes it is the abyss that is looking into me. I have my good days, and my bad. I think of the monsters on whose side my crime has put me, the killers, the torturers, the dirty little beasts who stand by and watch it happen, and I wonder if it would not be better simply to stop. But I have my task, my term. Today, in the work-shop, I caught her smell, faint, sharp, metallic, unmistakable. It is the smell of metal-polish – she must have been doing the silver that day. I was so happy when I identified it! Anything seemed possible. It even seemed that someday I might wake up and see, coming forward from the darkened room into the frame of that doorway which is always in my mind now, a child, a girl, one whom I will recognise at once, without the shadow of a doubt.

It is spring. Even in here we feel it, the quickening in the air. I have some plants in my window, I like to watch them, feeding on the light. The trial takes place next month. It will be a quick affair. The newspapers will be disappointed. I thought of trying to publish this, my testimony. But no. I have asked Inspector Haslet to put it into my file, with the other, official fictions. He came to see me today, here in my cell. He picked up the pages, hefted them in his hand. It was to be my defence, I said. He gave me a wry look. Did you put in about being a scientist, he said, and knowing the Behrens woman, and owing money, all that stuff? I smiled. It's my story, I said, and I'm sticking to it. He laughed at that. Come on, Freddie, he said, how much of it is true? It was the first time he had called me by my name. True, Inspector? I said. All of it. None of it. Only the shame.

THE SEA

To Colm, Douglas, Ellen, Alice

I

THEY DEPARTED, the gods, on the day of the strange tide. All morning under a milky sky the waters in the bay had swelled and swelled, rising to unheard-of heights, the small waves creeping over parched sand that for years had known no wetting save for rain and lapping the very bases of the dunes. The rusted hulk of the freighter that had run aground at the far end of the bay longer ago than any of us could remember must have thought it was being granted a relaunch. I would not swim again, after that day. The seabirds mewled and swooped, unnerved, it seemed, by the spectacle of that vast bowl of water bulging like a blister, lead-blue and malignantly agleam. They looked unnaturally white, that day, those birds. The waves were depositing a fringe of soiled yellow foam along the waterline. No sail marred the high horizon. I would not swim, no, not ever again.

Someone has just walked over my grave. Someone.

The name of the house is the Cedars, as of old. A bristling clump of those trees, monkey-brown with a tarry reek, their trunks nightmarishly tangled, still grows at the left side, facing across an untidy lawn to the big curved window of what used to be the living room but which Miss Vavasour prefers to call, in landladyese, the lounge. The front door is at the opposite side, opening on to a square of oil-stained gravel behind the iron gate that is still painted green, though rust has reduced its struts to a tremulous filigree. I am amazed at how little has changed in the more than fifty years that have gone by since I was last here. Amazed, and disappointed, I would go so far as to say appalled, for reasons that are obscure to me, since why should I desire change, I who have come back to live amidst the rubble of the past? I wonder why the house was built like that, sideways-on, turning a pebble-dashed windowless white end-wall to the road; perhaps in former times, before the railway, the road ran in a different orientation altogether, passing directly in front of the

front door, anything is possible. Miss V. is vague on dates but
thinks a cottage was first put up here early in the last century,
I mean the century before last, I am losing track of the millennia,
and then was added on to haphazardly over the years. That
would account for the jumbled look of the place, with small
rooms giving on to bigger ones, and windows facing blank walls,
and low ceilings throughout. The pitch pine floors sound a
nautical note, as does my spindle-backed swivel chair. I imagine
an old seafarer dozing by the fire, landlubbered at last, and the
winter gale rattling the window frames. Oh, to be him. To have
been him.

When I was here all those years ago, in the time of the gods,
the Cedars was a summer house, for rent by the fortnight or the
month. During all of June each year a rich doctor and his large,
raucous family infested it – we did not like the doctor's loud-
voiced children, they laughed at us and threw stones from behind
the unbreachable barrier of the gate – and after them a mysterious middle-aged couple came, who spoke to no one, and grimly
walked their sausage dog in silence at the same time every morning down Station Road to the strand. August was the most
interesting month at the Cedars, for us. The tenants then were
different each year, people from England or the Continent, the
odd pair of honeymooners whom we would try to spy on, and
once even a fit-up troupe of itinerant theatre people who were
putting on an afternoon show in the village's galvanised-tin
cinema. And then, that year, came the family Grace.

The first thing I saw of them was their motor car, parked on
the gravel inside the gate. It was a low-slung, scarred and battered
black model with beige leather seats and a big spoked polished
wood steering wheel. Books with bleached and dog-eared covers
were thrown carelessly on the shelf under the sportily raked back
window, and there was a touring map of France, much used. The
front door of the house stood wide open, and I could hear voices
inside, downstairs, and from upstairs the sound of bare feet running on floorboards and a girl laughing. I had paused by the gate,
frankly eavesdropping, and now suddenly a man with a drink in
his hand came out of the house. He was short and top-heavy, all
shoulders and chest and big round head, with close-cut, crinkled,
glittering-black hair with flecks of premature grey in it and a
pointed black beard likewise flecked. He wore a loose green shirt

unbuttoned and khaki shorts and was barefoot. His skin was so deeply tanned by the sun it had a purplish sheen. Even his feet, I noticed, were brown on the insteps; the majority of fathers in my experience were fish-belly white below the collar-line. He set his tumbler – ice-blue gin and ice cubes and a lemon slice – at a perilous angle on the roof of the car and opened the passenger door and leaned inside to rummage for something under the dashboard. In the unseen upstairs of the house the girl laughed again and gave a wild, warbling cry of mock-panic, and again there was the sound of scampering feet. They were playing chase, she and the voiceless other. The man straightened and took his glass of gin from the roof and slammed the car door. Whatever it was he had been searching for he had not found. As he turned back to the house his eye caught mine and he winked. He did not do it in the way that adults usually did, at once arch and ingratiating. No, this was a comradely, a conspiratorial wink, masonic, almost, as if this moment that we, two strangers, adult and boy, had shared, although outwardly without significance, without content, even, nevertheless had meaning. His eyes were an extraordinary pale transparent shade of blue. He went back inside then, already talking before he was through the door. 'Damned thing,' he said, 'seems to be ...' and was gone. I lingered a moment, scanning the upstairs windows. No face appeared there.

That, then, was my first encounter with the Graces: the girl's voice coming down from on high, the running footsteps, and the man here below with the blue eyes giving me that wink, jaunty, intimate and faintly satanic.

Just now I caught myself at it again, that thin, wintry whistling through the front teeth that I have begun to do recently. *Deedle deedle deedle*, it goes, like a dentist's drill. My father used to whistle like that, am I turning into him? In the room across the corridor Colonel Blunden is playing the wireless. He favours the afternoon talk programmes, the ones in which irate members of the public call up to complain about villainous politicians and the price of drink and other perennial irritants. 'Company,' he says shortly, and clears his throat, looking a little abashed, his protuberant, parboiled eyes avoiding mine, even though I have issued no challenge. Does he lie on the bed while he listens? Hard to picture him there in his thick grey woollen socks, twiddling

his toes, his tie off and shirt collar agape and hands clasped behind
that stringy old neck of his. Out of his room he is vertical man
itself, from the soles of his much-mended glossy brown brogues
to the tip of his conical skull. He has his hair cut every Saturday
morning by the village barber, short-back-and-sides, no quarter
given, only a hawkish stiff grey crest left on top. His long-lobed
leathery ears stick out, they look as if they had been dried and
smoked; the whites of his eyes too have a smoky yellow tinge.
I can hear the buzz of voices on his wireless but cannot make out
what they say. I may go mad here. *Deedle deedle.*

Later that day, the day the Graces came, or the following one, or
the one following that, I saw the black car again, recognised it at
once as it went bounding over the little humpbacked bridge that
spanned the railway line. It is still there, that bridge, just beyond
the station. Yes, things endure, while the living lapse. The car
was heading out of the village in the direction of the town, I shall
call it Ballymore, a dozen miles away. The town is Ballymore,
this village is Ballyless, ridiculously, perhaps, but I do not care.
The man with the beard who had winked at me was at the wheel,
saying something and laughing, his head thrown back. Beside
him a woman sat with an elbow out of the rolled-down window,
her head back too, pale hair shaking in the gusts from the window, but she was not laughing only smiling, that smile she
reserved for him, sceptical, tolerant, languidly amused. She wore
a white blouse and sunglasses with white plastic rims and was
smoking a cigarette. Where am I, lurking in what place of van-
tage? I do not see myself. They were gone in a moment, the car's
sashaying back-end scooting around a bend in the road with a
spurt of exhaust smoke. Tall grasses in the ditch, blond like the
woman's hair, shivered briefly and returned to their former
dreaming stillness.

I walked down Station Road in the sunlit emptiness of afternoon. The beach at the foot of the hill was a fawn shimmer under
indigo. At the seaside all is narrow horizontals, the world reduced
to a few long straight lines pressed between earth and sky.
I approached the Cedars circumspectly. How is it that in childhood everything new that caught my interest had an aura of the
uncanny, since according to all the authorities the uncanny is not
some new thing but a thing known returning in a different form,

become a revenant? So many unanswerables, this the least of them. As I approached I heard a regular rusty screeching sound. A boy of my age was draped on the green gate, his arms hanging limply down from the top bar, propelling himself with one foot slowly back and forth in a quarter circle over the gravel. He had the same straw-pale hair as the woman in the car and the man's unmistakable azure eyes. As I walked slowly past, and indeed I may even have paused, or faltered, rather, he stuck the toe of his plimsoll into the gravel to stop the swinging gate and looked at me with an expression of hostile enquiry. It was the way we all looked at each other, we children, on first encounter. Behind him I could see all the way down the narrow garden at the back of the house to the diagonal row of trees skirting the railway line – they are gone now, those trees, cut down to make way for a row of pastel-coloured bungalows like dolls' houses – and beyond, even, inland, to where the fields rose and there were cows, and tiny bright bursts of yellow that were gorse bushes, and a solitary distant spire, and then the sky, with scrolled white clouds. Suddenly, startlingly, the boy pulled a grotesque face at me, crossing his eyes and letting his tongue loll on his lower lip. I walked on, conscious of his mocking eye following me.

Plimsoll. Now, there is a word one does not hear any more, or rarely, very rarely. Originally sailors' footwear, from someone's name, if I recall, and something to do with ships. The Colonel is off to the lavatory again. Prostate trouble, I bet. Going past my door he softens his tread, creaking on tiptoe, out of respect for the bereaved. A stickler for the observances, our gallant Colonel.

I am walking down Station Road.

So much of life was stillness then, when we were young, or so it seems now; a biding stillness; a vigilance. We were waiting in our as yet unfashioned world, scanning the future as the boy and I had scanned each other, like soldiers in the field, watching for what was to come. At the bottom of the hill I stopped and stood and looked three ways, along Strand Road, and back up Station Road, and the other way, towards the tin cinema and the public tennis courts. No one. The road beyond the tennis courts was called the Cliff Walk, although whatever cliffs there may once have been the sea had long ago eroded. It was said there was a church submerged in the sandy sea bed down there, intact, with bell tower and bell, that once had stood on a headland that was

gone too, brought toppling into the roiling waves one immemorial night of tempest and awful flood. Those were the stories the
locals told, such as Duignan the dairyman and deaf Colfer who
earned his living selling salvaged golf balls, to make us transients
think their tame little seaside village had been of old a place of
terrors. The sign over the Strand Café, advertising cigarettes,
Player's Navy Cut, with a picture of a bearded sailor inside a life-
buoy, or a ring of rope – was it? – creaked in the sea breeze on its
salt-rusted hinges, an echo of the gate at the Cedars on which for
all I knew the boy was swinging yet. They creak, this present gate,
that past sign, to this day, to this night, in my dreams. I set off along
Strand Road. Houses, shops, two hotels – the Golf, the Beach –
a granite church, Myler's grocery-cum-post-office-cum-pub,
and then the field – the Field – of wooden chalets one of which
was our holiday home, my father's, my mother's, and mine.

If the people in the car were his parents had they left the boy
on his own in the house? And where was the girl, the girl who
had laughed?

The past beats inside me like a second heart.

The consultant's name was Mr Todd. This can only be considered a joke in bad taste on the part of polyglot fate. It could have
been worse. There is a name De'Ath, with that fancy medial
capital and apotropaic apostrophe which fool no one. This Todd
addressed Anna as Mrs Morden but called me Max. I was not at
all sure I liked the distinction thus made, or the gruff familiarity
of his tone. His office, no, his rooms, one says rooms, as one calls
him Mister not Doctor, seemed at first sight an eyrie, although
they were only on the third floor. The building was a new one,
all glass and steel – there was even a glass-and-steel tubular lift
shaft, aptly suggestive of the barrel of a syringe, through which
the lift rose and fell hummingly like a giant plunger being alter-
nately pulled and pressed – and two walls of his main consulting
room were sheets of plate glass from floor to ceiling. When Anna
and I were shown in my eyes were dazzled by a blaze of early-
autumn sunlight falling down through those vast panes. The
receptionist, a blonde blur in a nurse's coat and sensible shoes
that squeaked – on such an occasion who would really notice the
receptionist? – laid Anna's file on Mr Todd's desk and squeak-
ingly withdrew. Mr Todd bade us sit. I could not tolerate the

thought of settling myself on a chair and went instead and stood at the glass wall, looking out. Directly below me there was an oak, or perhaps it was a beech, I am never sure of those big deciduous trees, certainly not an elm since they are all dead, but a noble thing, anyway, the summer's green of its broad canopy hardly silvered yet with autumn's hoar. Car roofs glared. A young woman in a dark suit was walking away swiftly across the car park, even at that distance I fancied I could hear her high heels tinnily clicking on the tarmac. Anna was palely reflected in the glass before me, sitting very straight on the metal chair in three-quarters profile, being the model patient, with one knee crossed on the other and her joined hands resting on her thigh. Mr Todd sat sideways at his desk riffling through the documents in her file; the pale-pink cardboard of the folder made me think of those shivery first mornings back at school after the summer holidays, the feel of brand-new schoolbooks and the somehow bodeful smell of ink and pared pencils. How the mind wanders, even on the most concentrated of occasions.

I turned from the glass, the outside become intolerable now.

Mr Todd was a burly man, not tall or heavy but very broad: one had an impression of squareness. He cultivated a reassuringly old-fashioned manner. He wore a tweed suit with a waistcoat and watch chain, and chestnut-brown brogues that Colonel Blunden would have approved of. His hair was oiled in the style of an earlier time, brushed back sternly from his forehead, and he had a moustache, short and bristly, that gave him a dogged look. I realised with a mild shock that despite these calculatedly venerable effects he could not be much more than fifty. Since when did doctors start being younger than I am? On he wrote, playing for time; I did not blame him, I would have done the same, in his place. At last he put down his pen but still was disinclined to speak, giving the earnest impression of not knowing where to begin or how. There was something studied about this hesitancy, something theatrical. Again, I understand. A doctor must be as good an actor as physician. Anna shifted on her chair impatiently.

'Well, Doctor,' she said, a little too loudly, putting on the bright, tough tone of one of those film stars of the Forties, 'is it the death sentence, or do I get life?'

The room was still. Her sally of wit, surely rehearsed, had fallen flat. I had an urge to rush forward and snatch her up in my arms, fireman-fashion, and carry her bodily out of there. I did not stir. Mr Todd looked at her in mild, hare-eyed panic, his eyebrows hovering halfway up his forehead.

'Oh, we won't let you go quite yet, Mrs Morden,' he said, showing big grey teeth in an awful smile. 'No, indeed we will not.'

Another beat of silence followed that. Anna's hands were in her lap, she looked at them, frowning, as if she had not noticed them before. My right knee took fright and set to twitching.

Mr Todd launched into a forceful disquisition, polished from repeated use, on promising treatments, new drugs, the mighty arsenal of chemical weapons he had at his command; he might have been speaking of magic potions, the alchemist's physic. Anna continued frowning at her hands; she was not listening. At last he stopped and sat gazing at her with the same desperate, leporine look as before, audibly breathing, his lips drawn back in a sort of leer and those teeth on show again.

'Thank you,' she said politely in a voice that seemed now to come from very far off. She nodded to herself. 'Yes,' more remotely still, 'thank you.'

At that, as if released, Mr Todd gave his knees a quick smack with two flat palms and jumped to his feet and fairly bustled us to the door. When Anna had gone through he turned to me and gave me a gritty, man-to-man smile, and the handshake, dry, brisk, unflinching, which I am sure he reserves for the spouses at moments such as this.

The carpeted corridor absorbed our footsteps.

The lift, pressed, plunged.

We walked out into the day as if we were stepping on to a new planet, one where no one lived but us.

Arrived home, we sat outside the house in the car for a long time, loath of venturing in upon the known, saying nothing, strangers to ourselves and each other as we suddenly were. Anna looked out across the bay where the furled yachts bristled in the glistening sunlight. Her belly was swollen, a round hard lump pressing against the waistband of her skirt. She had said people would think she was pregnant – 'At my age!' – and we had laughed, not looking at each other. The gulls that nested in our chimneys had all gone back to sea by now, or migrated, or whatever it is they do. Throughout that drear summer they had wheeled above the rooftops all day long, jeering at our attempts to pretend that all was well, nothing amiss, the world continuous. But there it was, squatting in her lap, the bulge that was big baby De'Ath, burgeoning inside her, biding its time.

At last we went inside, having nowhere else to go. Bright light of midday streamed in at the kitchen window and everything had a glassy, hard-edged radiance as if I were scanning the room through a camera lens. There was an impression of general, tight-lipped awkwardness, of all these homely things – jars on the shelves, saucepans on the stove, that breadboard with its jagged knife – averting their gaze from our all at once unfamiliar, afflicted presence in their midst. This, I realised miserably, this is how it would be from now on, wherever she goes the soundless clapping of the leper's bell preceding her. *How well you look!* they would exclaim, *Why, we've never seen you better!* And she with her brilliant smile, putting on a brave face, poor Mrs Bones.

She stood in the middle of the floor in her coat and scarf, hands on her hips, casting about her with a vexed expression. She was still handsome then, high of cheekbone, her skin translucent, paper-fine. I always admired in particular her Attic profile, the nose a line of carven ivory falling sheer from the brow.

'Do you know what it is?' she said with bitter vehemence. 'It's inappropriate, that's what it is.'

I looked aside quickly for fear my eyes would give me away; one's eyes are always those of someone else, the mad and desperate dwarf crouched within. I knew what she meant. This was not supposed to have befallen her. It was not supposed to have befallen us, we were not that kind of people. Misfortune, illness, untimely death, these things happen to good folk, the humble ones, the salt of the earth, not to Anna, not to me. In the midst of the imperial progress that was our life together a grinning losel had stepped out of the cheering crowd and sketching a parody of a bow had handed my tragic queen the warrant of impeachment.

She put on a kettle of water to boil and fished in a pocket of her coat and brought out her spectacles and put them on, looping the string behind her neck. She began to weep, absent-mindedly, it might be, making no sound. I moved clumsily to embrace her but she drew back sharply.

'For heaven's sake don't fuss!' she snapped. 'I'm only dying, after all.'

The kettle came to the boil and switched itself off and the seething water inside it settled down grumpily. I marvelled, not for the first time, at the cruel complacency of ordinary things. But no, not cruel, not complacent, only indifferent, as how could they be otherwise? Henceforth I would have to address things as they are, not as I might imagine them, for this was a new version of reality. I took up the teapot and the tea, making them rattle – my hands were shaking – but she said no, she had changed her mind, it was brandy she wanted, brandy, and a cigarette, she who did not smoke, and rarely drank. She gave me the dull glare of a defiant child, standing there by the table in her coat. Her tears had stopped. She took off her glasses and dropped them to hang below her throat on their string and rubbed at her eyes with the heels of her hands. I found the brandy bottle and tremblingly poured a measure into a tumbler, the bottle-neck and the rim of the glass chattering against each other like teeth. There were no cigarettes in the house, where was I to get cigarettes? She said it was no matter, she did not really want to smoke. The steel kettle shone, a slow furl of steam at its spout, vaguely suggestive of genie and lamp. Oh, grant me a wish, just the one.

'Take off your coat, at least,' I said.

But why at least? What a business it is, the human discourse.

I gave her the glass of brandy and she stood holding it but did not drink. Light from the window behind me shone on the lenses of her spectacles where they hung at her collar bone, giving the eerie effect of another, miniature she standing close in front of her under her chin with eyes cast down. Abruptly she went slack and sat down heavily, extending her arms before her along the table in a strange, desperate-seeming gesture, as if in supplication to some unseen other seated opposite her in judgment. The tumbler in her hand knocked on the wood and splashed out half its contents. Helplessly I contemplated her. For a giddy second the notion seized me that I would never again be able to think of another word to say to her, that we would go on like this, in agonised inarticulacy, to the end. I bent and kissed the pale patch on the crown of her head the size of a sixpence where her dark hair whorled. She turned her face up to me briefly with a black look.

'You smell of hospitals,' she said. 'That should be me.'

I took the tumbler from her hand and put it to my lips and

drank at a draught what remained of the scorching brandy. I realised what the feeling was that had been besetting me since I had stepped that morning into the glassy glare of Mr Todd's consulting rooms. It was embarrassment. Anna felt it as well, I was sure of it. Embarrassment, yes, a panic-stricken sense of not knowing what to say, where to look, how to behave, and something else, too, that was not quite anger but a sort of surly annoyance, a surly resentment at the predicament in which we grimly found ourselves. It was as if a secret had been imparted to us so dirty, so nasty, that we could hardly bear to remain in one another's company yet were unable to break free, each knowing the foul thing that the other knew and bound together by that very knowledge. From this day forward all would be dissembling. There would be no other way to live with death.

Still Anna sat erect there at the table, facing away from me, her arms extended and hands lying inert with palms upturned as if for something to be dropped into them.

'Well?' she said without turning. 'What now?'

There goes the Colonel, creeping back to his room. That was a long session in the lav. Strangury, nice word. Mine is the one bedroom in the house which is, as Miss Vavasour puts it with a demure little moue, *en suite*. Also I have a view, or would have were it not for those blasted bungalows at the bottom of the garden. My bed is daunting, a stately, high-built, Italianate affair fit for a Doge, the headboard scrolled and polished like a Stradivarius. I must enquire of Miss V. as to its provenance. This would have been the master bedroom when the Graces were here. In those days I never got further than the downstairs, except in my dreams.

I have just noticed today's date. It is a year exactly since that first visit Anna and I were forced to pay to Mr Todd in his rooms. What a coincidence. Or not, perhaps; are there coincidences in Pluto's realm, amidst the trackless wastes of which I wander lost, a lyreless Orpheus? Twelve months, though! I should have kept a diary. My journal of the plague year.

A dream it was that drew me here. In it, I was walking along a country road, that was all. It was in winter, at dusk, or else it was a strange sort of dimly radiant night, the sort of night that there is only in dreams, and a wet snow was falling. I was determinedly on my way somewhere, going home, it seemed, although I did not know what or where exactly home might be. There was open land to my right, flat and undistinguished with not a house or hovel in sight, and to my left a deep line of darkly louring trees bordering the road. The branches were not bare despite the season, and the thick, almost black leaves drooped in masses, laden with snow that had turned to soft, translucent ice. Something had broken down, a car, no, a bicycle, a boy's bicycle, for as well as being the age I am now I was a boy as well, a big awkward boy, yes, and on my way home, it must have been home, or somewhere that had been home, once, and that I would recognise again, when I got there. I had hours of walking to do but I did not mind that, for this was a journey of surpassing but inexplicable importance, one that I must make and was bound to complete. I was calm in myself, quite calm, and confident, too, despite not knowing rightly where I was going except that I was going home. I was alone on the road. The snow which had been slowly drifting down all day was unmarked by tracks of any kind, tyre, boot or hoof, for no one had passed this way and no one would. There was something the matter with my foot, the left one, I must have injured it, but long ago, for it was not painful, though at every step I had to throw it out awkwardly in a sort of half-circle, and this hindered me, not seriously but seriously enough. I felt compassion for myself, that is to say the dreamer that I was felt compassion for the self being dreamed, this poor lummox going along dauntlessly in the snow at fall of day with only the road ahead of him and no promise of homecoming.

That was all there was in the dream. The journey did not end, I arrived nowhere, and nothing happened. I was just walking there, bereft and stalwart, endlessly trudging through the snow and the wintry gloaming. But I woke into the murk of dawn not as I usually do these days, with the sense of having been flayed of yet another layer of protective skin during the night, but with the conviction that something had been achieved, or at least initiated. Immediately then, and for the first time in I do not know how long, I thought of Ballyless and the house there on Station Road, and the Graces, and Chloe Grace, I cannot think why, and it was as if I had stepped suddenly out of the dark into a splash of pale, salt-washed sunlight. It endured only a minute, less than a minute, that happy lightsomeness, but it told me what to do, and where I must go.

I first saw her, Chloe Grace, on the beach. It was a bright, wind-worried day and the Graces were settled in a shallow recess scooped into the dunes by wind and tides to which their some-what raffish presence lent a suggestion of the proscenium. They were impressively equipped, with a faded length of striped canvas strung between poles to keep chill breezes off, and folding chairs and a little folding table, and a straw hamper as big as a small suit-case containing bottles and vacuum flasks and tins of sandwiches and biscuits; they even had real tea cups, with saucers. This was a part of the beach that was tacitly reserved for residents of the Golf Hotel, the lawn of which ended just behind the dunes, and indignant stares were being directed at these heedlessly interlop-ing villa people with their smart beach furniture and their bottles of wine, stares which the Graces if they noticed them ignored. Mr Grace, Carlo Grace, Daddy, was wearing shorts again, and a candy-striped blazer over a chest that was bare save for two big tufts of tight curls in the shape of a miniature pair of widespread fuzzy wings. I had never before encountered nor, I think, have I encountered since, anyone so fascinatingly hairy. On his head was clamped a canvas hat like a child's upturned sand bucket. He was sitting on one of the folding chairs, holding a newspaper open before him and at the same time managing to smoke a ciga-rette, despite the stiff wafts of wind coming in from the sea. The blond boy, the swinger on the gate – it was Myles, I may as well give him his name – was crouched at his father's feet, pouting moodily and delving in the sand with a jagged piece of sea-polished driftwood. Some way behind them, in the shelter of the dune wall, a girl, or young woman, was kneeling on the sand, wrapped in a big red towel, under the cover of which she was trying vexedly to wriggle herself free of what would turn out to be a wet bathing suit. She was markedly pale and soulful of expression, with a long, slender face and very black, heavy hair. I noticed that she kept glancing, resentfully, as it seemed, at the back of Carlo Grace's head. I noticed too that the boy Myles was keeping sidelong watch, in the evident hope, which I shared, that the girl's protective towel would slip. She could hardly be his sister, then.

Mrs Grace came up the beach. She had been in the sea and was wearing a black swimsuit, tight and darkly lustrous as seal-skin, and over it a sort of wraparound skirt made of some dia-phanous stuff, held at the waist with a single button and billowing open with each step she took to reveal her bare, tanned, rather thick but shapely legs. She stopped in front of her husband and pushed her white-rimmed sunglasses up into her hair and waited through the beat that he allowed to pass before he lowered the newspaper and looked up at her, lifting his hand that held the cigarette and shading his eyes against the salt-sharpened light. She said something and he put his head on one side and shrugged, and smiled, showing numerous small white even teeth. Behind him the girl, still under the towel, discarded her bathing suit that she had freed herself of at last and, turning her back, sat down on the sand with her legs flexed and made the towel into a tent around herself and rested her forehead on her knees, and Myles drove his stick into the sand with disappointed force.

So there they were, the Graces: Carlo Grace and his wife Constance, their son Myles, the girl or young woman who I was sure was not the girl I had heard laughing in the house that first day, with all their things around them, their folding chairs and tea cups and tumblers of white wine, and Connie Grace's reveal-ing skirt and her husband's funny hat and newspaper and ciga-rette, and Myles's stick, and the girl's swimsuit, lying where she had tossed it, limply wadded and stuck along one wet edge with a fringe of sand, like something thrown up drowned out of the sea.

I do not know for how long Chloe had been standing on the dune before she jumped. She may have been there all that time, watching me watching the others. She was first a silhouette, with the sun behind her making a shining helmet of her short-cropped hair. Then she lifted her arms and with her knees pressed together launched herself off the dune wall. The air made the legs of her shorts balloon briefly. She was barefoot, and landed on her heels, sending up a shower of sand. The girl under the towel – Rose, give her a name too, poor Rosie – uttered a little shriek of fright. Chloe wobbled, her arms still lifted and her heels in the sand, and it seemed she would fall over or at least sit down hard, but instead she kept her balance, and smiled sideways spite-fully at Rose who had sand in her eyes and was making a fish face and shaking her head and blinking. '*Chlo*-e!' Mrs Grace said, a reproving wail, but Chloe ignored her and came forward and knelt in the sand beside her brother and tried to wrest the stick from him. I was lying on my stomach on a towel with my cheeks propped on my hands, pretending to read a book. Chloe knew I was looking at her and seemed not to care. What age were we, ten, eleven? Say eleven, it will do. Her chest was as flat as Myles's, her hips were no wider than mine. She wore a white singlet over her shorts. Her sun-bleached hair was almost white. Myles, who had been battling to keep his stick, snatched it free of her grasp at last and hit her with it on the knuckles and she said 'Ow!' and struck him in the breastbone with a small, pointed fist.

'Listen to this advertisement,' her father said to no one in particular, and read aloud, laughing, from the newspaper. '*Live ferrets required as venetian blind salesmen. Must be car drivers. Apply box twenty-three.*' He laughed again, and coughed, and, coughing, laughed. 'Live ferrets!' he cried. 'Oh, my.'

How flat all sounds are at the seaside, flat and yet emphatic, like the sound of gunshots heard at a distance. It must be the muffling effect of so much sand. Although I cannot say when I have had occasion to hear a gun or guns being fired.

Mrs Grace poured wine for herself, tasted it, grimaced, and sat down in a folding chair and crossed one firm leg on the other, her beach shoe dangling. Rose was getting dressed fumblingly under her towel. Now it was Chloe's turn to draw her knees up to her chest – is it a thing all girls do, or did, at least, sitting that way in the shape of a zed fallen over on its front? – and hold her feet in her hands. Myles poked her in the side with his stick. 'Daddy,' she said with listless irritation, 'tell him to stop.' Her father went on reading. Connie Grace's dangling shoe was jiggling in time to some rhythm in her head. The sand around me with the sun strong on it gave off its mysterious, catty smell. Out on the bay a white sail shivered and flipped to leeward and for a second the world tilted. Someone away down the beach was calling to someone else. Children. Bathers. A wire-haired ginger dog. The sail turned to windward again and I heard distinctly from across the water the ruffle and snap of the canvas. Then the breeze dropped and for a moment all went still.

They played a game, Chloe and Myles and Mrs Grace, the children lobbing a ball to each other over their mother's head and she running and leaping to try to catch it, mostly in vain. When she runs her skirt billows behind her and I cannot take my eyes off the tight black bulge at the upside-down apex of her lap. She jumps, grasping air and giving breathless cries and laughing. Her breasts bounce. The sight of her is almost alarming. A creature with so many mounds and scoops of flesh to carry should not cavort like this, she will damage something inside her, some tender arrangement of adipose tissue and pearly cartilage. Her husband has lowered his newspaper and is watching her too, combing his fingers through his beard under his chin and coldly smiling, his lips drawn back a little from those fine small teeth and his nostrils flared wolfishly as if he is trying to catch her scent. His look is one of arousal, amusement and faint contempt; he seems to want to see her fall down in the sand and hurt herself; I imagine hitting him, punching him in the exact centre of his hairy chest as Chloe had punched her brother. Already I know these people, am one of them. And I have fallen in love with Mrs Grace.

Rose comes out of the towel, in red shirt and black slacks, like a magician's assistant appearing from under the magician's scarlet-lined cape, and busies herself in not looking at anything, especially the woman and her children at play.

Abruptly Chloe loses interest in the game and turns aside and flops down in the sand. How well I will come to know these sudden shifts of mood of hers, these sudden sulks. Her mother calls to her to come back and play but she does not respond. She is lying propped on an elbow on her side with her ankles crossed, looking past me narrow-eyed out to sea. Myles does a chimp dance in front of her, flapping his hands under his armpits and gibbering. She pretends to be able to see through him. 'Brat,' her mother says of her spoilsport daughter, almost complacently, and goes back and sits down on her chair. She is out of breath, and the smooth, sand-coloured slope of her bosom heaves. She lifts a hand up high to brush a clinging strand of hair from her damp forehead and I fix on the secret shadow under her armpit, plum-blue, the tint of my humid fantasies for nights to come. Chloe sulks. Myles goes back to delving violently in the sand with his stick. Their father folds his newspaper and squints at the sky. Rose is examining a loose button on her shirt. The little waves rise and plash, the ginger dog barks. And my life is changed forever.

But then, at what moment, of all our moments, is life not

utterly, utterly changed, until the final, most momentous change
of all?

We holidayed here every summer, my father and mother and I.
We would not have put it that way. *We came here for our holidays*,
that is what we would have said. How difficult now it is to speak
as I spoke then. We came for our holidays here every summer,
for many years, many years, until my father ran off to England,
as fathers sometimes did, in those days, and do still, for that
matter. The chalet that we rented was a slightly less than life-sized
wooden model of a house. It had three rooms, a living room at
the front that was also a kitchen and two tiny bedrooms at the
back. There were no ceilings, only the sloped undersides of the
tarpapered roof. The walls were panelled with unintentionally
elegant, narrow, bevelled boards that on sunny days smelled of
paint and pine-sap. My mother cooked on a paraffin stove, the
tiny fuel-hole of which afforded me an obscurely furtive pleasure
when I was called on to clean it, employing for the task a delicate
instrument made of a strip of pliant tin with a stiff filament of
wire protruding at a right angle from its tip. I wonder where it
is now, that little Primus stove, so sturdy and steadfast? There was
no electricity and at night we lived by the light of an oil lamp.
My father worked in Ballymore and came down in the evenings
on the train, in a wordless fury, bearing the frustrations of his day
like so much luggage clutched in his clenched fists. What did my
mother do with her time when he was gone and I was not there?
I picture her sitting at the oilcloth-covered table in that little
wooden house, a hand under her head, nursing her disaffections
as the long day wanes. She was still young then, they both were,
my father and my mother, younger certainly than I am now.
How strange a thing that is to think of. Everybody seems to be
younger than I am, even the dead. I see them there, my poor
parents, rancorously playing at house in the childhood of the
world. Their unhappiness was one of the constants of my earliest
years, a high, unceasing buzz just beyond hearing. I did not hate
them. I loved them, probably. Only they were in my way, obscur-
ing my view of the future. In time I would be able to see right
through them, my transparent parents.

   My mother would only bathe far up the beach, away from the
eyes of the hotel crowds and the noisy encampments of day

trippers. Up there, past where the golf course began, there was a permanent sandbank a little way out from shore that enclosed a shallow lagoon when the tide was right. In those soupy waters she would wallow with small, mistrustful pleasure, not swimming, for she could not swim, but stretched out full-length on the surface and walking along the sea–floor on her hands, straining to keep her mouth above the lapping wavelets. She wore a crimplene swimsuit, mouse-pink, with a coy little hem stretched across tight just below the crotch. Her face looked bare and defenceless, pinched in the tight rubber seal of her bathing cap. My father was a fair swimmer, going at a sort of hindered, horizontal scramble with mechanical strokes and a gasping sideways grimace and one starting eye. At the end of a length he would rise up, panting and spitting, his hair plastered down and ears sticking out and black trunks abulge, and stand with hands on hips and watch my mother's clumsy efforts with a faint, sardonic grin, a muscle in his jaw twitching. He splashed water in her face and seized her wrists and wading backwards hauled her through the water. She shut her eyes tight and shrieked at him furiously to stop. I watched these edgy larks in a paroxysm of disgust. At last he let her go and turned on me, upending me and grasping me by the ankles and pushing me forward wheelbarrow-fashion off the edge of the sandbank and laughing. How strong his hands were, like manacles of cold, pliant iron, I feel even yet their violent grip. He was a violent man, a man of violent gestures, violent jokes, but timid, too, no wonder he left us, had to leave us. I swallowed water, and twisted out of his grasp in a panic and jumped to my feet and stood in the surf, retching.

Chloe Grace and her brother were standing on the hard sand at the water's edge, looking on.

They wore shorts as usual and were barefoot. I saw how strikingly alike they were. They had been collecting seashells, which Chloe was carrying in a handkerchief knotted corner-to-corner to make a pouch. They stood regarding us without expression, as if we were a show, a comic turn that had been laid on for them but which they found not very interesting, or funny, but peculiar only. I am sure I blushed, grey and goosepimpled though I was, and I had an acute awareness of the thin stream of seawater pouring in an unstoppable arc out of the sagging front of my swimming trunks. Had it been in my power I would have cancelled my shaming parents on the spot, would have popped them like bubbles of sea spray, my fat little bare-faced mother and my father whose body might have been made of lard. A breeze smacked down on the beach and swarmed across it slantwise under a skim of dry sand, then came on over the water, chopping the surface into sharp little metallic shards. I shivered, not from the cold now but as if something had passed through me, silent, swift, irresistible. The pair on the shore turned and trailed off in the direction of the wrecked freighter.

Was it that day that I noticed Myles's toes were webbed?

Miss Vavasour downstairs is playing the piano. She maintains a delicate touch on the keys, trying not to be heard. She worries that she will disturb me, engaged as I am up here in my immense and unimaginably important labours. She plays Chopin very nicely. I hope she does not start on John Field, I could not bear that. Early on I tried to interest her in Fauré, the late nocturnes in particular, which I greatly admire. I even bought the scores for her, ordered them from London, at considerable expense. I was too ambitious. She says she cannot get her fingers around the notes. *Your mind*, more like, I do not reply. Recreant, recreant thoughts. I wonder that she never married. She was beautiful, once, in her soulful way. Nowadays she wears her long grey hair, that formerly was so black, gathered into a tight loop behind her head and transpierced by two crossed pins as big as knitting needles, a style that is to my mind suggestive, wholly inappropriately, of the geisha-house. The Japanese note is continued in the kimono-like belted silk dressing-gown that she wears of a morning, the silk printed with a motif of brightly coloured birds and bamboo fronds. At other times of the day she favours sensible tweeds, but at dinner-time she may surprise us, the Colonel and me, coming rustling to the table in a calf-length confection of lime-green with a sash, or in Spanish-style scarlet bolero jacket and tapered black slacks and neat little shiny black slippers. She is quite the elegant old lady, and registers with a muted flutter my approving glance.

The Cedars has retained hardly anything of the past, of the part of the past that I knew here. I had hoped for something definite of the Graces, no matter how small or seemingly insignificant, a faded photo, say, forgotten in a drawer, a lock of hair, or even a hair-pin, lodged between the floorboards, but there was nothing, nothing like that. No remembered atmosphere, either, to speak of. I suppose so many of the living passing through – it is a lodging house, after all – have worn away all traces of the dead.

How wildly the wind blows today, thumping its big soft ineffectual fists on the window panes. This is just the kind of autumn weather, tempestuous and clear, that I have always loved. I find the autumn stimulating, as spring is supposed to be for others. Autumn is the time to work, I am at one with Pushkin on that. Oh, yes, Alexander and I, Octobrists both. A general costiveness has set in, however, most unPushkinian, and I cannot work. But I keep to my table, pushing the paragraphs about like the counters in a game I no longer know how to play. The table is a small spindly affair with an undependable flap, which Miss V. carried up here herself and presented to me with a certain shy intentionality. *Creak, little wood thing, creak.* There is my sea-captain's swivel chair too, just like the one I used to have in some rented place where we lived years ago, Anna and I, it even groans in the same way when I lean back in it. The work I am supposed to be engaged in is a monograph on Bonnard, a modest project in which I have been mired for more years than I care to compute. A very great painter, in my estimation, about whom, as I long ago came to realise, I have nothing of any originality to say. Brides-in-the-Bath, Anna used to call him, with a cackle. *Bonnard, Bonn'art, Bon'nargue.* No, I cannot work, only doodle like this.

Anyway, work is not the word I would apply to what I do. Work is too large a term, too serious. Workers work. The great ones work. As for us middling men, there is no word sufficiently modest that yet will be adequate to describe what we do and how we do it. Dabble I do not accept. It is amateurs who dabble, while we, the class or genus of which I speak, are nothing if not professional. Wallpaper manufacturers such as Vuillard and Maurice Denis were every bit as diligent – there is another key word – as their friend Bonnard, but diligence is not, is never, enough. We are not skivers, we are not lazy. In fact, we are frenetically energetic, in spasms, but we are free, fatally free, of what might be called the curse of perpetuance. We finish things, while for the real worker, as the poet Valéry, I believe it was, pronounced, there is no finishing a work, only the abandoning of it. A nice vignette has Bonnard at the Musée du Luxembourg with a friend, it was Vuillard, indeed, if I am not mistaken, whom he sets to distracting the museum guard while he whips out his paintbox and reworks a patch of a picture of his own that had been hanging there for years. The true workers all die in a fidget of frustration. So much to do, and so much left undone!

Ouch. There is that pricking sensation again. I cannot help wondering if it might presage something serious. Anna's first signs were of the subtlest. I have become quite the expert in matters medical this past year, not surprisingly. For instance I know that pins-and-needles in the extremities is one of the early symptoms of multiple sclerosis. This sensation I have is like pins-and-needles only more so. It is a burning jab, or series of jabs, in my arm, or in the back of my neck, or once, even, memorably, on the upper side of the knuckle of my right big toe, which sent me hopping on one leg about the room uttering piteous moos of distress. The pain, or smart, though brief, is often severe. It is as if I were being tested for vital signs; for signs of feeling; for signs of life.

Anna used to laugh at me for my hypochondriacal ways. *Doctor Max*, she would call me. *How is Doctor Max today, is he feeling poorly?* She was right, of course, I have always been a moaner, fussing over every slightest twinge or ache.

There is that robin, it flies down from somewhere every afternoon and perches on the holly bush beside the garden shed. I notice it favours doing things by threes, hopping from a top twig to a lower and then a lower again where it stops and whistles thrice its sharp, assertive note. All creatures have their habits. Now from the other side of the garden a neighbour's piebald cat comes creeping, soft-stepping pard. Watch out, birdie. That grass needs cutting, once more will suffice, for this year. I should offer to do it. The thought occurs and at once there I am, in shirt-sleeves and concertina trousers, stumbling sweat-stained behind the mower, grass-haulms in my mouth and the flies buzzing about my head. Odd, how often I see myself like this these days, at a distance, being someone else and doing things that only someone else would do. Mow the lawn, indeed. The shed, although tumbledown, is really rather handsome when looked at with a sympathetic eye, the wood of it weathered to a silky, silvery grey, like the handle of a well-worn implement, a spade, say, or a trusty axe. Old Brides-in-the-Bath would have caught that texture exactly, the quiet sheen and shimmer of it. *Doodle deedle dee.*

Claire, my daughter, has written to ask how I am faring. Not well, I regret to say, bright Clarinda, not well at all. She does not telephone because I have warned her I will take no calls, even from her. Not that there are any calls, since I told no one save her where I was going. What age is she now, twenty-something, I am not sure. She is very bright, quite the bluestocking. Not beautiful, however, I admitted that to myself long ago. I cannot pretend this is not a disappointment, for I had hoped that she would be another Anna. She is too tall and stark, her rusty hair is coarse and untameable and stands out around her freckled face in an unbecoming manner, and when she smiles she shows her upper gums, glistening and whitely pink. With those spindly legs and big bum, that hair, the long neck especially – that is something at least she has of her mother – she always makes me think, shamefacedly, of Tenniel's drawing of Alice when she has taken a nibble from the magic mushroom. Yet she is brave and makes the best of herself and of the world. She has the rueful, grimly humorous, clomping way to her that is common to so many ungainly girls. If she were to arrive here now she would come sweeping in and plump herself down on my sofa and thrust her clasped hands so far down between her knees the knuckles would almost touch the floor, and purse her lips and inflate her cheeks and say *Poh!* and launch into a litany of the comic mishaps she has suffered since last we saw each other. Dear Claire, my sweet girl.

She accompanied me when I came down here to Ballyless for the first time, after that dream, the dream I had of walking homeward in the snow. I think she was worried I might be bent on drowning myself. She must not know what a coward I am. The journey down reminded me a little of the old days, for she and I were always fond of a jaunt. When she was a child and could not sleep at night – from the start she was an insomniac, just like her Daddy – I would bundle her in a blanket into the car and drive her along the coast road for miles beside the darkling sea, crooning whatever songs I knew any of the words of, which far from putting her to sleep made her clap her hands in not altogether derisory delight and cry for more. One time, later on, we even went on a motoring holiday together, just the two of us, but it was a mistake, she was an adolescent by then and grew rapidly bored with vineyards and chateaux and my company, and nagged at me stridently without let-up until I gave in and brought her home early. The trip down here turned out to be not much better.

It was a sumptuous, oh, truly a sumptuous autumn day, all Byzantine coppers and golds under a Tiepolo sky of enamelled blue, the countryside all fixed and glassy, seeming not so much itself as its own reflection in the still surface of a lake. It was the kind of day on which, latterly, the sun for me is the world's fat eye looking on in rich enjoyment as I writhe in my misery. Claire was wearing a big coat of dun-coloured suede which in the warmth of the car gave off a faint but unmistakable fleshy stink which distressed me, although I made no complaint. I have always suffered from what I think must be an overly acute aware-ness of the mingled aromas that emanate from the human con-course. Or perhaps suffer is the wrong word. I like, for instance, the brownish odour of women's hair when it is in need of wash-ing. My daughter, a fastidious spinster – alas, I am convinced she will never marry – usually has no smell at all, that I can detect. That is another of the numerous ways in which she differs from her mother, whose feral reek, for me the stewy fragrance of life itself, and which the strongest perfume could not quite sup-press, was the thing that first drew me to her, all those years ago. My hands now, eerily, have a trace of the same smell, her smell, I cannot rid them of it, wring them though I may. In her last months she smelt, at her best, of the pharmacopoeia.

When we arrived I marvelled to see how much of the village as I remembered it was still here, if only for eyes that knew where to look, mine, that is. It was like encountering an old flame behind whose features thickened by age the slender lineaments that a former self so loved can still be clearly discerned. We passed the deserted railway station and came bowling over the little bridge – still intact, still in place! – my stomach at the crest doing that remembered sudden upward float and fall, and there it all was before me, the hill, road, and the beach at the bottom, and the sea. I did not stop at the house but only slowed as we went by. There are moments when the past has a force so strong it seems one might be annihilated by it.

'That was it!' I said to Claire excitedly. 'The Cedars!' On the way down I had told her all, or almost all, about the Graces. 'That was where they stayed.'

She turned back in her seat to look.

'Why did you not stop?' she said.

What was I to answer? That I was overcome by a crippling shyness suddenly, here in the midst of the lost world? I drove on, and turned on to Strand Road. The Strand Café was gone, its place taken by a large, squat and remarkably ugly house. Here were the two hotels, smaller and shabbier, of course, than in my memory of them, the Golf sporting importantly a rather grandiose flag on its roof. Even from inside the car we could hear the palms on the lawn in front dreamily clacking their dry fronds, a sound that on purple summer nights long ago had seemed to promise all of Araby. Now under the bronzen sunlight of the October afternoon – the shadows were lengthening already – everything had a quaintly faded look, as if it were all a series of pictures from old postcards. Myler's pub-post-office-grocery had swelled into a gaudy superstore with a paved parking area in front. I recalled how on a deserted, silent, sun-dazed afternoon half a century ago there had sidled up to me on the gravelled patch outside Myler's a small and harmless-seeming dog which when I put out my hand to it bared its teeth in what I mistakenly took to be an ingratiating grin and bit me on the wrist with an astonishingly swift snap of its jaws and then ran off, sniggering, or so it seemed to me; and how when I came home my mother scolded me bitterly for my foolishness in offering my hand to the brute and sent me, all on my own, to the village doctor who, elegant and urbane, stuck a perfunctory plaster over the rather pretty, purplish swelling on my wrist and then bade me take off all my clothes and sit on his knee so that, with a wonderfully pale, plump and surely manicured hand pressed warmly against my lower abdomen, he might demonstrate to me the proper way to breathe. 'Let the stomach swell instead of drawing it in, you see?' he said softly, purringly, the warmth of his big bland face beating against my ear.

Claire gave a colourless laugh. 'Which left the more lasting mark,' she asked, 'the dog's teeth or the doctor's paw?'

I showed her my wrist where in the skin over the ulnar styloid are still to be seen the faint remaining scars from the pair of puncture marks made there by the canine's canines.

'It was not Capri,' I said, 'and Doctor ffrench was not Tiberius.'

In truth I have only fond memories of that day. I can still recall the aroma of after-lunch coffee on the doctor's breath and the fishy swivel of his housekeeper's eye as she saw me to the front door.

Claire and I arrived at the Field.

In fact it is a field no longer but a dreary holiday estate packed higgledy-piggledy with what are bound to be jerry-built bungalows, designed I suspect by the same cack-handed line-drawer who was responsible for the eyesores at the bottom of the garden here. However, I was pleased to note that the name given to the place, ersatz though it be, is the Lupins, and that the builder, for I presume it was the builder, even spared a tall stand of this modest wild shrub – *Lupinus*, a genus of the Papilionaceae, I have just looked it up – beside the ridiculously grand mock-gothic gateway that leads in from the road. It was under the lupin bushes that my father every other week, at darkest midnight, with spade and flashlight, muttering curses under his breath, would dig a hole in the soft sandy earth and bury the bucketful of slops from our chemical lavatory. I can never smell the weak but oddly anthropic perfume of those blossoms without seeming to catch behind it a lingering sweet whiff of nightsoil.

'Are you not going to stop at all?' Claire said. 'I'm starting to feel car sick.'

As the years go on I have the illusion that my daughter is catching up on me in age and that by now we are almost contemporaries. It is probably the consequence of having such a clever child – had she persisted she would have made a far finer scholar than I could ever have hoped to be. Also she understands me to a degree that is disturbing and will not indulge my foibles and excesses as others do who know me less and therefore fear me more. But I am bereaved and wounded and require indulging. If there is a long version of shrift then that is what I am in need of. *Let me alone*, I cried at her in my mind, *let me creep past the traduced old Cedars, past the vanished Strand Café, past the Lupins and the Field that was, past all this past, for if I stop I shall surely dissolve in a shaming puddle of tears.* Meekly, however, I halted the car at the side of the road and she got out in a vexed silence and slammed the door behind her as if she were delivering me a box on the ear. What had I done to annoy her so? There are times when she is as wilfully moody as her mother.

And then suddenly, unlikeliest of all, behind the huddle of the Lupins' leprechaun houses, here was Duignan's lane, rutted as it always was, ambling between tangled hedges of hawthorn and dusted-over brambles. How had it survived the depredations of lorry and crane, of diggers both mechanical and human? Here as a boy I would walk down every morning, barefoot and bearing a dented billycan, on my way to buy the day's milk from Duignan the dairyman or his stoically cheerful, big-hipped wife. Even though the sun would be long up the night's moist coolness would cling on in the cobbled yard, where hens picked their way with finical steps among their own chalk-and-olive-green droppings. There was always a dog lying tethered under a leaning cart that would eye me measuringly as I went past, teetering on tiptoe so as to keep my heels out of the chicken-merd, and a grimy white cart-horse that would come and put its head over the half-door of the barn and regard me sidelong with an amused and sceptical eye from under a forelock that was exactly the same smoky shade of creamy-white as honeysuckle blossom. I did not like to knock at the farmhouse door, fearing Duignan's mother, a low-sized squarish old party who seemed fitted with a stumpy leg at each corner and who gasped when she breathed and lolled the pale wet polyp of her tongue on her lower lip, and instead I would hang back in the violet shadow of the barn to wait for Duignan or his missus to appear and save me from an encounter with the crone.

Duignan was a gangling pinhead with thin sandy hair and invisible eyelashes. He wore collarless calico shirts that were antique even then and shapeless trousers shoved into mud-caked wellingtons. In the dairy as he ladled out the milk he would talk to me about girls in a suggestively hoarse, wispy voice – he was to die presently of a diseased throat – saying he was sure I must have a little girlfriend of my own and wanting to know if she let me kiss her. As he spoke he kept his eye fixed on the long thin flute of milk he was pouring into my can, smiling to himself and rapidly batting those colourless lashes. Creepy though he was he held a certain fascination for me. He seemed always teasingly on the point of revealing, as he might show a lewd picture, some large, general and disgusting piece of knowledge to which only

adults were privy. The dairy was a low square whitewashed cell
so white it was almost blue. The steel milk churns looked like
squat sentries in flat hats, and each one had an identical white
rosette burning on its shoulder where the light from the doorway
was reflected. Big shallow muslin-draped pans of milk lost in
their own silence were set on the floor to separate, and there was
a hand-cranked wooden butter churn that I always wanted to see
being operated but never did. The cool thick secret smell of milk
made me think of Mrs Grace, and I would have a darkly exciting
urge to give in to Duignan's wheedling and tell him about her,
but held back, wisely, no doubt.

Now here I was at the farm gate again, the child of those days
grown corpulent and half-grey and almost old. An ill-painted
sign on the gate-post warned trespassers of prosecution. Claire
behind me was saying something about farmers and shotguns but
I paid no heed. I advanced across the cobbles – there were still
cobbles! – seeming not to walk but bounce, rather, awkward as
a half-inflated barrage balloon, buffeted by successive breath-
robbing blows out of the past. Here was the barn and its half-
door. A rusted harrow leaned where Duignan's cart used to lean
– was the cart a misremembrance? The dairy was there too, but
disused, its crazy door padlocked, against whom, it was impossible to imagine, the window panes dirtied over or broken and
grass growing on the roof. An elaborate porch had been built on
to the front of the farmhouse, a glass and aluminium gazebo of a
thing suggestive of the rudimentary eye of a giant insect. Now
inside it the door opened and an elderly young woman appeared
and stopped behind the glass and considered me warily. I blundered forward, grinning and nodding, like a big bumbling
missionary approaching the tiny queen of some happily as yet
unconverted pygmy tribe. At first she stayed cautiously inside the
porch while I addressed her through the glass, loudly enunciating
my name and making excited gesticulations with my hands. Still
she stood and gazed. She gave the impression of a young actress
elaborately but not quite convincingly made-up to look old. Her
hair, dyed the colour of brown boot polish and permed into a
mass of tight, shiny waves, was too voluminous for her little
pinched face, surrounding it like a halo of dense thorns, and
looking more like a wig than real hair. She wore a faded apron
over a jumper that she could only have knitted herself, a man's

corduroy trousers balding at the knees, and those zippered ankle
boots of Prussian-blue mock-velvet that were all the rage among
old ladies when I was young and latterly seem exclusive to beggar
women and female winos. I bellowed at her through the glass
how I used to stay down here as a child, in a chalet in the Field,
and how I would come to the farm in the mornings for milk.
She listened, nodding, a pucker appearing and disappearing at
the side of her mouth as if she were suppressing a laugh. At last
she opened the door of the porch and stepped out on to the
cobbles. In my mood of half-demented euphoria – really, I was
ridiculously excited – I had an urge to embrace her. I spoke in a
rush of the Duignans, man and wife, of Duignan's mother, of
the dairy, even of the baleful dog. Still she nodded, a seemingly
disbelieving eyebrow arched, and looked past me to where Claire
stood waiting in the gateway, arms folded, clasping herself in her
big expensive fur-trimmed coat.

Avril, the young woman said her name was. Avril. She did not
volunteer a surname. Dimly, like something lifting itself up that
for a long time had seemed dead, there came to me the memory
of a child in a dirty smock hanging back in the flagged hallway
of the farmhouse, holding negligently by its chubby flexed arm
a pink, bald and naked doll and watching me with a gnomic stare
that nothing would deflect. But this person before me could not
have been that child, who by now would be, what, in her fifties?
Perhaps the remembered child was a sister of this one, but much
older, that is, born much earlier? Could that be? No, Duignan had
died young, in his forties, so it was not possible, surely, that this
Avril would be his daughter, since he was an adult when I was a
child and . . . My mind balked in its calculations like a confused
and weary old beast of burden. But Avril, now. Who in these parts
would have conferred on their child a name so delicately vernal?

I asked again about the Duignans and Avril said yes, Christy
Duignan had died – Christy? had I known that Duignan's name
was Christy? – but Mrs D. was living still, in a nursing home
somewhere along the coast. 'And Patsy has a place over near Old
Bawn and Mary is in England but poor Willie died.' I nodded.
I found it suddenly dispiriting to hear of them, these offshoots of
the Duignan dynasty, so solid even in only their names, so mun-
danely real, Patsy the farmer and Mary the emigrant and little
Willie who died, all crowding in on my private ceremony of

remembering like uninvited poor relations at a fancy funeral. I could think of nothing to say. All the levitant euphoria of a moment past was gone now and I felt over-fleshed and incommensurate with the moment, standing there smiling and weakly nodding, the last of the air leaking out of me. Still Avril had not identified herself beyond the name, and seemed to think that I must know her, must have recognised her – but how would I, or from where, even though she was standing in what was once the Duignans' doorway? I wondered that she knew so much about the Duignans if she was not one of them, as it seemed certain she was not, or not of the immediate family, anyway, all those Willies and Marys and Patsys, none of whom could have been her parent or doubtless she would have said so by now. All at once my gloom gathered itself into a surge of sour resentment against her, as if she had for some fell reason of her own set herself up here, in this unconvincing disguise – that hennaed hair, those old lady's bootees – intentionally to usurp a corner of my mythic past. The greyish skin of her face, I noticed, was sprinkled all over with tiny freckles. They were not russet-coloured like Claire's, nor like the big splashy ones that used to swarm on Christy Duignan's strangely girlish forearms, nor, for that matter, like the worrying ones that nowadays have begun to appear on the backs of my own hands and on the chicken-pale flesh in the declivities of my shoulders on either side of the clavicle notch, but were much darker, of the same shade of dull brown as Claire's coat, hardly bigger than pinpricks and, I regret to say, suggestive of a chronic and general lack of cleanliness. They put me uneasily in mind of something, yet I could not think what it was.

'It is just, you see,' I said, 'that my wife died.'

I do not know what came over me to blurt it out like that. I hoped Claire behind me had not heard. Avril gazed into my face without expression, expecting me to say more, no doubt. But what more could I have said? On some announcements there is no elaborating. She gave a shrug denoting sympathy, lifting one shoulder and her mouth at one side.

'That's a pity,' she said in a plain, flat tone. 'I'm sorry to hear that.' She did not seem to mean it, somehow.

The autumn sun fell slantwise into the yard, making the cobbles bluely shine, and in the porch a pot of geraniums flourished aloft their last burning blossoms of the season. Honestly, this world.

*   *   *

In the flocculent hush of the Golf Hotel we seemed, my daughter
and I, to be the only patrons. Claire wanted afternoon tea and
when I had ordered it we were directed to a deserted cold conser-
vatory at the rear that looked out on the strand and the receding
tide. Here despite the glacial air a muted hint of past carousings
lingered. There was a mingled smell of spilt beer and stale cigarette smoke, and on a dais in a corner an upright piano stood,
incongruously bespeaking the Wild West, its lid lifted, showing
the gapped grimace of its keys. After that encounter in the farm-
yard I felt quivery and vapourish, like a diva tottering off-stage
at the end of a disastrous night of broken high notes, missed
prompts, collapsing scenery. Claire and I sat down side by side
on a sofa and presently an awkward, ginger-haired boy tricked
out in a waiter's black jacket and trousers with a stripe down the
sides brought a tray and set it clattering on a low table before us
and fled, stumbling in his big shoes. The tea-bag is a vile inven-
tion, suggestive to my perhaps overly squeamish eye of something a careless person might leave behind unflushed in the
lavatory. I poured a cup of the turf-coloured tea and bolstered it
with a nip from my hip-flask – never to be without a ready supply
of anaesthetic, that is a thing I have learned in this past year. The
light of afternoon was soiled and wintry now and a wall of cloud,
dense, mud-blue, was building up from the horizon. The waves
clawed at the suave sand along the waterline, scrabbling to hold
their ground but steadily failing. There were more palm trees out
there, tousled and spindly, their grey bark looking thick and
tough as elephant hide. A hardy breed they must be, to survive
in this cold northern clime. Do their cells remember the desert's
furnace-heat? My daughter sat sunk in her coat with both hands
wrapped for warmth around her tea cup. I noted with a pang
her babyish fingernails, their pale-lilac tint. One's child is always
one's child.

I talked about the Field, the chalet, the Duignans.

'You live in the past,' she said.

I was about to give a sharp reply, but paused. She was right,
after all. Life, authentic life, is supposed to be all struggle, unflag-
ging action and affirmation, the will butting its blunt head against
the world's wall, suchlike, but when I look back I see that the
greater part of my energies was always given over to the simple

search for shelter, for comfort, for, yes, I admit, it, for cosiness. This is a surprising, not to say a shocking, realisation. Before, I saw myself as something of a buccaneer, facing all-comers with a cutlass in my teeth, but now I am compelled to acknowledge that this was a delusion. To be concealed, protected, guarded, that is all I have ever truly wanted, to burrow down into a place of womby warmth and cower there, hidden from the sky's indifferent gaze and the harsh air's damagings. That is why the past is just such a retreat for me, I go there eagerly, rubbing my hands and shaking off the cold present and the colder future. And yet, what existence, really, does it have, the past? After all, it is only what the present was, once, the present that is gone, no more than that. And yet.

Claire drew her head tortoise-fashion deep into the shell of her coat and kicked off her shoes and braced her feet against the edge of the little table. There is always something touching in the sight of a woman's stockinged feet, I think it must be the way the toes are bunched fatly together so that they might almost be fused. Myles Grace's toes were naturally, unnaturally, like that. When he splayed them, which he could do as easily as if they were fingers, the membranes between them would stretch into a gossamer webbing, pink and translucent and shot through leaf-like with a tracery of fine veins red like covered flame, the marks of a godling, sure as heaven.

I suddenly recalled, out of the evening's steadily densening blue, the family of teddy bears that had been Claire's companions throughout her childhood. Slightly repulsive, animate-seeming things I thought them. Leaning over her in the grainy light of the bedside lamp to bid her goodnight I would find myself regarded from above the rim of her coverlet by half a dozen pairs of tiny gleaming glass eyes, wetly brown, motionless, uncannily alert.

'Your *lares familiares*,' I said now. 'I suppose you have them still, propped on your maiden couch?'

A steep-slanted flash of sunlight fell along the beach, turning the sand above the waterline bone-white, and a white seabird, dazzling against the wall of cloud, flew up on sickle wings and turned with a soundless snap and plunged itself, a shutting chevron, into the sea's unruly back. Claire sat motionless for a moment and then began to cry. No sound, only the tears, bright beads of quicksilver in the last effulgence of marine light falling down from the high wall of glass in front of us. Crying, in that silent and almost incidental fashion, is another thing she does just like her mother did.

'You're not the only one who is suffering,' she said.

I know so little about her, really, my daughter. One day when she was young, twelve or thirteen, I suppose, and poised on the threshold of puberty, I barged in on her in the bathroom, the door of which she had neglected to lock. She was naked save for a towel wrapped tightly turban-fashion around her head. She turned to look at me over her shoulder in a fall of calm light from the frosted window, quite unflustered, gazing at me out of the fulness of herself. Her breasts were still buds but already she had that big melony behind. What did I feel, seeing her there? An inner chaos, overlaid by tenderness and a kind of fright. Ten years later she abandoned her studies in art history – Vaublin and the fête galante style; that's my girl, or was – to take up the teaching of backward children in one of the city's increasingly numerous, seething slums. What a waste of talent. I could not forgive her, cannot still. I try, but fail. It was all the doing of a young man, a bookish fellow of scant chin and extreme egalitarian views, on whom she had set her heart. The affair, if such it was – I suspect she is still a virgin – ended badly for her. Having persuaded her to throw up what should have been her life's work in favour of a futile social gesture, the blackguard absconded, leaving my misfortunate girl in the lurch. I wanted to go after him and kill him. At the least, I said, let me pay for a good barrister to prosecute him for breach of promise. Anna said to stop it, that I was only making matters worse. She was already ill. What could I do?

Outside, the dusk was thickening. The sea that before had been silent had now set up a vague tumult, perhaps the tide was on the turn. Claire's tears had stopped but stood unwiped, she seemed not to have noticed them. I shivered; these days whole churchyardsful of mourners traipse back and forth unfeelingly over my grave.

A large man in a morning coat came from the doorway behind us and advanced soundlessly on servant's feet and looked at us in polite enquiry and met my eye and went away again. Claire snuffled, and delving in a pocket brought out a handkerchief and stentorously blew her nose.

'It depends,' I said mildly, 'on what you mean by suffering.'

She said nothing but put the hankie away and stood up and looked about her, frowningly, as if in search of something but not knowing what. She said she would wait for me in the car, and walked away with her head bowed and her hands deep in the pockets of that coat-shaped pelt. I sighed. Against a blackening vault of sky the seabirds rose and dived like torn scraps of rag. I realised I had a headache, it had been beating away unheeded in my skull since I had first sat down in this glassed-in box of wearied air.

The boy-waiter came back, tentative as a fox cub, and made to take the tray, a carroty lock falling limply forward from his brow. With that colouring he could be yet another of the Duignan clan, cadet branch. I asked him his name. He stopped, canted forward awkwardly from the waist, and looked at me from under his pale brows in speculative alarm. His jacket had a shine, the shot cuffs of his shirt were soiled.

'Billy, sir,' he said.

I gave him a coin and he thanked me and stowed it and took up the tray and turned, then hesitated.

'Are you all right, sir?' he said.

I brought out the car keys and looked at them in perplexity. Everything seemed to be something else. I said that yes, I was all right, and he went away. The silence about me was heavy as the sea. The piano on the dais grinned its ghastly grin.

When I was leaving the lobby the man in the morning coat was there. He had a large, waxen, curiously characterless face. He bowed to me, beaming, hands clasped into fists before his chest in an excessive, operatic gesture. What is it about such people that makes me remember them? His look was unctuous yet in some way minatory. Perhaps I had been expected to tip him also. As I say: this world.

Claire was waiting by the car, shoulders hunched, using the sleeves of her coat for a muff.

'You should have asked me for the key,' I said. 'Did you think I wouldn't give it to you?'

On the way home she insisted on taking the wheel, despite my vigorous resistance. It was full night by now and in the wide-eyed glare of the headlamps successive stands of unleaving fright-trees loomed up suddenly before us and were as suddenly gone, collapsing off into the darkness on either side as if felled by the

pressure of our passing. Claire was leaning so far forward her nose
was almost touching the windscreen. The light rising from the
dashboard like green gas gave to her face a spectral hue. I said she
should let me drive. She said I was too drunk to drive. I said I was
not drunk. She said I had finished the hip-flask, she had seen me
empty it. I said it was no business of hers to rebuke me in this
fashion. She wept again, shouting through her tears. I said that
even drunk I would have been less of a danger driving than she
was in this state. So it went on, hammer and tongs, tooth and
nail, what you will. I gave as good, or as bad, as I got, reminding
her, merely as a corrective, that for the best part, I mean the worst
part – how imprecise the language is, how inadequate to its occasions – of the year that it took her mother to die, she had been
conveniently abroad, pursuing her studies, while I was left to
cope as best I could. This struck home. She gave a hoarse bellow
between clenched teeth and thumped the heels of her hands on
the wheel. Then she started to fling all sorts of accusations at me.
She said I had *driven Jerome away.* I paused. Jerome? Jerome? She
meant of course the chinless do-gooder – fat lot of good he did
her – and sometime object of her affections. Jerome, yes, that was
the scoundrel's unlikely name. How, pray, I asked, controlling
myself, how had I *driven him away?* To that she replied only with
a head-tossing snort. I pondered. It was true I had considered
him an unsuitable suitor, and had told him so, pointedly, on more
than one occasion, but she spoke as if I had brandished a horse-
whip or let fly with a shotgun. Besides, if it was my opposition
that had *driven him away,* what did that say for his character or his
tenacity of purpose? No no, she was better off free of the likes of
him, that was certain. But for now I said nothing more, kept my
counsel, and after a mile or two the fire in her went out. That is
something I have always found with women, wait long enough
and one will have one's way.

When we got home I went straight into the house, leaving
her to park the car, and got the number of the Cedars from the
telephone book and telephoned Miss Vavasour and told her that
I wished to rent one of her rooms. Then I went upstairs and
crawled into bed in my drawers. I was suddenly very tired. A fight
with one's daughter is never less than debilitating. I had moved
by then from what had been Anna's and my bedroom into the
spare room over the kitchen, which used to be the nursery and

where the bed was low and narrow, hardly more than a cot. I could hear Claire below in the kitchen, banging the pots and pans. I had not told her yet that I had decided to sell the house. Miss V. on the telephone had enquired how long I planned to stay. I could hear from her tone that she was puzzled, even distrustful. I maintained a deliberate vagueness. Some weeks, I said, months, perhaps. She was silent for a lengthy moment, thinking. She mentioned the Colonel, he was a permanent, she said, and set in his ways. I volunteered no comment on that. What were colonels to me? She could entertain an entire officer corps on the premises for all I cared. She said I would have to send out my laundry. I asked her if she remembered me. 'Oh, yes,' she said without inflexion, 'yes, of course, I remember you.'

I heard Claire's step on the stairs. Her anger had drained all away by now and she walked at a dragging, disconsolate plod. I do not doubt she too finds arguments tiring. The bedroom door was ajar but she did not come in, only asked listlessly through the gap if I wanted something to eat. I had not switched on the lamps in the room and the long, tapering trapezoid of light spilling across the linoleum from the landing where she stood was a pathway leading straight to childhood, hers and my own. When she was little and slept in this room, in this bed, she liked to hear the sound of my typewriter from the study downstairs. It was a comforting sound, she said, like listening to me think, although I do not know how the sound of me thinking could comfort anyone; quite the opposite, I should have said. Ah, but how far off, now, those days, those nights. All the same, she should not have shouted at me like that in the car. I do not merit being shouted at like that. 'Daddy,' she said again, with a note of testiness now, 'do you want dinner or not?' I did not answer, and she went away. Live in the past, do I.

I turned towards the wall and away from the light. Even though my knees were bent my feet still stuck out at the end of the bed. As I was heaving myself over in a tangle of sheets – I have never been able to cope with bedclothes – I caught a whiff of my own warm cheesy smell. Before Anna's illness I had held my physical self in no more than fond disgust, as most people do – hold their selves, I mean, not mine – tolerant, necessarily, of the products of my sadly inescapable humanity, the various effluvia, the eructations fore and aft, the gleet, the scurf, the sweat and other common leakages, and even what the Bard of Hartford quaintly calls the particles of nether-do. However, when Anna's body betrayed her and she became afraid of it and its alien possibilities, I developed, by a mysterious process of transference, a crawling repugnance of my own flesh. I do not have this sense of self-disgust all the time, or at least I am not all the time aware of it, although probably it is there, waiting until I am alone, at night, or in the early morning especially, when it rises around me like a miasma of marsh gas. I have developed too a queasy fascination with the processes of my body, the gradual ones, the way for instance my hair and my fingernails insistently keep growing, no matter what state I am in, what anguish I may be undergoing. It seems so inconsiderate, so heedless of circumstance, this relentless generation of matter that is already dead, in the same way that animals will keep going about their animal business, unaware or uncaring that their master sprawled on his cold bed upstairs with mouth agape and eyes glazed over will not be coming down, ever again, to dish out the kibble or take the key to that last tin of sardines.

Speaking of typewriters – I did, I mentioned a typewriter a minute ago – last night in a dream, it has just come back to me, I was trying to write my will on a machine that was lacking the word *I*. The letter *I*, that is, small and large.

Down here, by the sea, there is a special quality to the silence at night. I do not know if this is my doing, I mean if this quality is something I bring to the silence of my room, and even of the whole house, or if it is a local effect, due to the salt in the air, perhaps, or the seaside climate in general. I do not recall noticing it when I was young and staying in the Field. It is dense and at the same time hollow. It took me a long while, nights and nights, to identify what it reminds me of. It is like the silence that I knew in the sickrooms of my childhood, when I would lie in a fever, cocooned under a hot, moist mound of blankets, with the emptiness squeezing in on my eardrums like the air in a bathysphere. Sickness in those days was a special place, a place apart, where no one else could enter, not the doctor with his shiver-inducing stethoscope or even my mother when she put her cool hand on my burning brow. It is a place like the place where I feel that I am now, miles from anywhere, and anyone. I think of the others in the house, Miss Vavasour, and the Colonel, asleep in their rooms, and then I think perhaps they are not asleep, but lying awake, like me, glooming gaunt-eyed into the lead-blue darkness. Perhaps the one is thinking of the other, for the Colonel has an idea of our chatelaine, I am convinced of it. She, however, laughs at him behind his back, not entirely without fondness, calling him Colonel Blunder, or Our Brave Soldier. Some mornings her eyes are red-rimmed as if she had been crying in the night. Does she blame herself for all that happened and grieve for it still? What a little vessel of sadness we are, sailing in this muffled silence through the autumn dark.

It was at night especially that I thought about the Graces, as I lay in my narrow metal bed in the chalet under the open window, hearing the monotonously repeated ragged collapse of waves down on the beach, the solitary cry of a sleepless seabird and, sometimes, the distant rattling of a corncrake, and the faint, jazzy moanings of the dance band in the Golf Hotel playing a last slow waltz, and my mother and father in the front room fighting, as they did when they thought I was asleep, going at each other in a grinding undertone, every night, every night, until at last one night my father left us, never to return. But that was in winter, and somewhere else, and years off still. To keep from trying to hear what they were saying I distracted myself by making up dramas in which I rescued Mrs Grace from some great and general catastrophe, a shipwreck or a devastating storm, and sequestered her for safety in a cave, conveniently dry and warm, where in moonlight – the liner had gone down by now, the storm had abated – I tenderly helped her out of her sopping swimsuit and wrapped a towel around her phosphorescent nudity, and we lay down and she leaned her head on my arm and touched my face in gratitude and sighed, and so we went to sleep together, she and I, lapped about by the vast soft summer night.

In those days I was greatly taken with the gods. I am not speaking of God, the capitalised one, but the gods in general. Or the idea of the gods, that is, the possibility of the gods. I was a keen reader and had a fair knowledge of the Greek myths, although the personages in them were hard to keep track of, so frequently did they transform themselves and so various were their adventures. Of them I had a necessarily stylised image – big, nearly

naked plasticene figures all corded muscle and breasts like
inverted tundishes – derived from the works of the great masters
of the Italian Renaissance, Michelangelo especially, reproduc-
tions of whose paintings I must have seen in a book, or a maga-
zine, I who was always on the look-out for instances of bare flesh.
It was of course the erotic exploits of these celestial beings that
most took my fancy. The thought of all that tensed and tensely
quivering naked flesh, untrammelled save by the marmoreal folds
of a robe or a wisp of gauze fortuitously placed – fortuitous, perhaps, but fully and frustratingly as protective of modesty as Rose's
beach towel or, indeed, Connie Grace's swimsuit – glutted my
inexperienced but already overheating imagination with reveries
of love and love's transgressions, all in the unvarying form of
pursuit and capture and violent overmastering. Of the details of
these skirmishes in the golden dust of Greece I had scant grasp.
I pictured the pump and shudder of tawny thighs from which
pale loins shrink even as they surrender, and heard the moans
of mingled ecstasy and sweet distress. The mechanics of the act,
however, were beyond me. Once on my rambles along the
thistled pathways of the Burrow, as that strip of scrubland
between the seashore and the fields was called, I almost stumbled
over a couple lying in a shallow sandy pit making love under a
raincoat. Their exertions had caused the coat to ride up, so that
it covered their heads but not their tails – or perhaps they had
arranged it that way, preferring to conceal their faces, so much
more identifiable, after all, than behinds – and the sight of them
there, the man's flanks rhythmically busy in the upright wish-
bone of the woman's lifted, wide-flung legs, made something
swell and thicken in my throat, a blood-surge of alarm and
thrilled revulsion. *So this*, I thought, or it was thought for me, *so
this is what they do.*

Love among the big people. It was strange to picture them, to
try to picture them, struggling together on their Olympian beds
in the dark of night with only the stars to see them, grasping and
clasping, panting endearments, crying out for pleasure as if in
pain. How did they justify these dark deeds to their daytime
selves? That was something that puzzled me greatly. Why were
they not ashamed? On Sunday morning, say, they arrive at
church still tingling from Saturday night's frolics. The priest
greets them in the porch, they smile blamelessly, mumbling

innocuous words. The woman dips her fingertips in the font, mingling traces of tenacious love-juice with the holy water. Under their Sunday best their thighs chafe in remembered delight. They kneel, not minding the mournfully reproachful gaze the statue of their Saviour fixes on them from the cross. After their midday Sunday dinner perhaps they will send the children out to play and retire to the sanctuary of their curtained bedroom and do it all over again, unaware of my mind's bloodshot eye fixed on them unblinkingly. Yes, I was that kind of boy. Or better say, there is part of me still that is the kind of boy that I was then. A little brute, in other words, with a filthy mind. As if there were any other sort. We never grow up. I never did, anyway.

By day I loitered about Station Road hoping for a glimpse of Mrs Grace. I would pass by the green metal gate, slowing to the pace of a somnambulist, and will her to walk out of the front door as her husband had walked out that day when I caught my first sight of him, but she kept stubbornly within. In desperation I would peer past the house to the clothesline in the garden, but all I saw was the children's laundry, their shorts and socks and one or two items of Chloe's uninterestingly skimpy underthings, and of course their father's flaccid, greyish drawers, and once, even, his sand-bucket hat, pegged at a rakish angle. The only thing of Mrs Grace's I ever saw there was her black swimsuit, hanging by its shoulder straps, limp and scandalously empty, dry now and less like a sealskin than the pelt of a panther. I looked in at the windows, too, especially the bedroom ones upstairs, and was rewarded one day – how my heart hammered! – by a glimpse behind a shadowed pane of what seemed a nude thigh that could only be hers. Then the adored flesh moved and turned into the hairy shoulder of her husband, at stool, for all I knew, and reaching for the lavatory roll.

There was a day when the door did open, but it was Rose who came out, and gave me a look that made me lower my eyes and hurry on. Yes, Rose had the measure of me from the start. Still has, no doubt.

I determined to get into the house, to walk where Mrs Grace walked, sit where she sat, touch the things that she touched. To this end I set about making the acquaintance of Chloe and her brother. It was easy, as these things were in childhood, even for a child as circumspect as I was. At that age we had no small talk,

no rituals of polite advance and encounter, but simply put ourselves into each other's vicinity and waited to see what would
happen. I saw the two of them loitering on the gravel outside
the Strand Café one day, spied them before they spied me,
and crossed the road diagonally to where they were standing, and
stopped. Myles was eating an ice cream with deep concentration,
licking it evenly on all sides like a cat licking a kitten, while
Chloe, I suppose having finished hers, waited on him in an atti-
tude of torpid boredom, leaning in the doorway of the café with
one sandalled foot pressed on the instep of the other and her face
blankly lifted to the sunlight. I did not say anything, nor did they.
The three of us just stood there in the morning sunshine amid
smells of seawrack and vanilla and what passed in the Strand Café
for coffee, and at last Chloe deigned to lower her head and
directed her gaze towards my knees and asked my name. When
I told her she repeated it, as if it were a suspect coin she was
testing between her teeth.

'Morden?' she said. 'What sort of a name is that?'

We walked slowly up Station Road, Chloe and I in front and
Myles behind us, gambolling, I nearly said, at our heels. They
were from the city, Chloe said. That would not have been hard
for me to guess. She asked where I was staying. I gestured vaguely.

'Down there,' I said. 'Along past the church.'

'In a house or a hotel?'

How quick she was. I considered lying – 'The Golf Hotel,
actually' – but saw where a lie could lead me.

'A chalet,' I said, mumbling.

She nodded thoughtfully.

'I've always wanted to stay in a chalet,' she said.

This was no comfort to me. On the contrary, it caused me to
have a momentary but starkly clear image of the crooked little
wooden outhouse standing amid the lupins across from my bedroom window, and even seemed to catch a dry, woody whiff of
the torn-up squares of newsprint impaled on their rusty nail just
inside the door.

We came to the Cedars, stopped at the gate. The car was
parked on the gravel. It had been out recently, the cooling engine
was still clicking its tongue to itself in fussy complaint. I could
hear faintly from inside the house the melting-toffee tones of a
palm court orchestra playing on the wireless, and I pictured Mrs

Grace and her husband dancing together in there, sweeping around the furniture, she with her head thrown back and her throat bared and he mincing on his satyr's furred hind legs and grinning up eagerly into her face – he was shorter than she by an inch or two – with all his sharp little teeth on show and his ice-blue eyes alight with mirthful lust. Chloe was tracing patterns in the gravel with the toe of her sandal. There were fine white hairs on her calves but her shins were smooth and shiny as stone. Suddenly Myles gave a little jump, or skip, as if for joy but too mechanical for that, like a clockwork figure coming abruptly to life, and clipped me playfully on the back of the head with his open palm and turned and with a gagging laugh scrambled agilely over the bars of the gate and dropped down to the gravel on the other side and spun about to face us and crouched with knees and elbows flexed, like an acrobat inviting his due of applause. Chloe made a face, pulling her mouth down at one side.

'Don't mind him,' she said in a tone of bored irritation. 'He can't talk.'

They were twins. I had never encountered twins before, in the flesh, and was fascinated and at the same time slightly repelled. There seemed to me something almost indecent in such a predicament. True, they were brother and sister and so could not be identical – the very thought of identical twins sent a shiver of secret and mysterious excitement along my spine – but still there must be between them an awful depth of intimacy. How would it be? Like having one mind and two bodies? If so it was almost disgusting to think of. Imagine somehow knowing intimately, from the inside, as it were, what another's body is like, its different parts, different smells, different urges. How, how would it be? I itched to know. In the makeshift picture-house one wet Sunday afternoon – here I leap ahead – we were watching a film in which two convicts from a chain-gang made their escape still manacled together, and beside me Chloe stirred and made a muffled sound, a sort of laughing sigh. 'Look,' she whispered, 'it's me and Myles.' I was taken aback, and felt myself blush and was glad of the dark. She might have been admitting to something intimate and shameful. Yet it was the very notion of an impropriety in such closeness that made me eager to know more, eager, and yet loath. Once – this is an even longer leap forward – when I got up the nerve to ask Chloe straight out to tell me, because I longed to know, what it felt like, this state of unavoidable intimacy with her brother – her other! – she thought for a moment and then held up her hands before her face, the palms pressed almost together but not quite touching. 'Like two magnets,' she said, 'but turned the wrong way, pulling and pushing.' After she had said it she fell darkly silent, as though this time it was she who thought she had let drop a shaming secret, and she turned away from me, and I felt for a moment something of the same panicky dizziness that I did when I held my breath for too long underwater. She was never less than alarming, was Chloe.

The link between them was palpable. I pictured it as an invisibly fine thread of sticky shiny stuff, like spider's silk, or a glistening filament such as a snail might leave hanging as it crossed from one leaf to another, or steely and bright, it might be, and taut, like a harp-string, or a garotte. They were tied to each other, tied and bound. They felt things in common, pains, emotions, fears. They shared thoughts. They would wake in the night and lie listening to each other breathing, knowing they had been dreaming the same thing. They did not tell each other what was in the dream. There was no need. They knew.

Myles had been mute from birth. Or rather, simply, he had never spoken. The doctors could find no cause that would account for his stubborn silence, and professed themselves baffled, or sceptical, or both. At first it had been assumed he was a late starter and that in time he would begin to speak like everyone else, but the years went on and still he said not a word. Whether he had the ability to speak and chose not to, no one seemed to know. Was he mute or silent, silent or mute? Could he have a voice that he never used? Did he practise when there was no one to hear? I imagined him at night, in bed, under the covers, whispering to himself and smiling that avid, elfin smile of his. Or maybe he talked to Chloe. How they would have laughed, forehead to forehead and their arms thrown around each other's neck, sharing their secret.

'He'll talk when he has something to say,' his father would growl, with his accustomed menacing cheerness.

It was plain that Mr Grace did not care for his son. He avoided him when he could, and was especially unwilling to be alone with him. This was no wonder, for being alone with Myles was like being in a room which someone had just violently left. His muteness was a pervasive and cloying emanation. He said nothing but was never silent. He was always fidgeting with things, snatching them up and immediately throwing them down again with a clatter. He made dry little clicking noises at the back of his throat. One heard him breathe.

His mother treated him with a sort of trailing vagueness. At moments as she weaved abstractedly through her day – although she was not a serious drinker she always looked to be mellowly a little drunk – she would stop and seem to notice him with not quite recognition, and would frown and smile at the same time, in a rueful, helpless fashion.

Neither parent could do proper sign language, and spoke to Myles by way of an improvised, brusque dumb-show that seemed less an attempt at communication than an impatient waving of him out of their sight. Yet he understood well enough what it was they were trying to say, and often before they were halfway through trying to say it, which only made them more impatient and irritated with him. Deep down they were both, I am sure, a little afraid of him. That is no wonder either. It must have been like living with an all too visible, all too tangible poltergeist.

For my part, although I am ashamed to say it, or at least I should be ashamed, what Myles put me most in mind of was a dog I once had, an irrepressibly enthusiastic terrier of which I was greatly fond but which on occasion, when there was no one about, I would cruelly beat, poor Pongo, for the hot, tumid pleasure I derived from its yelps of pain and its supplicatory squirmings. What twig-like fingers Myles had, what brittle, girlish wrists! He would goad me, plucking at my sleeve, or walking on my heels and popping his grinning head repeatedly up from under my arm, until at last I would turn on him and knock him down, which was easy to do, for I was big and strong even then, and taller than he was by a head. When he was down, however, there was the question of what to do with him, since unless prevented he would be up again at once, rolling over himself like one of those self-righting toy figures and springing effortlessly back on to his toes. When I sat on his chest I could feel the wobble of his heart against my groin, his ribcage straining and the fluttering of the taut, concave integument below his breastbone, and he would laugh up at me, panting, and showing his moist, useless tongue. But was not I too a little afraid of him, in my heart, or wherever it is that fear resides?

In accordance with the mysterious protocols of childhood – were we children? I think there should be another word for what we were – they did not invite me into the house that first time, after I had accosted them outside the Strand Café. In fact, I do not recall under what circumstances exactly I managed eventually to get inside the Cedars. I see myself after that initial encounter turning away frustratedly from the green gate with the twins watching me go, and then I see myself another day within the very sanctum itself, as if, by a truly magical version of Myles's leap over the top bar of the gate, I had vaulted all obstacles to land up in the living room next to an angled, solid-seeming beam of brassy sunlight, with Mrs Grace in a loose-fitting, flowered dress, light-blue with a darker pattern of blue blossoms, turning from a table and smiling at me, deliberately vague, evidently not knowing who I was but knowing nevertheless that she should, which shows that this cannot have been the first time we had encountered each other face to face. Where was Chloe? Where was Myles? Why was I left alone with their mother? She asked if I would like something, a glass of lemonade, perhaps. 'Or,' she said in a tone of faint desperation, 'an apple . . .?' I shook my head. Her proximity, the mere fact of her thereness, filled me with excitement and a mysterious sort of sorrow. Who knows the pangs that pierce a small boy's heart? She put her head on one side, puzzled, and amused, too, I could see, by the tongue-tied intensity of my presence before her. I must have seemed like a moth throbbing before a candle-flame, or like the flame itself, shivering in its own consuming heat.

What was it she had been doing at the table? Arranging flowers in a vase – or is that too fanciful? There is a multi-coloured patch in my memory of the moment, a shimmer of variegated brightness where her hands hover. Let me linger here with her a little while, before Rose appears, and Myles and Chloe return from wherever they are, and her goatish husband comes clattering on to the scene; she will be displaced soon enough from the throbbing centre of my attentions. How intensely that sunbeam glows. Where is it coming from? It has an almost churchly cast, as if, impossibly, it were slanting down from a rose window high above us. Beyond the smouldering sunlight there is the placid gloom

of indoors on a summer afternoon, where my memory gropes
in search of details, solid objects, the components of the past. Mrs
Grace, Constance, Connie, is still smiling at me in that unfocused
way, which, now that I consider it, is how she looked at everything, as if she were not absolutely persuaded of the world's
solidity and half expected it all at any moment to turn, in some
outlandish and hilarious way, into something entirely different.

I would have said then that she was beautiful, had there been
anyone to whom I would have thought of saying such a thing,
but I suppose she was not, really. She was rather stocky, and her
hands were fat and reddish, there was a bump at the tip of her
nose, and the two lank strands of blonde hair that her fingers kept
pushing back behind her ears and that kept falling forward again
were darker than the rest of her hair and had the slightly greasy
hue of oiled oak. She walked at a languorous slouch, the muscles
in her haunches quivering under the light stuff of her summer
dresses. She smelled of sweat and cold cream and, faintly, of
cooking fat. Just another woman, in other words, and another
mother, at that. Yet to me she was in all her ordinariness as remote
and remotely desirable as any a painted pale lady with unicorn
and book. But no, I should be fair to myself, child though I was,
nascent romantic though I may have been. She was, even for me,
not pale, she was not made of paint. She was wholly real, thick-
meated, edible, almost. This was the most remarkable thing of
all, that she was at once a wraith of my imagination and a woman
of unavoidable flesh and blood, of fibre and musk and milk. My
hitherto hardly less than seemly dreams of rescue and amorous
dalliance had by now become riotous fantasies, vivid and at the
same time hopelessly lacking in essential detail, of being voluptuously overborne by her, of sinking to the ground under all her
warm weight, of being rolled, of being ridden, between her
thighs, my arms pinned against my breast and my face on fire, at
once her demon lover and her child.

At times the image of her would spring up in me unbidden,
an interior succubus, and a surge of yearning would engorge the
very root of my being. One greenish twilight after rain, with a
wedge of wet sunlight in the window and an impossibly un-
seasonal thrush piping outside in the dripping lupins, I lay face
down on my bed in such an intense suffusion of unassuageable
desire – it hovered, this desire, like a nimbus about the image of

my beloved, enfolding her everywhere and nowhere focused –
that I broke into sobs, lavish, loud and thrillingly beyond all
control. My mother heard me and came into the room, but said
nothing, uncharacteristically – I might have expected a brusque
interrogation, followed by a smack – only picked up a pillow that
the thrashings of my grief had pushed off the bed and, after the
briefest of hesitations, went out again, shutting the door soundlessly behind her. What did she imagine I was weeping for,
I wondered, and wonder again now. Had she somehow recognised my rapturously lovesick grief for what it was? I could not
believe it. How would she, who was merely my mother, know
anything of this storm of passion in which I was helplessly suspended, the frail wings of my emotions burned and blasted by
love's relentless flame? Oh, Ma, how little I understood you,
thinking how little you understood.

So there I am, in that Edenic moment at what was suddenly the
centre of the world, with that shaft of sunlight and those vestigial
flowers – sweet pea? all at once I seem to see sweet pea – and
blonde Mrs Grace offering me an apple that was however
nowhere in evidence, and everything about to be interrupted
with a grinding of cogwheels and a horrible, stomach-turning
lurch. All sorts of things began to happen at once. Through an
open doorway a small black woolly dog came skittering in from
outside – somehow now the action has shifted from the living
room to the kitchen – its nails making frantic skittling noises on
the pitch pine floor. It had a tennis ball in its mouth. Immediately
Myles appeared in pursuit, with Rose in turn pursuing him. He
tripped or pretended to trip over a rucked rug and pitched
forward only to tumble nimbly head over heel and leap to his feet
again, almost knocking into his mother, who gave a cry in which
were mingled startlement and weary annoyance – 'For heaven's
sake, Myles!' – while the dog, its pendent ears flapping, changed
tack and shot underneath the table, still grinningly gripping the
ball. Rose made a feint at the animal but it dodged aside. Now
through another doorway, like Old Father Time himself, came
Carlo Grace, wearing shorts and sandals and with a big beach
towel draped over his shoulders, his hairy paunch on show. At
sight of Myles and the dog he gave a roar of sham rage and
stamped his foot threateningly, and the dog let go of the ball, and
dog and boy disappeared through the door as precipitately as they

had entered. Rose laughed, a high whinny, and looked quickly at Mrs Grace and bit her lip. The door banged and in rapid echo another door banged upstairs, where a lavatory, flushed a moment previously, had set up its after-gulps and gurglings. The ball that the dog had dropped rolled slowly, shiny with spit, into the middle of the floor. Mr Grace, seeing me, a stranger – he must have forgotten that day of the wink – mugged a double-take, throwing back his head and screwing up his face at one side and sighting quizzically at me along the side of his nose. I heard Chloe coming downstairs, her sandals slapping on the steps. By the time she entered the room Mrs Grace had introduced me to her husband – I think it was the first time in my life I had been formally introduced to anyone, although I had to say my name since Mrs Grace had still not remembered it – and he was shaking my hand with a show of mock solemnity, addressing me as *My dear sir!* and putting on a cockney accent and declaring that any friend of his children's would always be welcome in *our 'umble 'ome*. Chloe rolled her eyes and gave a shuddering gasp of disgust. 'Shut *up*, Daddy,' she said through clenched teeth, and he, feigning terror of her, let go my hand and drew the towel shawl-like over his head and hurried at a crouch on tiptoe out of the room, making little bat-squeaks of pretend fright and dismay. Mrs Grace was lighting a cigarette. Chloe without even a glance in my direction crossed the room to the door where her father had gone out. 'I need a lift!' she shouted after him. 'I need—' The car door slammed, the engine started, the big tyres mashed the gravel. 'Damn,' Chloe said.

Mrs Grace was leaning against the table – the one with the sweet pea on it, for magically we are back in the living room again – smoking her cigarette in the way that women did in those days, one arm folded across her midriff and the elbow of the other cupped in a palm. She lifted an eyebrow at me and smiled wryly and shrugged, picking a fleck of tobacco from her lower lip. Rose stooped and wrinkling her nose picked up reluctantly the spit-smeared ball between a finger and thumb. Outside the gate the car horn tooted merrily twice and we heard the car drive away. The dog was barking wildly, wanting to be let in again to retrieve the ball.

By the way, that dog. I never saw it again. Whose can it have been?

* * *

Odd sense of lightness today, of, what shall I call it, of volatility. The wind is up again, it is fairly blowing a tempest out there, which must be the cause of this giddiness I am feeling. For I have always been strongly susceptible to the weather and its effects. As a child I loved to curl up by the wireless set of a winter eve and listen to the shipping forecast, picturing all those doughty sea-dogs in their sou'westers battling through house-high waves in Fogger and Disher and Jodrell Bank, or whatever those far-flung sea areas are called. Often as an adult, too, I would have that same feeling, there with Anna in our fine old house between the mountains and the sea, when the autumn gales groaned in the chimneys and the waves were coming over the sea wall in washes of boiling white spume. Before the pit opened under our feet that day in Mr Todd's rooms – which, come to think of it, did have about them something of the air of a sinisterly superior barber's shop – I was often surprised to ponder how many of life's good things had been granted me. If that child dreaming by the wireless had been asked what he wanted to be when he grew up, what I had become was more or less what he would have described, in however halting a fashion, I am sure of it. This is remarkable, I think, even allowing for my present sorrows. Are not the majority of men disappointed with their lot, languishing in quiet desperation in their chains?

I wonder if other people when they were children had this kind of image, at once vague and particular, of what they would be like when they grew up. I am not speaking of hopes and aspirations, vague ambitions, that kind of thing. From the outset I was very precise and definite in my expectations. I did not want to be an engine driver or a famous explorer. When I peered wishfully through the mists from the all too real then to the bliss-fully imagined now, this is, as I have said, exactly how I would have foreseen my future self, a man of leisurely interests and scant ambition sitting in a room just like this one, in my sea-captain's chair, leaning at my little table, in just this season, the year declining towards its end in clement weather, the leaves scampering, the brightness imperceptibly fading from the days and the street lamps coming on only a fraction earlier each even-ing. Yes, this is what I thought adulthood would be, a kind of long indian summer, a state of tranquillity, of calm incuriousness, with nothing left of the barely bearable raw immediacy of childhood, all the things solved that had puzzled me when I was small, all mysteries settled, all questions answered, and the moments dripping away, unnoticed almost, drip by golden drip, towards the final, almost unnoticed, quietus.

There were things of course the boy that I was then would not have allowed himself to foresee, in his eager anticipations, even if he had been able. Loss, grief, the sombre days and the sleepless nights, such surprises tend not to register on the prophetic imagination's photographic plate.

And then, too, when I consider the matter closely, I see that the version of the future that I pictured as a boy had an oddly antique cast to it. The world in which I live now would have been, in my imagining of it then, for all my perspicacity, different from what it is in fact, but subtly different; would have been, I see, all slouch hats and crombie overcoats and big square motor cars with winged manikins bounding from the bonnets. When had I known such things, that I could figure them so distinctly? I think it is that, being unable to conceive exactly what the future would look like but certain that I would be a person of some eminence in it, I must have furnished it with the trappings of success as I saw it among the great folk of our town, the doctors and solicitors, the provincial industrialists for whom my father humbly worked, the few remnants of Protestant gentry still clinging on in their Big Houses down the bosky side roads of the town's hinterland.

But no, that is not it either. It does not adequately account for the genteelly outmoded atmosphere that pervaded my dream of what was to come. The precise images I entertained of myself as a grown-up – seated, say, in three-piece pinstriped suit and raked fedora in the back seat of my chauffered Humber Hawk with a blanket over my knees – were imbued, I realise, with that etiolated, world-weary elegance, that infirm poise, which I associated, or which at least I associate now, with a time before the time of my childhood, that recent antiquity which was, of course, yes, the world between the wars. So what I foresaw for the future was in fact, if fact comes into it, a picture of what could only be an imagined past. I was, one might say, not so much anticipating the future as nostalgic for it, since what in my imaginings was to come was in reality already gone. And suddenly now this strikes me as in some way significant. Was it actually the future I was looking forward to, or something beyond the future?

The truth is, it has all begun to run together, past and possible future and impossible present. In the ashen weeks of daytime dread and nightly terror before Anna was forced at last to acknowledge the inevitability of Mr Todd and his prods and potions, I seemed to inhabit a twilit netherworld in which it was scarcely possible to distinguish dream from waking, since both waking and dreaming had the same penetrable, darkly velutinous texture, and in which I was wafted this way and that in a state of feverish lethargy, as if it were I and not Anna who was destined soon to be another one among the already so numerous shades. It was a gruesome version of that phantom pregnancy I experienced when Anna first knew she was expecting Claire; now it seemed I was suffering a phantom illness along with her. On all sides there were portents of mortality. I was plagued by coincidences; long-forgotten things were suddenly remembered; objects turned up that for years had been lost. My life seemed to be passing before me, not in a flash as it is said to do for those about to drown, but in a sort of leisurely convulsion, emptying itself of its secrets and its quotidian mysteries in preparation for the moment when I must step into the black boat on the shadowed river with the coin of passage cold in my already coldening hand. Strange as it was, however, this imagined place of pre-departure was not entirely unfamiliar to me. On occasion in the past, in moments of inexplicable transport, in my study, perhaps, at my desk, immersed in words, paltry as they may be, for even the second-rater is sometimes inspired, I had felt myself break through the membrane of mere consciousness into another state, one which had no name, where ordinary laws did not operate, where time moved differently if it moved at all, where I was neither alive nor the other thing and yet more vividly present than ever I could be in what we call, because we must, the real world. And even years before that again, standing for instance with Mrs Grace in that sunlit living room, or sitting with Chloe in the dark of the picture-house, I was there and not there, myself and revenant, immured in the moment and yet hovering somehow on the point of departure. Perhaps all of life is no more than a long preparation for the leaving of it.

For Anna in her illness the nights were worst. That was only to be expected. So many things were only to be expected, now that the ultimate unexpected had arrived. In the dark all the breathless incredulity of daytime – *this cannot be happening to me!* – gave way in her to a dull, unmoving amazement. As she lay sleepless beside me I could almost feel her fear, spinning steadily inside her, like a dynamo. At moments in the dark she would laugh out loud, it was a sort of laugh, in renewed sheer surprise at the fact of this plight into which she had been so pitilessly, so ignominiously, delivered. Mostly, however, she kept herself quiet, lying on her side curled up like a lost explorer in his tent, half in a doze, half in a daze, indifferent equally, it seemed, to the prospect of survival or extinction. Up to now all her experiences had been temporary. Griefs had been assuaged, if only by time, joys had hardened into habit, her body had cured its own minor maladies. This, however, this was an absolute, a singularity, an end in itself, and yet she could not grasp it, could not absorb it. If there were pain, she said, it would at least be an authenticator, the thing to tell her that what had happened to her was realler than any reality she had known before now. But she was not in pain, not yet; there was only what she described as a general sense of agitation, a sort of interior fizzing, as if her poor, baffled body were scrabbling about inside itself, desperately throwing up defences against an invader that had already scuttled in by a secret way, its shiny black pincers snapping.

In those endless October nights, lying side by side in the darkness, toppled statues of ourselves, we sought escape from an intolerable present in the only tense possible, the past, that is, the faraway past. We went back over our earliest days together, reminding, correcting, helping each other, like two ancients tottering arm-in-arm along the ramparts of a town where they had once lived, long ago.

We recalled especially the smoky London summer in which we met and married. I spotted Anna first at a party in someone's flat one chokingly hot afternoon, all the windows wide open and the air blue with exhaust fumes from the street outside and the honking of passing buses sounding incongruously like fog horns through the clamour and murk in the crowded rooms. It was the size of her that first caught my attention. Not that she was so very large, but she was made on a scale different from that of any woman I had known before her. Big shoulders, big arms, big feet, that great head with its sweep of thick dark hair. She was standing between me and the window, in cheesecloth and sandals, talking to another woman, in that way that she had, at once intent and remote, dreamily twisting a lock of hair around a finger, and for a moment my eye had difficulty fixing a depth of focus, since it seemed that, of the two of them, Anna, being so much the bigger, must be much nearer to me than the one to whom she was speaking.

Ah, those parties, so many of them in those days. When I think back I always see us arriving, pausing together on the threshold for a moment, my hand on the small of her back, touching through brittle silk the cool deep crevice there, her wild smell in my nostrils and the heat of her hair against my cheek. How grand we must have looked, the two of us, making our entrance, taller than everyone else, our gaze directed over their heads as if fixed on some far fine vista that only we were privileged enough to see.

At the time she was trying to become a photographer, taking moody early-morning studies, all soot and raw silver, of some of the bleaker corners of the city. She wanted to work, to do something, to be someone. The East End called to her, Brick Lane, Spitalfields, such places. I never took any of this seriously. Perhaps I should have. She lived with her father in a rented apartment in a liver-coloured mansion on one of those gloomy backwaters off Sloane Square. It was an enormous place, with a succession of vast, high-ceilinged rooms and tall sash-windows that seemed to avert their glazed gaze from the mere human spectacle passing back and forth between them. Her Daddy, old Charlie Weiss – 'Don't worry, it's not a Jew name' – took to me at once. I was big and young and gauche, and my presence in those gilded rooms amused him. He was a merry little man with tiny delicate hands and tiny feet. His wardrobe was an amazement to me, innumerable Savile Row suits, shirts from Charvet in cream and bottle-green and aquamarine silk, dozens of pairs of handmade miniature shoes. His head, which he took to Trumper's to be shaved every other day – hair, he said, is fur, no human being should tolerate it – was a perfect polished egg, and he wore those big heavy spectacles favoured by tycoons of the time, with flanged ear-pieces and lenses the size of saucers in which his sharp little eyes darted like inquisitive, exotic fish. He could not be still, jumping up and sitting down and then jumping up again, seeming, under those lofty ceilings, a tiny burnished nut rattling around inside an outsized shell. On my first visit he showed me proudly around the flat, pointing out the pictures, old masters every one, so he imagined, the giant television set housed in a walnut cabinet, the bottle of Dom Perignon and basket of flawless inedible fruit that had been sent him that day by a business associate – Charlie did not have friends, partners, clients, but only associates. Light of summer thick as honey fell from the tall windows and glowed on the figured carpets. Anna sat on a sofa with her chin on her hand and one leg folded under her and watched dispassionately as I negotiated my way around her preposterous little father. Unlike most small people he was not at all intimidated by us big ones, and seemed indeed to find my bulk reassuring, and kept pressing close up to me, almost amorously; there were moments, while he was displaying the gleaming fruits of his success, when it seemed that he might of a sudden hop up and settle himself all comfy in the cradle of my arms. When he had mentioned his business interests for the third time I asked what business it was that he was in and he turned on me a gaze of flawless candour, those twin fish-bowls flashing.

'Heavy machinery,' he said, managing not to laugh.

Charlie regarded the spectacle of his life with delight and a certain wonder at the fact of having got away so easily with so much. He was a crook, probably dangerous, and wholly, cheerfully immoral. Anna held him in fond and rueful regard. How such a diminutive man had got so mighty a daughter was a mystery. Young as she was she seemed the tolerant mother and he the waywardly winning manchild. Her own mother had died when Anna was twelve and since then father and daughter had faced the world like a pair of nineteenth-century adventurers, a riverboat gambler, say, and his alibi girl. There were parties at the flat two or three times a week, raucous occasions through which champagne flowed like a bubbling and slightly rancid river. One night towards the end of that summer we came back from the park – I liked to walk with her at dusk through the dusty shadows under the trees that were already beginning to make that fretful, dry, papery rustle that harbinges autumn – and before we had even turned into the street we heard the sounds of tipsy revelry from the flat. Anna put a hand on my arm and we stopped. Something in the air of evening bespoke a sombre promise. She turned to

me and took one of the buttons of my jacket between a finger
and thumb and twisted it forward and back like the dial of a safe,
and in her usual mild and mildly preoccupied fashion invited me
to marry her.

Throughout that expectant, heat-hazed summer I seemed to
have been breathing off the shallowest top of my lungs, like a
diver poised on the highest board above that tiny square of blue
so impossibly far below. Now Anna had called up to me ring-
ingly to *jump, jump!* Today, when only the lower orders and what
remains of the gentry bother to marry, and everyone else takes a
partner, as if life were a dance, or a business venture, it is perhaps
hard to appreciate how vertiginous a leap it was back then to
plight one's troth. I had plunged into the louche world of Anna
and her father as if into another medium, a fantastical one
wherein the rules as I had known them up to then did not apply,
where everything shimmered and nothing was real, or was real
but looked fake, like that platter of perfect fruit in Charlie's flat.
Now I was being invited to become a denizen of these excitingly alien deeps. What Anna proposed to me, there in the dusty
summer dusk on the corner of Sloane Street, was not so much
marriage as the chance to fulfil the fantasy of myself.

The wedding party was held under a striped marquee in the
mansion's unexpectedly spacious back garden. It was one of
the last days of that summer's heat wave, the air, like scratched
glass, crazed by glinting sunlight. Throughout the afternoon long
gleaming motor cars kept pulling up outside and depositing yet
more guests, heron-like ladies in big hats and girls in white lip-
stick and white leather knee-high boots, raffish pinstriped gents,
delicate young men who pouted and smoked pot, and lesser,
indeterminate types, Charlie's business associates, sleek, watchful
and unsmiling, in shiny suits and shirts with different-coloured
collars and sharp-toed ankle boots with elasticated sides. Charlie
bounced about amongst them all, his blued pate agleam, pride
pouring off him like sweat. Late in the day a huddle of warm-
eyed, slow-moving, shy plump men in headdresses and spotless
white djellabas arrived in our midst like a flock of doves. Later
still a dumpy dowager in a hat got stridently drunk and fell down
and had to be carried away in the arms of her stone-jawed
chauffeur. As the light thickened in the trees and the shadow
of the next-door house began to close over the garden like a

trapdoor, and the last drunken couples in their clown-bright clothes were shuffling around the makeshift wooden dance floor one last time with their heads fallen on each other's shoulders and their eyes shut and eyelids fluttering, Anna and I stood on the tattered edges of it all, and a dark burst of starlings out of nowhere flew low over the marquee, their wings making a clatter that was like a sudden round of applause, exuberant and sarcastic.

Her hair. Suddenly I am thinking of her hair, the long dark lustrous coil of it falling away from her forehead in a sideways sweep. Even in her middle age there was hardly a strand of grey in it. We were driving home from the hospital one day when she lifted a length of it from her shoulder and held it close to her eyes and examined it strand by strand, frowning.

'Is there a bird called a baldicoot?' she asked.

'There is a bandicoot,' I said cautiously, 'but I don't think it's a bird. Why?'

'Apparently I shall be as bald as a coot in a month or two.'

'Who told you that?'

'A woman in the hospital who was having treatment, the kind I am to have. She was quite bald, so I suppose she would know.' For a while she watched the houses and the shops progressing past the car window in that stealthily indifferent way that they do, and then turned to me again. 'But what is a coot?'

'That's a bird.'

'Ah.' She chuckled. 'I'll be the spitting image of Charlie when it has all fallen out.'

She was.

He died, old Charlie, of a blood clot in the brain, a few months after we were married. Anna got all his money. There was not as much of it as I would have expected, but still, there was a lot.

The odd thing, one of the odd things, about my passion for Mrs Grace is that it fizzled out almost in the same moment that it achieved what might be considered its apotheosis. It all happened on the afternoon of the picnic. By then we were going about everywhere together, Chloe and Myles and I. How proud I was to be seen with them, these divinities, for I thought of course that they were the gods, so different were they from anyone I had hitherto known. My former friends in the Field, where I no longer played, were resentful of my desertion. 'He spends all his time now with his grand new friends,' I heard my mother one day telling one of their mothers. 'The boy, you know,' she added in an undertone, 'is a dummy.' To me she wondered why I did not petition the Graces to adopt me. 'I won't mind,' she said. 'Get you out from under my feet.' And she gave me a level look, harsh and unblinking, the same look she would often turn on me after my father had gone, as if to say, *I suppose you will be the next to betray me.* As I suppose I was.

My parents had not met Mr and Mrs Grace, nor would they. People in a proper house did not mix with people from the chalets, and we would not expect to mix with them. We did not drink gin, or have people down for the weekend, or leave touring maps of France insouciantly on show in the back windows of our motor cars – few in the Field even had a motor car. The social structure of our summer world was as fixed and hard of climbing as a ziggurat. The few families who owned holiday homes were at the top, then came those who could afford to put up at hotels – the Beach was more desirable than the Golf – then there were the house renters, and then us. All-the-year-rounders did not figure in this hierarchy; villagers in general, such as Duignan the dairyman or deaf Colfer the golf-ball collector, or the two Protestant spinsters at the Ivy Lodge, or the French woman who ran the tennis courts and was said to copulate regularly with her alsatian dog, all these were a class apart, their presence no more than the blurred background to our intenser, sun-shone-upon doings. That I had managed to scramble from the base of those steep social steps all the way up to the level of the Graces seemed, like my secret passion for Connie Grace, a token of specialness, of being the one chosen among so many of the unelect. The gods had singled me out for their favour.

The picnic. We went that afternoon in Mr Grace's racy motor car far down the Burrow, all the way to where the paved road ended. A note of the voluptuous had been struck immediately by the feel of the stippled leather of the seat cover sticking to the backs of my thighs below my shorts. Mrs Grace sat beside her husband in front, half turned towards him, an elbow resting on the back of her seat so that I had a view of her armpit, excitingly stubbled, and even caught now and then, when the breeze from the open window veered my way, a whiff of her sweat-dampened flesh's civet scent. She was wearing a garment which I believe even in those demurer days was called, with graphic frankness, a halter top, no more than a strapless white woollen tube, very tight, and very revealing of the curves of her bosom's heavy undersides. She had on her film star's sunglasses with the white frames and was smoking a fat cigarette. It excited me to watch as she took a deep drag and let her mouth hang open crookedly for a moment, a rich curl of smoke suspended motionless between those waxily glistening scarlet lips. Her fingernails too were painted a bright sanguineous red. I was seated directly behind her in the back seat, with Chloe in the middle between Myles and me. Chloe's hot, bony thigh was pressed negligently against my leg. Brother and sister were engaged in one of their private wordless contests, tussling and squirming, plucking at each other with pincer fingers and trying to kick each other's shins in the cramped space between the seats. I never could make out the rules of these games, if rules there were, although a winner always emerged in the end, Chloe, most often. I recall, with even now a faint stirring of pity for poor Myles, the first time I witnessed them playing in this way, or fighting, more like. It was a wet afternoon and we were trapped indoors at the Cedars. What savagery a rainy day could bring out in us children! The twins were sitting on the living room floor, on their heels, facing each other, knee to knee, glaring into each other's eyes, their fingers interlocked, swaying and straining, intent as a pair of battling samurai, until at last something happened, I did not see what it was, although it was decisive, and Myles all at once was forced to surrender. Snatching his fingers from her steely claws he threw his arms around himself – he was a great clutcher of the injured or insulted self – and began to cry, in frustration and rage, emitting a high, strangled whine, his lower lip clamped over the upper and his eyes squeezed shut and spurting big, shapeless tears, the whole effect too dramatic to be entirely convincing. And what a gloatingly feline look victorious Chloe gave me over her shoulder, her face unpleasantly pinched and an eye-tooth glinting. Now, in the car, she won again, doing something to Myles's wrist that made him squeal. 'Oh, do stop, you two,' their mother said wearily, barely giving them a glance. Chloe, still grinning thinly in triumph, pressed her hip harder against my leg, while Myles grimaced, making a pursed O of his lips, this time holding back his tears, but barely, and chafing his reddened wrist.

At the end of the road Mr Grace stopped the car, and the hamper with its sandwiches and tea cups and bottles of wine was lifted from the boot and we set off to walk along a broad track of hard sand marked by an immemorial half-submerged rusted barbed-wire fence. I had never liked, even feared a little, this wild reach of marsh and mud flats where everything seemed turned away from the land, looking off desperately towards the horizon as if in mute search for a sign of rescue. The mud shone blue as a new bruise, and there were stands of bulrushes, and forgotten marker buoys tethered to slimed-over rotting wooden posts. High tide here was never more than inches deep, the water racing in over the flats swift and shiny as mercury, stopping at nothing. Mr Grace scampered ahead handily, a folding chair clutched under each arm and that comical bucket hat tilted over his ear. We rounded the point and saw across the strait the town humped on its hill, a toy-like lavender jumble of planes and angles surmounted by a spire. Seeming to know where he was going Mr Grace struck off from the track into a meadow thronged with great tall ferns. We followed, Mrs Grace, Chloe, Myles, me. The ferns were as high as my head. Mr Grace was waiting for us on a grassy bank at the edge of the meadow, under an umbrella pine. Unnoticed, a shattered fern stalk had gouged a furrow in my bare ankle above the side of my sandal.

On a patch of grass between the low grassy bank and the wall of ferns a white cloth was spread. Mrs Grace, kneeling, a cigarette clamped in a corner of her mouth and one eye shut against the smoke, laid out the picnic things, while her husband, his hat falling further askew, struggled to draw a resistant wine cork. Myles was already off among the ferns. Chloe sat frog-like on her haunches, eating an egg sandwich. Rose – where is Rose? She is there, in her scarlet shirt and dancing pumps and dancer's tight black pants with the straps that go under the soles of her feet, and her hair black as a crow's wing tied in a plume behind her fine-boned head. But how did she get here? She had not been in the car with us. A bicycle, yes, I see a bicycle asprawl in abandon among the ferns, handlebars turned sideways and its front wheel jutting up at a somehow unseemly angle, a sly prefiguring, as it seems now, of what was to come. Mr Grace clamped the wine bottle between his knees and strained and strained, his earlobes turning red. Behind me Rose sat down at one corner of the tablecloth, leaning on a braced arm, her cheek almost resting on her shoulder, her legs folded off to the side, in a pose that should have been awkward but was not. I could hear Myles running in the ferns. Suddenly the cork came out of the wine bottle with a comical pop that startled us all.

We ate our picnic. Myles was pretending to be a wild beast and kept running in from the ferns and snatching handfuls of food and loping off again, hooting and whinnying. Mr and Mrs Grace drank their wine and presently Mr Grace was opening another bottle, this time with less difficulty. Rose said she was not hungry but Mrs Grace said that was nonsense and commanded her to eat and Mr Grace, grinning, offered her a banana. The afternoon was breezy under an as yet unclouded sky. The crooked pine soughed above us, and there was a smell of pine needles, and of grass and crushed ferns, and the salt tang of the sea. Rose sulked, I supposed because of Mrs Grace's rebuke and Mr Grace's offer of that lewd banana. Chloe was engrossed in picking at the stipples of a ruby cicatrice just below her elbow where the previous day a thorn had scratched her. I examined the fern-wound on my ankle, an angry pink groove between translucent deckle edges of whitish skin; it had not bled but in the deeps of the groove a clear ichor glinted. Mr Grace sat slumped into himself in a folding chair with one leg crossed on the other, smoking a cigarette, his hat pulled low on his forehead, shadowing his eyes.

I felt a soft small thing strike me on the cheek. Chloe had left off picking at her scabs and had thrown a breadcrumb at me. I looked at her and she looked back without expression and threw another crumb. This time she missed. I picked up the crumb from the grass and threw it back, but I missed, too. Mrs Grace was idly watching us, reclining on her side directly in front of me on the shallow incline of the verdant bank, her head supported on a hand. She had set the stem of her wine glass in the grass with the bowl wedged at an angle against a sideways lolling breast – I wondered, as so often, if they were not sore to carry, those big twin bulbs of milky flesh – and now she licked a fingertip and ran it around the rim of the glass, trying to make it sing, but no sound came. Chloe put a pellet of bread into her mouth and wetted it with spit and took it out again and kneaded it in her fingers with slow deliberation and took leisurely aim and threw it at me, but the wad fell short. 'Chloe!' her mother said, a wan reproach, and Chloe ignored her and smiled at me her cat's thin, gloating smile. She was a cruel-hearted girl, my Chloe. For her amusement of a day I would catch a handful of grasshoppers and tear off one of their back legs to prevent them escaping and put the twitching torsos in the lid of a polish tin and douse them in paraffin and set them alight. How intently, squatting with hands pressed on her knees, she would watch the unfortunate creatures as they seethed, boiling in their own fat.

She was making another spit-ball. 'Chloe, you are disgusting,' Mrs Grace said with a sigh, and Chloe, all at once bored, spat out the bread and brushed the crumbs from her lap and rose and walked off sulkily into the shadow of the pine tree.

Did Connie Grace catch my eye? Was that a complicit smile? With a heaving sigh she turned and lay down supine on the bank with her head leaning back on the grass and flexed one leg, so that suddenly I was allowed to see under her skirt along the inner side of her thigh all the way up to the hollow of her lap and the plump mound there sheathed in tensed white cotton. At once everything began to slow. Her emptied glass fell over in a swoon and a last drop of wine ran to the rim and hung an instant glittering and then fell. I stared and stared, my brow growing hot and my palms wet. Mr Grace under his hat seemed to be smirking at me but I did not care, he could smirk all he liked. His big wife, growing bigger by the moment, a foreshortened, headless giantess at whose huge feet I crouched in what felt almost like fear, gave a sort of wriggle and raised her knee higher still, revealing the crescent-shaped crease at the full-fleshed back of her leg where her rump began. A drumbeat in my temples was making the daylight dim. I was aware of the throbbing sting in my gouged ankle. And now from far off in the ferns there came a thin, shrill sound, an archaic pipe-note piercing through the lacquered air, and Chloe, up at the tree, scowled as if called to duty and bent and plucked a blade of grass and pressing it between her thumbs blew an answering note out of the conch-shell of her cupped hands.

After a timeless minute or two my sprawling maja drew in her leg and turned on her side again and fell asleep with shocking suddenness – her gentle snores were the sound of a small, soft engine trying and failing repeatedly to start – and I sat up, carefully, as if something delicately poised inside me might shatter at the slightest violent movement. All at once I had a sour sense of deflation. The excitement of a moment past was gone, and there was a dull restriction in my chest, and sweat on my eyelids and my upper lip, and the damp skin under the waistband of my shorts was prickly and hot. I felt puzzled, and strangely resentful, too, as if I were the one, not she, whose private self had been intruded upon and abused. It was a manifestation of the goddess I had witnessed, no doubt of that, but the instant of divinity had been disconcertingly brief. Under my greedy gaze Mrs Grace had been transformed from woman into daemon and then in a moment was mere woman again. One moment she was Connie Grace, her husband's wife, her children's mother, the next she was an object of helpless veneration, a faceless idol, ancient and elemental, conjured by the force of my desire, and then something in her had suddenly gone slack, and I had felt a qualm of revulsion and shame, not shame for myself and what I had purloined of her but, obscurely, for the woman herself, and not for anything she had done, either, but for what she was, as with a hoarse moan she turned on her side and toppled into sleep, no longer a demon temptress but herself only, a mortal woman.

Yet for all my disconcertion it is the mortal she, and not the divine, who shines for me still, with however tarnished a gleam, amidst the shadows of what is gone. She is in my memory her own avatar. Which is the more real, the woman reclining on the grassy bank of my recollections, or the strew of dust and dried marrow that is all the earth any longer retains of her? No doubt for others elsewhere she persists, a moving figure in the waxworks of memory, but their version will be different from mine, and from each other's. Thus in the minds of the many does the one ramify and disperse. It does not last, it cannot, it is not immortality. We carry the dead with us only until we die too, and then it is we who are borne along for a little while, and then our bearers in their turn drop, and so on into the unimaginable generations. I remember Anna, our daughter Claire will remember Anna and remember me, then Claire will be gone and there will be those who remember her but not us, and that will be our final dissolution. True, there will be something of us that will remain, a fading photograph, a lock of hair, a few fingerprints, a sprinkling of atoms in the air of the room where we breathed our last, yet none of this will be us, what we are and were, but only the dust of the dead.

As a boy I was quite religious. Not devout, only compulsive. The God I venerated was Yahweh, destroyer of worlds, not gentle Jesus meek and mild. The Godhead for me was menace, and I responded with fear and its inevitable concomitant, guilt. I was a very virtuoso of guilt in those younger days, and still am in these older ones, for that matter. At the time of my First Communion, or, more to the point, the First Confession that preceded it, a priest came daily to the convent school to induct our class of fledgling penitents into the intricacies of Christian Doctrine. He was a lean, pale fanatic with flecks of white stuff permanently at the corners of his lips. I am recalling with especial clarity an enraptured disquisition he delivered to us one fine May morning on the sin of looking. Yes, looking. We had been instructed in the various categories of sin, those of commission and omission, the mortal and the venial, the seven deadly, and the terrible ones that it was said only a bishop could absolve, but here it seemed was a new category: the passive sin. Did we imagine, Fr Foamfleck scoffingly enquired, pacing impetuously from door to window, from window to door, his cassock swishing and a star of light gleaming on his narrow, balding brow like a reflection of the divine effluvium itself, did we imagine that sin must always involve the performance of an action? Looking with lust or envy or hate is lusting, envying, hating; the wish unfollowed by the deed leaves an equal stain upon the soul. Had not the Lord himself, he cried, warming to his theme, had not the Lord himself insisted that a man who looks with an adulterous heart upon a woman has as good as committed the act? By now he had quite forgotten about us, as we sat like a little band of mice gazing up at him in awed incomprehension. Although all this was as much news to me as it was to everyone else in the class – what was adultery, a sin that only adults could commit? – I understood it well enough, in my way, and welcomed it, for even at the age of seven I was an old hand, or should I say eye, at spying upon acts I was not supposed to witness, and knew well the dark pleasure of taking things by sight and the darker shame that followed. So when I had looked my fill, and look I did and filled I was, up the silvery length of Mrs Grace's thigh to the crotch of her knickers and that crease across the plump top of her leg under her bum, it was natural that I should immediately cast about for fear that all that while someone in turn might have been looking at me, the looker. Myles who had come in from the ferns was busy ogling Rose, and Chloe was still lost in vacant reverie under the pine tree, but Mr Grace, now, had he not been observing me, all along, from under the brim of that hat of his? He sat as though collapsed into himself, his chin on his chest and his furred belly bulging out of his open shirt, a bare ankle still crossed on a bare knee, so that I could see along his inner leg, too, up to the great balled lump in his khaki shorts squeezed to bursting between thick thighs. All that long afternoon, as the pine tree spread its steadily deepening purple shadow across the grass towards him, he hardly left his folding chair except to refill his wife's wine glass or fetch something to eat – I can see him, crushing half a ham sandwich between bunched fingers and thumb and stuffing the resultant mush at one go into the red hole in his beard.

To us then, at that age, all adults were unpredictable, even slightly mad, but Carlo Grace required a particularly wary monitoring. He was given to the sudden feint, the unexpected pounce. Sitting in an armchair and seemingly lost in his newspaper, he would shoot out a hand quick as a striking snake as Chloe was passing by and catch hold of her ear or a handful of her hair and twist it vigorously and painfully, with never a word or a pause in his reading, as if arm and hand had acted of their own volition. He would break off deliberately in the midst of saying something and go still as a statue, a hand suspended, gazing blank-eyed into the nothing beyond one's nervously twitching shoulder as if attending to some dread alarm or distant tumult that only he could hear, and then suddenly would make a sham grab at one's throat and laugh hissingly through his teeth. He would engage the postman, who was halfway to being a halfwit, in earnest consultation about the prospects for the weather or the likely outcome of an upcoming football match, nodding and frowning and fingering his beard, as if what he was hearing were the purest pearls of wisdom, and then when the poor deluded fellow had gone off, whistling pridefully, he would turn to us and grin, with lifted eyebrows and pursed lips, waggling his head in soundless mirth. Although all my attention seemed to have been trained upon the others, I think now that it was from Carlo Grace I first derived the notion that I was in the presence of the gods. For all his remoteness and amused indifference, he was the one

who appeared to be in command over us all, a laughing deity, the
Poseidon of our summer, at whose beck our little world arranged
itself obediently into its acts and portions.

Still that day of licence and illicit invitation was not done.
As Mrs Grace, stretched there on the grassy bank, continued
softly snoring, a torpor descended on the rest of us in that little
dell, the invisible net of lassitude that falls over a company when
one of its number detaches and drops away into sleep. Myles was
lying on his stomach on the grass beside me but facing in the
opposite direction, still eyeing Rose where she was still seated
behind me on a corner of the tablecloth, oblivious, as always, of
his beady regard. Chloe was still standing in the shadow of the
pine tree, holding something in her hand, her face lifted, looking up intently, at a bird, perhaps, or just at the latticework of
branches against the sky, and those white puffs of cloud that had
begun to inch their way in from the sea. How pensive she was
yet how vividly defined, with that pine cone – was it? – in her
hands, her rapt gaze fixed amongst the sunshot boughs. Suddenly
she was the centre of the scene, the vanishing point upon which
everything converged, suddenly it was she for whom these
patterns and these shades had been arranged with such meticulous artlessness: that white cloth on the polished grass, the leaning, blue-green tree, the frilled ferns, even those little clouds,
trying to seem not to move, high up in the limitless, marine sky.
I glanced at Mrs Grace asleep, glanced almost with contempt.
All at once she was no more than a big archaic lifeless torso, the
felled effigy of some goddess no longer worshipped by the tribe
and thrown out on the midden, a target for the village boys with
their slingshots and their bows and arrows.

Abruptly, as if roused by the cold touch of my scorn, she sat up
and cast about her with a blurred look, blinking. She peered into
her wine glass and seemed surprised to find it empty. The drop
of wine that had fallen on her white halter had left a pink stain, she
rubbed it with a fingertip, clicking her tongue. Then she looked
about at us again and cleared her throat and announced that we
should all play a game of chase. Everyone stared at her, even Mr
Grace. '*I'm* not chasing anyone,' Chloe said from her place under
the tree's shade, and laughed, a disbelieving snort, and when
her mother said she must, and called her a spoilsport, she came
and stood beside her father's chair and leaned an elbow on his

shoulder and narrowed her eyes at her mother, and Mr Grace, old grinning goat god, put an arm around her hips and folded her in his hairy embrace. Mrs Grace turned to me. 'You'll play, won't you?' she said. 'And Rose.'

I see the game as a series of vivid tableaux, glimpsed instants of movement all rush and colour: Rose from the waist up racing through the ferns in her red shirt, her head held high and her black hair streaming behind her; Myles, with a streak of fern-juice on his forehead like warpaint, trying to wriggle out of my grasp as I dug my claw deeper into his flesh and felt the ball of his shoulder bone grind in its socket; another fleeting image of Rose running, this time on the hard sand beyond the clearing, where she was being chased by a wildly laughing Mrs Grace, two barefoot maenads framed for a moment by the bole and branches of the pine, beyond them the dull-silver glint of the bay and the sky a deep unvarying matt blue all the way down to the horizon. Here is Mrs Grace in a clearing in the ferns crouched on one knee like a sprinter waiting for the off, who, when I surprise her, instead of fleeing, as the rules of the game say that she should, beckons to me urgently and makes me crouch at her side and puts an arm around me and draws me tight against her so that I can feel the softly giving bulge of her breast and hear her heart beating and smell her milk-and-vinegar smell. 'Ssh!' she says and puts a finger to my lips – to mine, not her own. She is trembling, ripples of suppressed laughter run through her. I have not been so close to a grown-up woman since I was a child in my mother's arms, but in place of desire now I feel only a kind of surly dread. Rose discovers the two of us crouching there, and scowls. Mrs Grace, grasping the girl's hand as if to haul herself up, instead pulls her down on top of us, and there is a melee of arms and legs and Rose's flying hair and then the three of us, leaning back on our elbows and panting, are sprawled toe to toe in a star shape amid the crushed ferns. I scramble to my feet, suddenly afraid that Mrs Grace, my suddenly former beloved, will wantonly display her lap to me again, and she puts up a hand to shade her eyes and looks at me with an impenetrable, hard, unwarm smile. Rose too springs up, brushing at her shirt, and mutters something angrily that I do not catch and strides off into the ferns. Mrs Grace shrugs. 'Jealous,' she says, and then bids me fetch her cigarettes, for all of a sudden, she declares, she is dying for a fag.

When we returned to the grassy bank and the pine tree Chloe and her father were not there. The remains of the picnic, scattered on the white cloth, had a look of deliberateness to them, as if they had been arranged there, a message in code for us to decipher. 'That's nice,' Mrs Grace said sourly, 'they've left the clearing-up to us.' Myles emerged from the ferns again and knelt and picked a blade of grass and blew another reed-note between his thumbs and waited, still and rapt as a plaster faun, the sunlight burnishing his straw-pale hair, and a moment later from far off came Chloe's answering call, a pure high whistle piercing like a needle through the waning summer day.

On the subject of observing and being observed, I must mention the long, grim gander I took at myself in the bathroom mirror this morning. Usually these days I do not dally before my reflection any longer than is necessary. There was a time when I quite liked what I saw in the looking-glass, but not any more. Now I am startled, and more than startled, by the visage that so abruptly appears there, never and not at all the one that I expect. I have been elbowed aside by a parody of myself, a sadly dishevelled figure in a Hallowe'en mask made of sagging, pinkish-grey rubber that bears no more than a passing resemblance to the image of what I look like that I stubbornly retain in my head. Also, there is the problem that I have with mirrors. That is, I have many problems with mirrors, but mostly they are metaphysical in nature, whereas the one I speak of is entirely practical. Because of my inordinate and absurd size, shaving mirrors and the like are always set too low for me on the wall, so that I have to lean down to be able to view the entirety of my face. Lately when I see myself peering out of the glass, stooped like that, with that expression of dim surprise and vague, slow fright which is perpetual with me now, mouth slack and eyebrows arched as if in weary astonishment, I feel I have definitely something of the look of a hanged man.

When I came here first I thought of growing a beard, out of inertia more than anything else, but after three or four days I noticed that the stubble was of a peculiar dark-rust colour – now I know how Claire can be a redhead – nothing like the hair on my scalp, and frosted with specks of silver. This rufous stuff, coarse as sandpaper, combined with that shifty, bloodshot gaze,

made me into a comic-strip convict, a real hard case, not yet
hanged perhaps but definitely on Death Row. My temples where
the greying hair has gone sparse are flecked with chocolatey,
Avrilaceous freckles, or liver spots, I suppose they are, any one
of which, I am all too well aware, might in a moment turn ramp-
ant at the whim of a rogue cell. I note too that my rosacea is
coming on apace. The skin on my brow is marked all over with
rubescent blotches and there is an angry rash on the wings of my
nose, and even my cheeks are developing an unsightly red flush.
My venerable and much-thumbed copy of *Black's Medical
Dictionary*, by the estimable and ever unflappable William A. R.
Thomson, M.D. – Adam & Charles Black, London, thirtieth
edition, with 441 black-and-white, or grey-and-greyer, illustra-
tions and four colour plates which never fail to freeze the cockles
of my heart – informs me that rosacea, a nice name for an unpleasant complaint, is due to *a chronic congestion of the flush areas of
the face and forehead, leading to the formation of red papules*; the resultant erythema, the name we medical men give to redness of the
skin, tends to wax and wane but ultimately becomes permanent,
and may, the candid Doctor warns, *be accompanied by gross enlargement of the sebaceous glands (see SKIN), leading to the gross enlargement
of the nose known as rhinophyma (qv) or grog blossoms*. The repetition
there – *gross enlargement . . . gross enlargement* – is an uncharacter-
istic infelicity in Dr Thomson's usually euphonious if somewhat
antiquated prose style. I wonder if he does house calls. He would
be bound to have a calming bedside manner and a fund of information on all sorts of topics, not all of them health-related.
Medical men are more versatile than they are given credit for.
Roget of *Roget's Thesaurus* was a physician, did important
research on consumption and laughing gas, and no doubt cured
the odd patient, into the bargain. But grog blossoms, now, that
is something to look forward to.

When I consider my face in the glass like this I think, naturally,
of those last studies Bonnard made of himself in the bathroom
mirror at Le Bosquet towards the end of the war after his wife
had died – critics call these portraits pitiless, although I do not
see why pity should come into it – but in fact what my reflection
most reminds me of, I have just realised it, is that Van Gogh self-
portrait, not the famous one with bandage and tobacco pipe and
bad hat, but that one from an earlier series, done in Paris in 1887,

in which he is bare-headed in a high collar and Provence-blue necktie with all ears intact, looking as if he has just emerged from some form of punitive dousing, the forehead sloped and temples concave and cheeks sunken as from hunger; he peers out from the frame sidewise, warily, with wrathful foreboding, expecting the worst, as so he should.

This morning it was the state of my eyes that struck me most forcibly, the whites all craquelured over with those tiny bright-red veins and the moist lower lids inflamed and hanging a little way loose of the eyeballs. I have, I note, hardly any lashes left, I who when young had a silky set a girl might have envied. At the inner extremity of the upper lids there is a little bump just before the swoop of the canthus which is almost pretty except that it is permanently yellowish at the tip, as if infected. And that bud in the canthus itself, what is that for? Nothing in the human visage bears prolonged scrutiny. The pink-tinged pallor of my cheeks, which are, I am afraid, yes, sunken, just like poor Vincent's, was made the more stark and sickly by the radiance reflected off the white walls and the enamel of the sink. This radiance was not the glow of a northern autumn but seemed more like the hard, unyielding, dry glare of the far south. It glinted on the glass before me and sank into the distemper of the walls, giving them the parched, brittle texture of cuttlefish bone. A spot of it on the curve of the hand-basin streamed out-ward in all directions like an immensely distant nebula. Standing there in that white box of light I was transported for a moment to some far shore, real or imagined, I do not know which, although the details had a remarkable dreamlike definition, where I sat in the sun on a hard ridge of shaly sand holding in my hands a big flat smooth blue stone. The stone was dry and warm, I seemed to press it to my lips, it seemed to taste saltily of the sea's deeps and distances, far islands, lost places under leaning fronds, the frail skeletons of fishes, wrack and rot. The little waves before me at the water's edge speak with an animate voice, whispering eagerly of some ancient catastrophe, the sack of Troy, perhaps, or the sinking of Atlantis. All brims, brackish and shining. Water-beads break and fall in a silver string from the tip of an oar. I see the black ship in the distance, looming imperceptibly nearer at every instant. I am there. I hear your siren's song. I am there, almost there.

II

WE SEEMED to spend, Chloe and Myles and I, the most part of our days in the sea. We swam in sunshine and in rain; we swam in the morning, when the sea was sluggish as soup, we swam at night, the water flowing over our arms like undulations of black satin; one afternoon we stayed in the water during a thunderstorm, and a fork of lightning struck the surface of the sea so close to us we heard the crackle of it and smelt the burnt air. I was not much of a swimmer. The twins had been taking lessons since they were babies and clove the waves effortlessly, like two pairs of gleaming shears. What I lacked of skill and gracefulness I made up for in stamina. I could go long distances without stopping, and frequently did, given any kind of audience, churning along steadily in sidestroke until I had exhausted not only myself but the patience of the watchers on the strand as well.

It was at the end of one of these sad little gala displays that I had my first inkling of a change in Chloe's regard for me, or, should I say, an inkling that she had a regard for me and that a change was occurring in it. Late in the evening it was, and I had swum the distance – what, a hundred, two hundred yards? – between two of the green-slimed concrete groynes that long ago had been thrown out into the sea in a vain attempt to halt the creeping erosion of the beach. I stumbled out of the waves to find that Chloe had waited for me, on the shore, all the time that I was in the water. She stood huddled in a towel, shivering in spasms; her lips were lavender. 'There's no need to show off, you know,' she said crossly. Before I could reply – and what would I have said, anyway, since she was right, I had been showing off – Myles came leaping down from the dunes above us on wheeling legs and sprayed us both with sand and at once I had an image, perfectly clear and strangely stirring, of Chloe as I had first seen her that day when she jumped from the edge of that other dune into the midst of my life. Now she handed me my towel. We three were the only ones on the beach. The misty grey air of evening had the feel of dampened ash. I see us turn and walk away towards the gap in the dunes that led to Station Road. A corner of Chloe's towel trails in the sand. I go along with my towel draped over one shoulder and my wet hair slicked down, a Roman senator in miniature. Myles runs ahead. But who is it that lingers there on the strand in the half-light, by the darkening sea that seems to arch its back like a beast as the night fast advances from the fogged horizon? What phantom version of me is it that watches us – them – those three children – as they grow indistinct in that cinereal air and then are gone through the gap that will bring them out at the foot of Station Road?

I have not yet described Chloe. In appearance there was not much difference between us, she and I, at that age, I mean in terms of what of us might have been measured. Even her hair, almost white but darkening when it was wet to the colour of polished wheat, was hardly longer than mine. She wore it in a pageboy style, with a fringe at the front overhanging her handsome, high-domed, oddly convex forehead – like, it suddenly strikes me, remarkably like the forehead of that ghostly figure seen in profile hovering at the edge of Bonnard's *Table in Front of the Window*, the one with the fruit bowl and the book and the window that itself looks like a canvas seen from behind propped on an easel; everything for me is something else, it is a thing I notice increasingly. One of the older boys from the Field assured me one day with a snicker that a fringe like Chloe's was the certain sign of a girl who played with herself. I did not know what he meant, but I felt sure that Chloe did not play, on her own or otherwise. Not for her the games of rounders or of hunt that I had formerly enjoyed with the other youngsters in the Field. And how she sneered, flaring her nostrils, when I told her that among the families in the chalets there were girls of her age who still played with dolls. She held the majority of her coevals in high scorn. No, Chloe did not play, except with Myles, and what they did together was not really play.

The boy who had remarked on her fringe – suddenly I see him, as if he were before me here, Joe somebody, a hulking, big-boned fellow with jug ears and horrent hair – also said that Chloe had green teeth. I was outraged, but he was right; there was, I saw, the next time I had the opportunity to take a close look at them, a faint tinge to the enamel of her incisors that was green indeed, but a delicate damp grey-green, like the damp light under trees after rain, or the dull-apple shade of the undersides of leaves reflected in still water. Apples, yes, her breath too had an appley smell. Little animals we were, sniffing at each other. I liked in particular, when in time I got the chance to savour it, the cheesy tang in the crevices of her elbows and her knees. She was not, I am compelled to admit, the most hygienic of girls, and in general she gave off, more strongly as the day progressed, a flattish, fawnish odour, like that which comes out of, which used to come out of, empty biscuit tins in shops – do shops still sell loose biscuits from those big square tins? Her hands. Her eyes. Her bitten fingernails. All this I remember, intensely remember, yet it is all disparate, I cannot assemble it into a unity. Try as I may, pretend as I may, I am unable to conjure her as I can her mother, say, or Myles, or even jug-eared Joe from the Field. I cannot, in short, see her. She wavers before my memory's eye at a fixed distance, always just beyond focus, moving backward at exactly the same rate as I am moving forward. But since what I am moving forward into has begun to dwindle more and more rapidly, why can I not catch up with her? Even still I sometimes see her in the street, I mean someone who might be she, with the same domed forehead and pale hair, the same headlong and yet curiously hesitant, pigeon-toed stride, but always too young, years, years too young. This is the mystery that baffled me then, and that baffles me yet. How could she be with me one moment and the next not? How could she be elsewhere, absolutely? That was what I could not understand, could not be reconciled to, cannot still. Once out of my presence she should by right become pure figment, a memory of mine, a dream of mine, but all the evidence told me that even away from me she remained solidly, stubbornly, incomprehensibly herself. And yet people do go, do vanish. That is the greater mystery; the greatest. I too could go, oh, yes, at a moment's notice I could go and be as though I had not been, except that the long habit of living indisposeth me for dying, as Doctor Browne has it.

'*Patient*,' Anna said to me one day towards the end, 'that is an odd word. I must say, I don't feel patient at all.'

When exactly I transferred my affections – how incorrigibly fond I am of these old-fashioned formulations! – from mother to daughter I cannot recollect. There was that moment of insight

and intensity at the picnic, with Chloe, under the pine tree, but
that was an aesthetic rather than amorous or erotic crystallisation.
No, I recall no grand moment of recognition and acknowledg-
ment, no slipping of Chloe's hand shyly into mine, no sudden
stormy embrace, no stammered profession of eternal love. That
is, there must have been some or even all of these, must have been
a first time we held hands, embraced, made declarations, but
these first times are lost in the folds of an ever more evanescent
past. Even that evening when with chattering teeth I waded out
of the sea and found her waiting for me blue-lipped on the strand
in the dusk I did not suffer the soundless detonation that love is
supposed to set off in even a boy's supposedly unsusceptible
breast. I saw how cold she was, and realised how long she had
waited, registered too the brusquely tender way in which she
drew the wing of the towel across my scrawny, goosefleshed ribs
and draped it on my shoulder, but saw and realised and registered
with little more than a mild glow of gratification, as though a
warm breath had fanned across a flame burning inside me somewhere in the vicinity of my heart and made it briefly flare. Yet
all along a transmutation, not to say a transubstantiation, must
have been taking place, in secret.

I do recall a kiss, one out of the so many that I have forgotten.
Whether or not it was our first kiss I do not know. They meant
so much then, kisses, they could set the whole kit and caboodle
going, flares and firecrackers, fountains, gushing geysers, the lot.
This one took place – no, was exchanged – no, was consum-
mated, that is the word, in the corrugated-iron picture-house,
which all along has been surreptitiously erecting itself for this
very purpose out of the numerous sly references I have sprinkled
through these pages. It was a barn-like structure set on a bit of
scrubby waste-land between the Cliff Road and the beach. It had
a steeply angled roof and no windows, only a door at the side,
hung with a long curtain, of leather, I think, or somesuch stiff
heavy stuff, to keep the screen from being whited-out when late-
comers slipped in during matinées or at evening while the sun
was shooting out its last piercing rays from behind the tennis
courts. For seating there were wooden benches – we called them
forms – and the screen was a large square of linen which any stray
draught would set languorously asway, giving an extra undula-
tion to some heroine's silk-clad hips or an incongruous quiver

to a fearless gunslinger's gun-hand. The proprietor was a Mr Reckett, or Rickett, a small man in a Fair Isle jumper, assisted by his two big handsome teenage sons, who were a little ashamed, I always thought, of the family business, with its taint of peep-shows and the burlesque. There was only one projector, a noisy affair with a tendency to overheat – I am convinced I once saw smoke coming out of its innards – so that a full-length feature required at least two reel changes. During these intervals Mr R., who was also the projectionist, did not raise the lights, thus affording – deliberately, I am sure, for Reckett's or Rickett's Picture-House had an invitingly disreputable reputation – the numerous couples in the house, even the under-age ones, an opportunity for a minute or two of covert erotic fumbling in the pitch-dark.

On that afternoon, the rainy Saturday afternoon of this momentous kiss I am about to describe, Chloe and I were sitting in the middle of a bench near the front, so close to the screen that it seemed to tilt out over us at the top and even the most benign of the black-and-white phantoms flickering across it loomed with a manic intensity. I had been holding Chloe's hand for so long I had ceased to feel it in mine – not the primal encounter itself could have fused two fleshes so thoroughly as did those early hand-holdings – and when with a lurch and a stutter the screen went blank and her fingers twitched like fishes I twitched too. Above us the screen retained a throbbing grey penumbral glow that lasted a long moment before fading, and of which something seemed to remain even when it was gone, the ghost of a ghost. In the dark there were the usual hoots and whistles and a thunderous stamping of feet. As at a signal, under this canopy of noise, Chloe and I turned our heads simultaneously and, devout as holy drinkers, dipped our faces towards each other until our mouths met. We could see nothing, which intensified all sensations. I felt as if we were flying, without effort, dream-slowly, through the dense, powdery darkness. The clamour around us was immensely far off now, the mere rumour of a distant uproar. Chloe's lips were cool and dry. I tasted her urgent breath. When at last with a strange little whistling sigh she drew her face away from mine a shimmer passed along my spine, as if something hot inside it had suddenly liquefied and run down its hollow length. Then Mr Rickett or Reckett – perhaps it was Rockett? – brought the projector to sputtering life again and the crowd subsided into more or less quiet. The screen flared white, the film clattered through its gate, and in the second before the soundtrack started up I heard the heavy rain that had been drumming on the iron roof above us suddenly cease.

Happiness was different in childhood. It was so much then a matter simply of accumulation, of taking things – new experiences, new emotions – and applying them like so many polished tiles to what would someday be the marvellously finished pavilion of the self. And incredulity, that too was a large part of being happy, I mean that euphoric inability fully to believe one's simple luck. There I was, suddenly, with a girl in my arms, figuratively, at least, doing the things that grown-ups did, holding her hand, and kissing her in the dark, and, when the picture had ended, standing aside, clearing my throat in grave politeness, to allow her to pass ahead of me under the heavy curtain and through the doorway out into the rain-washed sunlight of the summer evening. I was myself and at the same time someone else, someone completely other, completely new. As I walked behind her amid the trudging crowd in the direction of the Strand Café I touched a fingertip to my lips, the lips that had kissed hers, half expecting to find them changed in some infinitely subtle but momentous way. I expected everything to be changed, like the day itself, that had been sombre and wet and hung with big-bellied clouds when we were going into the picture-house in what had still been afternoon and now at evening was all tawny sunlight and raked shadows, the scrub grass dripping with jewels and a red sail-boat out on the bay turning its prow and setting off towards the horizon's already dusk-blue distances.

The café. In the café. In the café we.

It was an evening just like that, the Sunday evening when I came here to stay, after Anna had gone at last. Although it was autumn and not summer the dark-gold sunlight and the inky shadows, long and slender in the shape of felled cypresses, were the same, and there was the same sense of everything drenched and jewelled and the same ultramarine glitter on the sea. I felt inexplicably lightened; it was as if the evening, in all the drench and drip of its fallacious pathos, had temporarily taken over from me the burden of grieving. Our house, or my house, as supposedly it was now, had still not been sold, I had not yet had the heart to put it on the market, but I could not have stayed there a moment longer. After Anna's death it went hollow, became a vast echo-chamber. There was something hostile in the air, too, the growling surliness of an old hound unable to understand where its beloved mistress has gone and resentful of the master who remains. Anna would allow no one to be told of her illness. People suspected something was up, but not, until the final stages, that what was up, for her, was the game itself. Even Claire had been left to guess that her mother was dying. And now it was over, and something else had begun, for me, which was the delicate business of being the survivor.

Miss Vavasour was shyly excited by my arrival, two small round spots like dabs of pink crêpe paper glowed high on her finely wrinkled cheeks and she kept clasping her hands before her and pursing her lips to stop herself smiling. When she opened the door Colonel Blunden was there, bobbing behind her in the hallway, now at this shoulder now at that; I could see straight away he did not like the look of me. I sympathise; after all, he was cock of the walk here before I came and knocked him off his perch. Keeping a choleric glare directed at my chin, which was on his eye-level, for he is low-sized despite the ramrod spine, he pumped my hand and cleared his throat, all bluff and manly and barking comments about the weather, rather over-playing the part of the old soldier, I thought. There is something about him that is not quite right, something too shiny, too studiedly plausible. Those glossy brogues, the Harris tweed jacket with leather patches on the elbows and the cuffs, the canary-yellow waistcoat he sports at weekends, it all seems a little too good to be true. He has the glazed flawlessness of an actor who has been playing the same part for too long. I wonder if he really is an old army man. He does a good job of hiding his Belfast accent but hints of it keep escaping, like trapped wind. And anyway, why hide it, what does he fear it might tell us? Miss Vavasour confides that she has spotted him on more than one occasion slipping into church of a Sunday for early mass. A Belfast Catholic colonel? Rum; very.

In the bay of the window in the lounge, formerly the living room, a hunting table was set for tea. The room was much as I remembered it, or looked as if it was as I remembered, for memories are always eager to match themselves seamlessly to the things and places of a revisited past. The table, was that the one where Mrs Grace had stood arranging flowers that day, the day of the dog with the ball? It was laid elaborately, big silver teapot with matching strainer, best bone china, antique creamer, tongs for the sugar cubes, doilies. Miss Vavasour was in Japanese mode, her hair done up in a bun and pierced with the two big crossed pins, making me think, incongruously, of those erotic prints of the Japanese eighteenth century in which puffy, porcelain-faced matrons suffer imperturbably the gross attentions of grimacing gentlemen with outsized members and, I am always struck to notice, remarkably pliant toes.

The conversation did not flow. Miss Vavasour was nervous still and the Colonel's stomach rumbled. Late sunlight striking through a bush outside in the blustery garden dazzled our eyes and made the things on the table seem to shake and shift. I felt oversized, clumsy, constrained, like a big delinquent child sent by its despairing parents into the country to be watched over by a pair of elderly relatives. Was it all a hideous mistake? Should I mumble some excuse and flee to a hotel for the night, or go home, even, and put up with the emptiness and the echoes? Then I reflected that I had come here precisely so that it should be a mistake, that it should be hideous, that it should be, that I should be, in Anna's word, inappropriate. 'You're mad,' Claire had said, 'you'll die of boredom down there.' It was all right for her, I retorted, she had got herself a nice new flat – *wasting no time*, I did not add. 'Then come and live with me,' she said, 'there's room enough for two.' Live with her! Room for two! But I only thanked her and said no, that I wished to be on my own. I cannot bear the way she looks at me these days, all tenderness and daughterly concern, her head held to one side in just the way that Anna used to do, one eyebrow lifted and her forehead wrinkled solicitously. I do not want solicitude. I want anger, vituperation, violence. I am like a man with an agonising toothache who despite the pain takes a vindictive pleasure in prodding the point of his tongue again and again deep into the throbbing cavity. I imagine a fist flying out of nowhere and striking me full in the face, I almost feel the thud and hear the nose-bone breaking, even the thought of it affords me a grain of sad satisfaction. After the funeral, when people came back to the house – that was awful, almost unbearable – I gripped a wine glass so hard it shattered in my fist. Gratified, I watched my own blood drip as though it were the blood of an enemy to whom I had dealt a savage slash.

'So you're in the art business, then,' the Colonel said warily. 'A lot in that, yes?'

He meant money. Miss Vavasour, pinched-lipped, frowned at him fiercely and gave her head a reproving shake. 'He only writes about it,' she said in a whisper, gulping the words as she spoke them, as if that way I would be spared hearing them.

The Colonel looked quickly from me to her and back again and dumbly nodded. He expects to get things wrong, he is inured to it. He drinks his tea with a little finger cocked. The little finger of his other hand is hooked permanently flat against the palm, it is a syndrome, not uncommon, the name of which I have forgotten; it looks painful but he says it is not. He makes curiously elegant, sweeping gestures with that hand, a conductor calling up the woodwinds or urging a fortissimo from the chorus. He has a slight tremor, too, more than once the tea cup clacked against his front teeth, which must be dentures, so white and even are they. The skin of his weatherbeaten face and the backs of his hands is wrinkled and brown and shiny, like shiny brown paper that had been used to wrap something unwrappable.

'I see,' he said, not seeing at all.

One day in 1893 Pierre Bonnard spied a girl getting off a Paris tram and, attracted by her frailty and pale prettiness, followed her to her place of work, a *pompes funèbres*, where she spent her days sewing pearls on to funeral wreaths. Thus death at the start wove its black ribbon into their lives. He quickly made her acquaintance – I suppose these things were managed with ease and aplomb in the *Belle Époque* – and shortly afterwards she left her job, and everything else in her life, and went to live with him. She told him her name was Marthe de Méligny, and that she was sixteen. In fact, although he was not to discover it until more than thirty years later when he got round to marrying her at last, her real name was Maria Boursin, and when they had met she had been not sixteen but, like Bonnard, in her middle twenties. They were to remain together, through thick and thin, or rather say, through thin and thinner, until her death nearly fifty years later. Thadée Natanson, one of Bonnard's earliest patrons, in a memoir of the painter, recalled with swift, impressionistic strokes the elfin Marthe, writing of *her wild look of a bird, her movements on tiptoe*. She was secretive, jealous, fiercely possessive, suffered from a persecution complex, and was a great and dedicated hypochondriac. In 1927 Bonnard bought a house, Le Bosquet, in the undistinguished little town of Le Cannet on the Côte d'Azur, where he lived with Marthe, bound with her in intermittently tormented seclusion, until her death fifteen years later. At Le Bosquet she developed a habit of spending long hours in the bath, and it was in her bath that Bonnard painted her, over and over, continuing the series even after she had died. The *Baignoires* are the triumphant culmination of his life's work. In the *Nude in the Bath, with Dog*, begun in 1941, a year before Marthe's death and not completed until 1946, she lies there, pink and mauve and gold, a goddess of the floating world, attenuated, ageless, as much dead as alive, beside her on the tiles her little brown dog, her familiar, a dachshund, I think, curled watchful on its mat or what may be a square of flaking sunlight falling from an unseen window. The narrow room that is her refuge vibrates around her, throbbing in its colours. Her feet, the left one tensed at the end of its impossibly long leg, seem to have pushed the bath out of shape and made it bulge at the left end, and beneath the bath on that side, in the same force field, the floor is pulled out of alignment too, and seems on the point of pouring away into the corner, not like a floor at all but a moving pool of dappled water. All moves here, moves in stillness, in aqueous silence. One hears a drip, a ripple, a fluttering sigh. A rust-red patch in the water beside the bather's right shoulder might be rust, or old blood, even. Her right hand rests on her thigh, stilled in the act of supination, and I think of Anna's hands on the table that first day when we came back from seeing Mr Todd, her helpless hands with palms upturned as if to beg something from someone opposite her who was not there.

She too, my Anna, when she fell ill, took to taking extended baths in the afternoon. They soothed her, she said. Throughout the autumn and winter of that twelvemonth of her slow dying we shut ourselves away in our house by the sea, just like Bonnard and his Marthe at Le Bosquet. The weather was mild, hardly weather at all, the seemingly unbreakable summer giving way imperceptibly to a year-end of misted-over stillness that might have been any season. Anna dreaded the coming of spring, all that unbearable bustle and clamour, she said, all that life. A deep, dreamy silence accumulated around us, soft and dense, like silt. She was so quiet, there in the bathroom on the first-floor return, that I became alarmed sometimes. I imagined her slipping down without a sound in the enormous old claw-footed bath until her face was under the surface and taking a last long watery breath. I would creep down the stairs and stand on the return, not making a sound, seeming suspended there, as if I were the one under water, listening desperately through the panels of the door for sounds of life. In some foul and treacherous chamber of my heart, of course, I wanted her to have done it, wanted it all to be over with, for me as well as for her. Then I would hear a soft heave of water as she stirred, the soft splash as she lifted a hand for the soap or a towel, and I would turn away and plod back to my room and shut the door behind me and sit down at my desk and gaze out into the luminous grey of evening, trying to think of nothing.

'Look at you, poor Max,' she said to me one day, 'having to watch your words and be nice all the time.' She was in the nursing home by then, in a room at the far end of the old wing with a corner window that looked out on a wedge of handsomely unkempt lawn and a restless and, to my eye, troubling stand of great tall blackish-green trees. The spring that she had dreaded had come and gone, and she had been too ill to mind its agitations, and now it was a damply hot, glutinous summer, the last one she would see. 'What do you mean,' I said, 'having to be nice?' She said so many strange things nowadays, as if she were already somewhere else, beyond me, where even words had a different meaning. She moved her head on the pillow and smiled at me. Her face, worn almost to the bone, had taken on a frightful beauty. 'You are not even allowed to hate me a little, any more,' she said, 'like you used to.' She looked out at the trees a while and then turned back to me again and smiled again and patted my hand. 'Don't look so worried,' she said. 'I hated you, too, a little. We were human beings, after all.' By then the past tense was the only one she cared to employ.

'Would you like to see your room now?' Miss Vavasour enquired. Last spikes of sunlight through the bay window before us were falling like shards of glass in a burning building. The

Colonel was brushing crossly at the front of his yellow waistcoat where he had spilled a splash of tea. He looked put out. Probably he had been saying something to me and I had not been listening. Miss Vavasour led the way into the hall. I was nervous of this moment, the moment when I would have to take on the house, to put it on, as it were, like something I had worn in another, prelapsarian life, a once fashionable hat, say, an outmoded pair of shoes, or a wedding suit, smelling of mothballs and no longer fitting around the waist and too tight under the arms but bulging with memories in every pocket. The hall I did not recognise at all. It is short, narrow and ill-lit, and the walls are divided horizontally by a beaded runner and papered on their lower halves with painted-over anaglypta that looks to be a hundred years old or more. I do not recall there having been a hallway here. I thought the front door opened directly into – well, I am not sure what I thought it opened into. The kitchen? As I padded behind Miss Vavasour with my bag in my hand, like the well-mannered murderer in some old black-and-white thriller, I found that the model of the house in my head, try as it would to accommodate itself to the original, kept coming up against a stubborn resistance. Everything was slightly out of scale, all angles slightly out of true. The staircase was steeper, the landing pokier, the lavatory window looked not on to the road, as I thought it should, but back across the fields. I experienced a sense almost of panic as the real, the crassly complacent real, took hold of the things I thought I remembered and shook them into its own shape. Something precious was dissolving and pouring away between my fingers. Yet how easily, in the end, I let it go. The past, I mean the real past, matters less than we pretend. When Miss Vavasour left me in what from now on was to be *my room* I threw my coat over a chair and sat down on the side of the bed and breathed deep the stale unlived-in air, and felt that I had been travelling for a long time, for years, and had at last arrived at the destination to where, all along, without knowing it, I had been bound, and where I must stay, it being, for now, the only possible place, the only possible refuge, for me.

My friendly robin appeared a moment ago in the garden and I suddenly realised what it was that Avril's freckles reminded me of, that day of our encounter in Duignan's yard. The bird as usual

stops on its thirdmost perch in the holly bush and studies the
lay of the land with a truculent, bead-bright eye. Robins are a
famously fearless breed, and this one seems quite unconcerned
when Tiddles from next door comes stalking through the long
grass, and even gives what sounds like a sardonic cheep and ruffles
up its feathers and expands its blood-orange breast, as if to
demonstrate teasingly what a plump and toothsome morsel it
would make, if cats could fly. Seeing the bird alight there I
remembered at once, with a pang that was exactly the same size
and as singular as the bird itself, the nest in the gorse bushes that
was robbed. I was quite a bird enthusiast as a boy. Not the watching kind, I was never a watcher, I had no interest in spotting and
tracking and classifying, all that would have been beyond me, and
would have bored me, besides; no, I could hardly distinguish one
species from another, and knew little and cared less about their
history or habits. I could find their nests, though, that was my
specialty. It was a matter of patience, alertness, quickness of eye,
and something else, a capacity to be at one with the tiny creatures
I was tracking to their lairs. A savant whose name for the moment
I forget has posited as a refutation of something or other the asser-
tion that it is impossible for a human being to imagine fully what
it would be like to be a bat. I take his point in general, but I
believe I could have given him a fair account of such creature-
hood when I was young and still part animal myself.

I was not cruel, I would not kill a bird or steal its eggs, certainly
not. What drove me was curiosity, the simple passion to know
something of the secrets of other, alien lives.

A thing that always struck me was the contrast between nest
and egg, I mean the contingency of the former, no matter how
well or even beautifully it was fashioned, and the latter's com-
pletedness, its pristine fulness. Before it is a beginning an egg is
an absolute end. It is the very definition of self-containment.
I hated to see a broken egg, that tiny tragedy. In the instance I am
thinking of I must inadvertently have led someone to the nest.
It was in a clump of gorse on a slanted headland in the midst of
open fields, I would easily have been spotted going to it, as I had
been doing for weeks, so that the hen bird had grown used to
me. What was it, thrush, blackbird? Some such largish species,
anyway. Then one day I arrived and the eggs were gone. Two
had been taken and the third was smashed on the ground under

the bush. All that remained of it was a smear of mingled yolk and glair and a few fragments of shell, each with its stippling of tiny, dark-brown spots. I should not make too much of the moment, I am sure I was as sentimentally heartless as the next boy, but I can still see the gorse, I can smell the buttery perfume of its blossoms, I can recall the exact shade of those brown speckles, so like the ones on Avril's pallid cheeks and on the saddle of her nose. I have carried the memory of that moment through a whole half century, as if it were the emblem of something final, precious and irretrievable.

Anna leaning sideways from the hospital bed, vomiting on to the floor, her burning brow pressed in my palm, full and frail as an ostrich egg.

I am in the Strand Café, with Chloe, after the pictures and that memorable kiss. We sat at a plastic table drinking our favourite drink, a tall glass of fizzy orange crush with a dollop of vanilla ice cream floating in it. Remarkable the clarity with which, when I concentrate, I can see us there. Really, one might almost live one's life over, if only one could make a sufficient effort of recollection. Our table was near the open doorway from which a fat slab of sunlight lay fallen at our feet. Now and then a breeze from outside would wander in absent-mindedly, strewing a whisper of fine sand across the floor, or bringing with it an empty sweet-paper that advanced and stopped and advanced again, making a scraping sound. There was hardly anyone else in the place, some boys, or young men, rather, in a corner at the back playing cards, and behind the counter the proprietor's wife, a large, sandy-haired, not unhandsome woman, gazing off through the doorway in a blank-eyed dream. She wore a pale-blue smock or apron with a scalloped white edging. What was her name? What was it. No, it will not come – so much for Memory's prodigious memory. Mrs Strand, I shall call her Mrs Strand, if she has to be called anything. She had a particular way of standing, certainly I remember that, sturdy and four-square, one freckled arm extended and a fist pressed knuckles-down on the high back of the cash register. The ice cream and orange mixture in our glasses had a topping of sallow froth. We drank through paper straws, avoiding each other's eye in a new access of shyness. I had a sense of a general, large, soft settling, as of a sheet unfurling and falling on a bed, or a tent collapsing into the cushion of its own air. The fact of that kiss in the dark of the picture-house – I am coming to think it must have been our first kiss, after all – sat like an amazement between us, unignorably huge. Chloe had the faintest blond shadow of a moustache, I had felt its sable touch against my lip. Now my glass was almost empty and I was afraid the last of the liquid in the straw would do its embarrassing intestinal rattle. Covertly from under lowered lids I looked at Chloe's hands, one resting on the table and the other holding her glass. The fingers were fat to the first knuckle and from there tapered to the tip: her mother's hands, I realised. Mrs Strand's wireless set was playing some song to the swoony tune of which Chloe absently hummed along. Songs were so important then, moaning of longing and loss, the very twang of what we thought was love. In the night as I lay in my bed in the chalet the melodies would come to me, a faint, brassy blaring carried on the sea breeze from the ballrooms at the Beach Hotel or the Golf, and I would think of the couples, the permed girls in brittle blues and acid greens, the quiffed young men in chunky sportscoats and shoes with inch-thick, squashy soles, circling there in the dusty, hot half-dark. *O darling lover lonesome moonlight kisses heart and soul!* And beyond all that, outside, unseen, the beach in the darkness, the sand cool on top but keeping still the day's warmth underneath, and the long lines of white waves breaking on the bias, lit from inside themselves somehow, and over everything the night, silent, secret and intent.

'That picture was stupid,' Chloe said. She brought her face close to the rim of the glass, her fringe hanging free. Her hair was pale as the sunlight on the floor at her foot ... But wait, this is wrong. This cannot have been the day of the kiss. When we left the picture-house it was evening, an evening after rain, and now it is the middle of an afternoon, hence that soft sunlight, that meandering breeze. And where is Myles? He was with us at the pictures, so where would he have gone, he who never left his sister's side unless driven from it? Really, Madam Memory, I take back all my praise, if it is Memory herself who is at work here and not some other, more fanciful muse. Chloe gave a snort. 'As if they wouldn't have known that highwayman was a woman.'

I looked at her hands again. The one that had been holding the glass high up had slipped down to encircle the base, in which a spiked point of pure white light steadily burned, while the other, bending the straw to her lips delicately between a thumb and forefinger, cast a pale shadow on the table in the shape of a bird's beaked and high-plumed head. Again I thought of her mother, and this time I felt briefly something sharp and burning in my breast, as if a heated needle had touched my heart. Was it a twinge of guilt? For what would Mrs Grace feel, what would she say, if she were to spy me here at this table ogling the mauve shading in the hollow of her daughter's cheek as she sucked up the last of her ice-cream soda? But I did not really care, not deep down, deep past guilt and suchlike affects. Love, as we call it, has a fickle tendency to transfer itself, by a heartless, sidewise shift, from one bright object to a brighter, in the most inappropriate of circumstances. How many wedding days have ended with the tipsy and dyspeptic groom gazing miserably down on his brand new bride bouncing under him on the king-size bed of the honeymoon suite and seeing her best friend's face, or the face of her prettier sister or even, heaven help us, of her sportive mother?

Yes, I was falling in love with Chloe – had fallen, the thing was done already. I had that sense of anxious euphoria, of happy, helpless toppling, which the one who knows he will have to do the loving always feels, at the precipitous outset. For even at such a tender age I knew that there is always a lover and a loved, and knew which one, in this case, I would be. Those weeks with Chloe were for me a series of more or less enraptured humiliations. She accepted me as a suppliant at her shrine with disconcerting complacency. In her more distracted moods she would hardly deign to notice my presence, and even when she gave me her fullest attention there was always a flaw in it, a fleck of preoccupation, of absence. This wilful vagueness tormented and infuriated me, but worse was the possibility that it might not be willed. That she might choose to disdain me I could accept, could welcome, even, in an obscurely pleasurable way, but the thought that there were intervals when I simply faded to transparency in her gaze, no, that was not to be borne. Often when I broke in on one of her vacant silences she would give a faint start and glance quickly about, at the ceiling or into a corner of the room, anywhere but at me, in search of the source of the voice that had addressed her. Was this a heartless teasing or were these moments of blankness genuine? Galled beyond bearing

I would seize her by the shoulders and shake her, demanding that she see me and only me, but she would go slack in my hands and cross her eyes and let her head waggle like a rag doll's, laughing in her throat and sounding unnervingly like Myles, and when I flung her roughly from me in disgust she would fall back on sand or sofa and lie sprawled with limbs awry and pretend to be grotesquely, grinningly, dead.

Why did I put up with her caprices, her high-handedness? I was never one to suffer slights easily, and always made sure to get my own back, even on loved ones, or on loved ones especially. My forbearance in Chloe's case was due, I believe, to a strong urge of protectiveness that I had towards her. Let me explain, it is interesting, I think it is interesting. A nice, an exquisite, tactfulness was in operation here. Since she was the one on whom I had chosen, or had been chosen, to lavish my love, she must be preserved as nearly flawless as possible, spiritually and in her actions. It was imperative that I save her from herself and her faults. The task fell to me naturally since her faults were her faults, and she could not be expected to evade their bad effects by her own volition. And not only must she be saved from these faults and their consequences for her behaviour but she must be kept from all knowledge of them, too, insofar as it was possible for me to do so. And not just her active faults. Ignorance, incapacity of insight, dull complacency, such things too must be masked, their manifestations denied. The fact for instance that she did not know that she was later in my affections than her mother, of all people, made her seem almost piteously vulnerable in my eyes. Mark, the issue was not the fact of her being a late-comer in my affections, but her ignorance of that fact. If she were somehow to find out my secret she would likely be let down in her own estimation, would think herself a fool not to have seen what I felt for her mother, and might even be tempted to feel second to her mother in having been my second choice. And that must not be.

In case I should seem to be casting myself in too benevolent a light, I hasten to say that my concern and care in the matter of Chloe and her shortcomings was not for her benefit alone. Her self-esteem was of far less importance to me than my own, although the latter was dependent on the former. If her sense of herself were tainted, by doubt or feelings of foolishness or of lack of perspicacity, my regard for her would itself be tainted. So there must be no confrontations, no brutal enlightenments, no telling of terrible truths. I might shake her by the shoulders until her bones rattled, I might throw her to the ground in disgust, but I must not tell her that I had loved her mother before I loved her, that she smelled of stale biscuits, or that Joe from the Field had remarked the green tinge of her teeth. As I walked meekly behind her swaggering figure, my fond and fondly anguished gaze fixed on the blond comma of hair at the nape of her neck or the hairline cracks in the porcelain backs of her knees, I felt as if I were carrying within me a phial of the most precious and delicately combustible material. No, no sudden movements, none at all.

There was another reason why she must be kept inviolate, unpolluted by too much self-knowledge or, indeed, too sharp a knowledge of me. This was her *difference*. In her I had my first experience of the absolute otherness of other people. It is not too much to say – well, it is, but I shall say it anyway – that in Chloe the world was first manifest for me as an objective entity. Not my father and mother, my teachers, other children, not Connie Grace herself, no one had yet been real in the way that Chloe was. And if she was real, so, suddenly, was I. She was I believe the true origin in me of self-consciousness. Before, there had been one thing and I was part of it, now there was me and all that was not me. But here too there is a torsion, a kink of complexity. In severing me from the world and making me real-ise myself in being thus severed, she expelled me from that sense of the immanence of all things, the all things that had included me, in which up to then I had dwelt, in more or less blissful ignorance. Before, I had been housed, now I was in the open, in the clearing, with no shelter in sight. I did not know that I would not get inside again, through that ever straitening gate.

I never knew where I was with her, or what sort of treatment to expect at her hands, and this was, I suspect, a large part of her attraction for me, such is the quixotic nature of love. One day when we were walking along the beach at the water's edge searching after a particular kind of pink shell she needed to make a necklace she stopped suddenly and turned and, ignoring the bathers in the water and the picnickers on the sand, seized me by the shirt-front and pulled me to her and kissed me with such force that my upper lip was crushed against my front teeth and

I tasted blood, and Myles, behind us, did his throaty chuckle. In a moment she had pushed me away, in high disdain, it seemed, and was walking on, frowning, her eye as before moving sharply along the waterline where the bland, packed sand greedily inhaled the outrun of each encroaching wave with a sucking sigh. I looked about anxiously. What if my mother had been there to see, or Mrs Grace, or Rose, even? But Chloe seemed not to care. I can still recall the grainy sensation as the soft pulp of our lips was ground between our teeth.

She liked to throw down dares, but was vexed when they were taken up. Early one eerily still morning, with thunder clouds on the far horizon and the sea flat and greyly lucent, I was standing before her waist-deep in the warmish wash and about to dive and swim between her legs, if she would let me, which she sometimes did. 'Go on, quick,' she said, narrowing her eyes, 'I've just done a pee.' I could not but do as she urged, aspiring little gentleman that I was. But when I surfaced again she said I was disgusting, and leaned into the water to her chin and swam slowly away.

She was prone to sudden and unnerving flashes of violence. I am thinking of one wet afternoon when we were alone together in the living room at the Cedars. The air in the room was damply chill and there was the sad, rainy-day smell of soot and cretonne curtains. Chloe had come in from the kitchen and was crossing to the window and I stood up from the sofa and went towards her, I suppose to try to get my arms around her. Immediately at my approach she stopped and brought up her hand in a quick short arc and delivered me a slap full in the face. So sudden was the blow, so complete, it seemed a definition of some small, unique and vital thing. I heard the echo of it ping back from a corner of the ceiling. We stood a moment motionless, I with my face averted, and she took a step backward, and laughed, and then pouted sulkily and went on to the window, where she picked up something from the table and looked at it with a fierce frown.

There was a day on the beach when she fixed on a townie to torment. It was a blustery grey afternoon towards the end of the holiday, the faintest of autumnal notes already in the air, and she was bored and in malevolent mood. The townie was a pale, shivering fellow in sagging black swimming trunks, with a concave chest and nipples swollen and discoloured from the cold. We cornered him, the three of us, behind a concrete groyne.

He was taller than the twins, but I was taller still, and being eager to impress my girl I gave him a good hard push and knocked him back against the green-slimed wall, and Chloe planted herself in front of him and at her most imperious demanded to know his name and what he was doing here. He looked at her in slow bewilderment, unable to understand, it seemed, why he had been picked on, or what it was we wanted of him, which of course we did not know either. 'Well?' Chloe cried, hands on her hips and tapping one foot on the sand. He smiled uncertainly, more embarrassed than in fear of her. He had come down for the day, he said, mumbling, with his Mammy, on the train. 'Oh, your Mammy, is it?' Chloe said with a sneer, and as if that were a signal Myles stepped forward and smacked him hard on the side of the head with the flat of his hand, producing an impressively loud sharp *tock!* 'See?' Chloe said shrilly. 'That's what you get for being smart with us!' The townie, poor slow sheep that he was, only looked startled, and put up a hand and felt his face as if to verify the amazing fact of having been hit. There was a thrilling moment of stillness then when anything might have happened. Nothing did. The townie only gave a sort of resigned, sad shrug and shambled away, still with a hand lifted to his jaw, and Chloe turned on me defiantly but said nothing, while Myles only laughed.

What remained with me from the incident was not Chloe's glare or Myles's snigger, but the look the townie gave me at the end, before turning disconsolately away. He knew me, knew I was a townie too, like him, whatever I might try to seem. If in that look there had been an accusation of betrayal, of anger at me for siding with strangers against him, anything like that, I would not have minded, but would, in fact, have felt gratified, even if shamefacedly so. No, what unsettled me was the expression of acceptance in his glance, the ovine unsurprisedness at my perfidy. I had an urge to hurry after him and put a hand on his shoulder, not so that I might apologise or try to excuse myself for helping to humiliate him, but to make him look at me again, or, rather, to make him withdraw that other look, to negate it, to wipe the record of it from his eye. For I found intolerable the thought of being known in the way that he seemed to know me. Better than I knew myself. Worse.

I have always disliked being photographed, but I intensely

disliked being photographed by Anna. It is a strange thing to say, I know, but when she was behind a camera she was like a blind person, something in her eyes went dead, an essential light was extinguished. She seemed not to be looking through the lens, at her subject, but rather to be peering inward, into herself, in search of some defining perspective, some essential point of view. She would hold the camera steady at eye-level and thrust her raptor's head out sideways and stare for a second, sightlessly, it might be, as if one's features were written in some form of braille that she was capable of reading at a distance; when she pressed the shutter it seemed the least important thing, no more than a gesture to placate the apparatus. In our early days together I was unwise enough to allow her to persuade me to pose for her on a few occasions; the results were shockingly raw, shockingly revealing. In those half-dozen black-and-white head-and-shoulders shots that she took of me – and took is the word – I seemed to myself more starkly on show than I would have been in a full-length study and wearing not a stitch. I was young and smooth and not unhandsome – I am being modest – but in those photographs I appeared an overgrown homunculus. It was not that she made me look ugly or deformed. People who saw the photographs said they flattered me. I was not flattered, far from it. In them I appeared to have been grabbed and held for an instant on the point of fleeing, with cries of *Stop, thief!* ringing about me. My expression was uniformly winsome and ingratiating, the expression of a miscreant who fears he is about to be accused of a crime he knows he has committed yet cannot quite recall, but is preparing his extenuations and justifications anyway. What a desperate, beseeching smile I wore, a leer, a very leer. She trained her camera on a fresh-faced hopeful but the pictures she produced were the mug-shots of a raddled old confidence trickster. Exposed, yes, that is the word, too.

It was her special gift, the disenchanted, disenchanting, eye. I am thinking of the photographs she took in the hospital, at the end, at the beginning of the end, when she was still undergoing treatment and had strength enough to get up from her bed unaided. She had Claire search out her camera, it was years since she had used it. The prospect of this return to an old obsession gave me a strong yet unaccountable sense of foreboding. I found disturbing too, although again I could not have said exactly why, the fact that it was Claire, and not I, whom she had asked to fetch the camera, and in the tacit understanding, furthermore, that I was not to hear of it. What did it mean, all this secrecy and hugger-mugger? Claire, lately returned briefly from her studies abroad – France, the Low Countries, Vaublin, all that – was shocked to find her mother so ill, and was angry at me, of course, for not summoning her sooner. I did not tell her that Anna was the one who had not wanted her home. This too was odd, for in the past they had always been close, that pair. Was I jealous? Yes, a little, in fact more than a little, if I am to be honest. I am well aware of what I expected, what I expect, of my daughter, and of the selfishness and pathos of that expectation. Much is demanded of the dilettante's offspring. She will do what I could not, and be a great scholar, if I have any say in the matter, and I have. Her mother left her some money, but not enough. I am the big fat goose, and costive with the golden eggs.

It was by chance that I caught Claire smuggling the camera out of the house. She tried to pass it off casually, but Claire is not good at being casual. Not that she knew, any more than I did, why it should be a secret. Anna always had an underhand way of going about the simplest things, it was the lingering influence of her father and their rackety early life together, I suppose. There was a childish side to her. I mean she was wilful, secretive, and deeply resentful of the slightest interference or objection. I can talk, I know. I think it must be that we were both only children. That sounds odd. I mean that we were both the only children of our parents. That sounds odd too. Did I seem to disapprove of her attempts to be an artist, if taking snapshots can be considered artistry? In fact, I paid scant attention to her photographs, and she had no reason to think I would have kept the camera from her. It is all very puzzling.

Anyway, a day or two after I caught Claire with the camera I was called in by the hospital to be sternly informed that my wife had been taking photographs of the other patients and that there had been complaints. I blushed on Anna's behalf, standing in front of the Matron's desk and feeling like a schoolboy hauled up before the Head to account for someone else's misdeeds. It seemed Anna had been wandering through the wards, bare-foot, in her hospital-issue bleached white smock, wheeling her drip-feed stand – she called it her dumb waiter – in search of the more grievously marked and maimed among her fellow patients, by whose bedsides she would park the drip stand and bring out her Leica and snap away until she was spotted by one or other of the nurses and ordered back to her room.

'Did they tell you who complained?' she demanded of me sulkily. 'Not the patients, only the relatives, and what do they know?'

She had me bring the film for developing to her friend Serge. Her friend Serge, who at one time in the far past may possibly have been more than a friend, is a burly fellow with a limp and a mane of beautiful black hair which he tosses back from his forehead with a graceful sweep of both his big blunt hands. He has a studio at the top of one of those tall narrow old houses in Shade Street, by the river. He takes fashion photographs, and sleeps with his models. He claims to be a refugee from somewhere or other, and speaks with a lisping accent which the girls are said to find irresistible. He does not use a surname, and even Serge, for all I know, may be a *nom d'appareil*. He is the kind of person we used to know, Anna and I, in the old days, which were still new then. I cannot think now how I tolerated him; nothing like disaster for showing up the cheapness and fraudulence of one's world, one's former world.

There seems to be something about me that Serge finds irresistibly funny. He keeps up a stream of unamusing little jokes, which I am convinced are a pretext for him to laugh without seeming to be laughing at me. When I came to collect the developed prints he set off on a search for them amidst the picturesque disorder of the studio – it would not surprise me if he arranges the disorder, like a window display – picking his way about nimbly on his disproportionately dainty feet despite a violent list to the left at every other step. He slurped coffee from a seemingly bottomless mug and talked to me over his shoulder. The coffee is another of his trademarks, along with the hair and the limp and the Tolstoyan baggy white shirts that he favours. 'How is the beautiful Annie?' he asked. He glanced at me sidelong and laughed. He always called her Annie, which no one else did; I suppress the thought that it might have been his old love name for her. I had not told him of her illness – why should I? He was scrabbling about in the chaos on the big table he uses as a work desk. The vinegary stink of developing fluid from the darkroom was stinging my nostrils and my eyes. '*Any news of Annie*,' he warbled to himself, making a jingle of it, and gave another snuffly laugh down his nostrils. I saw myself run forward with a cry and hustle him to the window and heave him head-long down into the cobbled street. He gave a grunt of triumph and came up with a thick manila envelope, but when I reached out to take it he held back, considering me with a merrily speculative eye, his head cocked to the side. 'These things she is taking, they are some pictures,' he said, hefting the envelope in one hand and flapping the other limply up and down in his studied Mitteleuropean way. Through a skylight above us the sun of summer shone full on the work table, making the strewn sheets of photographic paper burn with a hot white glare. Serge shook his head and whistled soundlessly through pursed lips. 'Some pictures!'

From her hospital bed Anna reached up eagerly with fingers childishly splayed and snatched the envelope from my hands without a word. It was over-warm and humid in the room and there was a glistening grey film of sweat on her forehead and her upper lip. Her hair had begun to grow again, in a half-hearted fashion, as if it knew it would not be needed for long; it came out in patches, lank and black and greasy-seeming, like a cat's licked fur. I sat on the side of the bed and watched her tear impatiently with her fingernails at the flap of the envelope. What is it about hospital rooms that makes them so seductive, despite all that goes on in them? They are not like hotel rooms. Hotel rooms, even the grandest of them, are anonymous; there is nothing in them that cares for a guest, not the bed, not the refrigerated drinks cabinet, not even the trouser press, standing so deferentially at attention with its back to the wall. Despite all efforts of architects, designers, managements, hotel rooms are always impatient for us to be gone; hospital rooms, on the contrary, and without anybody's effort, are there to make us stay, to want to stay, and be content. They have a soothing suggestion of the nursery, all that thick cream paint on the walls, the rubberised floors, the miniature hand-basin in the corner with its demure little towel on a rail underneath, and the bed, of course, with its wheels and levers, that looks like a kiddie's complicated cot, where one might sleep and dream, and be watched over, and cared for, and never, not ever, die. I wonder if I could rent one, a hospital room, that is, and work there, live there, even. The amenities would be wonderful. There would be the cheery wake-up call in the mornings, meals served with iron regularity, one's bed made up neat and tight as a long white envelope, and a whole medical team standing by to cope with any emergency. Yes, I could be content there, in one of those white cells, my barred window, no, not barred, I am getting carried away, my window looking down on the city, the smokestacks, the busy roads, the hunched houses, and all the little figures, hurrying endlessly, to and fro.

Anna spread the photographs around her on the bed and pored over them avidly, her eyes alight, those eyes that by then had come to seem enormous, starting from the armature of the skull. The first surprise was that she had used colour film, for she had always favoured black-and-white. Then there were the photographs themselves. They might have been taken in a field hospital in wartime, or in a casualty ward in a defeated and devastated city. There was an old man with one leg gone below the knee, a thick line of sutures like the prototype of a zip fastener traversing the shiny stump. An obese, middle-aged woman was missing a breast, the flesh where it had been recently removed all puckered and swollen like a giant, empty eye socket. A big-bosomed, smiling mother in a lacy nightdress displayed a hydrocephalic baby with a bewildered look in its otter's bulging eye. The arthritic fingers of an old woman taken in close-up were knotted and knobbed like clusters of root ginger. A boy with a canker embossed on his cheek, intricate as a mandala, grinned into the camera, his two fists lifted and giving a double thumbs-up sign, a fat tongue cheekily stuck out. There was a shot angled down into a metal bin with gobs and strings of unidentifiable dark wet meat thrown into it – was that refuse from the kitchen, or the operating theatre?

What was most striking to me about the people pictured was the calmly smiling way in which they displayed their wounds, their stitches, their suppurations. I recall in particular a large and at first sight formal study, in hard-edged shades of plastic pinks and puces and glossy greys, taken from low down at the foot of her bed, of a fat old wild-haired woman with her slack, blue-veined legs lifted and knees splayed, showing off what I presumed was a prolapsed womb. The arrangement was as striking and as carefully composed as a frontispiece from one of Blake's prophetic books. The central space, an inverted triangle bounded on two sides by the woman's cocked legs and along the top by the hem of her white gown stretched tight across from knee to knee, might have been a blank patch of parchment in wait of a fiery inscription, heralding perhaps the mock-birth of the pink and darkly purple thing already protruding from her lap. Above this triangle the woman's Medusa-head seemed by a subtle trick of perspective to have been severed and lifted forward and set down squarely in the same plane as her knees, the clean-cut stump of the neck appearing to be balanced on the straight line of the gown's hem that formed the upturned base of the tri-angle. Despite the position in which it found itself the face was perfectly at ease, and might even have been smiling, in a humor-ously deprecating fashion, with a certain satisfaction and, yes, a certain definite pride. I recalled walking in the street with Anna one day after all her hair had fallen out and she spotted passing by on the opposite pavement a woman who was also bald. I do not know if Anna caught me catching the look they exchanged, the two of them, blank-eyed and at the same time sharp, sly, com-plicit. In all that endless twelvemonth of her illness I do not think I ever felt more distant from her than I did at that moment, elbowed aside by the sorority of the afflicted.

'Well?' she said now, keeping her eyes on the pictures and not bothering to look at me. 'What do you think?'

She did not care what I thought. By now she had gone beyond me and my opinions.

'Will you show them to Claire?' I asked. Why was that the first thing that came into my head?

She pretended not to have heard, or perhaps had not been listening. A bell was buzzing somewhere in the building, like a small insistent pain made audible.

'They are my dossier,' she said. 'My indictment.'

'Your indictment?' I said helplessly, feeling an obscure panic. 'Of what?'

She shrugged.

'Oh, everything,' she said, mildly. 'Everything.'

Chloe, her cruelty. The beach. The midnight swim. Her lost sandal, that night in the doorway of the dancehall, Cinderella's shoe. All gone. All lost. It is no matter. Tired, tired and drunk. No matter.

We have had a storm. It went on all night long and into the middle of the morning, an extraordinary affair, I have never known the like, in these temperate zones, for violence or duration. I enjoyed it outrageously, sitting up in my ornate bed as on a catafalque, if that is the word I want, the room aflicker around me and the sky stamping up and down in a fury, breaking its bones. At last, I thought, at last the elements have achieved a pitch of magnificence to match my inner turmoil! I felt transfigured, I felt like one of Wagner's demigods, aloft on a thunder cloud and directing the great booming chords, the clashes of celestial cymbals. In this mood of histrionic euphoria, fizzing with brandy-fumes and static, I considered my position in a new and crepitant light. I mean my general position. I have ever had the conviction, resistant to all rational considerations, that at some unspecified future moment the continuous rehearsal which is my life, with its so many misreadings, its slips and fluffs, will be done with and that the real drama for which I have ever and with such earnestness been preparing will at last begin. It is a common delusion, I know, everyone entertains it. Yet last night, in the midst of that spectacular display of Valhallan petulance, I wondered if the moment of my entrance might be imminent, the moment of my *going on*, so to say. I do not know how it would be, this dramatic leap into the thick of the action, or what exactly might be expected to take place, onstage. Yet I anticipate an apotheosis of some kind, some grand climacteric. I am not speaking here of a posthumous transfiguration. I do not entertain the possibility of an afterlife, or any deity capable of offering it. Given the world that he created, it would be an impiety against God to believe in him. No, what I am looking forward to is a moment of earthly expression. That is it, that is it exactly: I shall be expressed, totally. I shall be delivered, like a noble closing speech. I shall be, in a word, *said*. Has this not always been my aim, is this not, indeed, the secret aim of all of us, to be no longer flesh but transformed utterly into the gossamer of unsuffering spirit? Bang, crash, shudder, the very walls shaking.

By the way: the bed, my bed. Miss Vavasour insists it has always been here. The Graces, mother and father, was it theirs, is this where they slept, in this very bed? What a thought, I do not know what to do with it. Stop thinking it, that would be best; least unsettling, that is.

Another week done with. How quickly the time goes as the season advances, the earth hurtling along its groove into the year's sharply descending final arc. Despite the continuing clemency of the weather the Colonel feels the winter coming on. He has been unwell of late, has caught what he says is a cold on the kidneys. I tell him that was one of my mother's complaints – *one of her favourites, in fact*, I do not add – but he gives me a queer look, thinking I am mocking him, perhaps, as perhaps I am. What is a cold on the kidneys, anyway? Ma was no more specific than the Colonel on the subject, and even *Black's Medical* can offer no enlightenment. Maybe he wants me to think this is the reason for his frequent shufflings to the lavatory by day and night and not the something more serious that I suspect. 'I'm not the best,' he says, 'and that's a fact.' He has taken to wearing a muffler at mealtimes. He turns over his food listlessly and greets the mildest attempt at levity with a soulful, suffering glance that drops wearily away to the accompaniment of a faint sigh that is almost a moan. Have I described his fascinatingly chromatic nose? It changes hue with the time of day and the slightest variation of the weather, from pale lavender through burgundy to the deepest imperial purple. Is this rhinophyma, I suddenly wonder, are these Dr Thomson's famous grog blossoms? Miss Vavasour is sceptical of his complaints, and makes a wry face at me when he is not looking. I think he is losing heart in his attempts to woo her. In that bright-yellow waistcoat, the bottom button always punctiliously undone and the pointed flaps open over his neat little paunch, he is as intent and circumspect as one of those outlandishly plumed male birds, peacock or cock pheasant, who gorgeously stalk up and down at a distance, desperate of eye but pretending indifference, while the drab hen unconcernedly pecks in the gravel for grubs. Miss V. bats aside his ponderously coy attentions with a mixture of vexation and flustered embarrassment. I surmise, from the injured looks he throws at her, that previously she gave him some grounds for hope which were immediately whipped from under him when I came along to be a witness to her folly, and that now she is cross at herself and eager I should be convinced that what he may have taken for encouragement was really no more than a display of a landlady's professional politesse.

Often at a loss myself to know what to do with my time, I have been compiling a schedule of the Colonel's typical day. He rises early, for he is a poor sleeper, suggesting to us by expressive silences and tight-lipped shrugs a fund of battleground night-mares that would keep a narcolept from sleep, although I have an idea the bad memories that beset him were gathered not in the far-flung colonies but somewhere nearer home, for example on the boreens and cratered side roads of South Armagh. Breakfast he takes alone, at a small table in the inglenook in the kitchen – no, I did not recall an ingle, not to speak of a nook – solitude being the preferred mode in which to partake of what he fre-quently and portentously pronounces *the most important meal of the day.* Miss Vavasour is content not to disturb him, and serves him his rashers and eggs and black pudding in a sardonic silence. He keeps his own supply of condiments, unlabelled bottles of brown and red and dark-green sluggish stuffs, which he doles on to his food with an alchemist's niceness of measurement. There is a spread too that he prepares himself, he calls it slap, a khaki-coloured goo involving anchovies, curry powder, a great deal of pepper, and other, unnamed things; it smells, curiously, of dog. 'A great scourer for the bag,' he says. It took me a while to realise that this bag of which he often speaks, though never in Miss V.'s presence, is the stomach and environs. He is ever alive to the state of the bag.

After breakfast comes the morning constitutional, taken in all weathers down Station Road and along the Cliff Walk past the Pier Head Bar and back again the long way round by the light-house cottages and the Gem, where he stops to buy the morning paper and a roll of the extra-strong peppermints which he sucks on all day, and the faint sickly smell of which pervades the house. He goes along at a brisk clip with what I am sure he intends to be a military bearing, although the first morning I saw him setting off I noted with a jolt how at every step he swings out his left foot in a tight sideways curve, exactly as my long-lost father used to do. For the first week or two of my stay here he would still bring back from these route marches a token for Miss Vavasour, nothing fancy, nothing cissyish, a spray of russet leaves or a sprig of greenery, nothing that could not be presented as merely an item of horticultural interest, which he would place without remark on the hall table beside her gardening gloves and her big bunch of house keys. Now he returns empty-handed, save for his paper and his peppermints. That is my doing; my arrival put paid to the ceremony of the nosegays.

The newspaper consumes what is left of his morning, he reads it from first page to last, gathering intelligence, missing nothing. He sits by the fireplace in the lounge, where the clock on the mantelpiece has a hesitant, geriatric tick and pauses at the half-hour and the two quarter-hours to deliver itself of a single, infirm, jangling chime but on the hour itself maintains what seems a vindictive silence. He has his armchair, his glass ashtray for his pipe, his box of Swan Vestas, his footstool, his paper rack. Does he notice those brassy beams of sunlight falling through the leaded panes of the bay window, the desiccated bunch of sea-blue and tenderly blood-brown hydrangea occupying the grate where even yet the first fire of the season has not needed to be lit? Does he notice that the world he reads about in the paper is no longer the world he knew? Perhaps these days all his energies, like mine, go into the effort of not noticing. I have caught him furtively crossing himself when the tolling of the angelus bell comes up to us from the stone church down on Strand Road.

At lunchtime the Colonel and I must shift for ourselves, for Miss Vavasour retires to her room every day between noon and three, to sleep, or read, or work on her memoirs, nothing would surprise me. The Colonel is a ruminant. He sits at the kitchen table in shirtsleeves and an antique sleeveless pullover munching away at an ill-made sandwich – hacked lump of cheese or chunk of cold meat between two door-stoppers smeared with his slap, or a daub of Colman's fieriest, or sometimes both if he feels in need of a jolt – and tries out feints of conversation on me, like a canny field commander searching for a bulge in the enemy's defences. He sticks to neutral topics, the weather, sporting fix-tures, horse racing although he assures me he is not a betting man. Despite the diffidence his need is patent: he dreads the after-noons, those empty hours, as I dread the sleepless nights. He cannot make me out, would like to know what really I am doing here, who might be anywhere, if I chose, so he believes. Who that could afford the warm south – 'The sun's the only man for the pains and aches,' the Colonel opines – would come to do his grieving at the Cedars? I have not told him about the old days here, the Graces, all that. Not that all that is an explanation. I get up to leave – 'Work,' I say solemnly – and he gives me a desperate look. Even my unforthcoming company is preferable to his room and the radio.

A chance mention of my daughter provoked an excited response. He has a daughter too, married, with a pair of little ones, as he says. They are going to come for a visit any day now, the daughter, her husband the engineer, and the girls, who are seven and three. I have a premonition of photographs and sure enough the wallet comes out of a back pocket and the snaps are shown, a leathery young woman with a dissatisfied mien who looks not at all like the Colonel, and a little girl in a party frock who misfortunately does. The son-in-law, grinning on a beach with babe in arms, is unexpectedly good-looking, a big-shouldered southern type with an oiled quiff and bruised eyes – how did mousey Miss Blunden get herself such a he-man? Other lives, other lives. Suddenly somehow they are too much for me, the Colonel's daughter, her man, their girls, and I return the pictures hastily, shaking my head. 'Oh, sorry, sorry,' the Colonel says, harrumphing embarrassedly. He thinks that talk of family stirs painful associations for me, but it is not that, or not only that. These days I must take the world in small and carefully measured doses, it is a sort of homeopathic cure I am undergoing, though I am not certain what this cure is meant to mend. Perhaps I am learning to live amongst the living again. Practising, I mean. But no, that is not it. Being here is just a way of not being anywhere.

Miss Vavasour, so assiduous in other areas of her care of us, is capricious, not to say cavalier, in the matter not only of luncheon but of meals in general, and dinner especially at the Cedars can be an unpredictable refection. Anything might appear on the table, and does. Tonight for instance she served us breakfast kippers with poached eggs and boiled cabbage. The Colonel, sniffing, ostentatiously wielded his condiment bottles turn and turn about like a spot-the-pea artist. To these wordless protests of his Miss Vavasour's response is invariably one of aristocratic absent-mindedness verging on disdain. After the kippers there were tinned pears lodged in a gritty grey lukewarm substance which if childhood memory serves I think was semolina.

Semolina, my goodness. As we made our way through this stodge, with nothing but the clicking of cutlery to disturb the silence, I had a sudden image of myself as a sort of large dark simian something slumped there at the table, or not a something but a nothing, rather, a hole in the room, a palpable absence, a darkness visible. It was very strange. I saw the scene as if from outside myself, the dining room half lit by two standard lamps, the ugly table with the whorled legs, Miss Vavasour absently at gaze and the Colonel stooped over his plate and baring one side of his upper dentures as he chewed, and I this big dark indistinct shape, like the shape that no one at the séance sees until the daguerreotype is developed. I think I am becoming my own ghost.

After dinner Miss Vavasour clears the table in a few broad fanciful passes – she is altogether too good for this kind of menial chore – while the Colonel and I sit in vague distress listening to our systems doing their best to deal with the insults with which they have just been served. Then Miss V. in stately fashion leads the way to the television room. This is a cheerless, ill-lit chamber which has a somehow subterranean atmosphere, and is always dank and cold. The furnishings too have an underground look to them, like things that subsided here over the years from some brighter place above. A chintz-covered sofa sprawls as if aghast, its two arms flung wide and cushions sagging. There is an armchair upholstered in plaid, and a small, three-legged table with a dusty potted plant which I believe is a genuine aspidistra, the like of which I have not seen since I do not know when, if ever. Miss Vavasour's upright piano, its lid shut, stands against the back wall as if in tight-lipped resentment of its gaudy rival opposite, a mighty, gunmetal-grey Pixilate Panoramic which its owner regards with a mixture of pride and slightly shamed misgiving. On this set we watch the comedy shows, favouring the gentler ones repeated from twenty or thirty years ago. We sit in silence, the canned audiences doing our laughing for us. The jittering coloured light from the screen plays over our faces. We are rapt, as mindless as children. Tonight there was a programme on a place in Africa, the Serengeti Plain, I think it was, and its great elephant herds. What amazing beasts they are, a direct link surely to a time long before our time, when behemoths even bigger than they roared and rampaged through forest and swamp. In manner they are melancholy and yet seem covertly amused, at us, apparently. They lumber along placidly in single file, the trunk-tip of one daintily furled around the laughable piggy tail of its cousin in front. The young, hairier than their elders, trot contentedly between their mothers' legs. If one set out to seek among our fellow creatures, the land-bound ones, at least, for our very opposite, one would surely need look no further than the elephants. How is it we have allowed them to survive so long? Those sad little knowing eyes seem to invite one to pick up a blunderbuss. Yes, put a big bullet through there, or into one of those huge absurd flappy ears. Yes, yes, exterminate all the brutes, lop away at the tree of life until only the stump is left standing, then lovingly take the cleaver to that, too. Finish it all off.

You cunt, you fucking cunt, how could you go and leave me like this, floundering in my own foulness, with no one to save me from myself. *How could you.*

Speaking of the television room, I realise suddenly, I cannot think why it did not strike me before now, so obvious is it, that what it reminds me of, what the whole house reminds me of, for that matter, and this must be the real reason I came here to hide in the first place, is the rented rooms my mother and I inhabited, were forced to inhabit, throughout my teenage years. After my father left she was compelled to find work to support us and pay for my education, such as it was. We moved to the city, she and I, where she thought there would surely be more opportunities for her. She had no skills, had left school early and worked briefly as a shop-girl before she met my father and married him to get away from her family, nevertheless she was convinced that some-where there awaited her the ideal position, the job of jobs, the one that she and only she was meant to fill but maddeningly could never find. So we shifted from place to place, from lodging house to lodging house, arriving at a new one always it seemed on a drizzly Sunday evening in winter. They were all alike, those rooms, or are so at least in my memory of them. There was the armchair with the broken arm, the pockmarked lino on the floor, the squat black gas stove sullen in its corner and smelling of the previous lodger's fried dinners. The lavatory was down the hall, with a chipped wooden seat and a long brown rust-stain on the back of the bowl and the ring pull missing from the chain. The smell in the hall was like the smell of my breath when

I breathed and rebreathed it into my cupped hands to know what
it would be like to be suffocated. The surface of the table we
ate at had a tacky feel under the fingers no matter how hard she
scrubbed at it. After our tea she would clear away the tea things
and spread out the *Evening Mail* on the table under the wan glow
of a sixty-watt bulb and run a hairpin down the columns of job
ads, ticking off each ad and muttering angrily under her breath.
'*Previous experience essential . . . references required . . . must be university graduate . . .* Huh!' Then the greasy pack of cards, the matches
divided into two equal piles, the tin ashtray overflowing with her
cigarette butts, the cocoa for me and the glass of cooking sherry
for her. We played Old Maid, Gin Rummy, Hearts. After that
there was the sofa bed to be unfolded and the sour undersheet
pulled tight, and the blanket to be pinned up somehow from the
ceiling to hang along the side of her bed for privacy. I lay and
listened in helpless anger to her sighs, her snores, the squeaks of
broken wind that she let off. Every other night, it seemed,
I would wake to hear her as she wept, a knuckle pressed against
her mouth and her face buried in the pillow. My father was rarely
mentioned between us, unless he was late with the monthly
postal order. She could not bring herself to speak his name; he
was Gentleman Jim, or His Lordship, or, when she was in one of
her rages or had taken too much sherry, Phil the Flute-player, or
even Fart-arse the Fiddler. Her conceit was that he was enjoying
a lavish success, *over there*, a success he cruelly refused to share
with us as he should and as we deserved. The envelopes bringing
the money orders – never a letter, only a card at Christmas or on
my birthday, inscribed in the laboured copperplate of which he
had always been so proud – bore the postmarks of places which
even yet, when I am *over there* and see them signposted on the
motorways his labour helped to build, provoke in me a confusion
of feelings that includes a sticky sort of sadness, anger or its
aftershock, and a curious yearning that is like nostalgia, a nostalgia for somewhere I have never been to. Watford. Coventry.
Stoke. He too would have known the dingy rooms, the lino on
the floor, the gas stove, the smells in the hall. Then the last letter
came, from a strange woman – Maureen Strange, her name! –
announcing *the very sad news I have to tell you*. My mother's bitter
tears were as much of anger as of grief. 'Who's this,' she cried,
'this *Maureen*?' The single sheet of blue-lined notepaper shook

in her hand. 'Blast him,' she said through gritted teeth, 'blast him anyway, the bastard!' In my mind I saw him for an instant, in the chalet, as it happens, at night, turning back from the open door in the thick yellow glow of the paraffin lamp and giving me an oddly quizzical glance, almost smiling, a spot of light from the lamp shining on his forehead and beyond him through the doorway the velvety depthless dark of the summer night.

Last thing, when the television stations are about to plunge into their unacceptably lurid late-night schedules, the set is firmly switched off and the Colonel has a cup of herbal tea prepared for him by Miss Vavasour. He tells me he hates the stuff – 'Not a word, mind!' – but dares not refuse. Miss Vavasour stands over him as he drinks. She insists it will help him sleep; he is gloomily convinced the opposite is the case, yet makes no protest, and drains the cup with a doomed expression. One night I persuaded him to accompany me to the Pier Head Bar for a nightcap, but it was a mistake. He grew anxious in my company – I did not blame him, I grow anxious in it myself – and fidgeted with his tobacco pipe and his glass of stout and kept easing back his cuff surreptitiously to check the time by his watch. The few locals who were there glowered at us, and we soon left, and walked back to the Cedars in silence under a tremendous October sky of stars and flying moon and tattered clouds. Most nights I drink myself to sleep, or attempt to, with half a dozen bumpers of brandy from the jeroboam of best Napoleon I keep in my room. I suppose I could offer him a drop of that, but I think not. The idea of late-night chats with the Colonel about life and related matters does not appeal. The night is long, my temper short.

Have I spoken already of my drinking? I drink like a fish. No, not like a fish, fishes do not drink, it is only breathing, their kind of breathing. I drink like one recently widowed – widowered? – a person of scant talent and scanter ambition, greyed o'er by the years, uncertain and astray and in need of consolation and the brief respite of drink-induced oblivion. I would take drugs if I had them, but I have not, and do not know how I might go about getting some. I doubt that Ballyless boasts a dope dealer. Perhaps the Pecker Devereux could help me. The Pecker is a fearsome fellow all shoulders and barrel chest with a big coarse weathered face and a gorilla's bandy arms. His huge face is pitted all over from some ancient acne or pox, each cavity ingrained with its speck of shiny black dirt. He used to be a deep-sea sailor, and is said to have killed a man. He has an orchard, where he lives in a wheelless caravan under the trees with his scrawny whippet of a wife. He sells apples and, clandestinely, a cloudy, sulphurous moonshine made from windfalls that sends the young men of the village crazy on Saturday nights. Why am I speaking of him like this? What is the Pecker Devereux to me? In these parts the *x* is pronounced, *Devrecks*, they say, I cannot stop. How wild the unguarded fancy runs.

Our day today was lightened, if that is the way to put it, by a visit from Miss Vavasour's friend Bun, who joined us for Sunday lunch. I came upon her at noon in the lounge, overflowing a wicker armchair in the bay window, lolling as if helpless there and faintly panting. The space where she sat was thronged with smoky sunlight and at first I could hardly make her out, although in truth she is as unmissable as the late Queen of Tonga. She is an enormous person, of indeterminate age. She wore a sack-coloured tweed dress tightly belted in the middle, which made her look as if she had been pumped up to bursting at bosom and hips, and her short stout cork-coloured legs were stuck out in front of her like two gigantic bungs protruding from her nether regions. A tiny sweet face, delicate of feature and pinkly aglow, is set in the big pale pudding of her head, the fossil remains, marvellously preserved, of the girl that she once was, long ago. Her ash-and-silver hair was done in an old-fashioned style, parted down the centre and pulled back into an eponymous bun. She smiled at me and nodded a greeting, her powdered wattles joggling. I did not know who she was, and thought she must be a guest newly arrived – Miss Vavasour has half a dozen vacant rooms for rent at this off-peak season. When she tottered to her feet the wicker chair cried out in excruciated relief. She really is of a prodigious bulk. I thought that if her belt buckle were to fail and the belt snap her trunk would flop into a perfectly spherical shape with her head on top like a large cherry on a, well, on a bun. It was apparent from the look she gave me, of mingled sympathy and eager interest, that she was aware of who I was and had been apprised of my stricken state. She told me her name, grand-sounding, with a hyphen, but I immediately forgot it. Her hand was small and soft and moistly warm, a baby's hand. Colonel Blunden came into the room then, with the Sunday papers under his arm, and looked at her and frowned. When he frowns like that the yellowish whites of his eyes seem to darken and his mouth takes on the out-thrust blunt squareness of a muzzle.

Among the more or less harrowing consequences of bereavement is the sheepish sense I have of being an impostor. After Anna died I was everywhere attended upon, deferred to, made an object of special consideration. A hush surrounded me among people who had heard of my loss, so that I had no choice but to observe in return a solemn and pensive silence of my own, that very quickly set me twitching. It started, this singling-out, at the cemetery, if not before. With what tenderness they gazed at me across the grave-mouth, and how gently yet firmly they took my arm when the ceremony was done, as if I might be in danger of falling in a faint and pitching headlong into the hole myself. I even thought I detected a speculative something in the warmth with which certain of the women embraced me, in the lingering way they held on to my hand, gazing into my eyes and shaking their heads in wordless commiseration, with that melting stoniness of expression that old-style tragic actresses would put on in the closing scene when the harrowed hero staggered on stage with the heroine's corpse in his arms. I felt I should stop and hold up a hand and tell these people that really, I did not deserve their reverence, for reverence is what it felt like, that I had been merely a bystander, a bit-player, while Anna did the dying. Throughout lunch Bun insisted on addressing me in tones of warm concern, muted awe, and try as I might I could modulate no tone in response that did not sound brave and bashful. Miss Vavasour, I could see, was finding all this gush increasingly annoying, and made repeated attempts to foster a less soulful, brisker atmosphere at the table, without success. The Colonel was no help, although he did try, breaking in on Bun's relentless flow of solicitude with weather forecasts and topics from the day's papers, but every time was rebuffed. He was simply no match for Bun. Showing his tarnished dentures in a ghastly display of grins and grimaces, he had the look of a hyena bobbing and squirming before the heedless advance of a hippo.

Bun lives in the city, in a flat over a shop, in circumstances which, she would firmly have me know, are far beneath her, daughter of the hyphenated gentry that she is. She reminds me of one of those hearty virgins of a bygone age, the housekeeping sister, say, of a bachelor clergyman or widowed squire. As she twittered on I pictured her in bombazine, whatever that is, and button-boots, seated in state on granite steps before a vast front door in the midst of a tiered array of squint-eyed domestics; I saw her, the fox's nemesis, in hunting pink and bowler hat with a veil, astride the sagging back of a big black galloping horse; or there she was in an enormous kitchen with range and scrubbed deal table and hanging hams, instructing loyal old Mrs Grub on which cuts of beef to serve for the Master's annual dinner to mark the Glorious Twelfth. Diverting myself in this harmless fashion I did not notice the fight developing between her and Miss Vavasour until it was well under way, and I had no idea how it might have started or what it was about. The two normally muted spots of colour on Miss Vavasour's cheekbones were burning fiercely, while Bun, who seemed to be swelling to even larger proportions under the pneumatic effects of a growing indignation, sat regarding her friend across the table with a fixed, froggy smile, her breath coming in fast little plosive gasps. They spoke with vengeful politeness, barging at each other like an unfairly matched pair of hobby-horses. *Really, I fail to see how you can say . . . Am I to understand that you . . . ? The point is not that I . . . The point is that you did . . . Well, that is just . . . It most certainly is not . . . Excuse me, it most certainly is!* The Colonel, increasingly alarmed, looked wildly from one of them to the other and back again, his eyes clicking in their sockets, as if he were watching a tennis match that had started in friendly enough fashion but had suddenly turned murderous.

I would have thought Miss Vavasour would emerge the easy victor from this contest, but she did not. She was not fighting with the full force of the weaponry I am sure she has at her command. Something, I could see, was holding her back, something of which Bun was well aware and which she leaned upon with all her considerable weight and to her strong advantage. Although they seemed in the heat of the argument to have forgotten about the Colonel and me, the realisation slowly dawned that they were conducting this struggle at least partly for my benefit, to impress me, and to try to win me over, to one side or the other. I could tell this from the manner in which Bun's little eager black eyes kept flickering coyly in my direction, while Miss Vavasour refused to glance my way even once. Bun, I began to see, was far more sly and astute than I would at first have given her credit for. One is inclined to imagine that people who are fat must also be stupid. This fat person, however, had taken the measure of me, and, I was convinced, saw me clearly for what I was, in all my essentials. And what was it that she saw? In my life it never troubled me to be kept by a rich, or richish, wife. I was born to be a dilettante, all that was lacking was the means, until I met Anna. Nor am I concerned particularly about the provenance of Anna's money, which was first Charlie Weiss's and is now mine, or how much or what kind of heavy machinery Charlie had to buy and sell in the making of it. What is money, after all? Almost nothing, when one has a sufficiency of it. So why was I squirming like this under Bun's veiled but knowing, irresistible scrutiny?

But come now, Max, come now. I will not deny it, I was always ashamed of my origins, and even still it requires only an arch glance or a condescending word from the likes of Bun to set me quivering inwardly in indignation and hot resentment. From the start I was bent on bettering myself. What was it that I wanted from Chloe Grace but to be on the level of her family's superior social position, however briefly, at whatever remove? It was hard going, scaling those Olympian heights. Sitting there with Bun I recalled with an irresistible faint shudder another Sunday lunch at the Cedars, half a century before. Who had invited me? Not Chloe, surely. Perhaps her mother did, when I was still her admirer and it amused her to have me sitting tongue-tied at her table. How nervous I was, really terrified. There were things on the table such as I had never seen before, odd-shaped cruets, china sauce-boats, a silver stand for the carving knife, a carving fork with a bone handle and a safety lever that could be pulled out at the back. As each course arrived I waited to see which pieces of cutlery the others would pick up before I would risk picking up my own. Someone passed me a bowl of mint sauce and I did not know what to do with it – mint sauce! Now and then from the other end of the table Carlo Grace, chewing vigorously, would bend a lively gaze on me. What was life like at the chalet, he wanted to know. What did we cook on? A Primus stove, I told him. 'Ha!' he cried. 'Primus *inter pares*!' And how he laughed, and Myles laughed too, and even Rose's lips twitched, though no one save he, I am sure, understood the sally, and Chloe scowled, not at their mockery but at my haplessness.

Anna could not sympathise with my sensitivities in these matters, she being the product of a classless class. She thought my mother a delight – fearsome, that is, unrelenting, and unforgiving, but for all that delightful, in her way. My mother, I need hardly say, did not reciprocate this warm regard. They met no more than two or three times, disastrously, I thought. Ma did not come to the wedding – let me admit it, I did not invite her – and died not long afterwards, at about the same time as Charlie Weiss. 'As if they were releasing us, the two of them,' Anna said. I did not share this benign interpretation, but made no comment. That was a day in the nursing home, she suddenly began to speak about my mother, with nothing to prompt her that I had noticed; the figures of the far past come back at the end, wanting their due. It was a morning after storm, and all outside the window of the corner room looked tousled and groggy, the dishevelled lawn littered with a caducous fall of leaves and the trees swaying still, like hungover drunks. On one wrist Anna wore a plastic tag and on the other a gadget like a wristwatch with a button that when pressed would release a fixed dose of morphine into her already polluted bloodstream. The first time we came home for a visit – home: the word gives me a shove, and I stumble – my mother hardly spoke a word to her. Ma was living in a flat by the canal, a dim low place that smelled of her landlady's cats. We had brought her gifts of duty-free cigarettes and a bottle of sherry, she accepted them with a sniff. She said she hoped we were not expecting her to put us up. We stayed in a cheap hotel nearby where the bath water was brown and Anna's handbag was stolen. We took Ma to the Zoo. She laughed at the baboons, nastily, letting us know they reminded her of someone, me, of course. One of them was masturbating, with a curiously lackadaisical air, looking off over its shoulder. 'Dirty thing,' Ma said dismissively and turned away.

We had tea in the café in the grounds, where the blaring of elephants mingled with the clamour of the bank holiday crowd. Ma smoked the duty-free cigarettes, ostentatiously stubbing each one out after three or four puffs, showing me what she thought of my peace offerings.

'Why does she keep calling you Max?' she hissed at me when

Anna had gone to the counter to fetch a scone for her. 'Your name is not Max.'

'It is now,' I said. 'Did you not read the things I sent you, the things that I wrote, with my name printed on them?'

She gave one of her mountainous shrugs.

'I thought they were by somebody else.'

She could show her anger just by her way of sitting, skewed sideways on the chair, stiff-backed, her hands clamped on the handbag in her lap, her hat, shaped like a brioche and with a bit of black netting around the crown, askew on her unkempt grey curls. There was a little grey fuzz on her chin, too. She glanced contemptuously about her. 'Huh,' she said, 'this place. I suppose you'd like to leave me here, put me in with the monkeys and let them feed me bananas.'

Anna came back with the scone. Ma looked at it scornfully.

'I don't want that,' she said. 'I didn't ask for that.'

'Ma,' I said.

'Don't *Ma* me.'

But when we were leaving she wept, backing for cover behind the open door of the flat, lifting a forearm to hide her eyes, like a child, furious at herself. She died that winter, sitting on a bench by the canal one unseasonably mild mid-week afternoon. Angina pectoris, no one had known. The pigeons were still worrying at the crusts she had strewn for them on the path when a tramp sat down beside her and offered her a swig from his bottle in its brown-paper bag, not noticing she was dead.

'Strange,' Anna said. 'To be here, like that, and then not.'

She sighed, and looked out at the trees. They fascinated her, those trees, she wanted to go out and stand amongst them, to hear the wind blowing in the boughs. But there would be no going out, for her, any more. 'To have been here,' she said.

Someone was addressing me. It was Bun. How long had I been away, wandering through the chamber of horrors in my head? Lunch was done and Bun was saying goodbye. When she smiles her little face becomes smaller still, crinkling and contracting around the minute button of her nose. Through the window I could see clouds massing although a wettish sun low in the west still glared out of a pale sliver of leek-green sky. For a second I had that image of myself again, hunched hugely on my chair, pink lower lip adroop and enormous hands lying helplessly before me on the table, a great ape, captive, tranquillised and bleary. There are times, they occur with increasing frequency nowadays, when I seem to know nothing, when everything I did know seems to have fallen out of my mind like a shower of rain, and I am gripped for a moment in paralysed dismay, waiting for it all to come back but with no certainty that it will. Bun was gathering her things preparatory to the considerable effort of unbunging those mighty legs of hers from under the table and getting herself to her feet. Miss Vavasour had already risen and was hovering by her friend's shoulder – it was as big and round as a bowling ball – impatient for her to be gone and trying not to show it. The Colonel was at Bun's other side, leaning forward at an awkward angle and making vague feints in the air with his hands, like a removals man squaring up to a weighty and particularly awkward item of furniture.

'Well!' Bun said, giving the table a tap with her knuckles, and looked up brightly first at Miss Vavasour, then at the Colonel, and both pressed a step more closely in, as if they might indeed be about to put a hand each under her elbows and heave her to her feet.

We went outside into the copper-coloured light of the late-autumn evening. Strong gusts of wind were sweeping up Station Road, making the tops of the trees thrash and flinging dead leaves about the sky. Rooks cawed rawly. The year is almost done. Why do I think something new will come to replace it, other than a number on a calendar? Bun's car, a nippy little red model, bright as a ladybird, was parked on the gravel inside the gate. It gasped on its springs as Bun inserted herself rearways into the driving seat, first pushing in her enormous behind then heaving up her legs and falling back heavily with a grunt against the fake tiger-skin upholstery. The Colonel drew open the gate for her and stood in the middle of the road and directed her out with broad dramatic sweeps of his arms. Smells of exhaust smoke, the sea, the garden's autumn rot. Brief desolation. I know nothing, nothing, old ape that I am. Bun sounded the car horn gaily and waved, her pinched face grinning through the glass at us, and Miss Vavasour waved back, not gaily, and the car buzzed away lopsidedly up the road and over the railway bridge and was gone.

'That's a perisher,' the Colonel said, rubbing his hands and heading indoors.

Miss Vavasour sighed.

We would have no dinner, lunch having lasted so long and having been so fraught. Miss V. was still agitated, I could see, from that bandying of words with her friend. When the Colonel followed her into the kitchen, angling for afternoon tea, at least, she was quite sharp with him, and he scuttled off to his room and the commentary to a football match on the wireless. I too retreated, to the lounge, with my book – Bell on Bonnard, dull as ditch-water – but I could not read, and put the book aside. Bun's visit had upset the delicate equilibrium of the household, there was a sort of noiseless trilling in the atmosphere, as if a fine, taut alarm wire had been tripped and was vibrating still. I sat in the bay of the window and watched the day darken. Bare trees across the road were black against the last flares of the setting sun, and the rooks in a raucous flock were wheeling and dropping, settling disputatiously for the night. I was thinking of Anna. I make myself think of her, I do it as an exercise. She is lodged in me like a knife and yet I am beginning to forget her. Already the image of her that I hold in my head is fraying, bits of pigments, flakes of gold leaf, are chipping off. Will the entire canvas be empty one day? I have come to realise how little I knew her, I mean how shallowly I knew her, how ineptly. I do not blame myself for this. Perhaps I should. Was I too lazy, too inattentive, too self-absorbed? Yes, all of those things, and yet I cannot think it is a matter of blame, this forgetting, this not-having-known. I fancy, rather, that I expected too much, in the way of knowing. I know so little of myself, how should I think to know another?

But wait, no, that is not it. I am being disingenuous – for a change, says you, yes yes. The truth is, we did not wish to know each other. More, what we wished was exactly that, not to know each other. I said somewhere already – no time to go back and look for it now, caught up all at once as I am in the toils of this thought – that what I found in Anna from the first was a way of fulfilling the fantasy of myself. I did not know quite what I meant when I said it, but thinking now on it a little I suddenly see. Or do I. Let me try to tease it out, I have plenty of time, these Sunday evenings are endless.

From earliest days I wanted to be someone else. The injunction *nosce te ipsum* had an ashen taste on my tongue from the first time a teacher enjoined me to repeat it after him. I knew myself, all too well, and did not like what I knew. Again, I must qualify. It was not what I was that I disliked, I mean the singular, essential me – although I grant that even the notion of an essential, singular self is problematic – but the congeries of affects, inclinations, received ideas, class tics, that my birth and upbringing had bestowed on me in place of a personality. In place of, yes. I never had a personality, not in the way that others have, or think they have. I was always a distinct no one, whose fiercest wish was to be an indistinct someone. I know what I mean. Anna, I saw at once, would be the medium of my transmutation. She was the fairground mirror in which all my distortions would be made straight. 'Why not be yourself?' she would say to me in our early days together – *be*, mark you, not *know* – pitying my fumbling attempts to grasp the great world. *Be yourself!* Meaning, of course, *Be anyone you like.* That was the pact we made, that we would relieve each other of the burden of being the people whom everyone else told us we were. Or at least she relieved me of that burden, but what did I do for her? Perhaps I should not include her in this drive towards unknowing, perhaps it was only I who desired ignorance.

The question I am left with now, anyway, is precisely the question of knowing. Who, if not ourselves, were we? All right, leave Anna out of it. Who, if not myself, was I? The philosophers tell us that we are defined and have our being through others. Is a rose red in the dark? In a forest on a far planet where there are no ears to hear does a falling tree make a crash? I ask: who was to know me, if not Anna? Who was to know Anna, if not I? Absurd questions. We were happy together, or not unhappy, which is more than most people manage; is that not enough? There were strains, there were stresses, as how would there not be in any union such as ours, if any such there are. The shouts, the screams, the flung plates, the odd slap, the odder punch, we had all that. Then there was Serge and his ilk, not to mention my Sergesses, no, not to mention. But even in our most savage fights we were only violently at play, like Chloe and Myles in their wrestling matches. Our quarrels we ended in laughter, bitter laughter, but laughter all the same, abashed and even a little ashamed, ashamed that is not of our ferocity, but our lack of it. We fought in order to feel, and to feel real, being the self-made creatures that we were. That I was.

Could we, could I, have done otherwise? Could I have lived differently? Fruitless interrogation. Of course I could, but I did not, and therein lies the absurdity of even asking. Anyway, where are the paragons of authenticity against whom my concocted self might be measured? In those final bathroom paintings that Bonnard did of the septuagenarian Marthe he was still depicting her as the teenager he had thought she was when he first met her. Why should I demand more veracity of vision of myself than of a great and tragic artist? We did our best, Anna and I. We forgave each other for all that we were not. What more could be expected, in this vale of torments and tears? *Do not look so worried*, Anna said, *I hated you, too, a little, we were human beings, after all*. Yet for all that, I cannot rid myself of the conviction that we missed something, that I missed something, only I do not know what it might have been.

Lost track. Everything is mixed up. Why do I torment myself with these insoluble equivocations, have I not had enough of casuistry? Leave yourself alone, Max, leave yourself alone.

Miss Vavasour came in, a moving wraith in the shadows of the twilit room. She enquired if I was warm enough, if she should light a fire. I asked her about Bun, who was she, how had they met, just for the sake of asking something. It was a while before she gave an answer, and when she did it was to a question I had not asked.

'Well, you see,' she said, 'Vivienne's people own this house.'

'Vivienne?'

'Bun.'

'Ah.'

She bent to the fireplace and lifted the bunch of dried hydrangea, crackling, from the grate.

'Or perhaps it is she who owns it now,' she said, 'since most of her people have passed on.' I said I was surprised, I had thought the house was hers. 'No,' she said, frowning at the brittle flowers in her hands, then looked up, almost impish, showing the tiniest tip of a tongue. 'But I come with it, so to speak.'

Faintly from the Colonel's room we heard the crowd cheering and the commentator's excited squawks; someone had scored a goal. They must be playing in the almost dark by now. Injury time.

'And you never married?' I said.

She smiled a frugal smile at that, casting down her eyes again.

'Oh, no,' she said. 'I never married.' She glanced at me quickly and away. The two spots of colour on her cheekbones glowed. 'Vivienne,' she said, 'was my friend. Bun, that is.'

'Ah,' I said again. What else could I say?

She is playing the piano now. Schumann, *Kinderszenen*. As if to prompt me.

Strange, is it not, the way they lodge in the mind, the seemingly inconsidered things? Behind the Cedars, where a corner of the house met the tussocked lawn, under a crooked black drainpipe, there stood a water butt, long gone by now, of course. It was a wooden barrel, a real one, full-size, the staves blackened with age and the iron hoops eaten to frills by rust. The rim was nicely bevelled, and so smooth that one could hardly feel the joins between the staves; smoothly sawn, that is, and planed, but in texture the sodden grain-end of the wood there was slightly furry, or napped, rather, like the pod of a bulrush, only tougher to the touch, and chillier, and more moist. Although it must have held I do not know how many scores of gallons it was always full almost to the brim, thanks to the frequency of rain in these parts, even, or especially, in summer. When I looked down into it the water seemed black and thick as oil. Because the barrel listed a little the surface of the water formed a fat ellipse, that trembled at the slightest breath and broke into terror-stricken ripples when a train went past. That ill-tended corner of the garden had a soft damp climate all of its own, due to the presence of the water barrel. Weeds in profusion flourished there, nettles, dock leaves, convolvulus, other things I do not know the name of, and the daylight had a greenish cast to it, particularly so in the morning time. The water in the barrel, being rain water, was soft, or hard, one or the other, and therefore was considered good for the hair, or the scalp, or something, I do not know. And it was there one glittering sunny morning that I came upon Mrs Grace helping Rose to wash her hair.

Memory dislikes motion, preferring to hold things still, and as with so many of these remembered scenes I see this one as a tableau. Rose stands bent forward from the waist with her hands on her knees, her hair hanging down from her face in a long black shining wedge dripping with soap suds. She is barefoot, I see her toes in the long grass, and is wearing one of those vaguely Tyro-lean short-sleeved white linen blouses that were so popular at the time, full at the waist and tight at the shoulders and embroidered across the bust in an abstract pattern of red and Prussian-blue stitching. The neckline is deeply scalloped and inside it I have a clear glimpse of her pendent breasts, small and spiked, like the business ends of two spinning-tops. Mrs Grace wears a blue satin dressing-gown and delicate blue slippers, bringing an incongru-ous breath of the boudoir into the out-of-doors. Her hair is pinned back at the ears with two tortoiseshell clasps, or slides, I think they were called. It is apparent she is not long out of bed, and in the morning light her face has a raw, roughly sculpted look. She stands in the very pose of Vermeer's maid with the milk jug, her head and her left shoulder inclined, one hand cupped under the heavy fall of Rose's hair and the other pour-ing a dense silvery sluice of water from a chipped enamel jug. The water where it falls on the crown of Rose's head makes a bare patch that shakes and slithers, like the spot of moonlight on Pierrot's sleeve. Rose gives little hooting cries of protest – '*Oo! Oo! Oo!*' – at the cold shock of the water on her scalp.

Poor Rosie. I can never think of her name without that epithet attached. She was, what, nineteen, twenty at the most. Tallish, remarkably slender, narrow at waist and long of hip, she was possessed of a silky, sulky gracefulness from the height of her pale flat brow to her neat and shapely and slightly splay-toed feet. I suppose someone wishing to be unkind – Chloe, for instance – might have described her features as sharp. Her nose, with its tear-shaped, pharaonic nostrils, was prominent at the bridge, the skin stretched tight and translucent over the bone. It is deflected, this nose, a fraction to the left, so that when one looks at her straight-on there is the illusion of seeing her at once full-face and in profile, as in one of those fiddly Picasso portraits. This defect, far from making her seem misproportioned, only added to the soulful expressiveness of her face. In repose, when she was un-aware of being spied on – and what a little spy I was! – she would hold her head at an acute downward tilt, her eyes hooded and her shallowly cleft chin tucked into her shoulder. Then she would seem a Duccio madonna, melancholy, remote, self-forgetting, lost in the sombre dream of all that was to come, of all that, for her, was not to come.

Of the three central figures in that summer's salt-bleached triptych it is she, oddly, who is most sharply delineated on the wall of my memory. I think the reason for this is that the first two figures in the scene, I mean Chloe and her mother, are all my own work while Rose is by another, unknown, hand. I keep going up close to them, the two Graces, now mother, now daughter, applying a dab of colour here, scumbling a detail there, and the result of all this close work is that my focus on them is blurred rather than sharpened, even when I stand back to survey my handiwork. But Rose, Rose is a completed portrait, Rose is done. This does not mean she was more real or of more signifi-cance to me than Chloe or her mother, certainly not, only that I can picture her with the most immediacy. It cannot be because she is still here, for the version of her which is here is so changed as to be hardly recognisable. I see her in her pumps and sheer black pants and shirt of a crimson shade – although she must have had other outfits, this is the one she wears in almost every one of my recollections of her – posed among inconsequentials, the arbitrary props of the studio, a dull drape, a dusty straw hat with a blossom in the band, a bit of mossed-over wall that is probably made of cardboard, and, high up in one corner, an umber door-way where, mysteriously, deep shadows give on to a white-gold blaze of empty light. Her presence was not as vivid for me as that of Chloe or Mrs Grace, how could it be, yet there was something that set her apart, with that midnight-black hair of hers and that white skin the powdery bloom of which the strongest sunlight or harshest sea breeze seemed incapable of smudging.

She was I suppose what in the old days, I mean days even older than those of which I speak, would have been called a governess. A governess, however, would have had her modest spheres of power, but poor Rosie was helpless before the twins and their unheeding parents. For Chloe and Myles she was the obvious enemy, the butt of their cruellest jokes, an object of resentment and endless ridicule. They had two modes by which they treated her. They were either indifferent, to the point that she might have been invisible to them, or else they subjected everything she did or said, however trivial, to a relentless scrutiny and inter-rogation. As she moved about the house they would follow after her, crowding on her heels, watching closely her every action – putting down a plate, picking up a book, trying not to look at herself in a mirror – as if what she was doing were the most outlandish and inexplicable behaviour they had ever witnessed. She would ignore them for as long as she could bear but in the end would turn on them, flushed and trembling, and implore them please, please, to leave her alone, keeping her voice to an anguished whisper for fear the elder Graces should hear her losing control. This was just the response the twins had wanted, of course, and they would press up to her more closely still and peer eagerly into her face, feigning wonderment, and Chloe would bombard her with questions – what had been on the plate? was that a good book? why did she not want to see herself in the glass? – until tears welled up in her eyes and her mouth sagged askew in sorrow and impotent rage, and then the two of them would run off in delight, laughing like demons.

I discovered Rose's secret one Saturday afternoon when I came to the Cedars to call for Chloe. As I arrived she was getting into the car with her father and about to leave for a trip to town. I stopped at the gate. We had made an arrangement to go and play tennis – could she have forgotten? Of course she could. I was dismayed; to be abandoned like this on an empty Saturday afternoon was not a thing lightly to be borne. Myles, who was opening the gate for his father to drive through, saw my dismay and grinned, like the malignant sprite that he was. Mr Grace peered out at me from behind the windscreen and inclined his head towards Chloe and said something, and he also was grinning. By now the day itself, breezy and bright, seemed to exude derision and a generalised merriment. Mr Grace trod hard on the accelerator and the car with a loud report from its hindquarters bounded forward on the gravel so that I had to step smartly out of the way – although they shared nothing else, my father and Carlo Grace had the same truculently playful sense of fun – and Chloe through the side window, her face blurred behind the glass, looked out at me with an expression of frowning surprise, as if she had just that moment noticed me standing there, which for all I knew she had. I waved a hand, with as much carelessness as I could feign, and she smiled with downturned mouth in a fakely rueful way and gave an exaggerated shrug of apology, lifting her shoulders level with her ears. The car had slowed for Myles to get in and she put her face close to the window and mouthed something, and raised her left hand in an oddly formal gesture, it might have been a sort of blessing, and what could I do but smile and shrug too, and wave again, as she was borne away in a swirl of exhaust smoke, with Myles's severed-seeming head in the rear window, grinning back at me gloatingly.

The house had a deserted aspect. I walked past the front door and down to where the diagonal row of trees marked the end of the garden. Beyond was the railway line paved with jagged loose blue shale and giving off its mephitic whiff of ash and gas. The trees, planted too close together, were spindly and misshapen, their highest branches confusedly waving like so many arms upflung in wild disorder. What were they? Not oaks – sycamores, perhaps. Before I knew what I was doing I was clambering up the middlemost one. This was not like me, I was not daring or adventurous, and had, and have, no head for heights. Up I went, however, up and up, hand and instep, instep and hand, from bough to bough. The climb was exhilaratingly easy, despite the foliage hissing in scandalised protest around me and twigs slapping at my face, and soon I was as near the top as it was possible to go. There I clung, fearless as any Jack Tar astride the rigging, the earth's deck gently rolling far below me, while, above, a low sky of dull pearl seemed close enough to touch. At this height the breeze was a steady flow of solid air, smelling of inland things, earth, and smoke, and animals. I could see the roofs of the town on the horizon, and farther off and higher up, like a mirage, a tiny silver ship propped motionless on a smear of pale sea. A bird landed on a twig and looked at me in surprise and then flew away again quickly with an offended chirp. I had by now forgotten Chloe's forgetfulness, so exultant was I and brimful of manic glee at being so high and so far from everything, and I did not notice Rose below me until I heard her sobbing.

She was standing underneath the tree next to the one in which I was perched, her shoulders hunched and her elbows pressed into her sides as if to keep herself upright. Her agitated fingers clutched a wadded handkerchief, but so novelettishly was she posed, weeping there amidst the soughing airs of afternoon, that I thought at first it must be a crumpled love letter and not a hankie she was holding. How odd she looked, foreshortened to an irregular disc of shoulders and head – the parting in her hair was the same shade of off-white as the sodden handkerchief she was holding – and when she turned hastily at the sound of a step behind her she wobbled briefly like a ninepin that the bowl has succeeded only in striking a glancing blow. Mrs Grace was approaching along the pathway worn in the grass under the clothesline, her head bowed and her arms folded cruciform over flattened breasts and a hand clasped crosswise on each shoulder. She was barefoot, and wore shorts, and one of her husband's white shirts that was flatteringly far too big for her. She stopped a little way off from Rose and stood a moment silent, turning from side to side in quarter-turns on the pivot of herself, still with her hands on her shoulders, as if she too like Rose were holding herself up, herself a child that she was rocking in her arms.

'Rose,' she said in a playfully coaxing tone, 'oh, Rose, what is it?'

Rose, who had resolutely turned her face to the far fields again, gave a liquid snort of not-laughter.

'What is it?' she cried, her voice flying up on the final word and spilling over on itself. 'What is it?'

She blew her nose indignantly on the rim of the balled-up hankie and finished with a hair-tossing snuffle. Even from this angle I could see that Mrs Grace was smiling, and biting her lip. Behind me from afar came a hooting whistle. The afternoon train from town, matt-black engine and half a dozen green wooden carriages, was blundering towards us through the fields like a big mad toy, huffing bulbous links of thick white smoke. Mrs Grace moved forward soundlessly and touched a fingertip to Rose's elbow but Rose snatched her arm away as if the touch were burning hot. A flurry of wind flattened the shirt against Mrs Grace's body and showed distinctly the fat outlines of her breasts. 'Oh, come on now, Rosie,' she coaxed again, and this time managed to insinuate a hand into the crook of the girl's arm and with a series of soft tugs made her turn, stiff and unwilling though she was, and together they set off pacing under the trees. Rose went stumblingly, talking and talking, while Mrs Grace kept her head down as before and seemed hardly to speak at all; from the set of her shoulders and a stooping drag to her gait I suspected she was suppressing an urge to laugh. Of Rose's tremulous hiccupy words the ones I caught were *love* and *foolish* and *Mr Grace*, and of Mrs Grace's responses only a shouted *Carlo?* followed by an incredulous whoop. Suddenly the train was there, making the trunk of the tree vibrate between my knees; as the engine passed

I looked into the cabin and saw distinctly the white of an eye flash up at me from under a gleaming, smoke-blackened brow. When I turned back to them the two had stopped pacing and stood face to face in the long grass, Mrs Grace smiling with a hand lifted to Rose's shoulder and Rose, her nostrils edged with pink, gouging into her teary eyes with the knuckles of both hands, and then a blinding plume of the train's smoke blew violently into my face and by the time it cleared they had turned and were walking back up the path together to the house.

So there it was. Rose was lost in love for the father of the children in her charge. It was the old story, although I do not know how it was old for me, who was so young. What did I think, what feel? I recall most clearly the wadded handkerchief in Rose's hands and the blue filigree of incipient varicose veins on the backs of Mrs Grace's strong bare calves. And the steam engine, of course, that had come to a clanking stop over in the station, and stood now seething and gasping and squirting jets of scalding water from its fascinatingly intricate underparts as it waited impatiently to be off again. What are living beings, compared to the enduring intensity of mere things?

When Rose and Mrs Grace were gone I climbed down from the tree, a harder thing to do than climbing up had been, and went softly past the silent and unseeing house and walked down Station Road in the polished pewter light of the emptied afternoon. That train had pulled out of the station and by now was already somewhere else, somewhere else entirely.

Naturally I lost no time in telling Chloe of my discovery. Her response was not at all what I had expected it would be. True, she seemed shocked at first, but quickly assumed a sceptical air, and even appeared to be annoyed, I mean annoyed at me, for having told her. This was disconcerting. I had depended on her greeting my account of the scene under the trees with a delighted cackle, which in turn would have allowed me the assurance to treat the matter as a joke, instead of which I was forced to reflect on it in a more serious and sombre light. A sombre light, imagine that. But why a joke? Because laughter, for the young, is a neutralising force, and tames terrors? Rose, although nearly twice as old as we were, was still on this side of the gulf that separated us from the world of the adults. It was bad enough to have to entertain the thought of them, the real grown-ups, at their furtive frolics, but the possibility of Rose cavorting with a man of Carlo Grace's years – that paunch, that bulging crotch, that chest-fur with its glints of grey – was hardly to be entertained by a sensibility as delicate, as callow, as mine still was. Had she declared her love to Mr Grace? Had he reciprocated? The pictures that flashed before me of pale Rose reclining in her satyr's rough embrace excited and alarmed me in equal measure. And what of Mrs Grace? How calmly she had received Rose's blurted confession, with what lightness, what amusement, even. Why had she not scratched out the girl's eyes with her glistening, vermilion claws?

Then there were the lovers themselves. How I marvelled at the ease, the smooth effrontery, with which they masked all that was going on between them. Carlo Grace's very insouciance seemed now a mark of criminal intent. Who but a heartless seducer would laugh like that, and tease, and thrust out his chin and scratch rapidly in the grizzled beard underneath it, his fingernails making a rasping sound? The fact that in public he paid no more attention to Rose than he did to anyone else who happened to cross his path was only a further sign of his cunning and his skilful dissimulation. Rose had only to hand him his newspaper, and he had only to accept it from her, for it to seem to my hotly vigilant eye that a clandestine, indecent exchange had taken place. Her mild and diffident demeanour in his presence was to me that of a debauched nun, now that I knew of her secret shame, and images moved in the deeper reaches of my imagination of her glimmering pale form joined with him in dim coarse couplings, and I heard his muffled bellows and her muted moans of dark delight.

What had driven her to confess, and to her beloved's spouse, at that? And what did she think, poor Rosie, the first time her eye fell on the slogan that Myles scrawled in chalk on the gateposts and on the footpath outside the gate – *RV loves CG* – and the accompanying rudimentary sketch of a female torso, two circles with dots in the centre, two curves for the flanks, and, below, a pair of brackets enclosing a curt, vertical gash? She must have blushed, oh, she must have burned. She thought it was Chloe, not I, who had somehow found her out. Strangely, though, it was not Chloe whose power was thus increased over Rose, but the contrary, or so it seemed. The governess's eye had a new and steelier light when it fell on the girl now, and the girl, to my surprise and puzzlement, appeared cowed under that look as she had never been before. When I think of them like that, the one glinting, the other shying, I cannot but speculate that what happened on the day of the strange tide was in some way a consequence of the uncovering of Rose's secret passion. After all, why should I be less susceptible than the next melodramatist to the tale's demand for a neat closing twist?

The tide came up the beach all the way to the foot of the dunes, as though the sea were brimming over its bounds. In silence we watched the water's steady advance, sitting in a row, the three of us, Chloe and Myles and me, with our backs against the peeling grey boards of the disused groundsman's hut beside the first tee of the golf course. We had been swimming but we had given up, made uneasy by this waveless, unstoppable tide, the sinister, calm way it kept coming on. The sky was misted white all over with a flat, pale-gold disc of sun stuck motionless in the middle of it. Gulls swooped, shrieking. The air was still. Yet I distinctly recall how the single blades of marram grass growing up through the sand round about had each inscribed a neat half-circle in front of itself, which suggests a wind was blowing, or at least a breeze. Perhaps that was another day, the day I noticed the grass marking the sand like that. Chloe was in her swimsuit, with a white cardigan draped over her shoulders. Her hair was darkly wet and plastered to her skull. In that unshadowed milky light her face seemed almost featureless, and she and Myles beside her were as alike as the profiles on a pair of coins. Below us in a hollow in the dunes Rose lay on her back on a beach towel with her hands behind her head and seemed to be asleep. The sea's scummed edge was within a yard of her heels. Chloe considered her, smiling to herself. 'Maybe she'll be washed away,' she said.

It was Myles who got the door of the hut open, twisting the padlock until the bolt broke from its screws and came away in his hand. Inside, there was a single tiny room, empty, and smelling of old urine. A wooden bench seat was set along one wall, and above it there was a small window, the frame intact but the glass long gone. Chloe knelt on the bench with her face in the window and her elbows on the sill. I sat on one side of her, Myles on the other. Why do I think there was something Egyptian about the way that we were posed there, Chloe kneeling and looking out and Myles and I on the bench and facing into the

little room? Is it because I am compiling a Book of the Dead?
She was the Sphinx and we her seated priests. There was silence,
save for the crying of the gulls.

'I hope she gets drowned,' Chloe said, speaking through the
window, and gave one of her sharp little nicking laughs. 'I hope
she does' – *nick nick* – 'I hate her.'

Last words. It was early morning, just before dawn, when
Anna came to consciousness. I could not rightly tell if I had been
awake or just dreaming that I was. Those nights that I spent
sprawled in the armchair beside her bed were rife with curiously
mundane hallucinations, half dreams of preparing meals for
her, or talking about her to people I had never seen before, or
just walking along with her, through dim, nondescript streets,
I walking, that is, and she lying comatose beside me and yet
managing to move, and keep pace with me, somehow, sliding
along on solid air, on her journey towards the Field of Reeds.
Waking now, she turned her head on the damp pillow and looked
at me wide-eyed in the underwater glimmer of the nightlight
with an expression of large and wary startlement. I think she did
not know me. I had that paralysing sensation, part awe and part
alarm, that comes over one in a sudden and unexpected solitary
encounter with a creature of the wild. I could feel my heart beating in slow, liquid thumps, as if it were flopping over an endless
series of identical obstacles. Anna coughed, making a sound like
the clatter of bones. I knew this was the end. I felt inadequate to
the moment, and wanted to cry out for help. Nurse, nurse, come
quick, my wife is leaving me! I could not think, my mind seemed
filled with toppling masonry. Still Anna stared at me, still surprised, still suspicious. Away down the corridor someone unseen
dropped something that clattered, she heard the noise and
seemed reassured. Perhaps she thought it was something I had
said, and thought she understood it, for she nodded, but impatiently, as if to say *No, you're wrong, that is not it at all!* She reached
out a hand and fixed it claw-like on my wrist. That monkeyish
grasp, it holds me yet. I blundered forward from the chair in a
sort of panic and scrambled to my knees beside the bed, like one
of the dumbstruck faithful falling in adoration before an appari-
tion. Anna was still clutching my wrist. I put my other hand on
her brow, and it seemed to me I could feel her mind behind it
feverishly at work, making the last tremendous effort of thinking

its final thought. Had I ever looked at her in life, with such urgent attention, as I looked at her now? As if looking alone would hold her here, as if she could not go so long as my eye did not flinch. She was panting, softly and slowly, like a runner pausing who still has miles to run. Her breath gave off a mild, dry stink, as of withered flowers. I spoke her name but she only closed her eyes briefly, dismissively, as if I should know that she was no longer Anna, that she was no longer anyone, and then opened them and stared at me again, harder than ever, not in surprise now but with a commanding sternness, willing that I should hear, hear and understand, what it was she had to say. She let go of my wrist and her fingers scrabbled briefly on the bed, searching for something. I took her hand. I could feel the flutter of a pulse at the base of her thumb. I said something, some fatuous thing such as *Don't go*, or *Stay with me*, but again she gave that impatient shake of the head, and tugged my hand to draw me closer. 'They are stopping the clocks,' she said, the merest thread of a whisper, conspiratorial. 'I have stopped time.' And she nodded, a solemn, knowing nod, and smiled, too, I would swear it was a smile.

It was the deft, brusque way that Chloe shrugged off her cardigan that prompted me, that permitted me, to put my hand against the back of her thigh where she knelt beside me. Her skin was chill and stippled with gooseflesh but I could feel the busy blood swarming just below the surface. She did not respond to my touch but went on looking out at whatever it was she was looking at – all that water, perhaps, that inexorable slow flood – and cautiously I slid my hand upward until my fingers touched the taut hem of her bathing suit. Her cardigan, that had settled on my lap, now slithered off and tumbled to the floor, making me think of something, a spray of flowers let fall, perhaps, or a falling bird. It would have been enough for me just to go on sitting there with my hand under her bottom, my heart beating out a syncopated measure and my eyes fixed on a knot-hole in the wooden wall opposite, had she not in a tiny, convulsive movement shifted her knee a fraction sideways along the bench and opened her lap to my astonished fingertips. The wadded crotch of her swimsuit was sopping with seawater that felt scalding to my touch. No sooner had my fingers found her there than she clenched her thighs shut again, trapping my hand. Shivers like tiny electric currents ran from all over her into her lap, and with a wriggle she pulled herself free of me, and I thought it was all over, but I was wrong. Quickly she turned about and climbed down from the bench all knees and elbows and sat beside me squirmingly and turned up her face and offered me her cold lips and hot mouth to kiss. The straps of her swimsuit were tied in a bow at the back of her neck, and now without moving her mouth from mine she put up a hand behind her and undid the knot and tugged the wet cloth down to her waist. Still kissing her, I inclined my head to the side and looked with the eye that could see past her ear down along the ridges of her spine to the beginnings of her narrow rump and the cleft there the colour of a clean steel knife. With an impatient gesture she took my hand and pressed it to the barely perceptible mound of one of her breasts the tip of which was cold and hard. On her other side Myles sat with his legs loosely splayed before him, leaning his head back against the wall with his eyes closed. Blindly Chloe reached out sideways and found his hand lying palm-upwards on the bench and clasped it, and as she did so her mouth tightened against mine and I felt rather than heard the faint mewling moan that rose in her throat.

I did not hear the door opening, only registered the light altering in the little room. Chloe stiffened against me and turned her head quickly and said something, a word I did not catch. Rose was standing in the doorway. She was in her bathing suit but was wearing her black pumps, which made her long pale skinny legs seem even longer and paler and skinnier. She reminded me of something, I could not think what, one hand on the door and the other on the door-jamb, seeming to be held suspended there between two strong gusts, one from inside the hut driving against her and another from outside pressing at her back. Chloe hastily pulled up the flap of her swimsuit and retied the straps behind her neck, speaking that word again harshly under her breath, the word I could not catch – Rose's name, was it, or just some imprecation? – and made a low dive from the bench, fast as a fox, and ducked under Rose's arm and was gone through the door and away. 'You come back here, Miss!' Rose cried in a voice that cracked. 'Just you come back here this instant!' She gave me a look then, a more-in-sorrow-than-in-anger look, and shook her head, and turned and stalked off stork-like on those stilted white legs. Myles, still sprawled on the bench beside me, gave a low laugh. I stared at him. It seemed to me that he had spoken.

All that followed I see in miniature, in a sort of cameo, or one of those rounded views, looked on from above, at the off-centre of which the old painters would depict the moment of a drama in such tiny detail as hardly to be noticed amidst the blue and gold expanses of sea and sky. I lingered a moment on the bench, breathing. Myles watched me, waiting to see what I would do. When I came out of the hut Chloe and Rose were down on the little semicircle of sand between the dunes and the water's edge, squared up to each other and shrieking in each other's face. I could not hear what they were saying. Now Chloe broke away and stamped in a furious, tight ring around herself, churning the sand. She kicked Rose's towel. It is only my fancy, I know, but I see the little waves lapping hungrily at her heels. At last, with one last cry and a curious, chopping gesture of a hand and fore-arm, she turned and walked to the edge of the waves and, scissor-ing her legs, plumped down on the sand and sat with her knees pressed against her breast and her arms wrapped about her knees, her face lifted towards the horizon. Rose with hands on hips stood glaring at her back, but seeing she would get no response turned away and began angrily to gather up her things, pitching towel, book, bathing cap into the crook of her arm like a fishwife throwing fish into a creel. I heard Myles behind me, and a second later he passed me by at a headlong sprint, seeming to cartwheel rather than run. When he got to where Chloe was sitting he sat down beside her and put an arm across her shoulders and laid his head against hers. Rose paused and cast an uncertain glance at them, wrapped there together, their backs turned to the world. Then calmly they stood up and waded into the sea, the water smooth as oil hardly breaking around them, and leaned forward in unison and swam out slowly, their two heads bobbing on the whitish swell, out, and out.

We watched them, Rose and I, she clutching her gathered-up things against her, and I just standing. I do not know what I was thinking, I do not remember thinking anything. There are times like that, not frequent enough, when the mind just empties. They were far out now, the two of them, so far as to be pale dots between pale sky and paler sea, and then one of the dots dis-appeared. After that it was all over very quickly, I mean what we could see of it. A splash, a little white water, whiter than that all around, then nothing, the indifferent world closing.

There was a shout, and Rose and I turned to see a large red-faced man with close-clipped grey hair coming down the dunes towards us, high-stepping flurriedly through the sliding sands with comical haste. He wore a yellow shirt and khaki trousers and two-tone shoes and was brandishing a golf club. The shoes I may have invented. I am sure however of the glove that he wore on his right hand, the hand that held the golf stick; it was light brown, fingerless, and the back of it was punched with holes, I do not know why it caught my attention particularly. He kept shouting that someone should go for the Guards. He seemed extremely angry, gesturing in the air with the club like a Zulu warrior shaking his knobkerrie. Zulus, knobkerries? Perhaps I mean assegais. His caddy, meanwhile, up on the bank, an ageless emaciated runt in a buttoned-up tweed jacket and a tweed cap, stood contemplating the scene below him with a sardonic expression, leaning casually on the golf bag with his ankles crossed. Next, a muscle-bound young man in tight blue swimming trunks appeared, I do not know from where, he seemed to materialise out of the very air, and without preliminary plunged into the sea and swam out swiftly with expert, stiff strokes. By now Rose was pacing back and forth at the water's edge, three paces this way, stop, wheel, three paces that way, stop, wheel, like poor demented Ariadne on the Naxos shore, still clutching to her breast the towel, book and bathing cap. After a time the would-be life-saver came back, and strode towards us out of the waveless water with that swimmer's hindered swagger, shaking his head and snorting. It was no go, he said, no go. Rose cried out, a sort of sob, and shook her head rapidly from side to side, and the golfer glared at her. Then they were all dwindling behind me, for I was running, trying to run, along the beach, in the direction of Station Road and the Cedars. Why did I not cut away, through the grounds of the Golf Hotel, on to the road, where the going would have been so much easier? But I did not want the going to be easier. I did not want to get where I was going. Often in my dreams I am back there again, wading through that sand that grows ever more resistant, so that it seems that my feet themselves are made of some massy, crumbling stuff. What did I feel? Most strongly, I think, a sense of awe, awe of myself, that is, who had known two living creatures that now were suddenly, astoundingly, dead. But did I believe they were dead? In my mind they were held suspended in a vast bright space, upright, their arms linked and their eyes wide open, gazing gravely before them into illimitable depths of light.

Here at last was the green iron gate, the car standing on the gravel, and the front door, wide open as so often. In the house all was tranquil and still. I moved among the rooms as if I were myself a thing of air, a drifting spirit, Ariel set free and at a loss. I found Mrs Grace in the living room. She turned to me, putting a hand to her mouth, the milky light of afternoon at her back. This all is silence, save for the drowsy hum of summer from without. Then Carlo Grace came in, saying, 'Damned thing, it seems to be . . .' and he stopped too, and so we stood in stillness, we three, at the end.

Was't well done?

Night, and everything so quiet, as if there were no one, not even myself. I cannot hear the sea, which on other nights rumbles and growls, now near and grating, now afar and faint. I do not want to be alone like this. Why have you not come back to haunt me? It is the least I would have expected of you. Why this silence day after day, night after interminable night? It is like a fog, this silence of yours. First it was a blur on the horizon, the next minute we were in the midst of it, purblind and stumbling, clinging to each other. It started that day after the visit to Mr Todd when we walked out of the clinic into the deserted car park, all those machines ranked neatly there, sleek as porpoises and making not a sound, and no sign even of the young woman and her clicking high heels. Then our house shocked into its own kind of silence, and soon thereafter the silent corridors of hospitals, the hushed wards, the waiting rooms, and then the last room of all. Send back your ghost. Torment me, if you like. Rattle your chains, drag your cerements across the floor, keen like a banshee, anything. I would have a ghost.

Where is my bottle. I need my big baby's bottle. My soother.

Miss Vavasour gives me a pitying look. I blench under her glance. She knows the questions I want to ask, the questions I have been burning to put to her since I first came here but never had the nerve. This morning when she saw me silently formulating them yet again she shook her head, not unkindly. 'I can't help you,' she said, smiling. 'You must know that.' What does she mean by must? I know so little of anything. We are in the lounge, sitting in the bay of the bow window, as so often. The day outside is bright and cold, the first real day of winter we have had. All this in the historic present. Miss Vavasour is mending what looks suspiciously like one of the Colonel's socks. She has a wooden gadget, shaped like a large mushroom, on which she stretches the heel to darn the hole in it. I find it restful to watch her at this timeless task. I am in need of rest. My head might be packed with wet cotton wool and there is an acid taste of vomit in my mouth which all Miss Vavasour's plyings of milky tea and soldiers of thin-sliced toast cannot rid me of. Also there is a bruise on my temple that throbs. I sit before Miss V. sheepish and contrite. I feel more than ever the delinquent boy.

But what a day it was yesterday, what a night, and, heavens! what a morning-after. It all began with fair enough promise. Ironically, as it would turn out, it was the Colonel's daughter who was supposed to come down, along with Hubby and the children. The Colonel tried to be nonchalant, putting on his gruffest manner – 'We'll be rightly invaded!' – but over breakfast his hands shook so with excitement that he set the table to trembling and the tea cups rattling in their saucers. Miss Vavasour insisted that his daughter and her family should all stay for lunch, that she would cook a chicken, and asked what kind of ice cream the children would like. 'Oh, now,' the Colonel blustered, 'really, there's no need!' It was plain to see he was deeply affected, however, and was damp-eyed for a moment. I looked forward myself with some anticipation to getting a look at last at this daughter and her he-man husband. The prospect of the children was somewhat daunting, though; kiddies in general, I am afraid, bring out the not so latent Gilles de Rais in me.

The visit was due for midday, but the noontide bell tolled, and the lunch hour came and went, and no car had pulled up at the gate and no joyous shouts of the Little Ones had been heard. The Colonel paced, wrist clasped in a hand behind him, or stationed himself before the window, muzzle thrust forward, and shot a cuff and lifted his arm to eye-level and glared reproachfully at his watch. Miss Vavasour and I went about on tenterhooks, not daring to speak. The aroma of roasting chicken in the house seemed a heartless gibe. It was late in the afternoon when the

telephone in the hall rang, making us all start. The Colonel
leaned his ear to the receiver like a despairing priest in the confes-
sional. The exchange was brief. We tried not to hear what he was
saying. He came into the kitchen clearing his throat. 'Car,' he
said, looking at no one. 'Broke down.' Clearly he had been lied
to, or was lying now to us. He turned to Miss Vavasour with a
desolate smile. 'Sorry about the chicken,' he said.

I encouraged him to come out for a drink with me but he
declined. He was feeling a bit tired, he said, had a bit of a headache all of a sudden. He went off to his room. How heavy his
tread was on the stair, how softly he closed the bedroom door.
'Oh, dear,' Miss Vavasour said.

I went to the Pier Head Bar by myself and got sozzled. I did
not mean to but I did. It was one of those plangent autumn
evenings streaked with late sunlight that seemed itself a memory
of what sometime in the far past had been the blaze of noon.
Rain earlier had left puddles on the road that were paler than the
sky, as if the last of day were dying in them. It was windy and
the skirts of my overcoat flapped about my legs like Little Ones
of my own, begging their Da not to go to the pub. But go I did.
The Pier Head is a cheerless establishment presided over by a
huge television set, fully the match of Miss V.'s Panoramic,
permanently switched on but with the sound turned down. The
publican is a fat soft slow man of few words. He has a peculiar
name, I cannot remember it for the moment. I drank double
brandies. Odd moments of the evening stand out in my memory,
fuzzily bright, like lamp standards in a fog. I remember provok-
ing or being provoked into an argument with an old fellow at
the bar, and being remonstrated with by a much younger one,
his son, perhaps, or grandson, whom I pushed and who
threatened to summon the police. When the publican inter-
vened – Barragry, that is his name – I tried to push him, too,
lunging at him across the counter with a hoarse shout. Really,
this is not like me at all, I do not know what was the matter,
I mean other than what is usually the matter. At last they calmed
me down and I retreated grumpily to a table in the corner, under
the speechless television set, where I sat mumbling to myself and
sighing. Those drunken sighs, bubbly and tremulous, how like
sobs they can sound. The last light of evening, what I could see
of it through the unpainted top quarter of the pub window, was

of that angry, purplish-brown cast that I find both affecting and troubling, it is the very colour of winter. Not that I have anything against winter, indeed, it is my favourite season, next to autumn, but this year that November glow seemed a presagement of something more than winter, and I fell into a mood of bitter melancholy. Seeking to assuage my heaviness of heart I called for more brandy but Barragry refused it, advisedly, as I now acknowledge, and I stormed out in rageful indignation, or tried to storm but staggered really, and came back to the Cedars and my own bottle, which I have fondly dubbed the Little Corporal. On the stairs I met Colonel Blunden and had some converse with him, I do not know what about, exactly.

It was night by now, but instead of staying in my room and going to bed I put the bottle under my coat and went out again. Of what happened after that I have only jagged and ill-lit flickers of recollection. I remember standing in the wind under the shaking radiance of a street light awaiting some grand and general revelation and then losing interest in it before it could arrive. Then I was on the beach in the dark, sitting in the sand with my legs stuck out before me and the brandy bottle, empty now or nearly, cradled in my lap. There seemed to be lights out at sea, a long way from shore, bobbing and swaying, like the lights of a fishing fleet, but I must have imagined them, there are no fishing boats in these waters. I was cold despite my coat, the thickness of which was not enough to protect my hind parts from the chill dampness of the sand in which I was sitting. It was not the damp and the chill, however, that made me struggle to my feet at last, but a determination to get closer to those lights and investigate them; I may even have had some idea of wading into the sea and swimming out to meet them. It was at the water's edge, anyway, that I lost my footing and fell down and struck my temple on a stone. I lay there for I do not know how long, fluttering in and out of consciousness, unable or unwilling to move. It is a good thing the tide was on the ebb. I was not in pain, not even very much upset. In fact, it seemed quite natural to be sprawled there, in the dark, under a tumultuous sky, watching the faint phosphorescence of the waves as they pattered forward eagerly only to retreat again, like a flock of inquisitive but timorous mice, and the Little Corporal, as drunk it seemed as myself, rolling back and forth on the shingle with a grating sound, and hearing the wind above me blowing through the great invisible hollows and funnels of the air.

I must have fallen asleep then, or passed out even, for I do not remember the Colonel finding me, although he insists I spoke to him quite sensibly, and allowed him to help me up and walk me back to the Cedars. This must have been the case, I mean I must have been in some way conscious, for he would not have had the strength, surely, to get me to my feet unassisted, much less to haul me from the beach to my bedroom door, slung across his back, perhaps, or dragging me by the heels behind him. But how had he known where to find me? It seems that in our colloquy on the stairs, although colloquy is not the word, since according to him I did the most part of the talking, I had dwelt at length on the well-known fact, well known and a fact according to me, that drowning is the gentlest death, and when by a late hour he had not heard me returning, and fearing that I might indeed in my inebriated state try to make away with myself, he had decided he must go and look for me. He had to scout the beach for a long time, and had been about to give up the search, when some gleam from moon or brightest star fell upon my form, supine there on that stony littoral. When, after much meandering and many pauses for expatiation by me on numerous topics, we arrived at the Cedars at last, he had helped me up the stairs and seen me into my room. All this reported, for of that faltering anabasis I recall, as I have said, nothing. Later he had heard me, still in my room, being uproariously sick – not on the carpet but out of the window into the back yard, I am relieved to say – and then seeming to fall down heavily, and had taken it upon himself to come into my room, and there had discovered me, for the second time that night, in a heap, as they say, at the foot of the bed, lost to consciousness and, so he judged, urgently in need of medical attention.

I woke at some early hour of the still-dark morning to a strange and unnerving scene which I at first took to be an hallucination. The Colonel was there, spick as usual in tweed and cavalry twill – he had not been to bed at all – pacing the floor with a frown, and so, far more implausibly, was Miss Vavasour, who, it would turn out, also had heard, or felt, more likely, in the very bones of the old house, the crash I made as I collapsed after that bout of vomiting at the window. She was wearing her Japanese dressing-gown, and her hair was gathered under a hair-net the like of which I had not seen since I was a child. She sat on a chair a little way off from me, against the wall, sideways on, in the very pose of Whistler's mother, her hands folded on her lap and her face bowed, so that her eye sockets seemed two pits of empty blackness. A lamp, which I thought was a candle, was burning on a table before her, shedding a dim globe of light upon the scene, which overall – a dimly radiant round with seated woman and pacing man – might have been a nocturnal study by Géricault, or de la Tour. Baffled, and abandoning all effort to understand what was going on or how the two of them came to be there, I fell asleep again, or passed out again.

When I next awakened the curtains were open and it was day. The room had a chastened and somewhat abashed aspect, I thought, and everything looked pale and featureless, like a woman's unmade-up morning face. Outside, a uniformly white sky sat sulkily immobile, seeming no more than a yard or two higher than the roof of the house. Vaguely the events of the night came shuffling back shamefaced to my addled consciousness. Around me the bedclothes were tossed and twisted as after a debauch, and there was a strong smell of sick. I put up a hand and a shot of pain went through my head when my fingers found the pulpy swelling on my temple where it had struck upon the stone. It was only then, with a start that made the bed creak, that I noticed the young man seated on my chair, leaning forward with his arms folded on my desk, reading a book lying open before him on my leather writing pad. He wore steel-framed spectacles and had a high, balding brow and sparse hair of no particular colour. His clothes were characterless too, although I had a general impression of jaded corduroys. Hearing me stir he lifted his eyes unhurriedly from the page and turned his head and looked at me, quite composed, and even smiled, though cheerlessly, and enquired as to how I was feeling. Nonplussed – that is the word, surely – I struggled up in the bed, which seemed to wobble under me as if the mattress were filled with some thick and viscous liquid, and gave him what was intended to be an imperiously interrogative stare. However, he continued calmly regarding me, quite unruffled. The Doctor, he said, making it sound as though there were only one in the world, had been to see me earlier, while I was out – *out*, that was how he put it, and

I wondered wildly for a moment if I had been down to the beach again, without knowing it – and had said I seemed to be suffering from a concussion compounded by severe but temporary alcohol poisoning. Seemed? Seemed?

'Claire drove us down,' he said. 'She's sleeping now.'

Jerome! The chinless inamorato! Now I knew him. How had he wormed his way back into my daughter's favour? Had he been the only one she could think of to turn to, in the middle of the night, when the Colonel or Miss Vavasour, whichever of them it was, had called to tell her of the latest scrape her father had got himself into? If so, I thought, I shall be to blame, although I could not see exactly why. How I cursed myself, sprawled there on that doge's daybed, crapulent and woozy and altogether lacking the strength to leap up and seize the presumptuous fellow by the scruff and throw him out a second time. But there was worse to come. When he went out to find if Claire had wakened yet, and she came back with him, drawn and red-rimmed and wearing a raincoat over her slip, she informed me straight away, with the air of one hastily drawing fire so as to be able all the better to deflect it, that they were engaged. For a moment, befuddled as I was, I did not know what she meant – engaged by whom, and as what? – a moment which, as it proved, was sufficient for my vanquishment. I have not managed to bring up the subject again, and every further moment that passes further consolidates her victory over me. This is how, in a twinkling, these things are won and lost. Read Maistre on warfare.

Nor did she stop there, but, flushed with that initial triumph, and seizing the advantage offered by my temporary infirmity, went on to direct, a figurative hand cocked on her hip, that I must pack up and leave the Cedars forthwith and let her take me home – home, she says! – where she will care for me, which care will include, I am given to understand, the withholding of all alcoholic stimulants, or soporifics, until such time as the Doctor, him again, declares me fit for something or other, life, I suppose. What am I to do? How am I to resist? She says it is time I got down seriously to work. 'He is finishing,' she informed her betrothed, not without a gloss of filial pride, 'a big book on Bonnard.' I had not the heart to tell her that my Big Book on Bonnard – it sounds like something one might shy coconuts at – has got no farther than half of a putative first chapter and a notebook filled with derivative and half-baked would-be aperçus. Well, it is no matter. There are other things I can do. I can go to Paris and paint. Or I might retire into a monastery, pass my days in quiet contemplation of the infinite, or write a great treatise there, a vulgate of the dead, I can see myself in my cell, long-bearded, with quill pen and hat and docile lion, through a window beside me minuscule peasants in the distance making hay, and hovering above my brow the dove refulgent. Oh, yes, life is pregnant with possibilities.

I suppose I shall not be allowed to sell the house, either.

Miss Vavasour says she will miss me, but thinks I am doing *the right thing*. Leaving the Cedars is hardly of my doing, I tell her, I am being forced to it. She smiles at that. 'Oh, Max,' she says, 'I do not think you are a man to be forced into anything.' That gives me pause, not because of the tribute to my strength of will, but the fact, which I register with a faint shock, that this is the first time she has addressed me by my name. Still, I do not think it means that I can call her Rose. A certain formal distance is necessary for the good maintenance of the dainty relation we have forged, re-forged, between us over these past weeks. At this hint of intimacy, however, the old, unasked questions come swarming forward again. I would like to ask her if she blames herself for Chloe's death – I believe, I should say, on no evidence, that it was Chloe who went down first, with Myles following after, to try to save her – and if she is convinced their drowning together like that was entirely an accident, or something else. She would probably tell me, if I did ask. She is not reticent. She fairly prattled on about the Graces, Carlo and Connie – 'Their lives were destroyed, of course' – and how they, too, died, not long after losing the twins. Carlo went first, of an aneurysm, then Connie, in a car crash. I ask what kind of crash, and she gives me a look. 'Connie was not the kind to kill herself,' she says, with a faint twist of the lips.

They were good to her, afterwards, she says, never a reproach or the hint of an accusation of duty betrayed. They set her up at the Cedars, they knew Bun's people, persuaded them to take her on to look after the house. 'And here I am still,' she says, with a grim small smile, 'all these long years later.'

The Colonel is moving about upstairs, making discreet but definite noises; he is glad I am going, I know it. I thanked him for his help last night. 'You probably saved my life,' I said, thinking suddenly it was probably true. Much huffing and clearing of the throat – *Faugh, sir, only doin' me demned duty!* – and a hand giving my upper arm a quick squeeze. He even produced a going-away present, a fountain pen, a Swan, it is as old as he is, I should think, still in its box, in a bed of yellowed tissue paper. I am graving these words with it, it has a graceful action, smooth and swift with only the occasional blot. Where did he come by it, I wonder? I did not know what to say. 'Nothing required,' he said. 'Never had a use for it myself, you should have it, for your writing, and so on.' Then he bustled off, rubbing his white old dry hands together. I note that although it is not the weekend he is wearing his yellow waistcoat. I shall never know, now, if he really is an old army man, or an impostor. It is another of those questions I cannot bring myself to put to Miss Vavasour.

'It's her I miss,' she says, 'Connie – Mrs Grace – that is.' I suppose I stare, and she gives me another of those pitying glances. 'It was never him, with me,' she says. 'You didn't think that, did you?' I thought of her standing below me that day under the trees, sobbing, her head sitting on the platter of her foreshortened shoulders, the wadded hankie in her hand. 'Oh, no,' she said, 'never him.' And I thought, too, of the day of the picnic and of her sitting behind me on the grass and looking where I was avidly looking and seeing what was not meant for me at all.

Anna died before dawn. To tell the truth, I was not there when it happened. I had walked out on to the steps of the nursing home to breathe deep the black and lustrous air of morning. And in that moment, so calm and drear, I recalled another moment, long ago, in the sea that summer at Ballyless. I had gone swimming alone, I do not know why, or where Chloe and Myles might have been; perhaps they had gone with their parents somewhere, it would have been one of the last trips they made together, perhaps the very last. The sky was hazed over and not a breeze stirred the surface of the sea, at the margin of which the small waves were breaking in a listless line, over and over, like a hem being turned endlessly by a sleepy seamstress. There were few people on the beach, and those few were at a distance from me, and something in the dense, unmoving air made the sound of their voices seem to come from a greater distance still. I was standing up to my waist in water that was perfectly transparent, so that I could plainly see below me the ribbed sand of the sea bed, and tiny shells and bits of a crab's broken claw, and my own feet, pallid and alien, like specimens displayed under glass. As I stood there, suddenly, no, not suddenly, but in a sort of driving heave, the whole sea surged, it was not a wave, but a smooth rolling swell that seemed to come up from the deeps, as if something vast down there had stirred itself, and I was lifted briefly and carried a little way towards the shore and then was set down on my feet as before, as if nothing had happened. And indeed nothing had happened, a momentous nothing, just another of the great world's shrugs of indifference.

A nurse came out then to fetch me, and I turned and followed her inside, and it was as if I were walking into the sea.